By Richard S. Wheeler
from Tom Doherty Associates

*forthcoming

Praise for *Sierra*

"Wheeler proves himself, yet again, a fluid master of the Western."

—*Publishers Weekly*

"Another solid historical from the prolific Wheeler. . . . Absorbing and eventful, replete with authoritative details on the mortal risks, primitive conditions, and sometimes rich rewards awaiting those who joined the gold rush to California."

—*Kirkus Reviews*

"A rich tale. . . . Wheeler, as he did in *Goldfield,* re-creates the American frontier in fascinating detail, populates it with engaging characters, and, in the process, manages to personalize the great period of western expansion. . . . A wonderfully multifaceted portrayal of pioneer life."

—*Booklist*

"Wheeler has a long list of novels of the West to his credit and is a real master at capturing the history, atmosphere, and romance of 1850s California. This will appeal to readers of Westerns and general fiction alike. . . . Recommended."

—*Library Journal*

"Whether read as an adventure story, a love story, or a riveting fictional account of a watershed event in American history, *Sierra* is an outstanding novel with crackling good dialogue and unforgettable characters."

—*Roundup Magazine,* Western Writers of America

"Wheeler has mixed sound historical background into this tale of fortunes lost and won, of loves finally fulfilled, and too many wrongs left unpunished. Wheeler is an old hand at tales of our West. *Sierra* is his best so far."

—*Grand Rapids Press*

"This is an epic story of riches, greed, and love. . . . A riveting . . . . . period in American history. . . . a prize winner."

—*Tulsa World*

SIERRA

A Novel of
the
California Gold Rush

RICHARD S. WHEELER

A TOM DOHERTY ASSOCIATES BOOK
NEW YORK

This is a work of fiction. All the characters and events portrayed in this book are either products of the author's imagination or are used fictitiously.

SIERRA: A NOVEL OF THE CALIFORNIA GOLD RUSH

Copyright © 1996 by Richard S. Wheeler

A Forge Book
Published by Tom Doherty Associates, Inc.
175 Fifth Avenue
New York, NY 10010

Forge® is a registered trademark of Tom Doherty Associates, Inc.

ISBN: 0-812-54288-6
Library of Congress Card Catalog Number: 96-8305

First edition: September 1996
First mass market edition: May 1998

Printed in the United States of America

0 9 8 7 6 5 4 3 2 1

To my friend and literary agent,
Nat Sobel

Oh, rank is good, and gold is fair,
And high and low mate ill;
But love has never known a law
Beyond its own sweet will!

—John Greenleaf Whittier
Amy Wentworth

PART I

1849

CHAPTER 1

Oh Susanna, Oh, don't you cry for me.
For I'm off to California with a washbowl on my knee.

But cry she did, in the weeks before Ulysses left. When the moment came she didn't cry at all, but stood at the door, feeling as dreary and cold as the March sky, watching him lead the mules to the hitchrail. He was ending the honeymoon. He was abandoning the dreams they had forged together, the life they had planned, and the unborn child.

The sunniness in his face seduced her, as it always did. Even in this glowering morning, some golden light gathered around his face, as if a shaft of sun had pierced through, haloing and canonizing him. She hated that. Why couldn't he be as forlorn and love-stricken as herself?

The pair of big blue mules, young but well-broken to a plow, were wedding presents from her parents. But now he was taking them to California. He was going to walk two thousand miles through storms and heat, past wild Indians and buffalo, over mountains, crossing rivers deep enough to drown him. He was going to leave Susannah Strawbridge McQueen in Mount Pleasant, with nothing but an empty bed and a lonely house.

She blamed him, loved him, and kept back the tears this bitter dawn, and felt so much pain that she hardly knew herself. She had put on her gray dress, straight out of her trousseau. It felt tight now, and in a few weeks she couldn't wear it at all, but it flattered her. She wanted him to remember her looking her best. Let his last memory remind him of her love, her faithfulness, her yearning for him. She might never see him again, at least on earth.

He didn't seem to notice the way she had dressed, but she knew he did. She watched him brush the mules, taking care that nothing would gall the hide under the saddle blankets, and then load the packsaddles, each with a pair of panniers on it. Now and then he smiled at her, his frank, dark blue eyes surveying her with some inner fire that always melted her.

They had wed in September on a bright day she would always remember: the Reverend Mr. McCracken had bound them in the chapel of Iowa Wesleyan College in front of her family and his, and ninety others, all their friends and neighbors. Three months later her bliss came to an abrupt halt in the most unexpected way. On December 5, President Polk told Congress of a gold strike in newly won California, confirming the letters and rumors that had floated from that distant place for months. A few days later the first of the gold, fourteen pounds of it, arrived in Washington, and the rush was on. From that moment, Mount Pleasant, Iowa, could not contain Ulysses McQueen.

He read John C. Frémont's *Report of the Exploring Expedition to the Rocky Mountains in the Year 1842 and to Oregon and North California in the Years 1843–44*, memorizing every campsite and landmark. He found a copy of Edwin Bryant's *What I Saw in California*, and mastered every detail of the trip across "the Great American Desert." He studied each newspaper that floated into the college. Many of them printed letters from California trumpeting the bonanza; they ran maps, offered outfitting advice, and supplied copious information about the various routes, including the one across the Isthmus of Panama.

Ulysses changed. He seemed to gaze at distant horizons. It was as if he was shutting her out of his dreams, but she knew he didn't. He was just as caring as before, but suddenly she was standing at an abyss that had opened up in him like land riven by an earthquake. He was seeing gold, adventure, a sure-thing chance to grab a fortune and a life of luxury. The change in her new husband had shocked Susannah. Where was the Ulysses whose gold ring she wore? Was not the gold of wedded bliss, the gold of children, the gold of a fruitful farm next to the farms of his brothers and parents, and only two miles away from the farms of her parents and sisters and brothers, more gold than the gold of distant California? Wasn't the certainty of a sweet life in Mount Pleasant, surrounded by loved ones, better than a dangerous quest for gold?

Thus did Ulysses become a stranger. He had seemed a

stranger at the altar, but then she was looking forward to becoming his mate, of sharing life, of holding him within her arms at night, possessing him in all the sensuous and sacred ways; making coffee and cakes in the morning, sewing his clothes, milking the cow, churning the butter, bearing their children, feeding the harvest crews that would scythe the wheat and thresh it, or feeding the cornhuskers in the fall.

She didn't argue with him at first, knowing this foolishness would soon ebb away. And then, when the fever ate deeper into him, she did argue. But she never cried. Not then. Not yet.

At first it sounded like wistful dreaming.

"Some of those miners are washing a hundred dollars a day out of some rich bars," he had said. "I can go there, fill my pockets with rocks, and be back here in a year. We'll be comfortable the rest of our lives. I'm doing it for you, Susannah."

"Ulysses, we'll plant in the spring, and before we know it we'll be just as well off as our neighbors. Just like everyone here. We'll be together."

"I'd like to give you a big house and servants."

"I have all I want, Ulysses. You."

He had smiled, but there were visions dancing in his head that she couldn't fathom.

Next she had enlisted his parents and brothers. All through January she entertained, feeding them all at Sunday dinners after church. A word from Ulysses' father would surely bring Ulysses to his senses. Stanford McQueen was a force of nature, a pioneer who had fought for the land he still lived on. No graves filled a plot on McQueen's farm. It was as if he had forbidden death to abide there. No McQueen had died in Mount Pleasant, and they had been there three decades. She thought of the graves on the Strawbridge farm: a younger sister, an older brother, three grandparents, and a joint headstone waiting for her parents. Strawbridges died; other mere mortals died. But Stanford McQueen ruled over God and nature, and permitted no mortality on his dominions.

"Well, Ulysses, it won't be long now to spring planting. I'll tell you what to put in," the florid-faced older McQueen said, after a second helping of mince pie. "The sweet soil's fit for wheat or oats, and that's what you'll plant. There's a lot of men who'd say this country's fit for corn and hogs, but a McQueen should buck opinion and plant what's not being grown by others. That's how to make a market. How lucky we were to find this farm for you, just when old Greeley was ready to sell. Black loam and a creek, and well-drained fields—why, it's a young man's dream."

Ulysses had pushed back his chair from the great oak table, and smiled. "It is, sir; it's all that. But I think a man can do better, faster."

His father had stared, icily.

After that, Susannah resorted to the Strawbridges.

"Why, Ulysses," said her father one day, "those mules'll make work light for you. Well broke, near as big as Clydesdales, and gentle. I've seen mules with minds of their own, but I made a point of selecting a pair that'd worked together, and it'll make your labor light come spring."

"Thank you, sir," said Ulysses. "But this year I'll have it done on shares with my brothers."

After that she enlisted the Reverend Mr. McCracken and his slender wife, Philomena, who was as soft as iron. Susannah did not serve coffee to the Methodist minister or his wife because they believed the human body was a temple that should not be tampered with. They were good people. Maybe Ulysses was suffering a crisis of the spirit, and if so, they would surely reach him before it was too late.

"Ulysses, my son, consider the nature of gold and how it corrupts," the reverend began after raisin pie. "Now, gold itself is innocent, but the lust for it, a greed for wealth, can become an idol, a turning away from the Holy Spirit, and something to weigh carefully."

"Yes, sir," said Ulysses into the pregnant silence. Ulysses was smiling.

After that the tears flowed.

"Please, please, Ulysses. Please don't leave me," she cried.

"We'll be rich, Susannah! I'll come back here so loaded down with gold we can have anything we want. It's not for me—it's for you! And the baby!"

"All I want is you," she whispered, her tears wetting his shirt. "I won't ever see you again. You'll die out there. The Indians'll kill you."

"You just wait a year. Then you'll drive the fanciest gig in

Mount Pleasant, wear silks and satins, have a servant, too. And while you wait, my brothers'll look after you."

"You'll take sick, or those bandits in California, they'll shoot you—or worse. You'll fetch the cholera. Everyone's talking about it. I don't want to visit your grave."

"Well, there's no saying what'll happen. But if you don't try, you don't win. And who ever heard of a McQueen dying?"

"Don't you care for me?"

"You're like the sun to me."

"Then why do you leave me all alone?"

"You won't be alone. You've got my ma and pa, and your ma and pa, and Junior and Sarah and Jonathan and Lucy, and—"

"But not you," she said dully. "Why, Ulysses, why?"

"Because I must," he said.

"But that's no answer."

He smiled.

After that she had accepted the inevitable.

He finished cinching the packsaddles, and glanced knowingly at the overcast sky. "I'm glad I'm not taking a wagon," he said. "I'd be mired twenty times between here and Council Bluffs."

His burning blue eyes surveyed her, and she wished desperately she could be so beautiful he wouldn't even think of leaving her. Unconsciously her hand gripped her dress as he surveyed her.

"I reckon it's time," he said.

"Oh, Ulysses!"

"You just wait. Junior and Jonathan, they'll plow and plant and reap, and watch over the baby. They'll keep you just fine. You'll be snug as a bug. It's you I worry about, not me."

"Stay a while more, Ulysses." She felt as if she would break in two.

"Susannah, don't look at the clouds. I'm going to give us a life bigger than you ever dreamed of. I'll come back with twenty thousand dollars."

She eyed him skeptically.

"Dream a big dream, Susannah," he said.

He abandoned the mules and approached her at the doorway, and she knew if he hugged her she could never let go. But he came and hugged her, and she clutched his fine-muscled body as fiercely as she could.

"I want your blessing, Susannah," he said gravely.

She summoned her courage. "Yes, you have it, Ulysses. You're a brave man and I'm proud to be your wife. You'll show the whole world what you're made of. I admire you. You're doing what no one else in Mount Pleasant has the courage to do, and I'm with you every inch of the way. Go with my blessing."

"Look for me next summer. I'm taking the Panama boats home. That's what all the guidebooks say to do."

She pushed back a bit. "I have a gift for you," she whispered. She handed him a buckram-bound pasteboard packet tied with a blue ribbon. "I've written fifty-two letters, one for each week of the year. Open one each Sunday. I tried to imagine how I'll feel in six months, in nine months, in a year . . ."

He took the packet. "I'll read them each Sunday. They'll give me hope and remind me of you. I'll have the letters and your locket. Thank you. It'll be almost as good as real news." He tugged her to him again. "I'll be back soon."

"They're all I have to give you," she whispered. Then she made herself smile.

He let go, smiled apologetically, gave her hand a squeeze, and returned to his mules. Swiftly he slid her packet into his gear and lashed the canvas down. Then, almost too eagerly, he led his mules down the lane.

She watched him go, certain she would never see him again, and that her marriage died that day.

CHAPTER 2

Ulysses McQueen had one more stop to make, and it would be just as painful as his leave-taking from Susannah. He led the big mules, their backs dark and glossy from the mist, down the lane to his parents' farm. There he would say good-bye to them and his brothers and their wives and children. His new oilskins shed the mist comfortably, and his wide-brimmed beaver kept the wetness off his face and neck. But ere long his boots would soak through and he would walk on numb feet.

He tied the mules to the iron-ringed hitching post and climbed the three enameled white steps to the veranda. His family awaited him in the kitchen, but he saw no cheer in them as he made his way to the warmth of the stove. He took off his hat and smiled, shedding droplets on the worn wooden floor, eyeing them one by one, knowing they didn't approve—except his unmarried younger brother, Alexander. From that one ruddy face he caught a glint of delight.

"Well, sir," he said quietly to his stern father, "I'm off."

"It's the last we'll see of you," said Stanford Constable McQueen, an observation that Ulysses knew was laden with several meanings. The old gentleman possessed the sort of gravity that made him a respected elder in Mount Pleasant.

"Sir, you keep your health, and I'll do the same, and we'll be together in a year," Ulysses countered. He smiled benevolently at them, but they didn't return his cheer. He understood that. It wasn't that he was risking his life on a foolhardy quest, but that he had defied the patriarch. His every act had become an affront to the family.

They had created a comfortable cocoon for Ulysses: a fine neighboring farm, family help, a close-knit life with well-fixed friends and neighbors. The McQueens were known and respected. There in Mount Pleasant, Ulysses could enjoy a sweet life, live long, and die surrounded by beloved children and family. He was pitching all that aside—an act of such folly and insubordination that old Stanford McQueen had been embittered by it.

"I don't think God himself could turn your head," the elder McQueen said, carefully squeezing the testiness out of his voice. "I will send you off without my blessing. Write, and frequently, or I'll come hunt you down."

A paternal threat to hunt him down struck Ulysses as the heart of the problem, but he only smiled. He intended to live his own life, even if his brothers could not or would not. He turned to his mother, Henrietta, who stood beside her husband. She had strengths of her own. Long before, the pair of them had carved this place out of Iowa wilderness, braving Sac and Fox Indians, subduing the wilds and turning it into the biblical land of milk and honey. Her strength had risen from the Bible she now held in her hands. Her Delft-blue eyes fixed him in their gaze.

"Ulysses," she said, in a voice whose gravity matched her husband's, "no one can stop you. But we can urge you to conduct yourself in ways that win the favor of God and man. Remember the Sabbath. Read a chapter a day from the Good Book, and absorb every lesson. Avoid the sins that defile the body. If you should find wealth, don't squander it on riotous living. Remember your poor Susannah—my heart aches for her—and write us by every means. Don't expect all the letters to get through."

"Yes, Mother."

"All right, my dear boy," she said, and handed him a new, buckram-bound Testament. "It's inscribed. This evening, read my inscription. We've given you the compass of life and the character to make your way. You're a McQueen, and we know you'll do us honor."

She was paying him honor in her own way, and that was more than his father could manage. He accepted the Testament with a nod, and slid it deep into a pocket of his oilskin.

He shook hands with Jonathan, the choleric eldest son. "Take care of Susannah," he said.

"You give me no choice. Someone has to," Jonathan replied.

Ulysses ignored that, knowing it was a half-truth. Mostly, the Strawbridges would care for her, and see to her laying-in. Ulysses turned to Stanford Jr., the huskiest of the sons, and the family's workhorse. "I think my fields'll give you a fine crop. You'll profit."

"I'd prefer the time with my family," Junior replied.

Another rebuke. Neither brother wished him fortune. They were the obedient older sons, loyal and dutiful. Ulysses turned at last to Alexander, the bachelor caught in the parental nest, doing the heavy work that the senior Stanford McQueen could no longer manage. This brother, at least, wore a mischievous grin under his unruly thatch of red hair.

"Wish I could go with you," he said. "It'll be an adventure."

He laughed, and Ulysses joined him.

"I'll write," Ulysses promised. "You all write me care of Sutter's Fort, Sacramento River, California."

The McQueens weren't a hugging family, not even a kiss-on-the-cheek one—unlike the Strawbridges—so Ulysses shook hands with his sisters-in-law, Lucy and Sarah, patted three solemn children—Becky, Lizbeth, and Isaiah—on the head, shook hands with his parents, and gave Alex a clap on the back.

"You'll get it back, twice over," he said to Alex, alluding to the two hundred dollars that Alex had furtively lent him.

Alex nodded uneasily. The loan hadn't been a secret but it had certainly irked their father, and had become one of those unmentioned topics that families gently worked around in their daily talk.

"It's a long way to Kanesville," he said, by way of escaping that gloom-charged kitchen.

"We'll pray daily," said his mother.

"Oh, Ulysses," whispered chestnut-haired Sarah, who was Ulysses' favorite sister-in-law. Not even McQueen solemnity could savage her ebullience, and he sensed that his adventure secretly delighted her.

The family followed Ulysses out the door and stood on the veranda while he untied his mules. He waved cheerfully, and headed down the lane in a thicker mist, not turning to look back.

Not until he reached the western edge of the several McQueen farms did he begin to relax. He was off for California, in a cloud of disapproval. He marveled that he had found the courage to go, to break free of the endless bindings that had gently and tyrannically trapped him to Mount Pleasant. He loved his kin; that wasn't at issue. But he was going to live life his own way, and when he came home with a "pocketful of rocks," as the California-bound fellows were all saying, he would win some grudging respect from his father. Or would he?

He hiked across fields toward the pike that would take him west, through Lockridge and Batavia and Fairfield, on to Ottumwa, and out into half-settled prairie country where the road would become an elusive two-rut wagon trail, and he would have to ford streams, and there would be no corduroy roads across bogs. He faced a hike of almost three hundred miles just to get to Council Bluffs—some called it Kanesville now—one of the great marshaling and outfitting towns for those heading out the Platte River Road to California or Oregon.

He wished he could take a wagon, but he lacked the means. The little cast-off buckboard his family had given him at the time of his marriage wouldn't do, and besides, Susannah would need it. His best hope was to join a party with wagons. His precious cash would have to buy an outfit in Council Bluffs, food enough for six months on the trail, and provisions to keep him alive in the goldfields until he could stake a claim and begin digging up the rocks himself.

He had heard there would be packmule outfits going west, and he could always join one of them. They moved a lot faster than the ox-drawn wagons. Mules were cantankerous and contrary, but a good man could tame them well enough. When storms hit a packmule outfit, there would be no shelter. If a man took ill with dysentery or cholera, or broke a bone, or was wounded by an arrow, there would be no wagon to carry him. The wretch would be abandoned on the trail, awaiting whatever fate had in store.

Well, he thought, it wouldn't come to that. He would negotiate his passage with one of the many wagon companies heading for the goldfields. He reckoned he had the best mules in the county, and they'd get him to California one way or another.

The rain strengthened as he headed west. His body felt warm enough under the oilskins, but his boots had soaked through, and his feet felt like blocks of ice. As long as he kept walking he could bear the cold, but it wasn't going to be a picnic.

Doubts crowded him; he couldn't fight them back. He could quit right now, before he was committed beyond recall. Susannah would rejoice, smother him with attention, and before he knew it he'd be plowing the south field. His brothers might smirk, but his parents were too large for that, and would quietly welcome him home. His mother would ascribe his return to divine intervention.

He wiggled a set of cold toes within the chafing boot, and trudged grimly westward, ever west. It had been hard, and was still hard. Right now, Susannah would be trying to put a devastated life together, doing humdrum things, and probably thinking about him, just as he was intensely aware of her. Didn't she know he had to go? Had to try? She had never understood his vision, or saw what he saw, or realized what a golden chance it was for them both. Mysterious California enchanted him. This soaring adventure was what he had read about and dreamed of for many weeks. Whenever his neighbors gathered around the potbellied stoves of Mount Pleasant, the California gold was all they talked about, making much of every published account. He had grown wild with it, the images of the long trip west filling his mind, along with visions of the exciting scramble for nuggets in the canyons of California.

He loved Susannah and was glad she would wait for him. She would keep a hearth and home for him, and be there, with a feisty McQueen child, when he returned. It annoyed him that they were all saying they'd never see him again. He brimmed with health and strength, and was wise to the ways of nature, as any other farm-bred youth would be. He knew livestock, knew how to shoot, knew how to protect himself. No lily-livered city slicker was he.

But as he trudged through the muddy miles, and the cold stabbed his bones, he wondered.

CHAPTER 3

McQueen trudged through a gloomy day, but his spirits rose with each step. Excitement infused him. He had stepped down the lane a son and youth; now, a dozen miles west, he was a free adult. He scarcely noticed the thin rain, which rolled off his hat brim and down his oilskins. Only his cold feet reminded him that he would scarcely see the inside of a building for two thousand miles.

The dreary overcast denied him his sense of time. But when hunger overtook him, he judged it was time to eat. He nooned at a crossroads saloon. A mug of cider and a bowl of stew cost him three bits and a dozen questions from the nosy proprietress. Then he slogged on, into hilly country that made his pulse climb as he ascended, and finally into a thickening of the light, which heralded the end of that March day. He had hiked a good piece, and it was time to find a haven.

He wasn't worried. There would be places. At the next farmstead he turned into the lane, eyeing a rawboned whitewashed farmhouse with a commodious barn nearby.

A weathered man with his thumbs hooked under his galluses awaited him at the door.

"What brings you here, stranger?" the man asked.

"I'm looking for a place to put up my mules and spread a bedroll."

"I thought so. We get a few off the pike." He surveyed the mules. "Nice smooth animals, Missouri-bred, I'd reckon."

"Yes they are, sir."

"Where do you hail from?"

"Henry County, sir, Mount Pleasant."

"Well, you're hardly across the line. And where're you headed?"

"California, sir."

The man wheezed softly. "Another danged fool. You're the third in three days. You all figure you'll get rich." He came to some sort of decision. "Sure, there's a loft out there, and you can hay your mules for two bits. I'll want to know your name."

"Ulysses McQueen."

"McQueen's a name I know. All right, then. I'm Joshua Grey. The wife's not well so you'll have to rustle your own grub. It'll give you a little practice. You'll fix a lot of grub out there—if you ever get there."

McQueen paid the man with a quarter, visited with him a few minutes more, and drifted out to the sopping barnyard and into the cold barn. He heard the snort of horses as he entered, and made out a pair of Belgians, which peered at him from soft brown eyes.

He led his mules to a water trough supplied by a hand pump, cranked the handle until a good stream poured in, and let the mules drink. They weren't thirsty. They had snatched at brown grasses dripping with rainwater, all day. Then he put his mules into a single large stall, undid the cinches and britching, and pulled the heavy packsaddles and blankets off their backs. He found a currycomb on a windowsill and ran it over the slick backs of the mules, feeling their muscles spasm and dance as he loosened the packed-down hair.

McQueen clambered up a ladder to the loft, discovered a

diminished mound of hay—no doubt the loft had been full in the fall—and a pitchfork. He pitched hay into the manger below, doing it with a practiced hand, and watched the mules tackle their supper.

It was time to eat. He eased down the rungs, opened his packs, and dug out a wheel of cheese and some buns. He wanted a steaming meal after a cold day, but he would make do. He ate in decaying light, knowing he would have to settle himself quickly. He was loath to light a candle, an act that would bring swift eviction.

He hung the panniers from rafter hooks to keep rats out of them, dug out his bedroll, which consisted of double blankets and good tight duck cloth, climbed into the loft and spread the roll on some leveled hay. He probably would be warm enough with only the blankets, but a man could burrow into the hay if he had to. Then he unlaced his clammy boots, knowing that they wouldn't dry out overnight.

He rubbed his stockinged feet ruefully. They weren't blistered—he wasn't so dumb as to start across a continent in new boots—but they were sore and so cold he wondered if his toes would ever be warm. Then he slid into his bedroll. Tomorrow he would start raising a beard. There would be no point in shaving on the trail, and he'd heard that shaved men got burnt, chapped, frosted and blistered out there.

Thoughts of home crowded his mind. He wondered what Susannah was doing just now. Washing the supper dishes? He doubted she was alone. The Strawbridges would be with her. He ached to settle down beside her in the fourposter, as he always did, she in her white sleeping gown, her silky brown hair loose, her manner still shy. He ached for the moment when she would snuggle her head into the hollow of his shoulder, throw a slim arm across his chest, and talk quietly about all the things that had happened that day.

But as he lay in the straw, the larger dream enveloped him. He knew just what he would do when he got to California: he'd visualized it a thousand times. He would buy a goldpan, pick and shovel, and then head into the Sierras. He would go alone, and penetrate farther upstream than the rest, as close to the mother lode as he could get. He'd try the gravel in places the rest wouldn't touch because they were hard to reach. That's where the dust would be—down in some chasm he'd find a secret bar loaded with nuggets and flakes, and take out a fortune. In Mount Pleasant he'd heard some lucky ones were cleaning out a thousand dollars a day. He *knew* he could find one of those hidden spots, and it would only take a few weeks for him to make his fortune. It was all so clear to him that he even knew the chasm; he'd recognize it when he saw it. He'd show 'em.

"Susannah, just you wait and see!" he exclaimed into the creaking darkness of the barn. He heard a scurrying below, and supposed his outburst had frightened some small creature.

He was arguing with phantoms. He was on his own now, with no one to stop him. There was a new world a-building out there, a world where an ordinary fellow could become something. A world of beginnings. He didn't imagine he would spend long in that wild place. He'd get his gold and bring it back, and then he would not be beholden to his father.

He slept restlessly that night, at one point sharing his nest with a purring cat that snugged into his ribs.

"Susannah," he said, half awake.

He didn't wait for dawn. Upon the promise of light in the southeastern sky, he threw back his blankets, wolfed down some more cheese, and poked his feet into the clammy brogans. That turned out to be a torment, but he knew he wouldn't get to California if he let such discomforts rule him.

He hiked west, on the cusp of winter and spring, sometimes enjoying a seductive zephyr, more often enduring sharp cold. He slept in barns, ate in country saloons, bought provender in country stores, listened one night to prairie wolves as he slept in a haystack. Often he stopped to visit with people on the pike, listening to men in wagons, doffing his felt hat to women. Most of them laughed at him, especially the ones who had rooted into the land like great trees, never to budge again.

No matter where he was, the topic was California. Skeptics cited a long history of wild rumors and frauds. Visionaries thought that one could pluck up gold as if it were eggs lying in the grass, and walk away with burlap sacks full of it. A few dreamed of empire, Stars and Stripes on the Pacific. God's Promised Land. But the kind McQueen encountered most frequently were those who shook their heads sadly, and opined that the young man would surely perish of the cholera, die of snakebite, collapse from sunstroke, experience the bowel complaint after drinking alkali water, die of an arrow, croak of exhaustion or exposure, leave his bones on the prairie in a buffalo stampede or die on the horn of an angry ox. And if he got to California, the gold would all be gone, scooped up by those who'd arrived before.

He listened patiently to all that. Some people could talk themselves out of anything. Some people talked that way just to hide their own cowardice. He discovered that something separated him from them. He had the courage to try.

April arrived, and with it some coy warmth. A faint skim of green appeared in some meadows if one looked carefully, which McQueen did, with a farmer's eye. Not until that grass was up enough to feed the oxen could anyone leave for California. And not until the soupy roads dried out and hardened could anyone hope to take a wagon over them. He reckoned that his life on a farm was in his favor: he would know better than most when to start.

He arrived one sunny April noon at the outskirts of Council Bluffs, and found the place a madhouse. Men were living in rude tents and covered wagons, outfitting themselves, breaking green oxen to yoke or fractious mules to harness. He wandered through the motley crowds of sour-smelling males who were outfitting themselves, past smoky campfires that made his eyes run, past gaudy tent stores run by slick hucksters in silk hats, past smiths who were hammering iron onto the cloven feet of oxen. Raucous outfitters hawking goods from their tailgates accosted him. Traders eyed his good mules and bid for them as he passed, but he ignored them.

He found himself among hundreds of uprooted, unshaven, unwashed men, all of them waiting for the grass and looking for an edge or an angle. All of them scheming against the rest or forming alliances. All of them itching for the gold of California. All of them his rivals.

CHAPTER 4

E verywhere McQueen drifted, he came upon encampments chock-full of wagons, tents, horses, oxen, mules, and mountains of gear. He peered about him, flabbergasted. Thousands of people were about to head west.

Some camps were full of women and children, while others were all male. He realized that he was, after all, about to head out the Mormon Trail on the north bank of the Platte River. The camps with the families were those of Saints heading for Salt Lake. Each spring, since 1847, the Saints had gathered in Council Bluffs and headed west. But the all-male camps contained the gold-seekers, the "Californians." These men had formed themselves into companies, and had painted insignia on the sides of their wagon sheets. He came upon the Madison Badgers from Wisconsin, the Galena Miners, the Platteville, New York, Ramblers, who were all wearing gray uniforms with red piping, the Bethlehem Strutters, the Minnesota Rangers, the Marquette Company, on and on. Most of these fellows looked young, city-bred, and uncomfortable in their new boots and stiff woolen duds. He spotted a sprinkling of older men among them, some who might well be doctors or lawyers. One thing struck him forcefully: few were poor. These fine wagons and snowy tents and young saddlehorses and fat oxen had cost a young fortune.

The spectacle shocked him. If Council Bluffs contained so many, then Independence and St. Joseph, more accessible by river transport from all over the country, would contain a hundred times more. It was as if half the young men in the country were about to race for the bonanza gold.

He hiked westward until he found the bustling town of Kanesville. He still could not see the Missouri but the tilt of the land suggested it wasn't far. He led his packmules through the streets, discovering a bedlam of mercantiles, tent saloons, wagon-based purveyors of everything imaginable, hay and grain dealers, and bawling oxen and mules penned in rope corrals.

A chesty man in a silk top hat and brocaded vest stopped him. "Those mules for sale, son?" he asked.

"No, sir."

"Mighty fine flesh," the man said, disappointed. "Would you take two hundred apiece? In gold?"

The amount stunned McQueen. That was twice what he supposed they were worth. But he shook his head. "No, sir, these are personal, from my farm, not for sale."

"You'd better hope the redskins don't steal them. Are you with a packmule outfit?"

"No, sir, I arrived not a half hour ago and I'm just taking a look-see."

"Well, I'm not with an outfit either, and not inclined to join one. When I calculate the odds, I like them. I live by odds; I like the edge. Maybe we can team up. Where'll you be?"

McQueen studied the man for the first time, and found a topheavy older man with smoky eyes and a sardonic worldliness about him, a sort he had never seen in Mount Pleasant. This one styled his salted gray hair almost to his shoulders, wore a black cutaway coat, a high collar and cravat with a huge diamond stickpin in it, and polished boots. The man endured this survey with faint amusement. "My profession is cards," he said in a Missouri voice. "And you're a plowman."

"I own a good black-bottomed farm, Old Oak, in Ioway," McQueen replied stiffly. He knew enough to steer clear of a man like this. "I'm going to join a wagon company."

"Well, that's fine. My name's Asa Wall and I command the only decent hotel room in town—there." He pointed toward a hostelry called Kane House. "Look me up if you change your honorable mind."

McQueen escaped the gambler and perused the rest of town. Most prices seemed reasonable; competition from the tent merchants had driven prices down in spite of the huge demand for everything imaginable. He priced used rifles at fifteen or sixteen dollars, the same for revolvers. For another dollar and a half he could get a bullet mold, bar of lead, box of caps, wads, and a can of powder thrown in.

He left town reluctantly, knowing his first business was to

join an outfit. But finding the right men took some study. Some camps looked slovenly; others had been policed and kept clean. He finally settled on a Wisconsin group out of Beloit. Its men looked healthy and trim; some of the members were obviously farm people, solid as spreading oaks. He approached one who was shoeing an ox.

"I'm looking to join a company," he said.

The man straightened up, surveyed McQueen slowly, obviously studying his demeanor, age, and mules. "We're a wagon outfit," he said slowly. "I suppose you have one, and it's in top shape?"

"No, sir. Just the packmules."

"We've all paid a hundred into the company. The fees bought us two mess wagons, tents, and chow for a hundred twenty days. If you'd like, I'll take you to the captain. We'd vote on it this evening. I didn't catch your name."

"Ulysses McQueen, sir. Mountain Pleasant, Iowa. I farm."

"Deacon Howells, and so do I," the man said. They shook. Howells led McQueen to a goateed, pox-scarred man whose face was shaded by a spotless new slouch hat.

"Thorstein," said the man without preamble. "You want to join us, I take it?"

Howells made the introduction and let McQueen make his case.

Then the captain responded. "We've some requirements, you understand. All the companies going overland have organized themselves. Each man must have five hundred dollars cash. Each must purchase a portion of our mess with a hundred dollars, on an equal-share basis. That'll buy your food and supply our mess tents. Each must have a wagon in good condition, a sidearm and rifle. We've thirty-eight members. They've voted me their captain, and Howells the lieutenant, and each has expressly agreed to suffer our discipline and sign our articles. There'll be regular weekly meetings on the trail to handle problems. The company can expel members and return their share." The formidable Thorstein waited for McQueen to absorb all that. "Well, young man, do you wish to join us?"

"No, sir, I don't qualify," McQueen mumbled.

"Well, we've formed for our mutual protection. You'll want

to find a suitable company. Try the next grove. That's a pack-mule outfit from northern Missouri."

McQueen nodded. He headed for the Missourians, his mind full of what he had learned. He hadn't thought that going west would involve taking orders. He had imagined it would all be ganging together, like school friends. He didn't like what he'd heard. Thorstein had sounded all too much like his father.

The Missourians turned out to be rough-dressed frontiers-men, occupying a much less disciplined camp. About fifty mules stirred around a rope corral strung through some osage trees. All of the men sported luxuriant beards. Many wore but-ternut britches, or fringed leather jackets.

McQueen approached one who sat against a tree, honing the blade of a formidable sticker. "Who do I talk to about joining this outfit?" he asked.

"I don't reckon we want to be joined," the man said, squint-ing upward. "We're all family and kin, and you ain't Missoura, that's for plain sartin."

McQueen was not deterred. "This is a packmule outfit? Are you leaving soon?"

"We'll be packing," the man said. "We'll be walking our heels down. We'll be out in the middle of the weather. We'll freeze and sweat and cuss. But we'll walk to Californy before half these ox outfits git out on the prairie."

"That's what I want. I mean to get to the diggings and find a good claim ahead of the crowd."

The man laughed. "You ain't the only one. There's already a few dumb pukes gone, carrying a lot of oats because there ain't any grass up. It ain't so smart, though. I hear they're all mired down. It'll be a month before the trails pack down." He eyed McQueen. "Where do you hail from?"

"Henry County, Iowa. I farm."

"Cub like you don't hardly look old enough to push a plow through pillow feathers. I never had much use for Ioway."

McQueen could see how this was going. "I'd like to join."

"You good at taking orders, boy?"

"I'll make my own decisions. But I'm good at cooperating."

"That's what I mean. You ain't kith or kin or neighbor. And you don't take orders. If we take any outsider, he'd better obey.

If we say cut kindling, he cuts. If we say spit, he spits. If we say don't eat, he don't eat. Naw, you go find another outfit."

"You know of any pack outfit?"

The man shrugged, dismissively.

McQueen dealt with seven more outfits that afternoon, growing more and more discouraged. They all wanted a lot of money, and they all wanted him to knuckle under, or join some joint stock company and sign its articles, which often read like the Constitution of the United States, only six pages longer. The various anointed captains and majors ritually warned McQueen he'd die if he went alone; he'd end up with an arrow in his brisket, or gutted by the cholera. But he kept wondering about that. Why couldn't a man head west with a partner? He began looking for loners like himself, and found a few who were as independent as he was, but they looked like cutthroats.

He studied the Mormon camps longingly, but they would be slowest of all, laden with household stuff, women and children, and livestock. Most of them wouldn't roll until the trails hardened and plenty of grass was up. And in any case, Salt Lake was only halfway to California.

At dusk he headed back to Kanesville, grudgingly laid out two dollars to a feed dealer for skimpy baits of hay for his mules, and hunted for a campground, worried that someone would steal his mules while he slept. Through the day he had resisted several offers for them, and watched dozens of eyes silently survey his excellent animals. He felt hungry, tired, and discouraged.

He thought it might be safest to camp right in town. There'd be people around all night. None of the big outfits was camping close in, and he wondered if that was forbidden. He supposed he'd be chased out if it was. He picked a spot hardly a holler from the main street. It probably was private property, but he'd give it a try.

He picketed his mules, unsaddled them, laid out the bedroll, fought off loneliness, and suddenly remembered Susannah's letters. He dug into his kit, pulled out the fragrant packet, and extracted the first.

"My dear husband," she began. "Now we are apart. If we have the power to send our spirits along with our beloved, then I could be sure my spirit is walking beside you. I would like to comfort you on the trail, lighten your load, dream your dreams and hope your hopes. But I don't suppose my spirit is anywhere but in my bosom. I am proud of you. You have the courage to try new things and reach for the stars. You are the finest man a woman could have. I miss you. I hope you dream of me tonight. Your own Susannah."

What strange stuff that was, he thought. And yet the letter pleased him, even with all its odd speculations. Spirits outside of the body indeed. Tenderly he placed the letter to the rear of the sheaf, and tied the packet tight.

He needed chow but he didn't want to waste four bits in some tent beanery. He'd manage with a cold meal. He was pulling out his wheel of cheddar when the voice caught him:

"How'd it go, my upright young friend?" yelled the smoky-eyed gambler, Asa Wall, from a second-story window.

"It went just fine," McQueen answered.

CHAPTER 5

Moments later, Asa Wall strode through the dusk and settled himself on a stump. McQueen continued to make camp silently. The skies worried him. It might rain and he had no refuge.

"I can see you didn't connect, boy," Wall said.

McQueen didn't like being called boy, especially by a tinhorn. "I'll find an outfit tomorrow," he said.

"You had trouble, I take it. They want you to sign articles tougher than a temperance pledge."

Ulysses loosened the cinch of the second packsaddle, and lifted it off the mule. "I'm too poor for most of 'em."

"They require a wagon and outfit."

He had the sense that this wasn't entirely a social conversation, and he wondered how to fend off Wall. "I'm not cut out to sign articles and take orders," he said.

The gambler chuckled. "Neither am I. I'm not much of a follower. Nearly every sporting man I know bought passage to Panama. Nice easy sail down there, lots of pilgrims on board, looking for a little game; then fifty miles of land to cross, and a nice easy sail to California. All they have to do is survive the fevers and hope some ships miraculously appear on the Pacific side to pick them up and take them to California. I hear the Chagres fever is a killer. That and cholera, typhoid, and the ague."

"I wouldn't know."

"Anyway, the sports took the easy way and I'm taking the hard way. That's how I am."

McQueen pulled his bedroll open and let it air. He eyed the gambler, wary of him.

"What'll you do if you can't find a wagon outfit?" Wall asked.

"Join a packmule outfit, I guess."

"Those are organized like the others. You've got to sign on, pay in, and obey the captain."

"What are you getting at, Mr. Wall?"

"I'm looking for a partner."

"Sorry, I'm not your type."

That didn't seem to faze the gambler. "That's all to the good. I wouldn't want to partner with my type. I'm thinking of jumping off now and carrying some grain on a riding horse. Feed grain until the grass is up, then ride. I found three mules today. One'll carry my faro layout. The other two'll carry my gear. You're a farm boy—"

"I'm twenty, not a boy, and I'm Ulysses McQueen."

"—familiar with animals, not some city dude. Do you hunt?"

"No. I come from settled country. When we want meat we either buy it or slaughter it."

"You can slaughter?"

"It's not anything I enjoy."

"But you could dress game?"

McQueen nodded. It irritated him that Wall seemed to think the matter was settled. "It's not safe to go west alone. We have to go in armed parties or we'll be killed by the Indians. That's what everyone says."

Wall lifted his top hat and settled it. "I grew up in St. Louis, around the Planters Hotel, talking with all the mountain men. They wandered the whole west alone or in pairs."

"You know mountain men?"

"You name 'em. Bridger, Jed Smith, Joe Meek, Davy Jackson, Robert Campbell, the Sublettes . . ."

McQueen paused. "But you became a gambler."

Wall shrugged. "Dealing pasteboards is a lot easier than setting traps in icy streams. And a lot more profitable." He smiled. "And a lot more sociable. I like company."

That set McQueen to wondering. "What's your proposition?"

"We each get a saddle horse, load it with grain, and head out on foot along with our mules. When the grain's gone we ride. Beat the mob. There'll be ten or twenty thousand people at our heels. We've got to hurry; some outfits have left already, carrying grain."

"What happens if we run into redskins?"

"They don't move much until grass is up, just like us."

"What if they steal our stock?"

Wall shrugged. "You don't win if you don't bet. McQueen, risks are a part of life. High risks, high rewards. Getting out there first gives you a crack at the best gravel. There's only so much streambed to stake out. For me, getting there first means opening up my table ahead of the competition. It's worth a fortune to get there first."

"The ones going across the Isthmus will get there ahead of us. Some left in November. A lot in December."

"Some will—if they survive. And if they don't have to wait a couple of months in Panama City for a wandering whaler."

"I can't afford a horse."

"No one's taking horses west, so they're going begging. You can get a cheap plug. Fifty dollars. A saddle for ten."

"I don't know—"

"Let me tell you something, McQueen. There's only one ferry down there on the levee. When the grass is up, folks here'll be waiting for weeks to cross the Missouri. There's two thousand wagons here, they say, and more coming every day. Think on it. That ferry takes two wagons at a time, nearly an hour a trip. That's a mighty wide river. Right now there's no wait. A few smart people are moving over to the Indian country right now, completely outfitted and waiting there."

"What's the price?"

"I hear it's two dollars a head for livestock, one dollar a person. If you got a horse, you'd pay seven dollars for ferrying you and your stock."

McQueen felt tugged in several directions. Wall's proposition seemed good, but going west with a gambler seemed like just the sort of folly his mother had solemnly warned him to avoid. And he hadn't explored all the outfits.

Wall was grinning.

"I have to think about it. I don't know anything about you."

"That goes for both of us. You sleep on it. Let me know in the morning. We can get outfitted, pick up two plugs, buy grain, and be across the Missouri before dark."

McQueen nodded, utterly unsure. "Have you been out there—out west?"

The gambler didn't answer. He was staring at a black-bearded man slumped on a store porch, his back to the post. The man was groaning. His trousers were soaked with some sort of murky stain. The man's friends had gathered around him.

"Oh, no," Wall muttered.

"What is it?"

"See that fellow? He came up on the *Cairo Belle* with me two days ago. He's sick as a dog. See it?"

McQueen noticed a blue cast in the man's face. The man's mouth hung open and he sucked in air. "He sure isn't well," he muttered.

"McQueen. I've lived in river towns all my life. I'd lay hundred-to-one odds that poor devil's got cholera."

Cholera. The word shot terror through Ulysses.

"Those fellows with him haven't figured it out yet. They think it's dysentery. But that's cholera if ever I saw it."

"It came up the river on that boat?"

Wall nodded gravely. "You want to partner or not? Because I'm getting out of here before there's a rush on that ferry. I reckon we've a couple of hours to beat the mob."

Ulysses listened, astonished at the man's presumption. "What makes you think I'm going with you? And why should I trust you?"

"You'll trust me when you learn I deal off the top of the deck. If you don't like the way I deal when we get out in Indian country, drop out and wait for an outfit to come along. I'm not signing you to any compact. It's your decision, and you'll have to make it right now."

Impulsively, McQueen stuck out a hand, and Wall clasped it. "Do what you have to do. I'll do what I have to do. I'll meet you here in an hour. Let's hope the ferry stays open."

"I've got a lot to do, McQueen."

"So do I. We'll do better if we don't duplicate. I've got a skillet, coffeepot, kettle, tin plate, cup, and stuff. I've a fowling piece. One of us should have a hunting rifle and powder and all. I've a piece of duck cloth that's been waterproofed with linseed and beeswax; it'll make a half shelter. I'll load up on chow—flour, saleratus, sidepork, beans, and coffee. Some buckwheat, rice, molasses, sugar, and salt, too. I know what to get."

"I've a rifle. I'll get my hardware and mess gear from my room. I'll look for two plugs and some oats, and collect my mules; you buy chow. Meet you in front of that mercantile so we can load up the mules."

"Let's get going."

McQueen raced to a lamplit mercantile, tied his mules in front, and surveyed the heaped goods within. He made snap decisions, the items on the counter piling up with amazing speed. Years of living on a farm helped him. In twenty minutes he had completed the deal, astonishing the clerk by not haggling or complaining. He poured bank notes and quarter eagles and half eagles on the counter. There wasn't much change in his purse when he began loading his mules.

The street was quiet. The sick man had been helped away by his friends. Men walked calmly from store to store, as if no thunderhead loomed over them about to dash their hopes to bits. But McQueen knew the calm was deceptive. Any moment a howl might rise from the throat of Kanesville, and those who were smart and ready would head for the ferry.

He filled the panniers on his mules and waited. He saw no sign of Wall and grew impatient. A heap of goods still stood on the plank porch. Then at last he spotted the jaunty gambler, hurrying three sorry mules and two miserable saddle horses. Each horse carried a full duffel bag over its saddle.

"Laziest, most contrary clerk I ever dealt with," Wall grumbled. "I'd have liked to call his bluff. That idiot wanted me to dicker everything, and started sneering when I offered what he asked. 'All right, tinhorn,' he says, seeing a mark. I let him think it. He'll learn why in a few minutes." Wall peered around. "Nothing's stirred up yet, eh?"

McQueen shook his head, and began loading Wall's sullen mules. Daylight was waning. The ferrymen might quit. He worked furiously, balancing the loads, making sure the heaviest items sat low, desperately wondering what they had missed and would have no chance to buy until they reached Fort Kearney or even Laramie. It was up to him to remember everything because Wall wouldn't know much about living outdoors. McQueen stared at the gambler's waxen face, knowing it hadn't seen much weather.

"Where'd you get the horses, Mr. Wall?" he asked.

"Bought 'em on the spot from some kid for sixty apiece, saddles and all. They'll probably buck—I didn't try them out. The kid took me for a sucker, but I had my reasons. I already had the mules, but I was hoping to trade up. You owe me for one plug, bag of oats, and some hobbles, and I owe you for half the chow."

"I don't have much left."

"I have enough. Let's get across that river and then we'll worry about it."

They grabbed reins and led their little pack train through town and down the sharp slope to the Missouri River, which muscled its way south in the gloomy light. The far shore seemed an aching distance away. Ulysses made out the ferry in the middle of the river, slowly working its way west. It probably wouldn't be back to the east bank for an hour. So they were going to have to wait, while behind them the beast stretched its claws.

CHAPTER 6

A s they descended the dark bluff to the river bottoms, Ulysses McQueen spotted three white-sheeted wagons and some livestock gathered at the crossing. An outfit was ahead of them, waiting for the ferry. That meant another hour's delay. Wall smiled wryly. "Let's hope we get the jump on 'em," he said.

At the foot of the brooding cliff McQueen discovered a row of stores and houses that stretched along the flat only a few feet above the surly river. Lamplight glowed from the windows of a clapboard store. Next to it stood a darkened post office, which reminded him that he should write Susannah. He wouldn't have another chance.

But they hastened to the ferry landing, a muddy ramp that vanished into the sucking river. There an outfit consisting of a dozen men, three small covered wagons, and twenty or so oxen waited for the distant scow to complete its toilsome journey.

"Guess you're after us," one big fellow said.

"Yes, if the ferry operates at night," McQueen replied.

"It do. This hyar ferryman knows how his bread's buttered. He cusses the lot of us, but takes our coin. He'll take you, all right, cussing the darkness, and then he'll shut down unless some other bunch shows up. But no one does after it gets dark."

"You fellows planning to get an early jump on the road?" Wall asked casually, and McQueen knew the gambler was probing.

"No, we just reckon we'll wait on the yonder shore. There'll be a rush when it greens up, let me tell you."

"That's what we figure, too," McQueen said.

No talk of cholera. That was good.

"How long does it take to get across and back?" Wall asked.

"Oh, it's forty minutes if there's a bunch on board that'll do some smart poling. Longer otherwise."

"That's better than we thought," Ulysses said. "What's the price?"

"We don't rightly know, but it'll be too steep for my purse." The fellow turned to attend to an ox that was bellowing at something.

"Well, McQueen, I guess we've a couple of hours," Wall said. "You want to settle up?"

"I do," he said, relieved that the gambler wasn't going to stick him with the food bill. "And I want to look over those horses."

Wall pulled out his invoices for mess gear, powder, lead, and various hardware items, and a bill of sale for the two plugs.

Ulysses' cost for one horse, saddle and bridle, picket lines, halters, hobbles, oats, duffel bag, and some camping gear came to seventy-one dollars. Wall's share of the foodstuffs came to sixty-two and one bit.

"Guess you owe me eight and seven bits," Wall said.

McQueen dug into his bag, dismayed to find only an eagle and a few coins in it. He choked up. "I don't have enough to pay you. Or get across the Missouri," he muttered.

"How much do you have?"

"An eagle and some change. That's all I've got in the world."

"We're in this together, McQueen. I'll see you across the river, and you can owe me."

"I sure owe you more than cash. I'll repay somehow," he replied. He gave Wall the ten dollars to cover his debt and some of the cost of ferrying, and stared fearfully at the steep road up the bluff, half expecting a crazed mob to thunder down it and commandeer the ferry. But he saw nothing. He peered through the murk and discovered the ferry was returning, using a sail to take advantage of a westerly wind.

"I want to write a letter to my wife," he said to Wall. "Maybe I can do it in the store."

"Go ahead. I'll hold the place in line, kid."

Ulysses turned the mules over to the gambler and hastened into a lamplit mercantile, purchased a sheet of paper, an envelope, and a one-cent stamp from the old storekeep, and borrowed a pen from him. The white paper rebuked him. He didn't have a thing to say to Susannah. He hated to scratch out letters anyway. He'd written only two or three all his life.

"April 17, 1849," he began. "Dear Susannah, I have formed a partnership with Asa Wall of St. Louis, and we are leaving for California today. I am in good health. It has been cold. Write me at Sutter's Fort, Sacramento River, California. That is where I will get the mail. I will write you when I can. I will do well and bring home a pocket full of rocks. I miss you. I will be thinking about you and the baby, and praying for your health and comfort. Do not catch the catarrh." Then he added, "Your loving husband, Ulysses McQueen."

He glued the envelope shut, affixed the penny stamp and dropped the letter into the post-office mail slot. He had fourteen cents to his name.

Fearfully, he examined the road up the bluff again but saw no one. Up there, Kanesville brooded in the twilight, cloaking its murderous secret a little longer. But the last of the sand was running through the hourglass. "Just let Wall and me get across," he growled into the thickening dark.

He hurried back to the river where Wall was talking amiably with the other party, which was boarding the ferry. The rectangular flat-bottomed barge settled deeper as wagons and oxen and men boarded, until the weathered ferrymen called a halt. "The rest of them ox, they gonna wait," the operator bawled.

"You can squeeze 'em in."

"I can but I won't, and if there's an argument, ye can all get off."

With that, the overburdened barge slid into the night, leaving seven oxen and two men behind. One of them grinned. "Reckon you and us'll be shipmates," he said.

Itchily, Ulysses nodded. He consumed time by examining the plugs Wall had purchased, feeling hocks and pasterns for heat, lifting hooves, riding each a little, while Wall watched.

"One's wormy, and the other's probably twenty, judging from the set of his ribs, but they'll do," he said. "At least for two or three hundred miles."

"You can always go back and trade 'em for better. You're the farmer."

"Not on your life."

He itched to get across that black river. It seemed forever before the ferry returned, forever to load up the oxen, mules and horses. Then the ferryman collected. Wall pulled out his purse and paid for both of them. McQueen sighed, knowing he was starting across the continent beholden.

They shoved into the night, and hadn't poled twenty yards into the watery gloom when Wall pointed at the bluff. Men with lanterns were descending it.

"McQueen," he said, "you and your partner Asa Wall are a pair of lucky sons of bitches."

He nodded. He didn't like coarse talk. No one around Mount Pleasant talked like that. They pushed their poles into the mucky bottom until there was no bottom, and then they paddled beside the ferrymen until they were told to pole again. Finally the ferry bumped the far shore.

The west bank seemed like heaven to McQueen. He stepped off the ferry, pulled the reluctant stock with him, and stared back across the river, where lights bobbed. It had been that close. McQueen sighed, feeling peace steal through him at last.

"Let's walk to the top of the bluffs," he said to Wall. "There'll be a mob coming over all night and some might have cholera."

Wall nodded. They pushed through a moonless night, unable to see the trail at first, until McQueen's sharp eye began to discern it in starlight. He found a little swale, protected from the wind, with some scraggly trees nearby for firewood, and they settled down, feeling like freed prisoners of war.

This place seemed different. They were camping in Indian territory. He had entered this new world penniless and even a little in debt. He lacked cash to buy supplies at Fort Laramie for the second half of the great journey. And any more tolls would stump him. He couldn't even go home now unless he sold a horse or mule.

"Don't much like hard-ground sleeping," Wall said. "See you in the morning."

In the light of dawn they discovered scores of wagons on the river flats under the bluffs. Men labored around the encampments below, mending harness and packing gear. McQueen spotted Indians, jet-haired men with coppery faces, some wearing braids. He watched a moment and realized they were woodcutters, selling horseloads of firewood to the campers. Well, he thought, he was in Indian country. He would see Indians.

"McQueen," said Asa. "You fixing to camp here and see the sights, or take off?"

Suddenly civilization tugged at Ulysses, and he stared up the gulch into a transparent heaven burdened with cumulus clouds, reluctant to sever the final thread. He stood poised, on a knife-edge of spirit, adventure and a golden dream drawing him west while love tugged him east.

"It's a grand day. We can make a good piece," Wall said.

"Off to Californy," McQueen said.

They walked up the grade, avoiding the mucky road when they could, and found an undulating plain still winter-brown but with the faintest hint of green on south slopes. The trees surrendered to open land stretching to a horizon lost in spring haze.

They hiked side by side for a long while, saying nothing, absorbing the vastness of this country. There was no need to follow the miry wagon road, and they stayed far to its right. The pack animals came along easily. McQueen's heart lifted. They could walk thirty miles a day this way. Why stick with a slow outfit, lucky to do ten in the mud, or spend a week worrying wagons across a swollen creek? The world seemed very quiet, except when a zephyr eddied around him. But this world seemed intensely alive, too. Clouds plowed shadows across the land. Crows circled.

The road told an appalling story. The iron rims of wagon wheels had cut furrows two feet deep into the soft earth. Men driven by a lust for gold were wearing out their oxen so fast they would not last a hundred miles. McQueen confessed to himself that he shared that lust for gold, and it had carried him and Asa out into Indian country alone. Whose folly was worse? His and Asa's, or the wagon companies plowing the mud up ahead?

They watched a giant thunderhead build in the west, its belly black and angry, its glistening white top growing wider and wider and ever higher against a cobalt sky. It plunged the distant swells of prairie into a blue gloom. McQueen felt a subtle resistance in his picket line. His animals didn't like what they saw.

"Well, Ulysses, we're in for it," Asa said. "We've chosen the fastest way to California, but we're going to pay a price."

CHAPTER 7

S usannah read and reread the letter from Ulysses. It was written so stiffly that it didn't sound like him. It certainly had a guarded quality. Take this Asa Wall, for instance. Ulysses didn't say one word about this partner from St. Louis. That was utterly unlike him. Ulysses loved to describe people in great detail. Maybe it meant that this man was someone the family would not approve.

He was healthy, at least as of two weeks ago, thank God. Cholera had broken out in Independence among the thousands of men waiting for the grass to green. The disease had killed dozens, according to letters in the papers. And it had not spared St. Joseph, either, where thousands more "Californians" waited to start. Cholera struck down mortals like the angry hand of God, and no one had a remedy for it. The disease seemed to stalk through crowded places like the river packets, and hovered around camps where filth piled up. She dreaded the moment when it visited Council Bluffs, silently clawing at Ulysses.

She would write him at Sutter's Fort and let him know that all was well at home: the baby was swelling within her; she had the catarrh but was past it now; Jonathan was plowing and harrowing the fields, and would seed them shortly; the hay was running out but the milch cow would be on grass soon. She gazed out of her window, seeing Ulysses' elder brother toiling behind a pair of mules in the south field, and knew there were things she wouldn't tell Ulysses. The older brother never missed a chance to condemn the younger one as a wastrel.

Sutter's Fort seemed such an impossible distance away; it frightened her to think that Ulysses would travel clear across the continent to that barbarous country wrested from Mexico. Her letter would go by packet down the Mississippi to New Orleans, then by steamer to the Isthmus of Panama, then be taken across by mule, and picked up by a Pacific steamer and carried clear to California, and finally up the Sacramento River to Sutter's Fort. She could think of a thousand ways it might be lost, and another thousand ways Ulysses might be prevented from ever seeing it.

She felt a great ache for him, but what could she do? All she wanted was her husband at her side, sharing her choice chicken dumplings and gravy, scraping his face at the washbowl in the morning, going to services with her each Sunday dressed in his one suit, and she in her best finery. All she wanted was someone to talk to day by day, share her life with, plan for the child, and be close by when the midwife came.

The days had slid by with glacial slowness. Sometimes the McQueens called. Her sisters-in-law stopped by frequently, and that gladdened her. On Sundays one or another of her Strawbridge family came by in the buggy and took her to church, and there she smiled at her neighbors and pretended that she was happy.

From her window she saw Jonathan stop for the nooning. He unhitched the mules and led them to the shelter of Ulysses' barn. Then he headed toward the house. She braced herself. He was always at his most self-righteous when he had put in some hard work. She hurried to the kitchen, set out fresh-made bread and fresh-churned butter, and stirred the beef stew while he pumped water into a basin outside and washed. She had come to dread these moments.

She heard the door open and close, and he materialized in the kitchen.

"Good enough day," he said, settling himself. "I'll be ready to plant tomorrow if the rain stays off." He tackled the fresh warm bread and the new butter.

She set bowls of the steaming stew on the table. He was not a shy eater, and before he stood again the loaf would be demolished. She sat down and toyed with her bowl, not very hungry in spite of the heady aromas. She'd had a touch of morning sickness that day.

"Lucy says you got a letter from Council Bluffs," he said.

"Ulysses is well. That's a relief, with the cholera starting up again. I worry about him so."

"Aren't you going to share it?"

"Oh, there's no news. He's well." But something propelled her to a sideboard where the letter rested. She handed it to him.

He read it, never pausing in his eating.

"Asa Wall of St. Louis. Not a word what this fellow does. If I know Ulysses, he'll wind up in a jam. When it comes to judging a man's character, he can hardly tell which end of the elephant has the trunk."

"Oh, Jonathan, you're jumping to conclusions."

"No, I'm not. If Ulysses was proud of his partner, we'd be hearing the whole pedigree, along with two pages of the man's assets and accomplishments, right down to his church tithes."

Jonathan had a point, she thought. It annoyed her.

"He'll just get himself into trouble. The trouble is, my pa and ma let him get away with all get-out. The youngest son. So he got all the candy and none of the discipline. Now they let him loose, and he's skylarking his life away while responsible people try to make an honest living."

There it was again, the litany she heard most days her brothers-in-law worked Ulysses' fields. She remained silent, waiting for the rest, and was immediately rewarded.

"It's hard enough taking care of my own fields and feeding my own family without cleaning up after Ulysses," he said. "I hardly have time to spend with my own people."

She sipped some broth. Some days he was better; other days, like this one, he was worse. Junior was almost as bad. She would get the whole lecture this time.

"I didn't have a choice. He just expected Alexander and Junior and me to do it all, took us for granted. All so he could go chasing rainbows and moonbeams and making a fool of himself. Well, it's a burden."

"You and Junior get three-quarters of the crop, Jonathan," she said.

"Well, that's if we get a crop. Who knows if it'll rain? Or hail? Or freeze? Or whether we'll be grasshoppered out. I don't need it; the others don't need it."

"You could have said no to Ulysses," she said softly. "I wish you had . . . then you wouldn't have so much to complain about."

He laughed shortly, broke a piece of bread and used it to mop up the juices. "He would've hired some neighbor," Jonathan said. "The McQueens like to keep business in the family."

He settled back in his chair, having demolished everything set before him. "I'd like a siesta, but I can't take the time," he said. "A toiling man should take a long nooning, but younger brothers have their own designs on my time."

"All right!" she said sharply. "I'll pay you for your labor when the crop comes in, and I'll hire a man for the rest."

He glared. "You touchy or something? We McQueens always look after each other."

She felt a flush of temper, and pushed it back.

"I'm just jealous," he said. "That boy don't have to work for a living. It all drops into his soft white paws because he's got a big smile and a cheery way. There's a whole passel of people just itching to make him happy every time he wags his tail."

She pushed back her chair and plucked empty dishes from the checkered oilcloth.

"Here's what'll happen. You can count on it. We'll plant his fields. We'll take care of his gold-rush widow. We'll keep his place up. We'll pay his taxes. And then we'll have a bumper crop, a once-in-fifty-years harvest just when corn prices are high, and that happy-go-lucky cuss'll make more on his twenty-five percent than he would in any normal year. And Mount Pleasant'll welcome the prodigal home, and laugh at how the boy made money skylarking, and it'll become a famous story."

"If he lives," she said softly.

"He's too lucky to croak," Jonathan said. "Well, I'd better hitch up the mules again."

She poured hot water from the stove reservoir into a washbasin, and tackled the dishes angrily. Jonathan was simply voicing what they all thought. Didn't he know how it hurt her?

Was Ulysses just a skylarking boy? Had she made a dreadful mistake? Would she be doomed to a lonely life with a husband who vanished for endless periods while she wrestled with a family and the responsibilities of a home? Jonathan had triggered just such worries in her with each lunch; the whole McQueen family had expressed so many oblique opinions that she had been driven into self-imposed isolation. From the day Ulysses had left, she had felt a barrier between her in-laws and her.

She dried the dishes, crumbed the table, swept the kitchen floor, and faced her mending basket. She didn't feel like mending socks. She didn't feel like sewing, either, though she had a layette to make, and a dozen other things awaiting her. Jonathan had left her in a bleak mood.

She wasn't much at letter-writing, but she had attended female academy and had a good hand even if the words came slowly.

She found paper and an envelope, unstoppered the India, set out the blotter, and dipped into bottle with her steel nib.

"My dear, dear husband," she wrote. "When you receive this at Sutter's Fort you will be half a world away from me, in a strange land among strange people. I wonder whether this fragile sheet of paper will ever reach you. Whether you will survive the terrible trip across the plains and deserts and mountains, with wild Indians on the one hand, and cholera on the other.

"Your letter from Kanesville reached me, and I am heartened that you are in good health, and that you have found a partner. I would like to know more about him. You will need men of strength and courage and high moral standards with you as you face the wilderness. But you know that, and have surely selected a man who will be a true friend and ally when trouble comes. When I look at the maps or study the guidebook, I grow faint with worry.

"I miss you beyond what I can express in words. I wish you could be with me as the little spark of life in me grows. I am well, so far, but we haven't had heat. I wonder how I will survive the summer in such a condition. Jonathan has the south field almost ready for planting. Everyone is well except your mother, who has had the ague again.

"Find your gold and come home. I know how much it means to you to find it. You have great courage and will succeed because it is in you. Write me at every chance. Things are less fearsome when you tell about them, and you tame my awful imagination with your descriptions of your life. When I don't hear, my fears run wild. Take care of your dear, beloved self, and remember me in your thoughts and prayers. Your loving wife, Susannah."

On the envelope she wrote, "Ulysses McQueen, Sutter's Fort, Sacramento River, California."

That place seemed unimaginably far away.

CHAPTER 8

McQueen donned his black oilskins, while Asa Wall slipped into rubberized yellow rain gear. The first eddies of cold air slithered by, the iron scent of rain strong on the breeze. Light faded perceptibly. Ahead, a solid slate-colored wall loomed like a forbidden temple. Above, the white mass vanished into sullen gray overcast, and a few premonitory sprinkles beaded their rain gear.

The farmer and the gambler walked grimly into the gates of hell, knowing there would be no shelter on open prairie. Miles ago they had passed the last of the wooded ravines winding eastward to the Missouri. The horses and mules balked, wanting to turn their rumps to the storm.

The white sword of God shattered the gloom, followed by a rumble. The mules tugged on their picket line, and McQueen took a firmer grip. It wouldn't do to lose them in a storm.

"We could be back in my hotel room watching it through plate glass," Wall said, wild humor building in his face. "How much gold is this worth?"

It was an awful question that McQueen couldn't answer. He watched the staccato play of lightning. Any farmer knew enough to get out of his fields when a storm hit. Anything rising above the land drew the lightning down. He searched desperately for a gulch, and saw none. They were traversing flat country. The icy wind picked up, slicing into every cranny of his oilskins, chafing his face and eddying down his neck. He hunkered into the wind and yanked the reluctant horse and mules savagely.

The rain hit like grapeshot. McQueen felt it slap his face, worm its way into his tight-buttoned collar and chill his back. It came in fierce volleys, pelting them with giant drops that rattled off his slicker. He bent into the wind. The harder he walked, the warmer he would be, and the faster he would reach the end of the ordeal.

Asa Wall was laughing, and that puzzled McQueen. Was that how the gambler dealt with suffering? A shocking blaze of light followed by a crack and rolling thunder startled the animals, and McQueen hung on to the line as they bolted back. He fell, splashing into the soggy earth. But his grip on the picket line hadn't failed. Crossly, he picked himself up while his partner waited. His hands hurt. A rope burn tormented his right palm. There was no escape; they had no place to hide.

Water sluiced off the pack animals, blackening their hides, sliding off the packs, which McQueen devoutly hoped were turning the water. The canvas duffels carrying the grain worried him the most. He hiked grimly ahead, barely able to follow the rutted road, his feet numb and his boots as oozy as a chamois cloth. The animals hung their heads low, resisting every step.

The rain lessened for a few minutes, and McQueen thought the worst had passed. But then white pellets rattled off his oilskins, hammered at his hat brim, and smacked his hands; pea-sized hail, dumping down so fast the whole world whitened. It set up a great clatter, snare-drumming off the packs. His animals halted, fought his line.

"Turn 'em around," he yelled to Wall.

Wall did. McQueen wheeled his animals around until they could stand rump to storm, and there he stood as ice water collected around his boots, minute after minute, while the dead brown grasses vanished under a white burden.

He wrestled with misgivings. Was this the adventure he was seeking? Was this better than the quiet comfort of his farm, and the tenderness of Susannah's love? Somehow, he hadn't quite reckoned on this, even though he was a man of the soil and knew full well the rages of nature.

They stood a weary twenty minutes, though it felt like an hour to McQueen. The hail diminished into a stolid drizzle. He and Wall had passed through the worst. But the light was fading, and they faced a night on a soggy plain with no place even to sit down, much less lie down, and no means to warm themselves. It had turned sharply cold. Wall took the lead this time, walking through the drizzle. They were both looking for a stopping place, but the land yielded none.

They slogged quietly through a deepening gloom. The ground beneath them was soft and treacherous, especially on slopes, making each step perilous. Wall hiked along beside, keeping a companionable silence, and Ulysses paid him grudging homage. But they scarcely knew each other, he reminded himself, and he didn't doubt that if they got right down to comparing ideals, they wouldn't agree on anything.

A sense of danger sharpened McQueen's awareness. A chill could fever him, and there would be no roofed place for him to recover; he would mend or die under the dome of heaven. He rather liked that; he was on his own at last. Whatever else the storm achieved, it had hardened his will. There would be worse ahead, but he would deal with it. If he could weather this, he could weather anything.

The rain ceased but the overcast lingered, and light was draining away by the minute.

"We'll have to stop or lose the road," Wall said.

"It's a worry," McQueen replied. "I can't say I want to stand here and shiver all night. Let's keep on as long as we can. You know, we're hardly fifteen miles out from Kanesville."

The dusk thickened but they were able to perceive the trail. Wagons had plowed giant furrows in it, maybe even since the storm. The ruts were so deep and the mud so adhesive that McQueen wondered how even three yoke of fresh oxen could drag a wagon through it. They topped a considerable hill and beheld at a great distance an astonishing prick of orange light.

"Maybe we'll have us a hot supper after all," Wall said. They began a long muddy descent into a wooded flat, a watercourse of some kind. The fire grew brighter, until at last they beheld three ghostly wagons and various men sitting on logs before a fierce blaze that shot dancing light over the tableau.

"Hello the camp," Wall shouted.

"I think I hear a drowned rat," someone said.

"Two drowned rats," Wall responded.

Men laughed. "Californians, I reckon," someone said.

"Greedy gold-bugs," Wall retorted.

McQueen marveled at the easy camaraderie. He and Wall led their pack animals into a circle of young men, some of them sprouting fresh beards, most of them looking fairly dry.

"Well, this pair's smarter than we were," a fellow said. "We thunk to get a head start, but we're so mired we'll be here until the Fourth of July."

"Well, at least you've shelter. We were fixing to spend the night communing with nature," Wall said. "I'm Asa Wall of St. Louis, and my sidekick is Ulysses McQueen, late of Mount Pleasant, Ioway."

"Well, you've stumbled into some reckless fellows from Dubuque," a man said. "I'll get around to introductions. Fill your mugs; there's a pot of java still on. Lucky for us, we packed some dry firewood."

McQueen basked in the radiance from the fire as he sipped. In no time at all, it seemed, Wall had won an invitation to spend the night in a wagon. He and McQueen swiftly stripped the packs off the mud-soaked animals and hobbled them. McQueen began opening one of the duffel bags of oats.

"There's a fair amount of old grass in these bottoms. You might let 'em scrounge," offered a fellow named Davis. "And share our chow."

McQueen wanted to repay the kindness. "You're breaking out your sidepork and johnnycake batter; how would you like a gallon of oats from us?"

"Why, that's neighborly," said one. Swiftly the transaction was completed, much to McQueen's relief. He lacked the cash to offer these fellows for a meal.

McQueen wolfed down the hotcakes and bacon. Never had hot vittles felt so fine in his belly. Around him conversation whirled, and he realized Asa was a talker. The Dubuque outfit, it turned out, consisted mostly of mechanics, including a smith, riverboat fireman, wheelwright, harnessmaker, coachman, glass-blower, potter, street cleaner, some teamsters, and a dentist. Most were married and had left gold-rush widows behind. The outfit was captained by a veteran sergeant of the Mexican War, the man named Davis. Instead of crossing Iowa in winter, the outfit had caught a river packet to St. Louis, and another up the Missouri to Council Bluffs, and had provisioned there.

"And now we're axle-deep in mud," said one ruefully, waving a hand at wagons whose wheels were so caked McQueen could scarcely see the spokes. "Truth is, we were warned enough; a dozen experienced men told us to wait. Well, we got the gold fever. And besides, Bogwell and Kimberly are team-sters. And the oxen were fat, and we had a spare yoke for each outfit." He sighed. "We pretty near used up the oxen the first day, and now we'll have to rest them. Maybe go a mile tomor-rah, and let 'em rest. Maybe not even a mile. You fellers pack-ing, you've the right idea."

McQueen didn't respond. He and Wall had been on the brink of spending a cold night. There would be more cold and unshel-tered nights ahead, with danger from Indians besides.

"You putting out guards on the stock tonight?" Wall asked. "I reckon we could do our part."

"Naw," said one of them. "Not for another hundred miles.

Out amongst the Pawnee or the Otos or Omahas, then we'll worry."

McQueen felt weariness seep through him. In a single day he had walked twenty miles or so, battled a storm, and ended up in a cold, dripping valley with no dry ground for a bed.

But these fellows weren't going to call it a night. One of them found a banjo, another a fiddle, and almost before McQueen had scraped his tin plate clean, the whole outfit was singing. These fellows might be mired, but their spirits soared, and their laughter blotted away the damp cold and the predicament they faced. The fiddle player started with the lusty song of the gold rush, *"O, I'm off to Californy with a washbowl on my knee . . ."* And McQueen thought about Susannah, crying for him back home. He'd been so busy the last two days he had scarcely thought of her.

> Now old Dan Tucker's a fine old man,
> Washed his face in a frying pan.
> Combed his head with a wagon wheel,
> And died with a toothache in his heel.
>
> Get out the way old Dan Tucker,
> You're too late to get your supper.
> Get out the way, old Dan Tucker,
> You're too late to get your supper.
>
> Now old Dan Tucker he got drunk,
> Fell in the fire and kicked up a chunk.
> Red-hot coal got in his shoe,
> And oh my lawd how the ashes flew.

Why were they singing? Weren't they mired? Hadn't they worn down their oxen? Didn't they know California was four or five months away?

McQueen scarcely heard the rest of it. All he knew, in his weariness, was that these fellows, like so many Californians he'd met, were having an awfully good time. They were out on the wild trail at last, with only two thousand miles to go.

There was more than gold in this jamboree. He was having a good time, too. That's why he had come. But the thought made him uneasy, as if there were something wrong about leaving home.

CHAPTER 9

McQueen and Wall left the wagon outfit the next morning and hiked along a trail that showed no signs of recent travel. Now they were in the vanguard, although McQueen didn't doubt that some bold pack outfits had already left Independence or St. Joe, and were far out on the California Trail.

McQueen and Wall walked their horses and mules through rolling plains, still mostly winter-brown. Whenever they found a spot where the grass had pushed up a couple of inches, they let their stock graze. A heavy overcast marked this spring of 1849, plunging the world into a perpetual gloom, threatening rain that somehow held off as the two adventurers worked west.

They saw no Indians but McQueen worried that they might be stirring about. When he and Wall struck the valley of the Platte they began looking for signs of passage. That time of year every animal on the trail left hoofprints in the soft earth. There would be no way to hide from Indians.

Somewhere ahead, in the vicinity of Fort Kearny, the trails from Independence and St. Joe would strike the south bank of the Platte. Not until then, when McQueen and the tinhorn could stare across the broad, braided river, would they know whether they were the true vanguard of the great rush of '49, or whether they would see, across the flood, pack trains or white-sheeted wagons crawling along the south bank. But the trail took them along the Loup Fork for many days, and they never saw the Platte.

By day they were mostly silent, a mood that matched the mystery and loneliness of this country. They fed out the last of their oats and began riding their unburdened horses, glad not to walk anymore. Most days they managed thirty miles, twice what a wagon outfit could achieve. The farther west they penetrated, the fewer trees they found, and the sparser the grass. Soon they would be using buffalo chips for fuel. Each evening they chose their campsite carefully, avoiding places where their campfire could be seen at any distance. They let their horses and mules graze freely while they cooked up a supper, and then they picketed and hobbled the animals. At dawn they let the stock graze again. It was said that the Pawnee, in particular, could be vexatious, lifting anything not lashed down, but that all seemed an abstraction to McQueen. He and Wall saw no one, spotted no prints of unshod hooves in the soft earth, and grew ever more confident that the tribes were still in their villages waiting for the high sweet days of summer.

The evenings were best. McQueen relished the steaming tea they boiled up after they had nursed a tiny fire to life in the lee of an embankment to protect it from the relentless wind. They had seen little game, and were still digging into their flour and bacon. But soon they'd come upon buffalo, and would be roasting succulent meat. That was an advantage of being out in front. The shy bison would vanish when the traffic frightened them off. It was after these suppers that they got to know each other, each propped up against his saddle while absorbing the radiant heat of their campfire.

Asa Wall reminisced about his boyhood. He had been the son of a St. Louis wheelwright. His folks had emigrated west from Virginia, often dodging Shawnees on their way to Missouri. Then, one terrible August, cholera killed his father and mother, a sister and younger brother, but somehow spared Asa. Suddenly the man-child was alone and responsible for himself. A neighbor had tried to apprentice him an hour after the last funeral, but Asa had fled to the levee, wild and desperate, studying the packets that had steamed up from New Orleans, or down from Cairo, or across from Independence.

He had hired on as a cabin boy, a job that was little better than slavery. He possessed a cramped bunk near the thundering steam engine plus a uniform. But no cash. And he was indentured for seven years. The *Golden West* became his mother and father and home and life. He had slaved hard, suffering the abuse of passengers, the ship's master, and every crewman above him. He spent his youth cleaning berths, making bunks, hauling clean and dirty linens, serving food, collecting grubby dishes, running errands, fetching ardent spirits, emptying slop overboard, washing the water closets, and dodging the cuffs of a cruel boatswain.

"I learned something, Ulysses. I learned that I had only myself. I had to rely on my own wits, my own resources, my own courage. There was no one to help me. No one who cared about a boy named Asa Wall, except as a beast of burden. A few passengers gave me tips, but that was my sole income, and I had to hide my tiny hoard from the crew. But out of that I learned to make my way, rely on myself because that was all I had.

"You can guess the rest. I watched the gamblers. There were always a few on board. The river packet was their home. Some of them dressed in gaudy clothes, brocaded vests, black silk coats, white plumage about the neck, to advertise themselves. Others dressed like deacons, and pretended to be cotton brokers. Most of them were friendly, shrewd, and students of human nature. They coined money—dollars, shillings, doubloons, half eagles, eagles. How many times did I watch them pluck up a pile of cash at the end of a game, with a smile and a nod? I watched, learned, and began to practice. It was a way out of hell." He smiled at McQueen. "I don't suppose you approve of my way of getting a living—but at least you know how it came about."

"I—haven't thought much about how people end up what they are."

McQueen felt vaguely ashamed of his own life. He had been protected from the day he was born. He had never been put on his mettle. Asa Wall was a *man,* and McQueen knew he was not.

Wall eyed him kindly. "One thing I learned in my trade is to assess others. I form swift impressions. I saw you on the streets of Kanesville and knew you'd be a good man to partner with."

"What did you see?" McQueen asked, half dreading the response.

But Wall didn't reply. He just smiled.

In the next few days the grudging spring finally gave them warmth. The grass leapt up and the stock devoured it. McQueen could find no thinning of the horses and mules. This trip to California was turning out to be a lark. They struck the Platte at last, but could see no signs of travel on the far bank, nor anything resembling a fort there.

They spotted game now and then—antelope on a distant rise, white-tailed deer in the river flats, once an elk. But no sign of buffalo. One day they intersected the prints of unshod horses, perhaps a dozen, but neither of them could say for sure. McQueen stared, frightened. After that they were more watchful and silent. Still, they had yet to see an Indian.

Somewhere they had passed Fort Kearny but weren't sure when. It lay on the other side of the river. Often, from their north-bank trail, they could see little of the south bank, which was obscured by wooded islands and greening forests of willows and cottonwoods in the floodplains. By their reckoning they were making twenty-five to thirty miles a day, a smart pace that was putting them farther and farther ahead of the mob. With luck, they'd beat the overlanders, and face competition only from those who had sailed for Panama or around the Horn in the fall of 1848.

Timber dwindled, except for thick willow stands on islands in the Platte, and more and more they cooked with dried buffalo chips, which were plentiful. But one drizzling eve, in the midst of naked flats, they couldn't find a place to stop.

"We'd better keep on going," McQueen said. "It'll be better than lying in a puddle. There's not a dry chip in sight."

"I'm pretty tired," Wall said. "My horse is worn out. Maybe we should quit for today."

"We need to push, Asa. My plug isn't so good either, but we can rest them when we find the right place."

"This is harder work than I'd imagined back in Kanesville," Wall grumbled.

McQueen didn't reply. Wall had spent too much time shuffling decks and not enough time hardening himself. All his talk about meeting the mountain men when he was young didn't help him now. McQueen didn't know how far they could travel before night arrested them, but with some luck they might find a cutbank. Once before, a cutbank and their treated duck-cloth bedrolls had rescued them from a bad night. It meant leaving the trail and hiking along the bluffs a half mile north, but that didn't matter.

McQueen led Wall away from the Platte into rougher country, and about dusk spotted what they wanted: an overhanging bank in a horseshoe bend of a tiny tributary creek. And as a bonus, they found a handful of dry buffalo chips at the back of it.

Swiftly McQueen unloaded and hobbled the animals and turned them into a long ravine to graze. The grass looked good here, and the creek would water them. Hobbled, they wouldn't go far. He carried the packs to the cutbank and made a windbreak. Wall collected wet buffalo chips while McQueen fired the dry ones. Soon they had a smoky blaze going, enough to brew some tea and fry some cakes. It took a bushel of chips to cook a meal.

"We're lucky," Wall said. "If anything kills us, it'll be the weather."

"Or running out of food," McQueen said. They had dangerously depleted their supplies after only twenty days on the trail. Wall had turned out to be no hunter at all. McQueen had gone after game with Wall a few times, only to find that the gambler had no sense of where game lurked. And McQueen wondered whether Wall knew much about rifles.

"We've seen game enough," said Wall. "All we have to do is shoot it." A certain wry amusement lit his face. McQueen had come to understand that expression.

"I hope there's flour for sale at Laramie," McQueen said, darkly.

It had been another hard day, and they crawled into their bedrolls immediately after they had done their chores. The cutbank didn't protect them much. The slightest breeze doused them with rain. But it would do. McQueen kept his oilskins on, and pulled his duck cloth over his damp blankets. The ancient saddle made a brutal pillow, but he was growing inured to the discomfort. He hadn't expected the trip across two thousand miles of wilderness to be easy.

He drifted off to the blinking orange eye of a dying fire in the ashes of the buffalo chips, and the soft drip of light rain. It grew utterly black, without so much as a star to keep them company.

When he startled awake in the morning, with a clear sky above and dawn staining the world white, something felt wrong. Hurriedly he pulled on his damp boots and laced them.

Then he headed up the long coulee, looking for their livestock and knowing somehow he would not find it.

Twenty minutes later, having topped the bluffs and studied the moccasin tracks, and then the tracks of shod and unshod ponies mixed with the elongated hoofprints of their mules, he knew that he and Wall were afoot in the middle of nowhere, and in grave trouble.

CHAPTER 10

T hey followed the trail for an hour. It headed relent-lessly northeast, every print stamped indelibly in the soft earth. A small party of Indians had slipped close in the night, unbuckled the hobbles, and driven the two saddlers and the five mules away without arousing either man.

McQueen felt a sickening sense of defeat as he trudged along beside Wall. He carried his fowling piece and a spare bridle, while Wall carried his rifle and powderhorn. But the devils had escaped, and were now hours distant, unknown and unknow-able. McQueen felt like a fool. They should have waited and gone west with a large party. Why had he let the tinhorn talk him into leaving early?

Wall kept silent and seemed desolate. They reached the top of a low ridge, and saw nothing in the mid-morning sunlight.

"They're gone," Wall said. "May as well go back." McQueen agreed reluctantly, hating to give up. He worried the problem in his mind, feeling helpless and angry. He didn't know what to do. He felt Wall's gaze on him now and then, but neither man said anything.

When they reached their camp at the cutbank, McQueen eyed the packs bleakly. Some loaded panniers weighed over a hun-dred pounds. Others, that had carried their depleted food sup-plies, had grown lighter. They were half a mile from the Platte.

"Let's eat," McQueen said. He found some dead sagebrush that would do to start a fire. Silently Wall helped gather wet buffalo chips.

The smoky fire grudged its heat, but after ten minutes it gathered strength and began to consume the wet chips. Ulysses mashed some roasted coffee beans, threw them into the fire-blackened pot, and set it to boiling. Wall looked as if the world had come to an end, but said nothing, for which McQueen was grateful.

McQueen mixed some cornmeal, saleratus, water and salt, and started some johnnycakes. The sun was blessing the little canyon with sudden warmth. Above, a transparent sky stretched to infinity. Zephyrs sprung up, caressing the plains.

Quietly, McQueen handed Wall a cup filled with scalding coffee and then a tin plate full of the hotcakes, along with some fried sidepork.

"Well, Asa, what's the most important thing in your life?" McQueen asked.

"Staying alive, I guess. We're a long way from help."

"Do you want to go to California or not?" McQueen persisted.

"I don't see how we can. We can't carry this truck, and we can't live without it."

"Do you want to go back? Cross the river, find Fort Kearny and wait for an eastbound outfit?"

Wall stared into the quiet morning a long while. "There's no other way," he muttered.

"Yes there is. I'm going to California. I haven't come all this way just to turn tail."

"You've made your choice. But I'll head back."

"Just like that," McQueen said, an edge in his voice. "And what are you going to do? Play cards on the river packets again?"

"I didn't expect—"

"Come on, Asa, let's go to California."

"I don't know how," Wall said.

That was all the answer McQueen needed. He began to gather a load he could carry.

"What are you doing?" Wall asked.

"I'm going to haul this stuff back to the road, and wait. We're about halfway between Council Bluffs and Fort Laramie. A pack outfit's likely to show up first; maybe they'll have some spare mules."

"How'll you pay?"

"With extra work."

"And if they don't need you? Then what?"

McQueen shrugged. "Ditch most of my stuff. Then I'll walk west, carrying what I can, bedroll and some vittles, sticking with the pack outfit."

"You'll wear out."

"I've worked hard all my life. I've plowed and planted and hoed and reaped. I was wrestling a plow when I was ten. I'm not lazy, and I don't make some soft living with cards."

A wry humor crinkled Wall's tanned face, but he didn't reply. He stood, stared into a bright day, and stretched. "All right, Ulysses. I'll hike to California with you. Let's go. It's going to take all day to ferry this stuff to the road." He loosened a pannier from a packsaddle and hoisted it to his back, bending under the heavy weight. "I'm not used to this," he said, and headed across the floodplain toward the Platte.

McQueen watched the gambler go, knowing the man would not last a hundred yards, and then hoisted his pack to his shoulders. He strode easily, and soon overtook Wall.

"I hate to leave our stuff unprotected," he said. "The devils could get it. We're not even carrying the rifle."

Wall grunted, and set his load down. "I won't argue with you," he said.

"Asa, you leave your truck here. I'll get it in a few minutes. You just guard the camp. I'll find someplace near the trail to cache this out of sight."

"I'm obliged," said the gambler. Wall returned to the cutbank, while McQueen toted his load to the road with long, easy strides. He would have to divide some of the packs into several loads, but he could do it.

When he reached the trail, he studied it for signs of passage and found none. He left his load in a small depression fifty yards from the road, and returned for another. When he got to the cutbank, he found that Wall had divided the loads into manageable burdens, putting some gear into the empty duffel bags that had carried their oats.

By mid-afternoon he had hauled seven or eight hundred pounds of gear to the Platte road, even including Wall's faro layout. They rested on a sunny slope, enjoying a vibrant landscape, watching puffball clouds plow shadows across the vast land.

"Well, Ulysses, now it's your turn. What's the most important thing in *your* life?" Wall asked.

"I'm going to make something of myself," McQueen replied. "This morning I thought I might have to slink like a whipped dog into Mount Pleasant and live under a cloud the rest of my life. That's when I knew I was heading west."

Wall's gaze turned to horizons. "I'm thinking this isn't so bad," he said. "We're probably two weeks ahead of the crowd. We can hold out. One or another outfit'll let us join. The more manpower the better, as far as they're concerned." He turned to McQueen. "I'm going to California. You talked me into it. I want to see it. I've read Frémont's journals. It's a great country, with a mild climate. I've a notion that a man can carve out a paradise for himself there."

"You're not just going to try for a bonanza and go back?"

"Why would I go back?"

"Why—I'm going back to Mount Pleasant with a pocketful of rocks. I can just see the look in Susannah's eyes when I walk in and pour a pile of gold on the kitchen table. I can just see my brothers trying to belittle the whole trip, do anything but admit that I did the impossible. And my pa! He'll turn cold stone silent."

Wall laughed. "That's your dream. Mine is to go there and stay. I fancy I might find a woman there."

That shocked McQueen. "A Mexican woman?"

"Why not?"

"But they aren't, you know, fair-skinned. I mean like we are. They don't even talk English."

"That's why I fancy the idea."

"All I want is to clean up a gravel bar and go back. There's nothing like Mount Pleasant for a home."

Asa Wall grinned again.

"Well, let's get busy," McQueen said. "I noticed an island full of willows up ahead. There's our firewood if we can get to it. Maybe we can put up a shelter, make ourselves comfortable, and throw up a defense. The red devils might plague us again."

Wall nodded. Wordlessly McQueen plucked up one of the loads, while Wall collected a lighter one, and they hiked west until the island loomed offshore, separated by a gravelly shallows only inches deep. They found a campsite near the riverbank, not visible from the trail, and protected by a rocky ledge from the endless wind.

Wall was growing more cheerful as time passed, which pleased McQueen. Through that painful morning the gambler had progressed from despair to courage.

"I guess this'll be home for a while," Wall said. "At least until those slowpokes catch up. Let's see what a pair of adventurers can do to make camp comfortable."

CHAPTER 11

They cobbled together a shelter from whatever came to hand. With their camp ax they cut firewood on the island. Wall hunted without success but McQueen shot some mallards with his fowling piece.

A dozen times a day they climbed the nearest grade to see what might be coming along the trail, but all they saw was the aching emptiness of an endless plain. They had gotten farther ahead than they had imagined.

The spring weather held. They slept well on a thick carpet of reeds. McQueen dug out his awl and repaired a boot. They both worried about Indians, but they saw none. Once they thought they saw a thin white column of smoke. They studied the south bank of the Platte, but saw nothing. One night wolves barked for hours, destroying their sleep.

On the second afternoon Wall broke open a fresh deck of playing cards, and dealt himself solitaire. McQueen watched the gambler flip cards with deft economy of motion, and knew he was witnessing a way of life.

"Teach me some stuff, Asa," he said. "All those games you play."

Wall looked at him a long moment. "It runs against your religion," he said softly.

"Teach me anyway. I'm not playing for money."

"You want to learn how to throw away your gold."

"No, I just want to see 'em. Poker, vingt-et-un, faro, monte, euchre, all that stuff. I've never even seen a poker game."

"The better off you are, then."

"People win, or they wouldn't play. Isn't that right?"

Wall nodded. "Some win, sometimes. But in the end they lose. What makes you think it's worth knowing? Let me tell you something. If you don't gamble, you won't get hurt. You fill your pockets with rocks and go back to Iowa."

McQueen grinned. "Maybe I'll come try my luck at your tables when I get there. Double or nothing."

Wall stared back, unblinking, silent, somehow dangerous. "If you come to my table, you'll get no favors from me. I would hate to clean you out. Stay away. If you're going to throw it all away, donate it to some other tinhorn."

There was something so dark and menacing in that, it shot a chill through McQueen. "It's just luck, Asa. Maybe I'd set aside a dollar or two for a hand, just to tempt fate a little."

Wall shuffled the deck absently, a single fluid motion that fascinated McQueen. "All right," he said abruptly. "I'll give you some lessons. Faro's the least dangerous." He dug into his pack and extracted an oilcloth faro layout, a casebox with a tiger painted on it, a rack of chips, and a deck of cards. The man radiated something icy.

"Here are twenty chips. We'll say they're worth a dollar each," Wall said. He spread the oilcloth, which had images of the spade suit painted on it. "All bets are even. Suits don't count, only the numbers. You can bet to win by putting a chip on a card. You can bet to lose by putting one of these copper tokens on the chip, like this." He put a chip on the painted three of spades and a token on top of it.

"How do cards win or lose?" McQueen asked.

"I'll show you." Wall shuffled a deck. "The first and last cards, soda and hock, don't play." He dropped the deck into the casebox. "I'll pull two cards out of this slot in the side. The first loses, the second wins. If the cards are the same denomination—two sevens, say—I win; you lose no matter how you bet. That's my only advantage. It gives me half a percent. Not much advantage if the game's square."

"That's easy," said McQueen.

"There's more. There's a device with a lot of beads on wires. It's used to tell players what cards have been played, so they can see what's left in the deck. On a busy night a dealer's usually got a lookout on a perch above the table, keeping an eye out for late bets, and a casekeeper, recording what cards have been played. You ready to buck the tiger?"

"What does that mean?"

"Bet. It comes from the bengal painted on the side of the box. Playing faro is bucking the tiger."

McQueen shrugged. He tried a chip on the jack. Wall drew a trey and a seven. The chip remained in place.

McQueen added a second chip, this time on a deuce. Wall drew a nine and a deuce. He added a chip to McQueen's chip, and waited.

"I'm ahead," McQueen said cheerfully. He shifted his three chips to cover a four, eight, and king, and coppered the king. Wall drew the turn: a king, loser, and a queen, winner. He paid McQueen one chip on the coppered king.

"I was born lucky," McQueen said.

They played awhile. By late afternoon McQueen had multiplied his twenty chips to sixty-eight.

"I'll quit while I'm ahead," he said, shoving the pile toward the gambler. "Thanks for the lesson. Tonight, teach me vingt-et-un or poker."

Wall settled the chips into their rack with a practiced hand. "They're both games of skill," he said. "You'll need a lot more than luck." He eyed McQueen. "It would have been better if you'd lost. I can warn you, but I can see you've been bitten."

"Oh, pshaw, Asa, I'm just having fun."

"It's never fun. It's business. Don't bring your dust to my game, kid," Wall said, packing up the layout.

"I'm not gonna gamble," McQueen grumbled. Something in Wall's attitude irked him.

That evening, after more wearisome pancake fodder, McQueen got a lesson in the French game of vingt-et-un, and learned something about staying under the fatal twenty-one. He lost until dusk, and retired sullenly. Maybe he wasn't so lucky. Well, he wasn't going to gamble anyway. That was for fools.

In the morning, Wall dodged a poker lesson and went hunting alone, growling about making meat. At midday, life in camp suddenly changed. A pack outfit topped a knoll to the east. McQueen counted a dozen men, each leading a laden mule. He headed for the road and waited for them.

"Well, what wild tribe do ye belong to?" asked the lead man, a brown-bearded fellow.

"The Ioway, and my partner's from the Missouriah Tribe," McQueen responded.

"We thought we were first for Californy on the north bank," the man said. "But I guess we're second."

"You're first. We got separated from our mules by some Injuns, Pawnee probably. We thought maybe you could lend us a hand."

The man frowned. "We can lend you victuals if your belly's up against your backbone. We can't carry anything of yours. Each of us has one or two loaded mules, and none to spare. You can walk with us to Fort Laramie if'n it's what you want."

"We were looking for a few spare mules," McQueen muttered, wishing Wall was present. "I'm Ulysses McQueen, and my partner's Asa Wall. Noon with us if you've a mind."

"Pleased, I'm sure. I'm Gil Touhy, from Niles, Michigan. We're all Michiganders, out to conquer the wild West. We call it the Wolverine Pack Company."

One by one, they introduced themselves to McQueen. They were all young men, gold-seekers off across a continent on foot. He led them to the camp, and the pack outfit pulled the loads off the mules and set them to grazing the tender new grasses.

Touhy and his Wolverines had plenty of news. Cholera had scythed the huge tent camps outside of Independence, St. Joe, and Council Bluffs, and was killing people out on the California Trail. On the south side of the Platte there were dozens of wagon outfits far ahead. They had left early, when the ground was still frozen, carrying feedgrains for their oxen. Some of the advance guard would be close to Fort Laramie now.

"Fort Laramie! How do you know that?" McQueen asked.

"We paddled a raft across the river to Fort Kearny and found out. We were camping right across, and saw the lights over there. The army's counting wagons. They counted thirty through there a few days ago."

"What's behind you? Anyone else coming?"

"Oh, a whole army and then some. Tomorrah you'll see a wagon outfit from Illinois. It's mule-powered. Three wagons, four span to a wagon. They hauled feed in one wagon and then ditched it. . . . Maybe they'd pick up a couple of strays. But it's a race, and devil take the hindmost. Have you got something to trade?"

"I guess we do," McQueen said, doubtfully. "Our labor."

A while later he watched them throw their packs over the mules, tighten latigos, and walk out, a dozen men who would reach the goldfields ahead of most, and probably would outrun the deadly disease stalking westward as the days grew hotter.

"See you out there, McQueen," yelled Touhy as the outfit walked west.

A sudden melancholia engulfed McQueen. It would be tough to join any outfit, especially ones in the vanguard. Everything changed. He hated the camp. Itched to get moving. Considered loading up what he could carry and starting west. The gold fever tugged him, and a terror of the cholera bedeviled him.

Late in the afternoon Wall walked in without any game.

"Where've you been?" McQueen asked, an edge on his voice. "We had company. A pack outfit from Michigan."

"I know. I talked with them," Wall said. "It sounds like we can work something out tomorrow."

"We don't have anything to trade. Why should they take us on?"

Wall shrugged. "Most folk'll help another in trouble. This outfit offered to do what they could, didn't they?"

McQueen nodded. Wall pulled the cap off the nipple and slid his rifle into his stack of gear.

"You were sure gone a long time. And you didn't make meat."

"I wasn't really hunting."

"What were you doing?"

"I was dodging your itch to play cards. I have it in me not to lead you to perdition."

"What're you talking about?"

"You come from a straitlaced family, and you're young and full of hell and wanting to try out everything your folks warned against. That's the kind that's the easiest mark of all. I decided I wasn't going to help you along the road to hell."

"You're saying I can't take care of myself. I haven't got judgment enough for you. Well, you sound just like my brothers."

Wall grinned disarmingly and turned McQueen's unhappiness aside. "We'd better get set for tomorrow. That Illinois outfit won't stand around and wait for us. Touhy told me they'd be through here pretty early. Those outfits seem to know who's in front and who's behind."

McQueen grunted. This whole trip he'd shown the gambler how to live out-of-doors, bucked up the man's faltering spirits when the tinhorn was ready to quit and head east, done the cooking and camp chores, done the heavy hauling and hard work for them both, supplied some food with his fowling piece—but the gambler still thought he was a boy.

CHAPTER 12

T he Illinois outfit looked hard-used. Mud caked the felloes and spokes of the wheels and hung from the hubs. The mules had thinned, but looked sound enough. The train consisted of three mule-drawn wagons with fourteen men. Its captain, Virginius Dobbin, was a glaring, black-bearded man with a passion to reach the goldfields. The rest shared his madness, which is why it was the first wagon outfit out on the north bank of the Platte.

"We started with twenty-one, but we had some quitters," Dobbin said to Wall. "There's some that get into a little discomfort and hightail it home like whipped dogs. Others get fearful of redskins or the cholera or taking sick, and next thing you know, they're selling their shares and gitting out."

"Where're you from?" McQueen asked.

"Peru, Illinois. There's some from Streator, Ottawa, and LaSalle. It's California or bust, and we're going to get to the good dirt before it's all taken up."

"Well, we had that in mind until the redskins—don't know which—snuck in one night. We're looking for an outfit that'll take five packloads."

"We can do that, if you've a mess. We don't have victuals enough for you. And we'll settle on a price. The more men, the better the protection. We've some articles of agreement, too. You'll obey the captain—that's me—and the lieutenants. I don't have time for whiners. Do your duty and you'll get along."

McQueen didn't much like the sound of that. "What kind of cash?" he asked, doubtfully. "I'm strapped."

"Every man here contributed a hundred dollars for mess gear and vittles. We've two mess tents and sheet-metal stoves. One of these wagons is company-owned."

"Well, that's that," McQueen said, half relieved.

"Oh, I think we can trade a little, Ulysses," Wall said. He turned to Dobbin. "We've five packsaddles. McQueen has two and I have three. If your wagons break down they'll come in mighty handy. And we're a third of the way out, so maybe the price should be sixty-seven apiece, not a hundred."

"Packsaddles? Let's have a look," Dobbin said.

Wall showed him.

"Good enough. Packsaddles with saddle blankets. I'll take this to my men. Give me five minutes. You break camp. We wait for no man."

McQueen wasn't at all sure about this, but his doubts had been trumped. Wall had a knack for business even if he didn't have much trail savvy. McQueen found himself skedaddling around, throwing the skillet and mess gear into a pannier, yanking his duck-cloth ground cover from the roof of their hut and rolling up his blankets in it. He almost hated to abandon the camp.

"Rescued, McQueen," Wall said, stuffing his gear into his packs.

Just out of earshot, the young men who made up the outfit were engaged in serious debate. Then Dobbin approached.

"All right, they've accepted you, but on probation. You do your share and fit in, and you'll be welcome. You violate our rules, and you'll be left on the trail. And we keep the packsaddles." He eyed Wall. "What did you say you do?"

"I'm a gambler."

Dobbin stared a long time. "We don't drink, we don't curse, and we don't gamble. Every man does hard work—fetching firewood and chips, scrubbing pots, loading and unloading, harnessing spans of mules, herding them at night. There's no place among us for a lazy man. That's my rules."

Wall nodded, a faint smile flickering across his face.

"I'll be asking you more questions. If crimes are committed by any man in this company we'll mete out swift and appropriate justice. Is that understood?"

Wall nodded again.

"And you?" Dobbin asked McQueen.

"I farm in Mount Pleasant, Iowa."

"How did you two hitch up?"

"We met in Kanesville. We had the same intent. Go early, with pack animals."

"How are you armed?"

"Wall has a rifle; I have a fowling piece."

"Well, that's sensible. I never saw the use for a revolver out here. All right, pitch your gear into the mess wagon, that one there. We'll take that firewood, too. Put your vittles in with our chow. We mostly walk. You'd better have spare shoe leather."

"We do."

"All right, let's be off. We've lost time. We'll call it the nooning. You two walk with me. I want to know more about you."

Hastily Wall and McQueen heaped their packs into the wagon, while men they had yet to meet watched silently. Then they were off, sixteen men near the vanguard of the migration.

Uneasily, McQueen paced beside the captain. The train pulled out smartly, the mules obedient, their tall ears rotating to the hoarse commands and the crack of whips. Four men with each wagon walked beside the spans of mules, two on either side.

Dobbin and his lieutenant, a man he introduced as Oscar Clappe, walked ahead.

"What did you do before this, Mr. Dobbin?" asked Wall.

"I'm a stone mason. I was a corporal in the Mex War, under Winfield Scott."

"And you, Mr. Clappe?"

"I'm a minister of the gospel, sir. Of the Baptist sort."

"And you're after gold?"

"You bet I'm after gold, and lots of it. I've starved from passing the hat. If God scattered nuggets all over the west slope of the Sierras for any man to pluck up, then he meant for ministers of the gospel to collect them, same as any other man."

"You preach on Sundays?"

"We've abbreviated the matter. We honor the sabbath, of course, but the sooner I collect my pocketful of rocks, the sooner I can serve a congregation."

"What do the other gentlemen do?"

Dobbin answered. "Mixed group. Constable, brakeman, homeopathic doctor, wheelwright, smith, teamster, riverboat engineer, and some assorted young men."

McQueen studied the men walking behind. This evening, if Dobbin permitted any leisure, he would meet them. A few eyed him cheerfully. Maybe this wasn't going to be so bad.

"You're well equipped for breakdowns," McQueen said.

"Yes, but that's not what we're worrying about," Dobbin said. "It's the mules. They don't last. So we bought the best mules money could buy and we'll burn them up. When it's time, we'll abandon another wagon and put more spans of mules on the remaining two. And now you've given us a new option: if the mules weaken in harness, we'll use the packsaddles. If the mules break down, we'll shoot them."

"Shoot them?"

"So the next outfit doesn't get them. Every man behind us is a rival. What separates us from them is that we want the gold worse than they do, and we're willing to squander mules, wagons, shoe leather, and gear to have our pick of the gravel. I'll tell you something else: we'll burn pasture after we leave it. Whatever we can do to slow the mob behind us, we'll do."

"But animals'll starve if you burn pasture!" McQueen exclaimed.

"We do what's necessary."

Anger welled up in McQueen. "Captain Dobbin, sir, it's one thing to reach the goldfields first. It's another to burn pasture behind us. That grass'll keep animals alive."

"What're you, some saint, boy?"

"Sir, I'm a farmer. I respect my stock. My animals help make my living. They take me where I need to go."

"We're not farmers. It's every man for himself here, and if you don't like it—"

"You're talking about destroying life. Not just animals—men."

Dobbin veered toward McQueen until he loomed over the young man. "Take orders, keep your mouth shut—or get out," he said in a voice soft as velvet.

McQueen choked back the outrage that had welled through him, hot as lava. "It's not right," he said, bitterly.

Dobbin eyed him coldly. "You're on the edge, boy. You'll shut that noisy mouth. If I choose to abuse our stock, that's my privilege. If I choose to burn pasture, that's how it'll be. You understand?"

McQueen forced himself to talk softly. "There's lots of gold. That's what every report says."

"You can get rich or not," Dobbin said, measuring McQueen. "You want to quit us right now?"

"No, no, no," said Wall, swiftly intervening. "We're in, and you'll find us well worth your trouble."

"We'll see," Dobbin said, his sulphurous gaze on the gambler once again.

McQueen seethed. From childhood, he had been taught to care for livestock. No male McQueen ever sat down to a meal before making sure the horses or mules were cared for.

But there was something deeper and darker gnawing at McQueen as he walked west. These men were too ruthless. What kind were these, who would burn pasture to destroy rivals? Strand desperate men in a wilderness? The rush west didn't require scorched-earth tactics. He remembered, with a sudden yearning, the people of Mount Pleasant, his family and neighbors, the young people he had grown up with.

Dobbin and Clappe spent much of the afternoon grilling Asa Wall, trying to find reasons to abominate him. But Wall, glib and amiable, was equal to the occasion, and entertained them with recollections of the mountain men who came through St. Louis, and the giants of the fur trade, including the Chouteaus, Robert Campbell, and the Sublettes. Before the afternoon had passed, Wall had won grudging respect. McQueen detected a change of tone as time passed, and by evening, when they stopped, he realized that the gambler had won over the captain and his lieutenant.

At last, Dobbin called a halt in a broad valley filled with sparse grasses.

"You, McQueen," he said, dark as a thundercloud. "Take the mess-wagon mules, one span at a time, down to the river. Then pull the harness off and set it in order next to the wagon. Then loose-herd the mules over to that slope. That's good grass. Collect buffalo chips while you watch the herd. I want enough chips for breakfast. Two bushels. After supper halter and picket the mules close in. You'll do the first watch, until midnight, with that scattergun in hand. If you lose a mule to the redskins, you'll be in bigger trouble than you've ever been in before. Don't you quit your post until you're relieved. The cook'll get you up at four and you'll help him. Then you'll harness the four span you're responsible for. Get to know them. Two or three are tricky and stubborn. We keep that saddler tied to the wagon. If you can't find a mule, saddle up and find the animal. Then report to me."

McQueen waited, wondering what commands Dobbin would issue to the gambler.

"Wall, tonight I want you to tell me everything you know about this Platte River road," Dobbin said. "I'm glad we found you."

CHAPTER 13

The cook shook McQueen in the predawn dark. Wearily the young man pulled on his boots. The night watch had robbed him of sleep. He splashed water on his face and then helped the cook build a fire and start the coffee. After that he toiled at the chores, scrubbing pots and rinsing the tin mess service, aware all the while that Captain Dobbin was studying him with that flat, impenetrable gaze of his.

By dawn the outfit was ready to travel, mules harnessed, cooking gear loaded. McQueen had toiled nonstop.

"All right, McQueen," the captain said. "You'll fire these pastures."

The command jolted McQueen. He stood, staring.

"Can of coal oil in that wagon, and a mess of rags all torn up. Soak a few rags, and drop 'em in a row about two hundred yards long, and then put a lucifer to them. Nice west wind; it'll blow up a good fire."

Ulysses McQueen had come to a crossroads, and he knew the road he must travel. A number of the company watched, curiously.

"It runs against my conscience, sir."

"You disobeying me?"

McQueen didn't reply.

Captain Dobbin looked triumphant. "Well, now! *Disobeying*, the day after we rescued you." He waved an arm. "Out. Get your bedroll off the wagon. You're out."

Dobbin had obviously been waiting for this moment, plotting it since yesterday. McQueen looked at the silent men and sensed they didn't like this. Wearily, he walked to the wagon and pulled his bedroll from it—all he had in the world.

"Just a minute, captain," said a balding man. "You can't put a man out without giving him some food and a way to survive. It's a death sentence."

Dobbin turned to the man, grinning. "Well, well, Camden, you want to join McQueen?"

"This man deserves better," Camden said.

"You questioning my orders, Camden?"

"Yes, we all are. And if it comes down to it, we can vote you out of your job. It's in the articles."

"Ah! Ah! God bless us," bawled the Reverend Clappe hastily. "Let's put this woe aside. Why, I'll go fire the grass, and we'll just get a-going. Time's a-wasting. No time for woe if we're going to go for the gold."

Virginius Dobbin stared at the crowd, his eyes so opaque that McQueen hadn't the faintest idea what was passing through the captain's mind. Then Dobbin nodded, and a tense moment dissolved. Men turned to their waiting wagons and teams.

McQueen wasn't sure he wanted to stay. Especially when he watched the cheerful minister soak rags in coal oil and torch the tall, brown grass into a wall of yellow flame. He didn't know who Camden was, but he seemed to be the only good man in the outfit.

Dobbin drove McQueen maliciously the next days, requiring him to catch and harness eight mules each morning, unharness them each evening, night-herd them, get up at four to help the cook and collect buffalo chips, and walk beside the mules by day. At noon he was required to watch the mules while the rest ate.

He scarcely had time to eat, and sometimes had to skip a meal. He stumbled somnolently westward, scarcely aware of the company's daily progress, wrestling with blistering heat, wind, thundershowers, and long slopes that stretched beyond hazy horizons. Gnats swarmed him by day, mosquitoes by night. He lacked time to meet the rest of the company though he gradually attached names to faces. Dobbin contrived to keep him apart from the others during the supper hour and the precious moments when the outfit relaxed.

He bore it stubbornly, damned if he would cave in or complain. He knew what this hazing was all about. There were moral issues here. He had brought up the right and wrong of it, and enraged Dobbin.

Dobbin's scorching pace kept the Illinois outfit near the vanguard, but each day McQueen watched the mules thin down and burn out. It sickened him. The harness collars wore off the hair on their shoulders; hollows developed where powerful muscle had once been. The croups of the mules bore more and more whip scars. Some were footsore. Others limped because of splints and stone bruises. They pulled halfheartedly, and required more and more whipping.

McQueen had no idea what Dobbin was saying to the rest; he knew only that he was isolated and had no friend except Wall. Still, he found a few social moments during the days. A pair of young fellows named Charley and Will found time to visit with him, asking about his life in Iowa and sharing some of their own in Illinois. A few others surveyed him with assessing gazes, not hostile but not friendly. One fellow named Dave Otter complained constantly but always out of earshot of Dobbin and Clappe. McQueen knew the type. Otter would do half as much as the rest, and grouse twice as hard.

Dobbin scarcely spoke to McQueen, except to bark commands in a voice that brooked no response.

"You think I'm too tough on you, don't you? You'll never make it to the goldfields, McQueen. You don't have what it takes," Dobbin said one day after McQueen had summoned up his courage and asked for one full night of rest. "I know your

type. You've been pampered. You lack ambition. When you
have ambition, you do what it takes. If you don't like it, just say
the word and I'll pitch your bedroll out and you can wait for the
next suckers to pick you up. I never could stand whiners. I had
my fill of them in the army."

McQueen whirled away. He had never whined. He wasn't
soft; he worked harder than the rest, and his calloused hands
were the hallmark of a life spent behind a one-bottom plow and
swinging a scythe and planting corn.

He knew he had been singled out. He wondered why none of
the others came to his defense. He had gotten to know most of
them, although two remained a mystery. The older of the two
never spoke a word, but listened intelligently. The younger was
apparently the man's son, and between them, they had some
sort of private language consisting of gestures and the son's
conversation. McQueen learned that the older man was Basil
Lalique, and the fifteen-year-old son was Martin. But what had
plunged the father into a mute life remained a well-kept secret
in this company.

Asa Wall was one of a few who regularly visited with
McQueen.

"I don't like it. Dobbin's a swine, Ulysses. But there's not
much I can do. I'm the sinner in this crowd of saints."

A quiet smile was all that Wall could give him. The rest
didn't notice or care, except maybe a reserved man named
Theodore Bacon, who seemed to assess McQueen each day.
Bacon was forming his own opinions, and McQueen suspected
he might have a friend there. One thing McQueen knew after
two weeks of brutal toil: even his strong young body couldn't
endure much more punishment.

The land was changing though he had grown so weary he
scarcely noticed it. The grass grew shorter and in bunches. He
saw more prickly pear and some silvery sagebrush. Trees were
even scarcer, but some lucky nights they found a few cottonwoods or alders in gulches along the Platte and treated themselves to a hot fire. Some days wolves followed them, skulking
along distant horizons. Several times, the company killed dia-
mondback rattlers. Cactus stabbed the mules and swelled their
pasterns. Alkali dust whited man and beast and clogged
McQueen's nostrils.

He kept going, though his body cried for sleep, and he stumbled through his tasks. He hurt all over, slept on foot, measured time in terms of the next moment he could sit down for a few minutes, and yearned for cool shade, anyplace he might escape the blistering sun. One of his boots tore apart but he was too exhausted to repair it, and he stumbled westward with a flapping sole that threatened to take its leave. Fort Laramie loomed larger in his mind. He would abandon this outfit there, even if all they let him keep was his bedroll—even if they took that from him.

Then one dawn Julius Garwood, the cook, shook him, but McQueen couldn't get out of his bedroll, could not even open his eyes. He felt a weariness so profound that he no longer could defy his body. The cook shook him again, but McQueen didn't care. Let them abandon him here; let him die beside the trail.

The cook let him alone. He knew nothing until he felt a hand on his forehead, and opened his eyes to Homer Camden, the young homeopathic doctor, a man bald as an egg, with protruding unhappy eyes and a luxuriant mustache waxed into saberpoints.

"He's not feverish, but he's worn out," Camden pronounced, talking to someone behind him. "He needs a few days to recover."

McQueen opened his swollen eyes and discovered Wall standing over him.

"I'll give him an anodyne," Camden said.

"Ulysses," said Wall. "I'm going to do something about this. Get some rest."

Time drifted by and the daylight intensified. McQueen didn't care. He knew that men came, hovered over him, mumbled among themselves, and went. He heard Dave Otter complain that McQueen's slacking would mean more work for the others. It didn't matter. He could not go farther.

At one point he heard Dobbin. "Worthless slacker. I knew it the moment I laid eyes on him," he said. "Throw him out."

"He's a good man, Dobbin."

McQueen heard a short hard laugh. "That from a gambler," Dobbin said.

"He took it, and never complained," said someone who

sounded like Charley Pyle. McQueen opened his eyes, and beheld several men peering down at him.

"You go on. Leave me," he mumbled.

"That settles it," snapped Dobbin. "Time's a-wasting. It's a good dry day and we can make thirty miles."

"Hold up, captain," said Camden. "We're going to have a meeting and talk this over. We can carry McQueen in a wagon for a few days."

"Meet all you want; it won't change a thing," Dobbin snapped. "Leave him there. That's a command. Now get the mules and harness up. You can meet tonight."

"We'll meet now," Will Hoke said. "That's in the covenant. We're going to talk about this fellow and about the worn-out mules, and maybe about the leadership."

"You've all gone soft," Dobbin growled.

McQueen didn't care. He wanted to sleep. He needed sleep so much that nothing else mattered. He drifted back into oblivion again.

It seemed only a moment until someone was shaking him, but when he opened his eyes he beheld full daylight, and Wall and Camden squatting beside him.

"McQueen, there's been a meeting," said the doctor. "We're going to stay here two days. The mules need rest. You can sleep the whole time. And after we start, you'll do light duty until you feel ready for more.

"The company voted that all work's to be parceled out equally. We voted to rest the mules, too. We'll rest them every few days, whether we're first or not to the goldfields. Getting there is more important than being first. The company's put Dobbin on notice: he quits harassing you and he quits abusing the stock, or he loses his command."

McQueen supposed he should have been glad, but he only wanted to sleep. He muttered a thank-you and drifted off. Camden handed him a small pill and some water.

"This is some valerian," he said. "It's a sedative."

McQueen didn't want a sedative, but Camden urged it on him, so he lifted himself up, swallowed the pill, took some water, and drifted off. He woke up once in deep darkness, and was startled to realize he had slept that entire day. He discovered a sky alive with stars. The world seemed better; he had friends in this outfit, Will Hoke and Charley Pyle and Dr. Camden. He had endured every torment that Dobbin had thrown at him.

From the beginning, Dobbin had called him "boy." Wall called him that, too, and so did Clappe and Otter and Garfield, the cook. It mystified him. He was a married man of twenty, doing more than his share, but these men had a way of telling him he wasn't one of them, he wasn't grown. What did it take to be a man? Why did they think that way about him? Was it because he had spoken up against bad things, like burning pasture? Did only boys have consciences?

He slid into sleep again, still aching in his flesh, though his soul ached less now. When he awoke the next time, daylight had returned. This time he was ready to get up, and he was ravenous. He stumbled into a sweet dawn, discovered Cookie stoking up the cookfire with buffalo chips, saw the whole herd of mules grazing a slope a half mile away, none of them picketed, and realized that something had happened to this outfit. Maybe it wasn't so ruthless after all. There were good men in it, and now he would meet them.

They welcomed him cheerfully at the breakfast fire, glad to see him up. He stoked up on hotcakes with molasses poured over them, good coffee so stiff it'd float a spoon, and dried apples.

"You gonna sleep today, too?" asked Charley.

"Some," he said.

"We're having a little hoedown tonight. Ramsey brought his fiddle, but he ain't had a chance even to tighten the strings so far. We're gonna sing a leetle, and Clappe's gonna give us an inspiration message. He promised to hold 'er down when we told him we'd likely baptize him in the Platte if he got too talky."

"How's Captain Dobbin?"

"Sulky. But even he's admitting the mules needed the rest. About you he says nothing at all."

"Maybe he figures I'm a mule, too," McQueen said.

Charley laughed. "Come meet the fellows. Theo Bacon's been fixing your boot, and old Clappe himself took it upon him to rinse your duds and dry 'em, snorting about the Golden Rule."

CHAPTER 14

W ith rest, McQueen's young body recovered swiftly, and he spent a sunny day repairing his clothing, reading Susannah's notes—which he hadn't examined for weeks—and catnapping whenever he needed to doze. After one such nap, deep in the afternoon, he found Wall waiting for him.

"You some better?"

"I could sleep another week."

"They'll wagon you tomorrow if you want."

"I'll see."

"That meeting yesterday told me how the land lies in this outfit. Most of 'em don't like how Dobbin picks on you. A couple of them—Hoke and Pyle—said you'd never once complained and did everything you'd been asked until you dropped.

"They want the work divided up fair and square, and you're to rest until you can carry a fair load. Dobbin didn't like that. He said you're a sissy and need a lesson."

McQueen fumed. "Why does he think that?"

Wall shrugged. "He got some notion about you when we first met—from what you said about burning pasture. He's called you a silver-spooner boy, and a lot of little items like that."

"Do you think that's what I am?" McQueen asked sharply.

"No, but you've never seen the rough side of life."

"I am what I am. I've worked hard all my life."

Wall grinned. "You don't have to defend yourself to me. That's how the vote went. This outfit's badly split. Some, including Dobbin, Clappe, Otter, Noble, the Wallace brothers, and Garwood, want to get to the goldfields first, even if we waste every mule and wreck every wagon. Doc Camden's leaning that direction but he wants a little more moderation. The others say we'll never get there at all unless we respect the mules."

"Who's on the other side?"

"The ones wanting to rest the mules are Mulligan, Bacon,

Ramsey, Pyle, Hoke, and the Laliques. None of 'em can stomach the pasture-burning, and the mule-wrecking. They're the ones you should call friends."

"What's going to happen?"

"They're still fighting over it. The hell-for-leather bunch wanted to pull out this morning and leave you behind with a few provisions so the next outfit up the trail could pick you up."

"Ditch me?"

"That's what Dobbin means about being hard. He says you're dragging the whole outfit. Costing 'em a fortune. Otter and Garwood and Clappe believe it, too."

"They'll kill the mules and end up at the rear."

"Ulysses, just because you're with this outfit doesn't mean they'll sacrifice one day, one hour, for you. We're not in the lead. Another packmule outfit, ten Missouri fellows, walked by us while you slept, and it's driving Dobbin crazy. He was talking of pulling out right then. But cooler heads took over—Doc Camden for one. It got tough for a while. There's a bare majority for resting the mules, but they won—this time."

McQueen listened, not surprised by the strife that had torn the outfit while he slept. "Asa, there's right and wrong. Burning pasture's wrong. Call me what you want. If it's soft to be against evil, call me soft. If it's soft to help others who need it, call me soft. I don't care what they think."

"Whoa up. Most of this bunch'll come down on your side. But it's a struggle. The Missouri men told us there's two pack outfits on our heels, and one wagon train two days behind. And across the Platte, there's several wagon outfits and a dozen pack outfits ahead of us. No one can figure how they did it."

McQueen pondered all that. "How are the mules?" he asked at last.

"Well, you're a better judge than I am. I can usually tell when a poker player's bluffing, but not when mules are bluffing. I'd say they're bad. Homer Camden told me these mules dragged those wagons through mire a foot deep those first weeks. They got hung up at every creek, got into trouble climbing every hill, sometimes so bad that it took every mule in the outfit and a lot of whipping to tug one unloaded wagon up a muddy slope. They don't have the strength of oxen."

McQueen pondered that. "You say that preacher, Clappe, is on the hell-for-leather side?"

"That's why he's the lieutenant. I never saw a godly man so itchy for gold. He says he's done pulling buttons out of the collection plate."

Tiredness stole through McQueen again. "I guess every outfit's got its quarrels," he said.

Wall left him to his musings, and McQueen summoned up the strength to walk out to the mules. The rest hadn't helped them much. One limped visibly. Others sprawled on the ground, preferring sleeping to grazing. They had shrunk so badly their ribs looked like corduroy, and their flesh had sunk around their skeletons. Their croups bore the scars of whiplash. The sight disgusted him.

Around the supper fire that evening, McQueen spotted little of the division that was wracking the outfit, though Dobbin's scorn bore into McQueen from smoldering black eyes.

Buck Ramsey pulled a banjo from his wagon, and McQueen heard the ping of strings being stretched and plucked until they were true. The sun was far from quitting when the outfit gathered, but Ramsey started in with a thick, gravelly voice:

> Oh, don't you remember sweet Betsy from Pike,
> Who crossed the big mountains with her lover, Ike,
> With two yoke of cattle, a large yellow dog,
> A tall Shanghai rooster and one spotted hog?

> Saying good-bye Pike County
> Farewell for a while,
> We'll come back again,
> When we've panned out our pile!

That seemed pretty good to McQueen. He'd never heard it before. The boys settled in, enjoying this rare evening's entertainment. Ramsey tried another:

> Oh, Shenandoah, I long to see you,
> Away, you rolling river.
> Oh, Shenandoah, I long to see you,

Away, I'm bound away,
'Cross the wide Missouri.

Ulysses listened to that, lost in its melancholy sweetness.

We've formed our band, we are all well manned,
The journey afar to the promised land;
The golden ore is rich in store,
On the banks of the Sacramento shore.

Then ho, boys, ho! For California, O!
There's plenty of gold, so I've been told,
On the banks of the Sacramento.

No sooner had that song drifted into the silent wilderness than Oscar Clappe arose. McQueen waited for the piety, but Clappe surprised him. He had donned his black preacher's garb and looked like an overstuffed penguin, except for the unkempt salt-and-pepper beard he had been currying. For a man who liked his vittles, he had a swift, darting way about him, and an orotund style that lingered lovingly on every phrase.

"Now, brethren," he began gently, "I'm a preacher of the Gospel, and some Gospel you'll hear now. If the Good Lord so fashioned the world that He choose to scatter golden nuggets the size of goose eggs, the size of walnuts and marbles and peas and acorns, across the west slope of the Sierra Nevada, then He had in mind enriching those who get to this Golconda afore the rest.

"Now, plainly, what He had in mind was a great winnowing and sifting, in which the most determined of His children should reach Paradise ahead of assorted sinners, malcontents, louts, and other wastrels. Now it's clear there is Divine Design in all this. The Elect will pluck up his natural riches, left there for eons of time, unseen by redskins and Mexicans, unknown to all the unfavored races, but plain to the first white Yankees, namely a fellow named Marshall, who was destined from the beginning of Creation to discover in Sutter's millrace what had eluded whole populations of lesser races. Namely, we white men are the Elect, and as the Elect, we have a bounden duty to prove up our faith, as it were, by getting there ahead of the yahoos going over the

Isthmus or around the Horn; ahead of the dunderheads with their slavering oxen grinding over the prairies.

"Don't call it gold, boys, call it *empire*. Gold, it isn't nothing but soft yeller metal. Call it freedom. Call it dominion. I got a dream, and so do you, fellers. I'm going to have me an *empire*. I'll scrape an *empire* out of the rivers, and then I'll buy an *empire*. It'll have a twenty-room house on a hill, but it won't be big enough to hold everything that pleasures me. I'll see my own land to the farthest horizons, from every window, and on my land I'll see my own kine, my own steeds, my own white lambs, lambs like the Lamb of God. And I'll have perfumed ladies at hand to beautify my house and comfort me, servants so thick I'll have to brush 'em away, brats by the bushel—kept off where they won't bother me, of course—peacocks and bulldogs, fandangos in my own beer garden.

"Now, gents, I'm under duress to limit my sermon to two minutes or face a humbling baptism in the mighty Platte. Now, at the crack of dawn, I expect this entire company, bar none, to pack up and run. You've been given your chance at blessedness, with a little discipline from Dobbin and your humble servant, and now it's up to you."

Clappe sat down abruptly. A few whistled. McQueen supposed it was the most crassly materialistic mixture of greed and God and racial conceit he had ever heard. He eyed the rest of the company, and saw a few grins and a couple of frowns.

Buck Ramsey coaxed the banjo back to life again, and the crowd quieted. That familiar song, "Oh, Susanna," twanged from the little stringed pancake, but the words Ramsey sang were ones McQueen had never heard:

> We're sons of gallant fathers, boys,
>   And mothers kind and true,
> Who whispered as they wrung our hands,
>   "God bless and be with you."
> Wives, scores of sympathizing friends,
>   Who wish us hearty speed,
> Besides the world to back us, if
>   Our steps to fortune lead.

Oh, California!
  Thou land of glittering dreams,
Where the yellow dust and diamonds, boys,
  Are found in all thy streams!

And all of us—have we not left
  Our best of life for this?
But cheer we up! we will return
  Laden with gold and bliss!
Then saddle our mules! away we go
  With hopes by fancy led,
To where the Sacramento flows
  Over its glittering bed!

McQueen enjoyed the night. These men, ruthless as they seemed to him, had left wives and children and families behind, just as he had. It put him in mind of Susannah and the child she was forming within her. He wondered if it would be a boy or a girl, and what she would name the little one. It was odd, how little he had thought of her on the trail.

The remembrance of her melted him. He was so far away now, almost to Fort Laramie and the beginning of the Rockies. Far across the wide Missouri she waited each day, growing heavy with his first child, the fruit of the sweetest moments he had ever known. Now she was on the other side of the river, and he sat in a wilderness, almost alone, and penniless.

A loneliness for her pierced him so deeply that he wanted to weep. Tomorrow would take him farther from her, and farther into a harsh world he had never imagined in his protected life in Mount Pleasant. He would have a little more time now, and he resolved that he would read one of her little letters each evening. With that, he retreated to his bedroll, wanting desperately to draw her to him as once he did so long ago. But then he dreamed of gold.

CHAPTER 15

E very day, the news from St. Joe and Independence grew worse. And the word from Council Bluffs was almost as bad. A few deaths from cholera there. Susannah read it in the reports and letters that had been reprinted by papers across the country. Cholera and dysentery had scythed through the gold-rush camps that had mushroomed around the jump-off and outfitting towns. Thousands had died, and more were succumbing each day.

No one understood the mysterious disease or knew what to do about it. Mass graves swallowed hundreds. The stench of death and dysentery and disease shrouded the camps. Worse, cholera had crawled out the California Trail, silently felling men who thought they had escaped the carnage on the banks of the Missouri.

A stream of correspondence flooded the nation, carried eastward by men who had enough of trail life. They carried letters sent by gold-rushers who wanted to assure their loved ones they were well. These had been printed and reprinted clear across the country, painting a portrait of pestilence so terrible that Susannah could scarcely bear to read them.

She ached for news from Ulysses. She could bear anything, endure loneliness, but she could not endure his silence. But no letter came. She hadn't heard from him since he left Council Bluffs. He was out there somewhere, maybe alive or maybe buried under cold sod, maybe sick and alone, and she could not comfort him or receive the benediction of his bright smile.

She took the view that no news was good news; that if something awful happened, she would hear soon enough. The best thing she could do was to wish him happiness and success, and prepare for her baby. This trip west was something he needed to do, and she had chosen to bless it and rejoice in his courage. That's what love was all about. But sometimes it was hard even to remember what Ulysses was like. It all seemed an abstraction; committing herself to a life with a man, marrying, moving into the commodious house, sharing her bed with a stranger. When she was single and living with her parents, there were always friends and family about, companionship, jokes, anecdotes, gossip, churchgoing, barn raisings, husking bees, and potluck suppers. But now? She rattled around the house, her routines scarcely altered by the occasional visits of the McQueens.

How they loved to drop a sheaf of newspapers on her kitchen table, with pursed lips, well aware that she would devour every published report. It was as if Ulysses' brothers and parents were more interested in saying "I told you so" than in fearing for the life of their son and brother. He had defied them, and that was the first and worst sin in the patriarchal McQueen family. He had made his own choices, cast aside their counsel, and now they circled Ulysses—and her—like wolves, waiting for their judgment to be confirmed.

She understood this harsh cast of mind and found the charity not to despise them for it. Old Stanford McQueen was an autocrat whose word was never to be questioned. Except by Ulysses. Susannah was finding Stanford McQueen more and more insufferable. She had not, in all these taut months of waiting for word of her husband's health, heard his family worry about him. Did they love him at all? Had they no tenderness? Only Mother McQueen acted as if she cared. Did the male McQueens really want Ulysses to die, stricken by the scourge of the gold rush, so they could say they were right? Susannah had the sickening feeling that at least the older brothers felt something like that.

They had, with ruthless perfection, maintained Ulysses' fields, as if to show her—and themselves—that they were the responsible members of the family, dutifully looking after the tangled affairs of the wastrel brother. Susannah looked out upon orderly croplands. The wet spring had slowed the planting. But now tender rows of corn poked up from black loam, and spring wheat, amazingly blue, pushed resolutely toward the coy sun, and in distant fields the barley and oats sprang upward. To be sure, the corn wouldn't be knee-high by the Fourth of July, but it was all planted. She almost hated the message in those well-hoed, well-weeded, well-plowed and -harrowed and -planted rows.

The nausea crawled up her belly again, and she hurried to the gray horsehair sofa, where she could arrange the throw pillows and lie back. She wished she could have some tea. Most mornings it helped. But the weather had been warm and she had let the fire in the kitchen range die. The pregnancy hadn't been bad, so far. She had thickened some, but she was far from ungainly, and the grim final month seemed far away. She wore loose smocks now, and was sewing a warm fall skirt with plenty of waist in it. She waited patiently for the nausea to pass, her gaze out the wavery glass upon boundless blue skies and a mysterious western horizon that hid her vanished husband. Her older sister, April, had told her that Strawbridge women had hard pregnancies and easy deliveries, but that didn't console her.

The morning sickness invariably drained away her buoyancy, and then she scolded herself for not being as resolute and courageous as she should be. She hadn't expected to marry a man who could not be anchored to a plot of good farmland, but if that was what he was, she intended to be the true wife who would walk beside him. At least that was what she often told herself. But in other moments she struggled against doubt.

There was some truth in the McQueens' indictment of Ulysses, as much as she hated to admit it. If he loved her, he would be at her side. She knew he was having the time of his life, skylarking westward through wild lands while she lay imprisoned, not only by the farm, the house, and his family, but by the sacred little bundle within her; the child of their passion.

A nauseous hour slid by, and then she arose weakly, cross that a woman must endure such things. This June day her courage failed her. She buried her head in her hands, feeling her fingers pierce her crown of long brown hair, and closed her eyes. She wanted to return home—home had become the Strawbridge farm again, not this alien place. She wanted to be pampered. She sighed, knowing she couldn't go home. She was no longer a virgin daughter.

Was this all that life would give her?

She recognized her mood for what it was, a melancholia mixed with anger. Only this day it was worse. Impulsively she stood, feeling the heaviness of her belly tug her downward, and then walked steadily to the dark oak escritoire she had received from Lucy McQueen. One of the few things that helped was writing letters. But they were always such a struggle because she had to censor her disappointment, and write only the most encouraging words.

She opened a sheaf of good cotton-matte stationery, a Christmas gift from her parents, found a pen with a new steel nib, uncorked the ink bottle and set the ugly green blotter with all its stains beside her. This letter, like the others, would be addressed to Sutter's Fort, and only God knew whether Ulysses' eyes would ever read it. She dipped her nib, shook it gently, and scratched "June 7, 1849," and "Mount Pleasant, Iowa."

"My darling Ulysses," she wrote, and wondered what to say after that. She wanted to write, "Please come home immediately before I go mad with loneliness," but she didn't. These days, all she did was censor herself, not only in her letters to Ulysses, but in the company of every McQueen and every Strawbridge.

She wanted him to see her strength and her faith in him. She was strong in most ways, and it seemed to her that it would be best to hide her doubts and weaknesses, and help him be serene in his quest for the gold.

"There are so many reports of the cholera in the papers that I yearn to hear from you, to know you are alive and in good health. Every day I pray that the author of the tides of history may preserve you from the scourge that now terrifies the nation," she said. That sounded awfully formal, she thought. It wasn't the way she and Ulysses whispered to each other in the night, or bantered over the supper table.

"I don't know where you are, but I fancy you are in the mountains now, having passed the first awful hurdle of the plains and their fierce Indians. My darling, I want you to pursue your course with joy, with zest, and with diligence, so that all that you hope for and strive toward may be fulfilled. Someday you will return in triumph, and then we will rejoice. You will shame the doubters, and show yourself a courageous man and a visionary who climbed the highest mountain. I am very proud you are my husband, proud that you have the courage to do great things. I am at your side, rejoicing in your success.

"My dear Ulysses, do not worry about me. I am well. The child grows. I am strong. No summer complaint or ague has come here, and no cholera, either. Mount Pleasant has been favored with a cool spring. Your family is well. The crops are in, and your brothers have been most diligent attending to your affairs, and they have made sure I lack nothing.

"But my dear Ulysses, I lack something, and it can only be recovered when you and I are united once again. I face life each day, dutiful in my conduct, serene in spirit, but cleaved in half, for only part of me is here. The other half abides in your bosom, where we share a spiritual and sacred union until death, and then forever.

"Go to the farthest corners of the continent, with my love and blessings upon you, and my prayers protecting you. And in the deeps of the night, my dear Ulysses, when you are thinking of me and perhaps missing me, know of my love.

"Write me when you can. Send it by any eastbound means, across the Isthmus, across the continent, around the Horn, and if possible, in duplicate so that if the sea should take one letter, or the wild Indians take another, or bandits rob the mails, there is yet a good chance that one copy will reach me.

"I am yours, and like the biblical Ruth, whither thou goest, there go I, if not in flesh, then in spirit. Your loving wife, Susannah."

She felt better for having written it; it pleased her to give him the blessing and encouragement his family had denied him. She would give Ulysses all she could; she would bury her anguish; she would love with selfless love, as well as *amour*, the passion of the heart.

CHAPTER 16

F rom the north bank of the Platte, the Illinois company could not make out the famous landmarks of the Oregon Trail they had read about in Lansford Hastings' *The Emigrants' Guide to Oregon and California* or in John C. Frémont's famous *Report*. They knew they were passing Courthouse Rock, Chimney Rock, and Scott's Bluff, but these were all concealed in the haze-veiled vistas. Soon they would be opposite Fort Laramie, the American Fur Company post.

They would have to cross the Platte to visit the fort. Many members hoped to post letters that would be taken east by someone. Would there be a ferry, as they had been told? And what would be the news? That in spite of their pell-mell dash across the vast plains, wagon outfits out of St. Joe and Independence had beaten them?

The country had changed radically. They drove through arid grasslands broken by outcrops and angular bluffs. Browns and tans drove other colors from the eye, and greens slinked down to the riverbanks. Swarms of buffalo gnats made men miserable, along with parching days, whining mosquitoes at night, horse flies that tormented the mules, and alkaline water that purged animal and man.

McQueen endured all this as he toiled west, still weary from his ordeal. He was doggedly doing more than his share. The gritty food laced with sand, the restless nights on cast-iron ground, the endless walking had all reduced him to bone and corded muscle. He had lost so much weight he scarcely recognized himself, and his ragged clothes flapped with each step. But the company seemed friendly now, except for the studied disdain of Dobbin.

About the time the road plunged into forbidding hills, the weary company reached the Fort Laramie ferry. Across the turbid water of the North Platte, they could see the post, an adobe rectangle lording over brown tents and blue-clad soldiers, as well as a host of lodges of wild Indians.

The ferry consisted of a scow that could be poled across, held on course by a ragged hemp guy line that looked as if it might fray apart at any moment. Some shouts and a gunshot finally elicited some action. A bearded fellow in tan buckskins, his face shaded by a broad-brimmed slouch hat, poled the scow slowly toward the north bank. It dawned on McQueen that the man would exact a toll, and he didn't have a shilling to his name.

Wall must have read his mind. "I'll take care of it, McQueen," he said. "You can pay me out in the goldfields when you make your pile."

McQueen mumbled his thanks, embarrassed to borrow again.

The scow finally bumped into a clay bank, and the ferryman stared at the crowd. "Hit's one bit one-way, two bits across and back, harses and mules and oxen one dollar. I can't take aught but a spring wagon or buggy, and that's two dollars."

Dobbin said, "Does the Mormon Trail end here?"

The weather-stained ferryman hawked and spat into the river. "A pilgrim can keep right on a-going, around them black hills—they ain't really black but the jack pine makes 'em look black—and hook up yonder a hundred miles, with the Orygon Trail. I arter charge for advice to pork-eaters. Well, are you coming, or do I pole this scow back without ye?"

Dobbin peered around at his men. "Two'll have to stay here and watch." His gaze slid over McQueen, held a moment, and slid past. "Pyle and Ramsey, you stay here an hour; McQueen, Hoke, you come back in an hour so these others can go."

That seemed fair enough. McQueen, Wall, and the rest crowded into the tippy barge and felt it bob under them. The ferryman collected his due, and pointed at half a dozen poles lying in the bilge. "You get to push," he said. "I'm plumb tired."

No one minded. McQueen grabbed the heavy pole, and found purchase on the river bottom. Swiftly he and others propelled the creaky scow to the south bank, where it bumped into land near the post.

"I suppose you'll have a lot of back-and-forthing," the ferryman said. "That's tolerable, as long as you do the poling. I'm too stove-up to do 'er myself."

But McQueen barely heard. He had only an hour. He raced toward the fort, past soldiers weathered to the color of ancient saddles. He didn't know a cavalry troop from an infantry company, but he guessed he was looking at foot soldiers.

Fort Laramie, or Fort John as the fur company called it, seemed a shabby old place, but strangely exciting to McQueen. He discovered blanket Indians everywhere, staring at him impassively from Asiatic faces. He wondered what tribe they were, and why they were allowed to wander freely through the place, and whether they would slit his throat if he made the wrong gesture.

The yard, within the tall adobe walls, was rank with the odor of buffalo hides, mixed with the fragrance of cookery. Bastions arose at two corners, but seemed almost comical. Nothing here needed defending. Along with the rest of the company, he crowded into the big, cluttered trading room, popping with questions.

The next moments answered most of them for him. "Yes," said the traders, "those are Oglala Sioux. We call them the fort loafers. That's what they do." McQueen learned that the army was about to buy the place, and it had sent a garrison company, which was waiting for the sale to become official.

And yes, there was an entrepreneur at the post taking east-bound mail for two bits a letter. When he got enough he would send an express east and mail the letters in St. Joe, paying the penny postage out of the two bits. A man could buy paper and envelope, and use the nibs and ink over yonder, for one bit. That seemed a shocking amount of money for some paper and ink, but McQueen grasped that things were dear here, and these opportunists would make the most of it.

He could write Susannah. He caught up with Wall, who was surveying decks of playing cards, and asked for three bits. Wall dug into his purse, found half a dollar, and bestowed it on McQueen. "Pay me when you can," was all he said.

But getting a letter written in his allotted hour proved harder than McQueen supposed. He had to wait while others employed the three nibs and the bottle of ink set on the trading counter. Many Illinoisans, and a crowd of strangers who were with a wagon company parked on the Oregon Trail, had the same notion. McQueen wished he had thought to bring some paper, a nib and ink with him. He watched as the scribblers coaxed words from their travel-addled brains and scratched them onto paper, blotting and dipping the nibs, and addressing envelopes. Some awkwardly rubbed away tears from sun-weathered cheeks. Sorley Mulligan kissed the envelope he held in his shaking hands. A man from another outfit prayed over his letter before surrendering it to its dubious fate. Homer Camden posted a letter he had written long before. The silent Basil Lalique stood staring.

Precious time skidded by. McQueen itched to see what was in all the rude rooms lining the walls of the post, itched to talk to the ruffians who lived in this improbable outpost six hundred miles from the western edge of the States. He wanted to learn something of the road ahead and what he would need. Not that he could afford anything. The traders were peddling sacks of flour or shoe leather or needles and thread, or awls at what they called "mountain prices," supposedly because of the long distances. But McQueen suspected it had more to do with the lack of competition.

Time slid by, and McQueen agonized. He rehearsed what he would scribble in the few minutes allotted to him. He didn't want to tell Susannah he had lost the prize Missouri mules and a saddle horse, too. Nor to tell her he was flat broke and owing money, heading for California without cash even to buy a pick and shovel and goldpan. Nor to tell her his clothes were rags. Nor to tell her he had partnered up with a gambler. Nor that he had been so exhausted by an abusive captain that he had collapsed.

But he might say he was with an Illinois outfit out of Peru. And he might tell her he was well, which was mostly true. He boogered all these around in his head: tell her this, stay quiet about that, and figure exactly what to scribble in the diminishing time he had. One by one, men finished up their notes, sealed envelopes, and gave the pen to the next fellow. The queues shortened until at last there was only one man ahead of him.

He felt unhappy about keeping some harsh realities from Susannah but he didn't want her to worry, especially when she was carrying the child. He was "seeing the elephant," as they all said, and this life wasn't the elephant he had in his mind when he walked down the lane in Mount Pleasant.

"All right, McQueen, get back across, now. You've had more than an hour," Clappe said. "You let those other fellows have a good time, too."

Stricken, McQueen eyed the crowd waiting for a pen. "But, but—" The protest died in his throat. "All right, sir," he said, surrendering his place. If he could find Asa and have Asa write just a note saying that McQueen has made Fort Laramie, McQueen is fine, McQueen sends his love . . .

But he couldn't find Wall. McQueen sighed, hurried through the massive double doors and into the glare of a hot sun. He found Will Hoke on the scow, waiting for him. Silently they poled across the North Platte, while the ferryman cut some plug and stuffed it into his mouth. At the north bank Pyle and Ramsey were waiting.

"Mules are quiet; we watered 'em, and there's even some grass around here, this side of the river. A couple of redskins wandered by, but all they did was have a look-see," Pyle said. "Watch out for them thievin' devils. Shoot if you must. If they clean us outa mules, Dobbin'll skin you alive and I couldn't even slow him down."

Moments later the ferry pulled away, and McQueen and Hoke walked silently to the wagons and the listless mules that stood with heaving flanks, enduring flies and heat. Ulysses sorrowed. He had missed his one chance in two thousand miles to send a letter.

Still . . . He cheered himself up with the thought that someplace along the way, they probably would encounter an eastbound party, or a gold-rusher turning tail, or a freight outfit going back to the states, or a party of sick and injured men. And then, maybe, he could scribble a note and send it back.

A couple of hours later Dobbin and Clappe hurried the rest of the outfit across the Platte.

McQueen found Wall and returned the four-bit piece.

"Keep it, kid," Wall said.

But McQueen wouldn't. "I don't want to owe," he said, thrusting the grubby coin into Wall's hand. He would try again when he got to California. It couldn't be very far now, he told himself.

Captain Dobbin called them together around the wagons.

"I found out that there's been thirty-seven wagons through here already, not including that Tennessee outfit parked there now. Some were even oxen outfits. I don't know how they got here so fast," Dobbin told them. "Figuring five to a wagon, that's almost two hundred ahead of us, and that's just wagon companies. No one knows how many more mule-pack outfits have whipped us. Maybe five hundred in all. And every one is getting to the gravel ahead of us. We're gonna make up the lost time now, you understand? If you think I've been pushing hard, you haven't seen anything. From now on, we'll go night and day. We're going to catch up and get to the gold first." He glared sulphurously at McQueen. "Anyone who don't like it can stay here."

PART II

1847

S tephen Lancaster Jarvis tucked the discharge into his haversack and pocketed the eagle. He had reached freedom and his twentieth birthday at the same time. The Mexican War had actually ended on September 14, but word hadn't arrived in Monterey until late in October. After that, he and the rest of Lieutenant Colonel Jonathan Stevenson's New York Volunteers waited an eternity for the paymaster to arrive so they could be mustered out. Now he was a free man three thousand miles from home.

He paused at the presidio gate, not certain which way to go. He was suddenly responsible for his own life, a continent away from his widowed mother, Althea Lancaster Jarvis, his two brothers and sister, the graves of his father, Hiram, and three sisters who had died of typhoid—an eternity from the settled life along the Hudson River. But that was how he wanted it. He lacked nineteen when he enlisted; he had barely passed twenty now, but his vision hadn't changed. Everything lay before him, and this land whispered sonnets in his ears.

Around him, the mustered-out members of his garrison were clotting into groups. Most were heading for San Diego or the Pueblo de Nuestra Señora de los Angeles de Porciuncula, the largest town in the province. A few talked of sailing to Yerba Buena, and then to Sutter's Fort at the confluence of the American and Sacramento Rivers, where the Swiss grandee Johann Augustus Sutter was said to be hiring all who sought employment. That's where a lot of Sam Brannan's Mormons had repaired, having discovered that Brigham Young was not inclined to establish his Zion in California, especially now that it had become U.S. territory.

"You heading north, Stephen?" asked Will Boles, a fellow private. "We're catching that schooner in the harbor. She's bound for Yerba Buena."

"No, Will," Jarvis replied. "I'm going to look for land."

"Suit yourself, amigo. It's been dandy to know ya. Maybe we'll meet again."

"I guess so," said Jarvis. They shook hands.

Other New Yorkers politely invited Jarvis to join them, and he turned them down. They knew he would, and didn't argue. He had never been close to any of them. From childhood he had been plagued by a painful shyness that imprisoned him within himself and separated him from company.

He had enlisted in the summer of 1846 for the duration of the war, with the understanding that he and all the rest would stay on in new-won California and anchor it to the United States. That had sounded like a cheerful proposition to a shy, homely string-bean cooper's apprentice in Troy. He had not yet finished his three-year apprenticeship with Jasper Riggins, maker of fine casks, barrels, and hogsheads. By enlisting, he forfeited Riggins' esteem as well as the right to call himself a journeyman. But cutting and shaping and hooping staves had bored him. Riggins loved the craft and his tight barrels showed it, but Stephen could barely summon up the energy to perform his daily chores, and often won sharp rebukes from the master cooper.

The call to arms, published with a grand fanfare in several New York papers, had sounded like the Trumpets of the Lord to Jarvis. He had no future in Troy. The girls avoided an awkward apprentice mechanic with big ears that poked out of brown hair, a splash of freckles over his long sallow face, and an unconquerable gawkiness. He didn't sneak out of his indenture, exactly. He had simply stammered his newly discovered patriotic fervor to the master one day, with ruffles and flourishes about serving the Republic, and departed down the Hudson to the port of New York.

Naval transport had carried him clear around Cape Horn and up the Pacific coasts of South and North America, and had deposited him and his nine hundred–strong regiment in the sleepy village of Yerba Buena in March. California had already been conquered twice, the first time by Stockton and the topographical engineer Captain Frémont, the second time by Stephen Watts Kearny and the others. It remained only to disperse the regiment around the new territory for garrison duty.

Jarvis looked back upon his brief military career as boredom, humiliation by sergeants, rotten swill, dysentery, and drill, punctuated by rare moments of excitement. He had never fired a shot in battle or faced an enemy. Around the white-limed presidio barracks in Monterey he had basked in bright cold sun, performed his duties without a murmur, watched sea otters, and stared endlessly at Monterey Bay, which in certain lights seemed a field of glittering diamonds.

At first he spent his free time in the cantinas wistfully eyeing the California women he was destined never to win, soaking up Spanish words, and yearning for things he could hardly imagine. But that palled, and so did life with his New York barracksmates. Without really intending to, he grew more and more isolated, and eventually his fellows left him to his own devices. He didn't seem to hear them, and always seemed to gaze at infinity.

What absorbed him was wild California itself. Monterey, the capital, had been built on a headland overlooking the blue-green bay. Many of its white adobe homes had red tile roofs. Pine forests abounded. The customshouse and the plaza and the presidio drew Californios and Yankees alike. He found the climate brisk and refreshing, often more chilly than warm. He enjoyed watching the polyglot population, with Californios predominating, but numerous Yankees, Englishmen, Chileans, Kanakas from the Sandwich Islands, and sailors from all over the world.

The Californios fascinated Jarvis. They flaunted showy clothes, the men in loose shirts open at the throat, embroidered vests, black velvet pants slit to the knee, red sashes, and dark ponchos or gaudy wool serapes in rainbow colors, while the señoritas and señoras wore loose silk or cotton dresses that bared the arms and were often gauded with silver spangles and velvet. They completed their ensembles with kid slippers, bright satin sashes, earrings and necklaces, and tasseled rebozos of bright hue.

The "greasers" were mostly amiable and didn't seem to mind being conquered so long as their conquerors governed them lightly. More to the point, they conquered the conquerors. They enticed the New York troops into the grog shops, cantinas, and gambling parlors, where flirtatious señoritas and audacious gamblers sucked every cent out of them. The Californios loved fine horses, had a great many of them, and pranced them along the clay streets in the gaudiest manner. Even the poorest of them, without a *real* in his pocket, managed to look like a grandee. Not a one of the privileged classes performed manual labor if he could help it, and even the humblest could afford an Indian or two to cut firewood, cook, shop, and clean their homes.

The Californios had strung their settlements along the coastal piedmont and had relied on ships for transport. They had scarcely penetrated the interior except around San Francisco Bay, where the great rivers connected them to the world. Much of the vast interior was unknown, and Jarvis yearned to know it.

For most of 1847 Jarvis's fellow Volunteers had chased the ladies, drunk bad claret imported from Boston and sold for one *real* a glass, and gambled away their scant pay at monte. The señoritas didn't mind being conquered. The insulted young señors fired fusillades of ferocious circulars at the conquerors, denouncing the barbaric Yankee invasion, while their elders smiled, entertained at their ranchos, and invited their conquerors in for strong spirits and *cigarros*.

If Stephen Jarvis had escaped all this, it was not because he wasn't tempted, but because something larger and only half discerned seduced him. Unlike the rest, he had wandered to the customshouse and found a few books there, including Richard Henry Dana's *Two Years Before the Mast*, a seafaring California story that had enthralled him. He had somehow befriended a man of parts, the tough, practical Thomas O. Larkin, once U.S. Consul to the Californios and now a powerful import-export merchant and adviser to the military government. Larkin patiently described the local inhabitants and their customs, lent him books, and encouraged Jarvis to do something with his coopering skills.

"We need artisans here, Jarvis," he said. "The Californios avoid skilled labor and import almost everything. Journeyman skills aren't in their blood."

"I don't want to be a mechanic, sir," he had replied.

Out of Stephen Jarvis's barracks reading and his acquaintance with Larkin had come a restlessness for something grander than the hell-raising of his garrison. The result was a six-month barracks education in fiction, international politics, economics, trade, diplomacy, and the peculiar customs of the Mexicans; a hoarding of half his miserable pay; and a restless vision as broad and tall and wide and deep as this giant province. He had scarcely hobnobbed with the rest of the boys. So, at that moment of separation, they smiled, bid him farewell, and left him standing utterly alone.

He had given much thought to where he might go, and what he might do, but it all had dizzied him. He stood paralyzed, the haversack growing heavier, as if adult responsibility had been stowed in that canvas. He walked toward the camino, the oxcart-wide royal road that meandered up the coast, spastically veering toward one after another of Father Junipero Serra's missions and the Mexican settlements. He rebuked himself. If this was adulthood, and he could exercise his will without authority over him, he was failing miserably at making decisions.

He had only one notion in mind: find land and lots of it. He would need the help of the Californios. He would need to learn Spanish. He liked the tongue; he enjoyed the way the Californio serving girls in the cantinas rattled it from their saucy lips, in staccato, like the sound of hail on a roof, except for moments when their crooning turned whispery or voluptuous, charged with volcanic emotion. He would become a grandee like Sutter, own a vast ranch stocked with horned cattle, find a wife when he had something to offer one, sire a family, raise everything he needed, and become a man of parts.

If only he knew how.

Theoretically he was entitled to a veteran's allotment, forty acres of land somewhere, but the unsettled condition of California prevented a claim. It was simply conquered land, not even an organized territory. The wealthier Californios held vast grants, some of them recently bestowed by Governor Pio Pico, and the smallest of these was an entire league, over four thousand acres. A veteran could hardly know where to stake a claim in a place under military occupation, or whether a claim established by squatting would hold up. And the ten dollars burning a hole in his trousers wouldn't fetch him a cattle herd or a plow or a house, not even combined with the seven he had managed to save.

The haversack was bearing down on him like a pig of lead, and he set it down. A carreta approached, a rattletrap affair pulled by a scarred and dusty mule, its solid wheels made out of a slab of a giant tree. The coppery peon, part Indian unlike the Californio upper crust, smiled at his Yankee conqueror and pounded past.

"Por favor, señor—" Stephen said, at a loss for words. But with considerable gesturing, he won himself a ride inland in exchange for a dozen spare brass buttons intended for his blue uniform. He tossed his bag into the bed, amid a residue of fragrant hay, and settled himself with his feet dangling over the tail. That gained him five miles and squandered the afternoon. He could have walked the distance twice as fast. The carreta rattled through brown hills, forded a fierce creek where man and mule drank, circumnavigated an estuary of the glittering turquoise bay, and passed cultivated bean fields, at one of which the wiry master of the cart shrugged, and turned into a lane.

"Caballo. Have you *caballo* for sale?" Jarvis asked.

The brown fellow looked puzzled. *"Ah, caballo! Nada, señor, no rico!"* He pointed east. *"Rancho Estrada, cinco leguas. Muchos caballos."*

Jarvis despaired. Five leagues carrying that haversack. If a Spanish league was the same as an English one, it meant walking fifteen miles just to find out whether the ranchero would part with a horse and saddle and bridle for ten or twelve dollars. Another idea occurred to him.

"Ah, the mule—packsaddle?" He pointed at the flap-eared old beast, and at his sack, and waited.

The man grinned, gap-toothed.

Jarvis could not come up with the words he needed. But the man beckoned, and Stephen followed down the lane toward a small adobe house nestled in an oak grove. There, the man trudged into a pen, caught up a fat parti-colored burro not much larger than a Saint Bernard dog, and slipped a crude rope halter onto it. The creature yawned. The man vanished into an adobe shed, and emerged with an ancient wood-and-rawhide contraption that proved to be an *aparejo*, or packsaddle. His next trip to the shed yielded an ancient *jerga*, or saddlecloth, and a mangy *salea*, or sheepskin. All of these he loaded onto the burro, and drew up the cinch.

"Cuanto cuesta?" Jarvis asked in what he imagined was Spanish.

"Diez reales."

That would reduce his worldly wealth by a dollar and a quarter, the *real* being worth twelve and a half cents. It seemed a good bargain. Now he could walk unburdened. Maybe he could still buy a saddler.

He swiftly completed the transaction, and wondered whether to bother with a horse now that he was freed from his haversack. He eyed his stiff double-soled military boots, which simultaneously threatened to fall apart and abrade his heels, and decided a man traversing California needed a Rosinante, and it could be of any shape or description as long as it had four working hooves.

He turned toward the Estrada ranch after absorbing his host's puzzled gesticulations and finger-pointing, following a two-rut lane that wended eastward into an endless crease in arid hills streaked with pine and live oak. The rancho would be somewhere in the foothills of the Sierra de Salinas. The walk would get him there tomorrow, and still might prove feckless if the rich Estradas resented their Yankee conqueror, or if ten or twelve dollars would buy only a hoof or a tail or an ear of some equine transport.

It seemed to be a beginning, though he couldn't imagine where it might lead, or what fate had in store.

CHAPTER 18

Not until the following afternoon did Stephen Jarvis reach the great rancho of the Estradas. He had spent the night in a haystack crawling with vermin, purchased a slab of beef and frijoles from the wizened wife of a bean farmer, fried his supper over a snapping blaze beside a languid creek, and continued onward, his blue footsoldier's uniform rumpled and dusty. He regretted wearing the uniform of the conquerors; it might be hard to explain, since he could speak no Spanish. But he had refused to spend a *real* on civilian clothing.

He supposed he was on the Estrada rancho when the hardscrabble farms vanished and the hilly terrain turned into pastureland dotted with mottes of live oak, thick groves of pine, manzanita in the brushy ravines, and spring-fed pools alive with fish. Everywhere multicolored long-horned cattle grazed. Herds of noble horses, coppery and dun and black, scattered uproariously at the sight of him, loving the disruption in their stolid lives.

The cattle wore elaborate and ornate brands, while the long-maned horses looked so wild he wondered if they had ever been tamed. The rutted road careened around golden hills, lurched into gulches and creeks, occasionally topped a divide that afforded vast views into eastern mountains and western grades plunging toward the distant coast, and finally led the sojourner into a long valley snugged into steep mountains. There, the Estrada *estancia* lorded over an empire that extended beyond every horizon that could be seen from its tall real-glass windows.

A vast silence enveloped the place. Jarvis heard not even the soft hum of a breeze. He spotted no fences, but some distance from the wide adobe casa stood a complex of pens and small outbuildings, also of mud-dried brick. Half a dozen humbler homes, some with dead laundry hanging like condemned criminals, lay to the north, making this Californio rancho almost a village. The red roof tiles of Monterey weren't evident here, and the adobe buildings hadn't been whitewashed with ground gypsum, either, at least on the outside. Horses dozed in the shade of mottes, heads low and legs cocked, stock-still except for the flick of their tails brushing away flies. Many were haltered and dragged ropes. Maybe there would be one for sale.

Jarvis walked ahead, seeing not the slightest sign of life. Was this private empire standing empty? Surely forty or fifty people must live here, but not one emerged from a door to greet him, and the whole plateau slumbered in the early afternoon of a cool October day. It puzzled him, and he had the eerie feeling he was being discourteous arriving when he did and without invitation.

He tied his burro to a hitchrail and contemplated the broad facade of the building. On the west side it was shaded by a shingled gallery, almost a veranda except that the posts had been set directly into the earth, giving the whole a rusticity that Jarvis rather enjoyed. A low pine door, elaborately carved and decorated with black ironwork, reached from the packed clay to the level of his neck; a door for midgets, apparently. He found no knocker on it, and was about to rap sharply, when the realization struck him:

Siesta.

He backed away. He didn't know the customs of these people, but if he wished to buy a horse from them, he ought to take pains not to offend. He would wait. Maybe he could use these soft silent hours to examine the innumerable horses he had seen on the flats. But he wondered about that, too. They might suppose he was stealing one, or at the very least, failing to mind his business.

Some split-log benches stood beside the massive door, and he settled upon one. But the deep shade chilled him, and he retreated back to the wan California sun. At any moment the first of the great autumnal storms would come, and this tan and buff and brown panorama would green up swiftly. The somnolence of the place gripped him, and he felt sleepy. Obviously, this strange climate required a midday rest or these people wouldn't do it. He felt the quietness slide through him. The Californios lived their lives never far from slumber. He was tired from a night in a haypile full of crawling things, and a day of weary walking. He decided to find a sunny corner near the elaborate pens, pole structures bound together with iron-hard rawhide. He found in the nearest pen a few weaned and freshly branded calves and one dozing sorrel with saddle marks on its back.

He tied his burro and settled into an ell in the pole corral, propped his back against the poles, and prepared to wait. But he had scarcely settled into his vigil before he beheld a vision he knew he would remember the rest of his life. In a rush he grasped an entire universe, a theology. With a start he realized that he had plunged into one of those transforming moments that come but once in a life; a hinge of Fate.

No woman he had ever met set his soul soaring like this one. She stood over him with bright curiosity in her honey-colored face and the faintest smile lifting the corners of her soft lips. Perhaps she was eighteen; he couldn't say. Slim as a whip she was, and as trim. Her hair, unlike that of so many of the Californios, was a bold brown with a hint of red, almost chestnut, and was gathered at the nape of her neck with a tortoiseshell comb. Liquid brown eyes, wise as a doe's, surveyed him with the frankest curiosity, dwelling a moment on his blue soldier's coat. A wry smile failed to tell him what she thought of that, but created a soft furrow in smooth cheeks that knew no lines, neither of sadness nor delight.

She apparently was going to go riding. She wore culottes of the softest tan doeskin, trimmed with velvet, and a creamy silk blouse with puffed sleeves, under an ornately embroidered waistcoat. He saw everything at once, a thunderbolt of sensation coursing through him; saw, felt his heart swell and his breath catch. He met the frankness of her gaze, met her curiosity with his own, and scrambled to his feet, feeling himself the subject of a silent audition. What could she be seeing in him? What he saw in her sent him soaring like an eagle climbing to the sun.

Only then did he notice the small braided leather crop in a small hand, with a leather popper on its end.

"Señor?" she asked.

He could not reply.

"Qué desea usted?"

"I came to buy a horse—ah, *caballo*. Ah, señorita . . ." It didn't register. "Ah, purchase a horse. Ah, royals, *reales*, for *caballo*." He ached to know her tongue. In one mesmerizing moment, he knew that his failure to learn Spanish in Monterey had cost him Paradise.

She frowned faintly, and tapped the riding crop in the palm of her left hand. *"No hablo inglés,"* she said in a voice so sweet and light that it sounded like chimes. She gestured to him to stay there, and then strode purposefully around the pens toward a small sorrowful adobe beyond them.

Presently she reappeared with an ancient, wire-haired black man in tow, the first Stephen had seen in California.

"Miss Estrada come sayin' she's got her a Yank," the old man grated, "and she don't know a word you're saying, except *caballo.* She favors that you want to buy you a horse. Is it for yoah army?"

"I—didn't catch your name," Stephen said, suddenly wanting the transaction to stretch out for as long as possible.

"Ah'm no name to you, and how Ah got here is none of yoah business."

"I understand perfectly. You probably didn't welcome us. I'm from New York, if that's a comfort to you."

"Yoah pokin' around. Now, is she right?"

"Yes, I'd like to buy a horse. I was mustered out yesterday, and I'm a private citizen now, seeking to make a life here. Would you introduce us?"

The old man squinted yellow-eyed at Stephen, and then translated, using a sibilant Spanish that didn't sound like the language the Californios spoke. Eventually she replied, and then the old man turned sternly to Stephen. "She's the señorita Estrada, Rita Concepción, but that's not the way for a footsoldier to address her. She's the daughter of the *ranchero*, the *patrón*, Juan Carlos Benito Estrada y Portola. To you, she's *'the señorita.'* If it's a horse yo' want, she says pick any out theah, and leave fifty *reales* with me. Theah mostly broke and ready to go."

"I'll need a saddle and bridle."

"That comes with it. Theah's a mountain of them yondah in that shed. That's all Californios do every time it storms is braid reins and stretch rawhide over saddletrees."

"Ah, I'd like her to give me a little information about the horses—the age, how well broken they are, things like that, sir."

The black man spoke to his *patrona* again, and turned to Stephen. "She says she will, but if yoah any sort of *caballero*, you'll know. If yoah not a caballero, the Estrada horses aren't for you."

Stephen's moment of truth had come. He had ridden a horse only two or three times in his life. He ached to lie to her, but some steely voice within him told him not to. "Tell the señorita I've been on a horse only once or twice; that I was a cooper's apprentice in Troy, New York, a country village near the Atlantic Coast." The words had burst out of him. "Tell her I'd like a horse anyway, because I've come all the way from Monterey looking for one, and because a man who intends to become a good Californio himself needs one, along with land and courage and a dream. Ask her, ah, if she'll pick the perfect one for a clumsy Yankee full of dreams."

From the flash of her eyes he thought perhaps she understood a little. It wouldn't surprise him. Monterey had become a city of cosmopolites. He watched while the black man slowly translated all that, sounding like a file scraping iron, and was rewarded with a soft laugh. She motioned him out into the tawny fields, her gaze raking him frequently as he strode beside her. The old man trailed behind.

He felt something tingle through him with each glance he gave her; saw the grace of her throat and the clean line of her jaw, and the shape of her thin nose. She wasn't exactly beautiful if beauty could be defined as classic features, but if it might be defined as grace and radiance and unbridled good humor and lively spirits, she was breathtaking.

She would not understand a thing. His heart lurched. He could say any blessed thing he wanted, for once, and she wouldn't laugh at him. He could untie his tongue, for once. He could speak with the eloquence of Daniel Webster. So he spoke to the sweet dream walking beside him, his words soft on the quiet afternoon. This time he didn't even blush. It was an ecstasy not to turn the color of a beet.

"I came here and in two minutes you changed my life," he said, wild emotion tripping over his wary tongue. "I'll never be the same. I'll dream of you. I'll master Spanish in a month for you. I'll come back someday, not as a mustered-out Yankee soldier, but as an eligible man. You must have a hundred suitors, handsome *caballeros*, seeking your hand. I'm just a shy Yank mechanic you can't even understand. That's how come I'm carrying on. But I only wish you'd wait, give me time, give me just one year . . . because from the moment I saw you, I knew . . ."

Too late, he realized the old black man had been listening. Stephen stopped abruptly, the blood roaring up his neck and into his cheeks. She turned to him, her eyes aware of something, though he couldn't say what. He'd been a fool.

They arrived at a group of horses, some of them mares and foals, two of them yearlings. She eased quietly among them, and while they edged away, they didn't run. One yawned, bar-ing grass-yellowed teeth. She caught the braided halter of a linebacked dun gelding, and handed it to him with that small quizzical smile.

He nodded gravely, wondering whether she had somehow translated his reckless words and was enjoying his folly. But her face was as earnest as his. She spoke briefly to the black man. *"Eso es un buen caballo, muy dócil y obediente. Dígale al yanqui que el caballo es muy simpático—tiene huesos fuertes y uñas duras. No necesita herraduras si no va aquel yanqui a recorrer tanto. Y dígale a él, que el caballo cuesta solamente treinta reales. Tenga la bondad de decirle que con el patrón, este caballo fuera de costar sesenta reales."*

"She says this dun's gentle and obedient, sound in every way, has good hard hooves that don't need shoe iron if you don't ride too much. He's eight, lots of good service left but not young and skittish. And for you, because she enjoys the Yank soldier, it's thirty *reales*. Her father, the *patrón*, would charge you sixty."

She smiled at him, and then one by one lifted the dun's feet to show him the good hooves and the animal's obedience.

"Thirty royals!" he said. "Tell the señorita I accept, and hope she can change a ten-dollar gold piece."

"Sí," she said softly, trumping the translator, and his pulse leapt.

CHAPTER 19

R ita Concepción Josefa Estrada y Portola eyed the young *yanqui* cheerfully, wishing she could entice him to stay awhile. He fascinated her. But it was just as well the young man was leaving; her father and brothers didn't take the conquest of California lightly, the way so many Californios did. Juan Carlos would have sent the young *soldado* away without the horse even though her family had more horses than it knew what to do with, maybe seven hundred, and this one would never be missed. No one rode it anyway; it was too tame, and never set the pulse pounding.

A *yanqui* who couldn't ride a horse. Why, that was as bad as being without legs. Doomed to crawl across the earth like a snail. She could hardly imagine it, and pitied the poor fellow. But all that was not of import. The only thing that mattered was his serious demeanor, and the quiet glances. He devoured her with his eyes, even blushed, while he struggled for politeness and distance. He was a grave and shy man.

It tugged at her. She had felt drawn to him, as if some *bruja* had given her a secret love potion. She laughed within herself, and could barely contain her merriment. Such a predicament. A mad tug of the *corazón* from some common *soldado* who had scarcely been on a horse, and probably would have to be told how to mount. A *yanqui* she could not even talk to or tease. It was no use. She had so many *novios*—beaus—that life had become complicated. It was an entertainment, *coqueteando*, flirting with one, discouraging another, leading another on *sin verguenza*, shamelessly, with little *piropos*, the flattering compliments. But they were all just *niños*, *cholos* fiery with their needs and ignorant of hers. She did not care for a single one.

She turned to the gaunt black man, Cullum. "Ask him what he calls himself. I wish to write him a *recibido*. He might need it, with our brand on the horse."

Cullum talked *inglés* to the fellow a moment. "He calls himself Stephen Jarvis."

"Yarvis? How do I spell this name?"

The young man understood, reached into his breast pocket and extracted a document. He pointed at his name, and dropped the ten-dollar gold coin into her hand to seal the transaction. The touch of his hand shot currents through her.

"Ah! Estéban Harvis. *Un momento*," she said, hastening to the house where her father's great escritoire stood in his shadowed den. She could read and write a little, though her brothers and father discouraged it. They discouraged everything: they discouraged her suitors, discouraged her from wearing her culottes and riding, discouraged her education, and would discourage her from selling this *yanqui* a horse if they knew about it. She hoped no one had arisen from his siesta yet; they would give her trouble, and maybe even embarrassment. Maybe even undo the sale, just to show her she shouldn't be selling Estrada horses, and to show the young *soldado* where he stood with a great Californio family.

It maddened her, this attitude. She had been in Monterey enough to know that other peoples did not think like this. Other peoples sometimes said, *"Sí, bueno, dejanos a cambiar"*—let us change. Here was a *yanqui* who wished to own a gentle horse. Why not? She entered the chilly hacienda and passed through the long, whitewashed *sala*, with its massive, richly carved chairs, their upright backs intended to exact penance from all who sat in them. She genuflected slightly as she passed the niche containing the lovely porcelain *bulto* of Our Lady of Guadalupe with the golden sunburst behind her, and headed for her papa's bower.

No one stirred. Outside, Cullum would entertain the young man. Cullum could speak that harsh English tongue, so gutteral and irregular she could not fathom it. But Cullum might be rude. He dreaded the *norteamericanos*. He had never told the Estradas his entire story, but over several years they had pieced it together. Cullum had been a slave in a province called Louisiana, and had fled toward Texas one night, slipped into Mexico just ahead of the bloodhounds, worked his way west, dodging Comanches, *federales*, and all sorts of others who could think of ways to profit from a fugitive slave. He ended up in Mexican California—and what he thought was safety, until the *yanquis* came.

Slowly, Rita traced the letters into words: "Be it known that Señor Stephen Jarvis has purchased one dun gelding bearing the Estrada mark and car notch, the fifteenth of October, this Year of Our Lord Eighteen Hundred and Forty-seven." She signed it, blotted it.

She dug into the drawer where her papa kept a sandalwood box decorated with Spanish marquetry and filled with coins—royals, pesos, doubloons, silver pieces of eight worth eight royals, or a dollar. Any Estrada could take some. He never kept ledgers or counted his cattle or horses; what a waste of time that would be on a great rancho so bountiful that it offered everything they needed ten times over. She would need to make change. She had sold the horse for thirty *reales*. Eight made one dollar. His ten-dollar gold piece was worth eighty *reales*. Therefore she owed him fifty *reales*. She started counting out the little silver coins in heaps of ten—and then stopped. She brightened and stuffed the coin bag back into its nest without making change.

It was a strange name, Harvis. Stephen Harvis. Odd how enunciating it sent small thrills through her body. She hurried into the pale fall sun. She was in no hurry, even though she might not ride today if she did not finish this business. But Plata, her silvery mare, could wait. The *yanqui* was more important. The young soldier was waiting beside the motte, just as before.

"*Ten*, Stephen Harvis," she said, handing him the receipt. Then she handed him his ten-dollar piece, and turned to Cullum. "Tell him I could not find the *reales* to divide the gold piece, and he will just have to take the horse and return someday when he can give me thirty *reales*." The stratagem filled her with bubbling pleasure.

Jarvis listened gravely. "Thank you," he replied. He didn't smile. Something was troubling him.

"Tell him, if he cannot pay, he must not worry about it. We have too many horses."

Again the discharged soldier listened, and then Cullum translated his response in his abominable Spanish. "He refuses to be in the debt, so he will ride back to Monterey and make the change and return. He likes the horse, and will pay for it the day after tomorrow. He does not want to be under obligation because he is not sure he will return."

That stunned her. Californios were casual about money, but this strange *yanqui* was so serious. She felt trapped by her own cleverness. She could not very well go to the hacienda and make the change. Impulsively, she addressed Cullum. "Tell him the dun horse is a *régalo*—a gift—of the family Estrada y Portola. We would not want him to ride back to Monterey to change the money. Let him think kindly upon us."

Stephen Jarvis listened gravely, studied her a moment, and nodded. He wanted to say something, but couldn't seem to summon the words.

Cullum said, "He is grateful. He thanks the señorita."

She grew bolder. "Find out where he is going, Cullum."

They talked a considerable while, while she waited impatiently. Surely all this talk had to do with more than the man's plans.

"What does he say?" she asked, impatiently.

Cullum eyed her fiercely. "He says he is a Northern man and abominates slavery, and hopes I have escaped the whip here, and asked whether he could help me. I told him that here I can pack up my blanket and leave, and that is what matters. I told him the Estradas and the señorita have been kind and good masters."

"Oh," she said, puzzled, wondering what business it was of Harvis to inquire about such things. But she liked what he had said. Stephen Harvis was a kind man, but too serious.

Then Cullum told her in his harsh Spanish that Jarvis intended to ride to the great *estancia* of Johann Augustus Sutter, the Helvetian on the Rio del Sacramento. He would ask for a job there. Some of his countrymen worked there, including some Mormons who spoke his tongue.

She pursed her lips. "Tell the señor Harvis he should learn the Spanish tongue. When he comes to California, he must become a Californio." She hadn't meant to be so bold, but the sight of him made her mind unruly, like the madness of the fandango, when she danced until she was giddy.

Stephen Harvis squirted out words in little bursts. They popped through his lips as if they had been in a prison. What an *hombre timido*.

"The Yankee says that he will learn the Spanish tongue with rapidity if she would want him to."

Joy engulfed her. Why did this *yanqui* pummel her soul so? "Tell Señor Harvis he must come back and visit me and try out his Spanish. I will introduce him to my papa and my *hermanos*."

What was it about this ex-soldier? Why did he not smile? He looked almost forlorn as he whispered something.

"He says he is not ready for that, not yet. He will make his fortune and then return to talk with you."

She shrugged, puzzled and disappointed. "*Está bien.* Tell him to bring his horse. We will find for him an old saddle."

She walked toward the corrals, and Stephen Jarvis followed meekly. The barriers maddened her. She could not talk with this man from New York who made her lips hunger. She marched past rows of saddles and chose a rather old, plain vaquero saddle with a big roping horn and a high cantle, found a ragged serape that could be folded into a blanket, and a braided bridle with the usual high-port iron bit, punishing if it was used too hard. All these she handed to Cullum, who saddled swiftly and then handed the reins of the linebacked dun to Estéban Harvis.

She hid her disapproval as he mounted clumsily and settled himself in the saddle. The stirrups were too high, but he didn't know it. She nodded to Cullum, who unlaced the leathers and lowered the stirrups for the New Yorker.

The ex-footsoldier looked frustrated, as if he wanted to say many things to her. *"Un mil de gracias,"* he said. He knew that much Spanish, anyway.

"No hay de que," she replied.

He didn't want to leave. She didn't want him to go. She wanted him to touch her. She knew he wanted to touch her. He sat in his saddle while the dun swatted flies with its tail. She stood, paralyzed by the lack of a common tongue. Then he rode away and she watched him until he disappeared.

She turned to the black man, whose face betrayed wry amusement. "What did he say? When you were behind us?"

"Nothin'. *Nada.*"

"Cullum."

"Oh, he confessed he is a common soldier and of no account, and said you knocked him over, and how he would like to come back someday and show you he has made something of himself."

"And what else?"

"Oh, nothing worth saying, señorita."

She glared at him, and then Cullum confirmed the thing that she sensed: "He is loco for you. He was hoping you would wait for him one year."

"Wait for him?" Her heart leapt.

"You had better find one of your own kind," Cullum said.

"You do not approve."

"I have no permission to approve what you do or not. I am not a bounden man, but I am a man under the *patrón* and it is almost the same." He glared. "You catch Plata for your canter and I will saddle the horse up for you."

"You did not really answer me."

"You do not want my notions, not some old black servant."

"Señor Cullum . . ."

He grinned fiercely at her. When he grinned that way his lips pulled back into a snarl, and it always chilled her. "You and Jarvis, you have some heat in your bellies, so hot it will scald you. It will not come to any good. You do not know what he is like. Maybe he is a cutthroat. The *patrón*, he would lock you up in a convent if he knew how you feel. You cannot conceal it from me; you have the fever so bad you would go after the Yankee if you had Plata saddled up and ready to run. You want to know what I think, do you? Well, now you do."

She reddened.

"Maybe you should not ride today. You would just go tearing after him," Cullum added. He grinned, his face in a snarl again.

She shook her head imperiously. "You have no reason," she said. "I do not care for *yanquis*. What would I want with a common soldier? I cannot even talk to him. We had a struggle just trying to barter."

Cullum grinned. "Thirty *reales*. You would not give him change. Now you will wait for him to come back."

"You have too much imagination."

She turned her back on him and walked around the corrals to Plata's pen. She bridled the silvery roan and curried him, all the while ignoring his sardonic stare. He saddled the quivering horse, drew the cinch tight, tugged again, and tucked the spare latigo. She mounted smoothly, felt the powerful horse gather itself between her legs, and rode away, choosing a trail into the Sierra de Salinas, as far away from Stephen Harvis's path as she could go. She pressed her thighs against the saddle skirts, felt the strength of the animal, and knew riding Plata and flirting with callow caballeros were not enough for her, and never again would be.

CHAPTER 20

S tephen Jarvis felt the tug of so many conflicting feelings he couldn't sort them out. He didn't want to leave the lordly Estrada place, yet he had no reason to stay. He was drawn to the Californio woman, Rita Concepción, yet he felt frightened and shy. He couldn't even talk with her. The sudden choke of passion had been nothing but romantic fancy. What folly. A striking daughter of a powerful Californio wouldn't be drawn to an army private and apprentice cooper, yet the smile on her face and the warm lamps of her eyes told him otherwise.

She had almost paralyzed him. He had kept his wits only because he didn't have to make conversation. If she had spoken English, he would have been tongue-tied. He couldn't say what had galvanized him: she wasn't a great beauty, though she radiated beauty in all her ways. It wasn't friendship, for they couldn't even speak to each other, and yet he knew that somehow they were lifelong friends. It wasn't common interests, for he knew nothing of horses or rural life, yet he sensed that in those few minutes together they had shared an aching vision of paradise.

He decided it was only lust, and felt ashamed of himself. He had yearned to touch her, hold her, kiss her. Yes! That's what it was, and it wasn't something he was proud of. He didn't think women should be mere objects of men's desires. To reduce the encounter to lust was to debase something holy and sacred, like a stained-glass window. But it was infinitely more. He decided he had been single too long, and was at that age when women fevered his heart.

He rode nervously, unsure of himself in the saddle, afraid that the horse would bolt away with him. But the dun proved to be a gentle and amiable friend. It shied now and then at imagined frights, sometimes almost unseating Stephen, but on those occasions he grasped the horn and the moment passed. He tugged his laden burro behind him, feeling more and more like a lord, his faithful transport taking him wherever he chose in this vast and unknown land.

He knew he had much to learn about horses, and tests would come when he dismounted, unsaddled, let the horse graze, tried to catch his mount in the morning and saddle up. He had watched all these things being done; any boy anywhere in the country knew all about them. He knew the lore, too; anyone did. He must brush the horse before saddling to make sure its back was clean so it wouldn't gall. He must cinch up tight or the saddle could rotate, spilling him. He must learn how to put the bit in the horse's mouth and buckle the bridle, all without alarming the animal. He must check the hooves and clean pebbles out of them and make sure they were shod properly.

But for now he was all right. He didn't doubt that the plug would eventually figure him out, and become less and less obedient with such a helpless master upon him, so he made a brave show of steering the steed and tapping its ribs with his heels.

He wasn't quite sure how to get to Sutter's Fort, which lay some vast distance to the north in the great central valley of this province. All anyone could tell him was to return to the coast, take the Camino Real north to Yerba Buena on San Francisco Bay, and there catch a sloop that would carry him up the Sacramento River. But he wanted to explore the mysterious interior of California, where he might find unclaimed land. That meant he must ride across the coastal ranges to the San Joaquin River, cross it and head north. He knew he would need to find a ferry to cross a river so vast, and he would have to circumnavigate huge tules, or swamps, which would take him far out of his way.

The rancho road took him toward Monterey but he wanted to go east, over the Salinas Mountains. He hesitated, then remembered that a mile or so below the Estrada buildings there had been a fork, one arm going to the rancho, the other continuing into the foothills. He retraced his steps, found the fork, and was satisfied that he was heading in a generally eastward direction. What madness, trying to find his way through a land he didn't know, unable to ask directions or explain his intent. He could see, in the distance and far below, the Estrada hacienda, and felt its tug, which he resisted. She had been only a dream.

He walked his horse for an hour, afraid to trot or canter for fear he could not slow it down, or that it would buck and throw him off. Finally, when his thighs ached beyond what he could endure, he knew he had to step down and rest. Maybe he would walk, leading his animals. Carefully he swung over the saddle, and avalanched to the ground. He knew, ruefully, he had much to learn about riding.

He found himself in a land of noble ridges, mostly grassed but with various shiny-leafed trees dotting the slopes, and thickets of manzanita. He pulled on his reins and rope, and his animals came along. He hadn't quite realized how steep the road was and how much labor it took to advance toward whatever mountain pass lay ahead. He pushed ahead determinedly, grateful he wasn't hiking through mud. The famous monsoon season had not yet come but loomed like a guillotine blade above his neck.

The animals followed obediently, so light on the lines he scarcely had to lead them. That evening he would need to water and feed them. For the first time in his short life, other living creatures depended on him for sustenance. Animals were a responsibility. He had never thought of them that way. He might be a lord of California, riding where he would, but he must be a servant, too.

Ahead of him, skylined on a ridge, a horseman sat a bright light horse, awaiting him. Good! Maybe he could get directions. He knew a few Californio words. But when he toiled up the last steep gravelly grade to the notch ahead he discovered, dizzily, that *she* was waiting for him, on a sleek silvery horse so spirited it seemed to float, even while standing still.

She wore a soft felt hat with a broad brim, and under it her huge brown eyes surveyed him cheerfully. Then she laughed, lightly, silvery in the high air.

"A dónde va usted?" she asked.

He could not answer. She was mesmerizing him, turning him into a tongue-tied boy.

"Rio del Sacramento, sí?"

He nodded. She frowned, and then broke into a rattle of Spanish while he stared blankly at her. She saw his bewilderment and laughed softly. Easily she slid off her horse, letting its reins dangle, found a stick and drew him a map in the dust. From it, he comprehended he was heading the right way; cross this range first, then another she called Diablo, and then the great valley. She gazed at him, questions in her eyes. *"Comprende?"* she asked. Had he understood? He nodded, his mind barely on the map. Her loose silk blouse had tightened about her as she drew lines in the dust. She paused, knowing where his attention lay, and smiled wryly at him.

"Un mil de gracias," he said softly.

She nodded, touched his hand shyly, and loosed a flood of things he couldn't understand, obviously enjoying the very fact that he couldn't. She was turning tables on him. First he had poured out his foolishness upon her uncomprehending ears, and now she was doing the same. Then she surveyed him with long, measured glances, as if to memorize one she would never see again. He stood quietly, feeling her sadness, feeling his own heart surrender to the impossible.

"I love you," he said. "I guess I'm crazy. We call it love at first sight."

She said nothing. A breeze played with a few strands of her silky brown hair. He gazed so intently at her he could see the pulse at her throat. He felt as if he had been turned to wax. Her soft brown lips opened slightly and she seemed to come to some decision.

She stepped into his arms, hugged him swiftly and hard, crushing herself to him—and then sprang back, her eyes dancing, before he could enfold her. His pulse climbed, but even as he registered the wild sweetness of her hug, she had stepped back, a piquant expression upon her face.

"Mi pobrecito yanqui, mi querido," she said. *"Te quiero mucho."*

He didn't know what else she said, though she said a lot, which tumbled about him in cascades and rills and melodies. But he could translate it perfectly. She was saying to come back to her soon, never forget her, and that she would wait for him. That she *loved* him. He wondered whether sometimes something happened between a man and a woman that transcended language. He had translated her words as clearly as if they both had been born to the same tongue.

"I know this is crazy, but I love you," he whispered.

She turned to leave after one last contemplating look. Her silvery horse accepted her so easily, he marveled. He clambered clumsily over his saddle after starting the whole business with the wrong foot. She was wreathed in mirth.

Then her horse streaked away and she didn't look back. He sat quietly, his gaze following her course down a long slope, until she vanished behind a grassy shoulder of land. A chill afternoon breeze sliced at him. In the California valleys it was summer. Up in the mountains, it was fall.

The mystery of their attraction was as profound as the mystery of God. What had he to do with Rita Concepción Estrada? How could this be love? This could not be love, for love did not alight like a bird of passage on a ship's spar.

But it was love.

Moodily, he walked his horse upward, topping one ridge and then riding toward a higher ridge ahead, all the while reliving a sublime moment that had transformed his uneventful life.

He would come back.

CHAPTER 21

J arvis tugged the reins of the dun and stared at an amazing sight. Sutter's Fort loomed ahead, a white adobe rectangle with bastions at opposing corners, the late-afternoon sun blistering two sides with light while plunging the rest in gloom.

The great edifice stood on a rise a mile or so from the Rio del Sacramento, surrounded by cultivated plots and the beginnings of a village. No mountains were visible in the haze; only the vast central valley of the province, stretching endlessly into twilight, somehow serene and mysterious in the dying light. What a shock to the senses it was, after traversing vast tracts of wilderness. One thing he knew: California might have been governed by the Californios for generations, but they had never tamed it. Johann August Sutter had erected an impenetrable bastion, a haven from the wild Indians in the area.

Jarvis kicked the weary dun. He and his horse and burro would cover the remaining two miles and arrive at the vaulting gates at dusk. He wondered what lay within, or if this Swiss grandee could offer him a future.

He had become a competent horseman the hard way, through weeks of hard riding, learning to sit the horse in ways that hurt him and it the least. He had crossed mountains and penetrated a central valley larger than many an Eastern state. He had made his mistakes with his animals, lamed the horse one day and been forced to walk for three because he had neglected to pluck a piece of rock that had lodged against the frog of the off fore hoof.

At first he had been overly zealous about tying them up at night so they wouldn't stray, but at last some horse wisdom penetrated his habits, and it made him an adequate if inexpert rider. Managing his stock had been only the beginning of his hardships. He would ever more perceive this vast province as the land of great rivers. Every one of them had posed a barrier to his progress. The faint two-rut trails he followed led him at last to the San Joaquin, and there at bankside he beheld a half mile of water roving between tule marshes along both banks. It offered no way to cross. How did the Californios manage it?

He rode upstream and down, finding no ferry, not even signs of life. Was this California nothing but wilderness? Would these arteries of water defeat him? He began to plan a raft, knowing it would take a week to build. A profusion of trees grew along the banks: oaks, cottonwoods, sycamores, and many others he couldn't identify. He had a hatchet, hardly the tool with which to construct a raft, but one day he had set about chopping the irregular thick limbs of a live oak, wondering whether he would ever reach Sutter's Fort.

A sloop saved him. He hailed the trim craft and it veered over to him. Two men, whose European tongue he couldn't speak, grasped his need, and cheerfully transported the nervous, blindfolded horse, the burro, and Jarvis to the east bank for one *real*. He never knew who they were or what they did.

California's thin population was riven not only by aching distances, but languages.

On the east shore he headed north again, but this time not alone. In thick groves of live oak he met groups of golden-fleshed bare-breasted Indian women who were harvesting acorns, gathering them into reed baskets. They watched him, as wary as does. They wore skirts either of cloth or some sort of native fiber that had been softened and woven into a fabric. They were mostly short and stocky, but handsome, even so.

Shyly they had invited him to stay with them, and he received in turn a coarse bread made from leached acorn meal. He found the cakes filling and nut-flavored. He gave them a spare knife in return. After that, he had faced more formidable rivers pouring icy snow-water out of the Sierras, and each of these had accosted him with troubles. On one he did find a ferryman, an ancient Californio with a scow. At another he found a rowboat and appropriated it, forcing his reluctant horse and burro to swim. Just getting his horses to enter the water and head across that torrent had cost him a day.

The first winter storm caught him where he could not hide, and he rode numbly through bone-chilling drizzle and fog, over slippery ground until he found an oak grove with numerous dead limbs, found some shelter there, and a way to build a fire. He was grateful for the heat. Sometimes life itself depended on dumb luck.

He rode through vast tracts of manzanita, an evergreen shrub with edible berries, which formed a thick wall of chaparral in places, requiring him to detour. The mighty San Joaquin had fathered great bogs, thick with tules and wildlife, especially fowl, ducks and geese of every description. In this bountiful land he encountered arrowhead, biscuit-root, camas, sego lilies, wild onions, buckeye, sunflowers, currants, grapes, raspberries, clover, watercress, and scores more plants everywhere. A man could live like Adam in Eden, he thought, never gripping a plow or hoeing a garden.

But most of all he wrestled the rivers, their cold crystal water tumbling out of the mysterious Sierra Nevada which he sometimes could see in the hazy east, an ominous wall that isolated this Eden from the rest of North America. One day he had come upon a formidable stream he had to swim because there was no sign of habitation or help. He stripped, tucked his clothes in his haversack, and plunged into the icy current, hoping he would not panic and the animals would not fight him. He made it, thrashing his way to a far bank bristling with spiky plants that lacerated his feet and ankles, and hastily struck a fire with his flint and steel to warm himself. The swim had, oddly, left him exhilarated.

Then one day he had encountered two men from the Stevenson Regiment, men he didn't know, who said they had been posted at Sonoma barracks. They camped together, but some unspoken barrier rested between him and his fellow New Yorkers, who casually named themselves Tom and Phil, and didn't offer last names. He suspected they had deserted. The gossip around the Monterey presidio was that over three hundred New York Volunteers had slipped their tethers and vanished into the vast backcountry, never to be tracked.

"Why did ye come the hard way?" Phil asked. "Ye could've boarded a coaster from Monterey to Yerba Buena, and a sloop to Sutter's Fort, and never lifted a finger or crossed a creek or spent a cold night in the tules."

Jarvis wanted to answer that he was destined by Fate to meet the woman he loved and would marry, and that was the entire reason. But instead he dwelled on the dreams that had filled his mind from the time at the presidio when he was pondering his future:

"A man can't get to know the country from the decks of a boat," he replied softly. "I'm going to Sutter for work, but I'm mastering the land. When the time comes . . . I'll stake the best country in California."

From these two he learned he was three short December days from Johann Sutter's fabled seat of New Helvetia. He could have gotten there three weeks earlier by water. The vast Bay of San Francisco, and the two great navigable streams feeding it, gave the Californios a magnificent interior transportation system he had scorned.

Still, the overland route had not delayed him long. He had acquired a keen sense of the territory, and maybe he could put that to use. Not only that, but the travel had turned him into a horseman of sorts, and a man who could survive in the wilds.

Time and time again, as he traveled and toiled, he thought of his enchanting Rita, remembered her wry smile, her glowing brown eyes, her lustrous brown hair. The imprint of her body, learnt by his own in three wild seconds, remained as vivid and holy to him as it had when she had impulsively hugged and released him, smiling things that he could translate, even if he could grasp almost nothing of what she spoke.

The rest of the journey he pondered the mystery of love at first sight. How could two people be drawn to each other with scarcely a glance? Did they have the faintest intimacy? Had they shared dreams? Had they attended Sunday picnics, gone for strolls arm in arm, danced the waltz or the quadrille? Had he sacrificed for her, given everything he possessed to her? Could he name the names of her brothers and sisters or her parents? Could she name his?

But whatever his doubts, he knew he was mad with love, and wild to win her. He lived for no other purpose than to love and delight a young woman with whom he had spent only one hour. It made no sense, but nothing about life had ever made much sense to him.

That final dwindling afternoon his powerful dun covered level ground dotted with Sutter's cattle huddled under mottes of live oak, and rode up to the arrogant gates. He was motioned in immediately by men he took to be Sutter's clerks, and found himself in a rectangular yard, with all manner of shops and warehouses and residences built under the brooding walls of the post. A clerk directed him to a door.

Within, he found a dark-hued man with moist eyes and unruly thick hair, dressed elegantly, behind a counter, and knew this was the famous Swiss himself. Sutter spoke passable English, and plainly had the Swiss gift of tongues:

"Ah! It is another of the Yankees who walks through my gates. Welcome to New Helvetia, young man. You are welcome here. We are both a long ways from home, no?"

"Yes," said Jarvis shyly. The affable founder of New Helvetia didn't stint on hospitality, and almost before Jarvis could inquire about prices and terms, hostlers were leading away his animals and toting his haversack into a comfortable apartment with an earthen floor and a corner fireplace with an aromatic stack of pine and cedar kindling waited his pleasure.

"Supper when the bell rings. We'll be expecting you," Sutter said amiably. "There is just time for you to wash. Is it that you are a Latter-Day Saint?"

"No, sir. Just discharged from the Stevenson Volunteers."

"Ah! So! I am now a captain in the Yankee militia. We have this to share. You will sit beside my wife and me, and we will find out what we can do for each other."

Moments later, Jarvis found himself seated at a plank table, being served juicy slabs of rib roast by handsome Indian women the color of coffee. He was introduced to so many men, mostly Americans, he couldn't remember their names, although one dignified young man with a knowing way about him, introduced as John Bidwell, struck Jarvis as a fellow to get to know.

The former private of volunteers wolfed the dripping pink haunch of beef, devoured new potatoes, a salad of fresh spinach and lettuce and carrots, various cakes and pastries made from Sutter's own wheat, a glass of fresh milk, newly churned butter, and a hard-boiled egg. He could scarcely believe he was eating what was coming to mouth. Nor was that all. Before him was a glass of fine red claret, Boston sardines, and an empty glass for strong spirits if he wished them.

"I think maybe you are the second or third who has come to New Helvetia overland," Sutter said. "All the others, by boat, never lifting a finger. What do you do?"

Swiftly Stephen told of his past—hesitating at first to admit he had been a cooper's apprentice—but then describing the outlines of an uneventful and ordinary life. Sutter nodded, his gaze intent.

"And what is it you wish to be in this land? I employ any mechanic for any useful art."

"Not a cooper," Jarvis said hastily.

"That is one thing I could not employ you to do, without first shipping in the barrelworks," Sutter said.

"Anything else, sir. I know wood."

"Then it's settled. You can be a carpenter. In fact, I have recently contracted with a gentleman named Marshall, James Marshall, to build a sawmill some distance from here in the Coloma Valley, near good wood. I intend to get into the lumber business. California starves for good lumber. Would you care to join him? The pay—it is always the same for mechanics—is fifteen Yankee dollars a month and board."

"Would I be bounden, sir?"

Sutter laughed. "In this land, no man is bound. I hire by the day, the week, or the month, but usually by the month."

"It's what I want, sir."

"Good! Now tell me more about Stephen Jarvis, from New York, and a young man's dreams. Maybe I can help."

"Maybe we can help each other, sir," Jarvis replied.

Sutter beamed.

CHAPTER 22

T he bleak prospect before Jarvis didn't hold much promise. Ahead of him, in an obscure valley drained by the South Fork of the Rio de los Americanos, a square-built, dour carpenter named James Marshall was slowly erecting a sawmill, employing an undershot waterwheel for power. Marshall and his foreman lived in a sturdy cabin; his motley crew in large tents, one of them a kitchen and mess. The future mill was located on a sharp bend of the rushing river. The millrace would cut across the neck, taking advantage of the drop.

Sutter had explained the arrangement: he himself was paying the help and supplying board. Marshall was to build and operate the sawmill, taking a quarter of the sawn lumber as his share of the profits. Now, with winter closing in, the usually sunny skies heavily overcast and threatening, and the prospect before Jarvis of hard, cold, wet outdoor labor, he pondered his future.

At Sutter's Fort, Jarvis had glimpsed what California might offer an ambitious man. Sutter employed platoons of motley men who hoed his vegetable gardens, cultivated two acres of the roses of Castile that had been planted from slips the Franciscan fathers had given him, grew wheat and other grains,

operated a cattle and hide business. The great fort functioned as
a hotel and store and restaurant, supplying wayfarers with their
every need. Sutter's blacksmiths could repair a wagon or forge
ship's furniture for the sloops and cutters plying the river. His
mechanics could repair a wheel, reset a tire, build a new hub, or
fashion a new tongue. Sutter's table groaned with wines from
Spain, spices from around the world, preserved fish from New
England, his own beef, pork, chicken and eggs; milk, butter and
cream from his own dairy. What's more, Sutter was a man of
parts—esteemed by the Californios, a citizen of Mexico before
the conquest, and a Yankee captain now. And all of it achieved
since his arrival in 1839.

Would California offer the same bounty to a cooper's
apprentice from Troy? No, at least not for a while, until the
unsettled condition of the province had passed by. No peace
treaty had been signed with Mexico, and the province was held
by conquest alone. How could a man claim land, start a great
ranch, go into business? Where were the maps describing
the metes and bounds of the numerous holdings of the
Californios?

He would have to wait. That was what he learned in his several days enjoying Sutter's cheerful hospitality. Meanwhile, he
would have only his mechanic's skills to sustain him; that or
common labor out in the wheat fields or herding the long-
horned beef cattle.

Thus he rode into the miserable encampment huddled in the
gloomy valley under brooding foothills and wintry prospects.
Off to the east, the Sierra Nevada vaulted higher and higher,
blockading California from the world. It was almost like living
on an island.

He touched the ribs of the dun with his heels, and rode out
to the construction site, ignoring the sharp wind. Maybe he
was born to be a mechanic. Maybe dreams were for visionaries, men with wild self-importance, and not for shy appren-
tices from the banks of the Hudson River. He didn't know; he
knew only that Johann Sutter's rude mill on the racing river
would be his refuge for a while. If he spent nothing of his fifteen a month, he would have forty-five dollars in three months,
ninety dollars in six months, and by then a warm spring would

be beckoning him to adventure. Surely in that empty land he had traversed, there would be a rancho awaiting him—if he had courage.

He found the crew at work, and found Marshall boring a log with his auger. Some of the men were deepening the millrace, shoveling away dirt, prying out rock. Others were erecting a framework of posts and beams that would support the water-wheel being constructed by some skilled artisans.

Marshall paused, eyed the newcomer, and nodded.

"Mr. Sutter's sent me. I'm to be employed by the month."

"Well, I can use any hand I can get. What's your name and trade?"

"I'm Stephen Jarvis. I was mustered out of the Stevenson Regiment a few weeks ago. I was a cooper's apprentice."

Marshall grunted. "All right. Stow your truck in that wall tent. Put your horse and burro out somewhere. The Indians'll steal them, so don't waste time picketing them. And then you can start shoveling. They'll show you." He nodded toward a few men.

"I'm skilled with wood, sir."

"Soaking staves, bending them in a jig, and planing. You'll shovel for now. I've some journeymen working on the wheel and the cradle. Work hard and you'll make out. My foreman's name is Pete Wimmer, and his wife does the cooking. You'll report to him."

Thus did Stephen Jarvis return to the life of an ordinary mechanic, all the while bewildered about the turns of Fate. He shoveled alongside a crew, and learned that some were Saints, discharged from Kearny's Mormon Battalion and en route to the great Salt Lake, where Brigham Young had founded their Zion. Every cent of their army salaries had been taken by the Prophet's emissaries, and they were laboring to put together a kit that would sustain them on their trip eastward in the spring. Two others who talked with the intonation of the city kept silent around Jarvis, and he suspected they were deserters from the New York Volunteers. The remaining man kept silent also, and glared about him.

The men with shovels labored in silence, unlike the carpenters working on the mill. Jarvis envied their camaraderie, their cheerful banter, their pleasure in their craftsmanship. Day by day he shoveled away the hardpan, broke up rock with an iron pike, and deepened the headrace. In the evenings he lay in one of the crude tents and enjoyed the company around him. Azariah Smith and Bill Johnson, the tree-fellers, usually played monte, sometimes with Alec Stephens and Jim Barger, while the Mormon, Henry Bigler, stayed apart and avoided any of the long list of things he considered dissolute.

In December the rains came gusting down, rattling the tent like grapeshot, sometimes delaying work. Those days they risked catarrh or worse as they dug, sawed, bolted, planed and draw-knifed until they were numb. The tents lacked stoves, but when six men crowded into one, they warmed up tolerably. Jarvis toiled away his days feeling more and more melancholic. He did not follow Marshall's counsel and kept his horse and burro close at hand, moving the picket stakes each day. Marshall himself came to see the value of it, and on occasion borrowed the dun to ride over to Sutter's Fort to report his progress or pick up some ironwork.

In mid-December they completed digging the headrace and lined its sides with thick hand-sawn plank to keep the rushing water from caving in the banks. Then Jarvis and the rest began work on the tailrace, which would drain the water back to the river after it had muscled the blades of the wheel.

He scarcely had time to think about Rita. He and the crew toiled through the short days and fell asleep soon after darkness engulfed them, too weary and cold to stay up. She had dissolved into a dream. He barely remembered what she looked like, or the timbre of her voice. He could summon up her smile, though, and the bright humor in her brown eyes, and her moment of generosity—if that's what it was—giving him the dun. He could not hope for the hand and heart of the daughter of a great land owner, a Californio who probably had never seen the outer reaches of his holdings. That's what he told himself through the winter evenings, as he tried to cope with the deepening hollowness of his life.

He knew himself for an ordinary man. What grandiose dreams he had once possessed! A great ranch, wealth, and the love of a glorious young Mexican woman. Ah, what folly to have even thought it. He had been born a mechanic; he would die a mechanic. All that separated him from the rest of his kind was a passion for reading, but reading wouldn't stake a claim for a one-square-league rancho. If anything, the novels and poems had only made him more romantic: He had enjoyed James Fenimore Cooper's *The Deerslayer,* Tennyson's *Morte d'Arthur,* and *The Count of Monte Cristo* by Dumas *père,* and Emily Brontë's *Wuthering Heights.* Just before he was discharged he had read Prescott's *History of the Conquest of Mexico.* His reading had stirred his imagination and made him unhappy with his present estate.

Unexpectedly, the one man whom he befriended in that wilderness valley was James Marshall himself. The carpenter, usually taciturn, was forever assessing his crew with knowing eyes. He dealt quietly and amiably with his men, perhaps aware that any harshness on his part would cause them to melt away like snow in spring. Jarvis discovered that Marshall was from New Jersey, no great distance from Troy, and that made them almost neighbors here. The carpenter had a practical bent, and sought to know something of all the trades and arts and mechanics of the times. He wanted to know about the cooper's arts, and Hudson River steam packets, and Jarvis obliged him. The young man, in turn, learned that his employer had a headful of practical learning, and could have flourished in a dozen other occupations.

By Christmas the carpenters had the mill up, and had built the cradle that would slide the sawlogs into the great toothed blade. Marshall was telling them the mill would be operating in a month, and after that they would be making siding and shingles.

One icy day he pulled Jarvis off the digging detail. "We need to shingle the mill," he said. "You can start splitting shingles."

Delighted to be free of the backbreaking digging, Jarvis sawed cedar logs and then split them with wedges and a maul. He barely kept up with the carpenters, who were nailing up the shingles on top of the open-sided mill as fast as he could split them. The tailrace grew like a long black snake, and one late January day the digging crew broke through ground to the riverbank. Hastily, the entire crew lined the tailrace with the thick planks that would channel the stream. All the rest stood ready; the big wheel hung on its axle, connected by pulleys and leather belts to the saw blade. The log cradle stood on its iron rails, ready to carry the huge California sugar pines and other timber into the whirring blade.

Exuberantly, the crew broke a cofferdam at the head of the headrace and watched a stream of the Rio de los Americanos boil through the race. The great wheel creaked on its iron bearings, and turned gently. The leather belts chattered and slipped, and the saw blade turned. A little. Something wasn't right. Marshall studied the mill and saw the difficulty. The tailrace wasn't deep enough. Water was pooling under the wheel instead of plunging through the mill. He set his entire crew to work. Jarvis dug furiously, eager to see the mill functioning. But lowering the tailrace would take two or three days.

The next day Marshall seemed agitated, barely civil, and Jarvis supposed the man was irritated with the delay. The day after that Marshall seemed half mad, pacing the millrace, peering into the mucky bottom, fingering stones in it, all the while mumbling to himself. The crew whispered. The boss had slid into some sort of wildness. Each day the crew dug frantically, lowering the tailrace until at last Marshall got a good head of pressure, and the wheel spun and shuddered crazily, its thunder echoing up and down the Coloma Valley like a Trumpet of Fate.

"I have to go report to Sutter," Marshall announced. "Start cutting lapboard. Jarvis, I'd like to borrow the dun."

With that, Jarvis's employer vanished for a few days. He had picked a strange moment to go, when storms raged one after another up the valley, shooting icy rain into the encampment, but when he returned, James Marshall was a different, brighter man.

"Mr. Sutter's sitting on a gold mine," he said to the crew expansively. "There's been grains of gold in the tailrace for days. We don't know how much. I've been cleaning them out. These things get exaggerated. I sifted about an ounce and a half of it, and took it to him. It passed all our tests. It's soft, it doesn't dissolve in lye, we can hammer it without shattering it—and it's heavy."

He paused. "This is Sutter's gold, of course. And not much of it. We'll continue to saw wood; that's what we're here for.

But Mr. Sutter has a request: He'd like you each to pledge your silence. And in return, he's doubling your wage."

Doubling the wage. Jarvis didn't know what to do. He itched to look for his own gold, and the same thoughts obviously were crowding the minds of the others. They were all struggling with this astonishing turn of events. Double wages was a sure thing; a fool's rush for elusive gold, which none of them knew how to mine, was another. Especially in the dead of winter. In the end, every man opted to stay and work—for the time being.

Jarvis thought he would stay on—also for the time being. Thirty dollars a month plus board could not be lightly dismissed, and the prospect of finding a bonanza somewhere else was minimal. He would wait and see. Anything else would be harebrained. He knew what he would do: take two days off and go talk to Sutter and Sutter's right-hand man, John Bidwell. Somehow, there might be opportunity in this.

Maybe the chance he was waiting for had come much faster than he had dreamed possible.

CHAPTER 23

Padre Tecolote arrived at the Estrada rancho on the afternoon of All Saints' Day, as he had for many years. Rita could hardly wait to find a private moment with him. She had urgent things to talk about—and maybe even confess. Things she could not share with her father and brothers.

Before the feast there would be the mass. All Saints' Day had been carefully kept by the Estradas for as long as Rita could remember. That and All Souls' Day, the Day of the Dead, that followed. There were always prayers for Rita's mother and three sisters, who had died in 1838 of a bilious fever, in spite of all the holy supplications of the family and priests. No male Estrada had been touched. Among the women, only Rita and a venerable grandmother survived.

On this holy day she would visit the rancho graveyard, where

so many Estradas lay forever in their glory, each grave encom-
passed by a black iron fence brought from distant Durango; the
head of each grave marked by an ornate black iron cross, with
the letters INRI upon it above a small iron plaque announcing
who lay there. She never knew what INRI stood for, but her
brother Hector once told her it drove away ghosts. There were
so many graves, all grown over with grass and weeds, poorly
tended. She always meant to clear the grave of her mother of its
sour yellow weeds and put poppies on it, and talk with her, but
she wasn't a dutiful daughter and her intentions never became
acts of devotion. So many graves, and in another plot so many
graves of servants—adults, *niños*—all the humble in service to
her family. No fences protected those graves and often the
horses and burros grazed the grass on them. On this day she and
all the rest would follow Padre Tecolote to the ancient plots
where he would bless the souls of the dead.

Of course Father Owl was not the real name of the secular
priest attached to the Franciscan mission at Carmel, San Carlos
Borromeo. Rita could barely remember his real name, which
was Juan Montalvo Pérez. Long ago, soon after the revolution,
he had been sent by the archbishop of Durango to enforce the
Republic's dispersal of mission lands.

Theoretically, the huge estates of the mission churches were
held in trust for the Indians who were being brought to the
faith, those they called novices. Actually, the system had
plunged the Indians into peonage. They slaved for the padres
for no wages, but the mission padres took care of them. The
infant Republic of Mexico didn't think much of that, and
required the missions to divest their lands—half directly to the
novices, divided into plots; the other half in trust, held by
trustees such as the Estradas who would use the proceeds of the
estates to further the well-being of the Indians.

It had been one of those foolish and visionary schemes that
fell apart as fast as it was promulgated. The Indians bartered
their new plots for strong spirits and trinkets; the trustees soon
held the land as their own and did nothing to help the Indians.
Thus the Indians ended up worse off than before.

Padre Tecolote, the strong arm of the archbishop, had done
his job and stayed on in Monterey, serving a parish church. And
he had become the family priest of the Estradas, marrying and

burying them, and keeping all the feast days. He looked just like an owl, with a small hooked beak and big staring eyes, a pale face, and a mysterious dignity laced with unfathomable power. The name had followed him from Durango, and now people called him that and he permitted himself the faintest upturn of lips. That was a concession from a man who never smiled.

Always, Padre Tecolote rode up to the ranch in a black-lacquered buggy imported from New England, and driven by a good trotter. He said that the Protestants who made it didn't know God but they knew California roads. When Rita Concepción saw the familiar buggy rolling up to the casa, she raced to meet him. She admired this grave, unblinking man, and loved the spiritual wisdom he imparted. The padre always gave her reasons when she needed them, even if the reason was only obedience to the wisdom of the church. Unlike other padres, he explained things to her instead of brusquely dismissing her questions.

He would answer her questions about the *yanqui*, questions she could not pose to her father or brothers. Would it be sinful to fall in love with the heretic? Must he become a Catholic to marry her? She loved her church and all things holy and true and Spanish, and knew it was the true path to God and to all her relatives in heaven. But now she loved a Protestant she had spent one hour with but fully intended to marry because that is what her heart told her to do.

Padre Tecolote emerged from his buggy, rocking it gently, carrying the black pigskin bag that contained the sacred vessels of the mass and the Host and holy oils, and another containing his personal effects.

Rita stood to one side as befitted her place, while her father, Juan Carlos, performed the greetings, and Hector, the eldest brother, offered the sacerdote his attendance.

"Ah, you have arrived upon the hour, as always, Father Montalvo. *Bienvenidos a nuestra casa,*" Estrada said gravely. When it came to sacred matters, Juan Carlos Estrada y Portola could be as solemn as the sacerdote. After the padre left, he would become choleric and impatient again.

"The chapel is ready, and I've gathered all our *indios,*" Hector announced. "But first you will wish to rest, and dust yourself off. There is an *olla* of cool water in your room."

"It is so," said the padre. "And you, my dear Rita, are you ready to honor the saints, known and unknown?"

She nodded. It always took awhile for her to gather her nerve around this powerful man who could deny her the sacraments or condemn her never to meet her mother in Heaven, or see God; or doom her to the fires of hell—even though Padre Tecolote had never been anything but kind.

She hoped desperately that the casa gleamed. She had worked furiously at it, alongside the Indian servants, preparing for the feast day and the visit of the man who held the keys to life and death, sanctification or disgrace. She had broomed the gessoed white walls, dusted the carved furniture with its Valencian red velvet and gold-tasseled seats, wiped and beeswaxed the *vargueño*, with its honeycomb of little drawers and inlaid ivory, removed each revered *bulto* from its niche—her family's beloved saints included Juan, carrying his staff and his lamb, Veronica holding the veil, and especially Our Lady of Sorrow, wearing her black *rebozo*, her lips caught in grief—and featherdusted them. Had she missed anything? Had she failed in her duty and piety?

Hector showed the padre to his chamber, newly scrubbed by Luz and Tio, and then the family waited. The Owl always took his time, and it was said he first prayed in his room and sought blessings upon the casa, and for this he was regarded with great esteem by all the Estradas. When he emerged at last, he wore a white silk stole and carried the embroidered vestments lovingly sewn for him by Estrada women.

Rita slid her ivory silk Chantilly lace mantilla over her brown hair. She loved that mantilla, one she had inherited from her mother. For many years that mantilla had covered her mother's beautiful face and hair in church, and now it covered Rita's, a reverence to God.

They all followed the padre to the adobe chapel attached to the casa, a vaulting cruciform building lovingly built by Rita's grandfather long ago at the end of the Spanish times. All the family's servants waited there, even Cullum, whose presence was required. Of course, should anyone refuse the sacraments of the Holy Faith he would no longer be employed here.

For the next hour, the padre heard confessions and assigned small penances. Of course, Juan Carlos went into the confessional first, then Hector and Benito and Santiago, then herself, all in proper order; it seemed to go as slowly as ever, and she decided her family had much to confess this time, especially her brothers.

When her turn came, she slid into the confessional, spoke through the grille to Padre Tecolote, pronounced the ritual words, "Forgive me, father, for I have sinned," and then got down to it.

"I have fallen in love with a *yanqui*."

"That is not a sin, my daughter, but it is an occasion for caution when a heretic is involved."

"I have impure thoughts about him."

"That is very close to being a sin. But you've committed no indiscretion?"

"I embraced him when I told him to go with God."

"That is a delicate matter, but it is not a sin. We will talk of this later. Have you anything else to place before God?"

She did. She had been mean to several of the servants, especially Cullum, ever since the American left, and angry at her brother Hector, and impatient with the authority of her father.

Swiftly the padre assigned her Acts of Contrition, and absolved her with the familiar Latin words, *"Ego te absolvo,"* and turned to the next penitent, the first of the many Estrada servants.

Sometime later, very late in the afternoon, all souls at the Estrada rancho sat on the rough pine pews of the chapel and heard the priest say the Latin mass. Usually that was a high point for her, a time of great holiness and elevation. But this afternoon her mind drifted elsewhere, her thoughts punctuated by the responses of the little congregation. She thought of Jarvis, his shyness, his homeliness, and his gaze that transcended language and spoke to her of love as sacred as the mass she was hearing. When she received the Host on her tongue, she could not focus her mind upon the sacrament. Then, suddenly, Padre Tecolote was offering the benediction, and only the redolence of snuffed candles remained.

Not until after the supper, and the political talk, and the scorn Hector, Benito and Lugo heaped on the vile invaders and all their works, did she have her chance with her confessor.

"I have come many leagues, and must retire. But before I do,

I would enjoy the company of the señorita for a little stroll," he said.

She drew a soft silk rebozo about her against the twilight chill. She had so few fine things, and her male family didn't seem to notice or care. But this shawl had come from her pitying aunt, and she wore it for its bright carmine beauty. Tonight it warmed her bare arms and neck and fell loosely over her stiff bosom, and the silver crucifix dangling there, adding to her respectful modesty.

"Now then," he said. "You seem unusually quiet. And bursting with a need to talk about your young man."

"*Verdad*, it is so," she said. Swiftly she told the priest about her strange encounter with the discharged American private.

"Ah, it is a familiar event in the life of a young woman," he said. "How long have you known this man who struck you with the darts of love?"

"*Quién sabe? Una hora, no más.* Maybe one hour."

"Ah! This question answers itself. He will fade from memory in a few days."

"No, something happened. I cannot explain it. I grow weak and foolish when I think of him."

"Ah! A dream. You will nurture the dream, and avoid the true world. Very familiar. What drew you to this fine young *yanqui?*"

"I do not know, padre."

"Is he handsome?"

"No, he is plain."

"Did he display strong character? Did he have the marks of valor? Perhaps he had medals on his uniform?"

"*No, nada de esos.* But yes, there was something. His gaze. He looked straight into my soul. And I looked into his. He possesses great tenderness and respect. He is very shy and has never loved a woman before. I could tell. We—you will tease me—we talked without having words."

"I would not tease you, child. I am here to be of service."

"It all happened without words. Something opened the light in his eyes as he beheld me, as if he had waited for me from the beginning of time. And I felt drawn to him. He is very serious, not like all the caballeros who preen and parade and do nothing with themselves. *Sí*, that is it. He will do something

with himself and lay his gift before me. No caballero would do
that."

"But you do not know these things."

"Pero sí. Yo sé!"

The padre pondered it, and then his voice hardened slightly.
"Now, think about this. He is a common soldier, not suitable for
you. He is a Protestant—at least we can assume it—and not
suitable to marry."

"But I could marry him, *no es verdad?"*

Padre Tecolote smiled gravely. "Yes, you could. You would
have to be married in the church, and you would raise your
niños in the church, and you would be tempted in many ways
to turn your back upon the Holy Faith. But yes, you could with
the blessings of the church—but probably not the blessings of
your father or your family."

"Would you oppose me?"

"There is nothing to oppose. You will never see this man
again. Ah, my child, I have learned not to oppose the darts of
Cupid. If I do, young people run away, and everything is worse.
I have come to this wisdom: Let things alone and God will
swiftly impose his mercies. I will not tell you no. I won't tell
you anything. You will wait, and if your beau returns to your
casa to present himself to you and your family, you will see him
in a new light, and if you introduce him to your father and
brothers, you will see him in yet another light. And when you
learn his tongue and he learns yours, so you can converse and
share your lives, you will discover still another man. And then,
if you still love him and he loves you, perhaps this is a match
blessed by God, and who am I to oppose it?"

She drew her rebozo tighter, wanting to steal warmth from it.
The birds had grown still. The scents of cedar and sunbaked
earth hung in the chill air. A blue band lingered in the western
skies. With each step she felt her roots. She was a Californio,
and this arid land of cedars and dry hills and the Holy Faith was
her inheritance. *"Un millón de gracias, padre,"* she said. "I
cannot ever become a *yanqui.* Maybe this man, Stephen Jarvis,
will become a Californio."

"Maybe so," said the priest. "The Faith is always inviting
people to join it, at the prompting of the heart. Maybe your
young man will become a *católico,* make you a home; maybe

he will become a beloved member of the family Estrada. There are other *yanquis* married to Californios all across the province. I will not oppose this, nor can the church. But of course prudence and caution are necessary, my dear child. And one must always stay pure and avoid indiscretions that wound your body, your reputation, and your family."

"*De seguro,*" she said wistfully. "I am of age, and that is very hard."

"*Sí,*" said the priest, "that is always hard. No one knows that better than I."

"I will wait; I told him I would wait," she said. "He said he had to make of himself a man of substance, and then he would come to me."

"That is good. That is how the will of God will perfect itself. We will see, maybe on All Saints' Day next year. But my little one, do not pine; do not let your soul starve, do not despair, and do not curse God if God's will is otherwise. Remember how near to us is the death."

"Stephen Jarvis will come back to me," she said. In spite of the priest's counsel, she was pining. "*Tanto duele mi corazón para tí, mi yanqui, mi amor.*"

How much my heart aches for you, my Yankee love.

CHAPTER 24

Through the month of February, Jarvis and the rest of the crew at Sutter's sawmill toiled at their tasks. With the completion of the mill, they began cutting timber, dragging the logs to the mill, and sawing them into planks.

But Stephen Jarvis's mind wasn't on milling. He was thinking about the gold, as was every other member of that crew. No one quit; that would be reckless, especially in the gloom of winter. But each evening they watched Marshall scrape gold from behind the riffles, or strips of wood, installed in the tailrace, and they knew it came to one or two ounces a day. It was Sutter's gold; his mill, on his New Helvetia holdings, though

Jarvis suspected Marshall had a stake in it. One day Sutter himself showed up, examined the tailrace, scraped up the flakes and nodules of gold, and rode back to the banks of the Rio del Sacramento.

The crew sawed logs, but they talked gold. The secret leaked out; Sutter himself had been spreading the word, and occasionally visitors showed up, examined the tailrace, and vanished, pensive looks on their faces. One of them was a wiry fellow named Isaac Humphrey, one of Sutter's employees on the Sacramento. He had once mined gold in Georgia, and knew about these things. He talked about goldpans—any good metal washbowl would do—and about a thing he called a rocker, which looked like a baby's crib, and also about a sluicing device called a long tom, which took several men to operate but could yield a lot of gold in a short time.

Jarvis listened intently, and then got the Georgian to draw him a diagram of a rocker. Jarvis knew he could build one easily from all the bits and pieces of lumber lying about. He would need some screws to hold it together and a piece of perforated sheet metal, but everything else would be easy for a former cooper. When the weather warmed, it might be worth his time to do some prospecting. If the Sierra Nevada yielded gold on the south fork of the American, then it might yield gold on the scores of other streams draining the vast range. But no one could say for sure.

He could get his pieces of perforated metal from the smith at Sutter's Fort, and maybe a washbowl, too. A Mormon fellow named Brannan had started up a little mercantile on the bank of the Sacramento at a place called Suttersville, intending to outfit the trickle of migrants from the States. If Sutter himself didn't have a pick and shovel for sale, Brannan's new store would.

He took two days off, rode the dun down to Sutter's Fort, and invested in the equipment. Shrewdly he bought two picks, two shovels, and two washbowls, as well as some camping gear. If a rush started, he could sell the spare tools for a mighty fine profit. He ran into Sutter's friend and former employee John Bidwell, and they talked gold and rockers and washbowls, and before the visit had ended, Jarvis had an order from Bidwell to build another rocker.

It seemed a little reckless, investing seventeen of his precious dollars in equipment that might be worthless if Sutter's gold proved to be an isolated pocket. But he had learned something about risks, and didn't mind taking chances. He had left a moldering life in Troy, New York, for a term in the Volunteers. He had abandoned the settled coastal districts of California for the wild interior, also on a risky quest for something grand, though he knew not what. And now he would risk a large part of his capital on some precious equipment—and see what would happen.

In the last days of February and on into March, he built two rockers in his free time, delivered one to Bidwell at his vast Rancho Chico on Butte Creek, and collected a three-dollar profit.

Bidwell looked it over, rocked it from side to side on its runners, and declared himself pleased.

"Jarvis, I'm fixing to go out prospecting. You care to join me? I'm going to leave right quick, soon as I can get my traps together, and some flour in from Pete Lassen's ranch," Bidwell said. "I'm aiming at April first and I'm going to try the Rio de las Plumas, the Feather, with a few friends. With your rocker and mine, we should be able to clean out a few gravel bars. If there's gold, we'll have a good crack at it."

"Yes, sir, I'd like that. But whose land is it? Can we take the gold?"

"Some of it's Sutter's. That's his other grant. He has two, you know. Some'll be unclaimed. Who knows?"

Jarvis liked Bidwell. The amiable man had come overland in 1841 on the Platte River route, winning his way to California in spite of terrible hardships. If anyone could find and mine gold, Bidwell would be the one. Jarvis felt flattered even to be invited by a man who had conquered the wilderness.

He quit the sawmill, telling Marshall he was going out to try his luck. He was not the first. The others had watched him build his rockers and outfit himself, and some followed suit. By late March, three had succumbed to the gold fever and had drifted off, leaving the Mormons, who were earning cash to get them to Salt Lake. Sutter's lumber operation was coming to a halt as one by one his men quit.

Jarvis sensed that Sutter's dream of an empire of cattle,

grain, vegetables, manufactured goods, and lumber was about to collapse. Almost every day now, sharp-eyed strangers drifted to the sawmill, took a silent look at the glowing yellow flakes and pea-sized nuggets collecting behind the riffles, or at the heavy bottles stuffed with nuggets and dust accumulating in Marshall's cabin, and caught the fever. The word was out—but Jarvis saw no signs of a rush. The Californios and the Anglo settlers watched and waited, properly skeptical. But an immediate shortage of picks and shovels and metal washpans had driven up the prices of these items. Jarvis knew he could sell his spares for ten times what he had paid weeks before—and any smith capable of manufacturing them could get rich.

In late April 1848, the Bidwell party, finally outfitted properly, set out for the Feather River. It numbered half a dozen men. Jarvis entertained no wild notions of striking it rich, nor did anyone else. Sutter's mill had yielded some gold, but hardly in bonanza quantities. Jarvis liked this crew, especially Bidwell, who was not much older than the rest, but led the group with courtesy.

The forks of the Feather drained a vast area of the Sierra Nevada north of Sutter's great grasslands empire. John Bidwell chose the river, partly because it was closest to his Rancho Chico, but also because it was among the most remote from the settlements. They had the place to themselves.

Jarvis never forgot those early days. They panned along the Feather and found gold everywhere; not in large quantities, but gold nonetheless, fine-grained and very light. He swiftly mastered the art of panning. He scooped sand into his pan, plucked the stones out, added water, swirled the mixture to settle the heavy gold particles while whirling off the lighter sand and gravel. None of them knew much about it, but they learned fast. Gold did that to them—fevered them to learn. Each pocketed a bit of concentrate, gold dust mixed with the heaviest black sand they couldn't wash away. Humphrey had said the next step was to amalgamate the particles with quicksilver, which would form a metallic substance that would not include the sand. But no one had brought any quicksilver, and no one knew how to get it. For now, the concentrate would have to do.

"It's here, boys," was all Bidwell said. "Let's go upstream

and see if we find nuggets. The closer to the mother lode, the more we should find."

No one disputed that. That spring they worked upstream, finding gold everywhere, stuffing their proceeds into their leather pokes. Jarvis loved it. The country had grown rough and wild. The river boiled through chasms that warmed only when the sun briefly visited the bottoms. Cliffs vaulted upward. Often the men had to detour, leading their pack animals around roaring canyons until they could find another flat where they could dip a pan. They rarely used the rockers; this was a prospecting time.

Gold! Jarvis could hardly believe the weight of his heavy pouch. After amalgamating, he would have many ounces of pure dust. It was here for the plucking. Anyone could. He marveled at his good fortune. It was as if being a cooper's apprentice had destined him to build two rockers, which had destined him to join Bidwell's exploration into wild, rough foothill country no white man had ever seen before.

But apparently it didn't satisfy two of Bidwell's Rancho Chico neighbors, Potter and Williams. They'd been muttering for a day or two, and then announced their intention to pull out.

"This is light gold, mostly flakes. We'll go over to the American, where Sutter's proved up heavy gold," Potter said. With that, the pair left, leaving Bidwell, Northfield, Dickson, and Jarvis.

Bidwell watched the pair head over a steep ridge and vanish. "Pickings always seem richer somewhere else," he said. "I get the itch myself sometimes."

Jarvis liked that. Bidwell hadn't condemned the departing pair at all. In John Bidwell the party had a fair and cheerful leader, Jarvis thought. "We're getting into heavier gold each day, seems like," he said. "One of these days we'll hit some real nuggets."

Relentlessly, Bidwell pushed deeper into the Sierras all through May and into June, always finding gold, but nothing exciting. They met no one, and had no idea what was happening on other drainages. For all they knew, the Yuba or the American or a dozen other rivers had proven to be Golcondas, and all of California had rushed in. They talked about this not-knowing, this isolation, this wild fear that they were missing the boat, this envy of others who were reaping imagined bonanzas. Sometimes they wrestled with the idea of sending one of their number back out just to find out what was happening, and whether they should be racing toward some better stream. But Bidwell himself always put the quietus to it.

"Let's see what we have here," he argued logically. "Boys, once we've tried this stream, we'll know one way or the other. The Sierra's a mighty range, and we'll not miss much, and we'll be satisfied we've left nothing behind us here."

Jarvis agreed to it, even though a part of him crawled with the need to bolt for the Yuba or some other place.

It turned hot, and they no longer had to huddle around fires to warm up after a numbing day working in snowmelt. Wildflowers bloomed in profusion—rakish purple, brilliant orange and yellow, searing blues—carpets of them that dazzled Jarvis and reminded him that gold wasn't all; he was seeing a paradise that sent his heart soaring. Surely the Californios didn't know what sort of paradise they possessed.

The thought reminded him of Rita. Nothing had changed. She hadn't faded from mind. He felt a curious sense of destiny; that the strands of his fate had swiftly gathered together here. He could laugh at himself: What had he to do with a lovely young woman whose tongue he didn't know, whose aristocratic family would dismiss him instantly? But all those forebodings didn't amount to anything compared to his joy at the thought of her, the comfortable feel of gold in his pouch, and the dream of taking it to her, showing her that he had become a man of substance.

June came and went, and Bidwell's diminished party pushed farther upstream, passing the mouth of the north fork. The placer gold deposits actually got richer and coarser as they went, luring them onward with its fabulous promise.

Then, on the Fourth of July, 1848, they came upon a sweeping bend of the river, lying in a broad flat, where multiple bars of gravel projected into the swift, murky torrent. Whatever else this place would provide, it was idyllic for camping and a good spot to pasture the pack animals.

Jarvis scooped up a load with his pan, added a little more water, and began swirling. The gravel spilled away, and he added a bit more water, whirled the sand out, added water again, and repeated the procedure. Then he peered into the bottom to see what he had found. Glittering in the basin was an amazing two or three ounces of bright yellow gold, coarse nuggets, large flakes, one convoluted piece the size of an acorn.

He whooped so loud he scarcely heard the whoops of the others there at John Bidwell's bar.

CHAPTER 25

T rembling, Jarvis tried a pan farther toward the stream, and found another two or three ounces in his bowl. He peered about sharply, looking for interlopers, and found only his friends, each whirling gravel. The bar covered several acres, and actually formed a flat. Maybe some other spot would be richer. He leapt toward a likely place, threw sand into his bowl, and found less gold, but one big nugget. He retreated, headed upstream, and tried another spot, crazed with greed. Around him the others pursued the same mad quest, except for Bidwell, who seemed content to pan the first area he had tested.

The nooning was forgotten. All that day the foursome panned gold. Jarvis was too heated and excited to unpack his rocker, screw it together, and begin serious mining. It would take an hour or two, and that would cost him hundreds of dollars. He had no idea of how much gold he collected that frenzied afternoon, but toward dusk, he knew that several pounds of uncleaned dust and nuggets burdened his leather pouch. He had made more in an afternoon than he had made in his prior life.

Bidwell called the halt. "Let's eat and talk this over, gentlemen," he said quietly. "There's no one here and it's not likely anyone'll show up for weeks. We don't need to wear ourselves down, take sick, and die for gold."

Jarvis laughed, and so did the other two, Dickson and Northfield, but no one except Bidwell stopped digging. The leader gathered dry driftwood, built a fire, and began making camp. The aroma of coffee finally brought Jarvis to his senses, and he quit for a while, wondering whether moonlight would let him continue.

Sheepishly the fevered men gathered and sipped coffee. Bidwell got out a small scale and weighed his take: He had seven pounds of uncleaned gold in his bag; the rest had three or four. It dawned on Jarvis he had wasted time scrambling all over the sandy flats to find the best diggings, and so had the rest, while their calm leader had quietly harvested pan after pan of gold.

"I'm rich!" cried Northfield. "I'll shoot the first bloody rat that tries to steal my gold." Then he laughed gleefully. "Think what Potter and Williams cut themselves out of. They'll kick and curse the rest of their lives, or maybe come back and try to barge in, saying they was part of the party."

"Let's talk about that," said Bidwell quietly. "Men'll be coming. And they'll want what we found. And if they outnumber us, we'll be driven out. We need to set up claims, record them, and draw up some rules. I asked Humphrey how it's done, and he said you need to define the boundaries of the claims, give the discoverers an extra claim apiece, and submit disputes to miners' meetings. A man holds his claim by leaving his tools on it. If he doesn't work it for more than three days, or hire someone to do it, he loses it."

Bidwell's quiet talk brought Jarvis back to reality. Yes, they would need to draw up some rules, fast—before the four of them got into a fierce fight.

"I guess you're right, John," Northfield said. "We went crazy. Me, I'm gonna get my pocketful of rocks, buy me a big white house on the banks of the Wabash, put a little pink woman in it, and raise sorghum and barley."

"You won't get no pocketful of rocks if some bunch of rowdies takes this away from us," Dickson said. "That's why we better organize. I figure if we have written-down rules, and dates of discovery, and all that, we've a better chance when the mob arrives."

"If there *is* a mob. We might clean out the whole bar and get to be millionaires before one outside coon shows up," Northfield said. "Especially with those rockers."

"Stephen and I both have rockers," Bidwell said. "We can work them alone, or we can pair up. There's four of us. I'm told a pair using a rocker can move five or six yards of gravel a day, while a man panning by himself can barely wash one yard in a long day. The two of us who've invested in the rockers should get something for our investment." He turned to Dickson and Northfield, who were sipping the scalding coffee. "Want to make an offer?"

"I'll wash my own," said Dickson instantly, but Northfield paused.

"I'll study on it," Northfield said. "I want to see what you come up with tomorrow. Right now, I'd like to draw up some rules and go stake my claim before it gets dark."

"We can stake claims in the morning," Bidwell said. "We'll each get two."

"Well, make 'em big!"

"As big as we can get away with when others arrive," Bidwell said. "You can bet they're coming."

"I wish we had some news," Jarvis said. "We've been back here for weeks."

"We'll get news. We have to go for supplies in a few days," Bidwell said ominously. "Flour's low, bacon's gone, parched corn—we have a sufficiency for now. Coffee beans almost out. Sugar's low, and so are the beans. And no one wants to hunt."

"But who'll go?" Northfield asked. "Whoever goes'll lose a fortune."

"We can cover whoever goes," Bidwell said. "The three of us will pool and then divide the gold by four while one person fetches provisions."

"Well, let's get on with it," Dickson snapped. "I want to stake my claims."

Jarvis eyed Dickson thoughtfully. The man had been transformed, and not for the better, by gold fever.

Bidwell studied Dickson too. "All right. This is now a miners' meeting, and the majority vote carries. Tie votes fail. Stephen, you record the minutes."

Jarvis nodded, dug into his kit and produced a small bound notebook and a pencil.

"I've been thinking about this all afternoon," Bidwell said. "This bar's below the banks and is sometimes submerged. I'd like to propose that each claim run bank-to-bank, twenty feet wide. Then we each get one, plus a discovery claim, so that we have forty feet of the bar apiece."

"That's not so much. I'm planning to get rich," said Dickson. "There's four or five acres of gravel, and you're giving us a few feet."

Bidwell nodded. "Men'll be coming here soon, as sure as we're sitting here. What'll they tolerate?"

They argued it awhile, and Jarvis could see Dickson digging in and resisting, wanting hundred-foot claims bank-to-bank. But when Bidwell called for the vote, Dickson found himself alone. Jarvis recorded that the discovery party had voted for twenty-foot claims.

They decided to stake the claims at dawn, and number them and record them in the ledger. After that, the meeting didn't take long. Dickson turned sullen—as if gold had destroyed his civility—but voted along with the rest on the ways to protect claims when absent, resolve disputes, appoint a clerk— Jarvis—and keep a record.

They boiled some parched corn into mush, seasoned it with a little salt, and then spent some time making a rudimentary camp. It shocked Jarvis to realize he had not taken care of his animals. Gold fever had smitten him and he had panned wildly all day, leaving the bridle in the dun's mouth. He found his animals a hundred yards off. The dun's bridle was fouled with saliva-slimed grass. He exchanged the bridle for a halter and picketed the horse, watching it eat greedily.

What does gold do to a man? he asked himself. It had turned him from a caring man who treated his livestock well into a negligent one. What would it do to Dickson when others arrived here? Jarvis didn't doubt others would come, maybe sooner than expected. He let the burro graze freely, knowing it wouldn't venture far from the horse. So far, they had encountered none of the local tribesmen, but that could change at any moment. Bidwell had taken care of his mules early in the day, calmly taking the time to do so while the rest had been gold-mad. And yet this man had panned over a pound more gold than the rest. Jarvis knew what it was that made Bidwell a leader, and what traits had enabled the man to traverse a wild continent and arrive in this mountain-girt Eden safely.

He set up his bedroll, eyed the bold skies for rain, decided not to erect a tent, and then sat down with his heavy buckskin bag of gold. He spread his duck cloth and poured the gold onto it, marveling at the sight in the long summer's twilight. He found himself plucking out waste rock, grains of sand, detritus, but it didn't clean the gold much. He filled a bucket and brought it to his camp, and quietly panned the gold again, using the delicacy that took too much time by day. This time, he reduced the waste noticeably, and when he packed away his gold at last, it was largely pure, except for some black sand he couldn't swirl out of his bowl. Quicksilver would do the rest, when he could buy some. He had heard of a cinnabar mine in the province; maybe some could be found.

Even before sunrise, the restless four laid out the first eight claims, using a tape measure, and built corner cairns out of river rock. Dickson scorned breakfast, and went off to pan on his own. Northfield eyed Jarvis apologetically.

"John Bidwell's an old Rancho Chico neighbor of mine, and I've asked to join him and work his rocker together. He'll take sixty and I'll take forty of what we produce. I guess that leaves you alone, Stephen, least until Dickson comes to his senses and decides to hitch up with you."

Jarvis nodded. He didn't mind. He had two rich claims and a rocker, one of only a handful in the Sierras. He followed Bidwell's lead, and ate a hearty breakfast of biscuits and grease, with some stinging coffee to wake him up. He unpacked and assembled his rocker, and set it near the roaring river, at a little slant. He had been told the riffle box should sit a couple of inches below the hopper. He paused a moment, in the sweetness of the dawn, the silence broken only by the rushing green water of the river. The events of the last hours—and weeks—stunned him. The discharged private, the cooper's apprentice, the wayfarer with a horse and burro had already ripped a one-day fortune out of the Feather River.

Then he set to work. He shoveled wet sands into the hopper of the rocker, picked out the waste rock by hand, and then added water bit by bit with his goldpan, gently rocking the apparatus. The watery sand and muck dribbled through the metal screen and rushed over the riffles and into the ground. Behind each riffle, shining gold accumulated. He wondered if this were faster than panning. He poked around the residue in the hopper, found a nugget too large to go through the perforations, and then threw out the rest. He scraped up the gold lodged behind the riffles, and poured it into his tin mess-plate. He gawked at the sight. He was holding maybe three or four troy ounces, an amount equal to his entire pay in the Volunteers.

At the end of that day, he reckoned he had collected around fifteen hundred dollars of dust and nuggets, and he was just getting started. It seemed unbelievable; too good to be true.

But Bidwell and Northfield reported twenty-five hundred, roughly twenty troy pounds of uncleaned gold, and Dickson wasn't saying.

Jarvis felt exultation and foreboding at the same time.

CHAPTER 26

During the next week they toiled through daylight, did their chores at night, and scarcely slept. Jarvis began to rewash his gold in the pan each evening, patiently plucking out grit, never quite satisfied. In two days he filled two leather pokes with cleaned gold. They felt fat and heavy in his hand. He begged an empty tea canister from Bidwell, and began storing his bonanza in that.

They saw no one. He ached to learn whether a gold rush was on, or whether they were alone. They all itched for news. If there had been a rush, the rivers below them might be crawling with miners. Word was out, and a few thousand Californians, Yankees, Mexicans, Kanakas, and others would try their luck sooner or later.

"Hope they stay away," growled Dickson. "They come in here, they'll steal from us. Bunch of brigands."

"Most men are honorable," Bidwell replied, mildly.

"Gold makes 'em thieves," Dickson retorted.

Jarvis studied the man. Dickson had grown more and more truculent and solitary, working alone, bolting down Bidwell's victuals, retreating to his own camp, as if the rest had become his mortal enemies.

And yet Dickson was in the same boat as the rest: they were on the brink of starving and their clothes were falling apart. The

last of the flour went into pancakes one bright morning a week
after they arrived. They ground up the last roasted coffee-bean
that evening. The sidepork was long gone. Jarvis tried hunting
one evening but found nothing. These harsh slopes didn't support game and he wasn't much of a hunter in any case. They
had heard tell of salmon in these rivers, but they lacked hooks
and lines, or nets. It was too early for berries, but in time there
would be wild grapes and plums there for the plucking. The last
of the meal went into flapjacks one evening, leaving only
parched corn that could be boiled into mush.

Jarvis toiled at his rocker each day, finding that the day's take
varied sharply, depending on what he was shoveling into the
battered hopper. He wasn't getting any more clever about
where to shovel, either, and he concluded that luck was a factor. Nature dealt the cards facedown, and you couldn't know
what lay in the sands or where the whirling floods had dropped
the gold. Each long day he shoveled sand and gravel into his
hopper, rocked his cradle, plucked out debris, and scraped gold
from behind the riffles. The gold came in endless shapes:
flakes, fine dust, pea-sized nodes, twisted and tortured pieces,
acorn-sized nuggets, and pinhead bits that glittered in black
sand. On his worst days he added around five hundred dollars
to his kitty, figuring his take at thirteen or fourteen dollars an
ounce for uncleaned gold. On his best days, he accumulated as
much as fifteen hundred. He had so much gold he scarcely
knew how to store it, and eventually sewed up some stout
pouches cut from his bedroll duck cloth.

He knew from the hang of his clothing he was losing weight.
The relentless toil exhausted him. His boots were falling apart
where the soles joined the uppers from being in water so much.
He sensed he needed greens and vegetables and meat, but none
were to be had except for some dandelions. He suspected he
was on the brink of scurvy. Scrapes and cuts didn't heal well,
and his gums bled. The others lost weight too. Bidwell looked
gaunt and shrunken. Northfield seemed to fold in his clothing.
Only Dickson, built like a bulldog, seemed the same. They
fought mosquitoes and sand flies, spiders and creatures with
glowing eyes that invaded their camps in the night. One day,
Northfield lay abed, wrestling with a headache and pains in his
chest.

One evening, after they had wolfed down some more corn mush, Bidwell raised the issue that was on their minds. "Someone has to go for provisions *right now*," he said. "We're close to starving. If no one goes right now, we'll be lucky to walk out of here alive—and we'll lose our claims."

"I'm not going," Dickson snapped. "I'm falling behind the rest of you as it is, me with just a goldpan."

Jarvis said nothing. Dickson could have partnered with him on any reasonable terms. The man had grown more and more solitary and wild-eyed, his only comments directed toward imaginary mobs who were about to overrun the bar and drive him off.

Bidwell knew his man, and didn't argue. "How about you, Simon?" he asked Northfield. "Would you go? I'll keep on working, and you'll get your share. We'll all contribute something."

"Not me," said Dickson. "Get some vittles and I'll buy them with dust, ten percent over your invoice. That's all I'm offering."

"Not enough, Dickson," Bidwell said mildly. "You're asking a man to leave the diggings for a week, for a profit of a few dollars."

"Then I won't buy anything," Dickson snapped. "There's Miwak and Yokuts Indians around. They've got that acorn meal. I'll get all I need in one day."

"Acorn meal's not a bad idea," Bidwell said levelly. "But look at us. Shoes falling apart. Clothing in rags. Fevered and starved. No coffee, no sugar, no beans, no meat, no lard, no fruits—and no news. We want news as much as anything." He turned to Northfield. "We'd make it up to you."

"I've been fevered, and that's a hard trip, mostly up and down."

Bidwell said nothing, and then turned to Jarvis. "How about it, Stephen? You've got a saddle horse. We have packmules. We'll work your claim with your rocker two hours each day. If you go, I think you'd better head for the Sacramento, not Pete Lassen's place. It's over a hundred miles each way, but Sutter'll have what we need. We'll have quite a shopping list."

Jarvis pondered it. In truth, he was ready to get out for a while. He ached for news. He itched for an ordinary hot bath.

His bones howled for a mattress. He needed more than food. He eyed the three others, knowing he could trust Bidwell, Northfield and Dickson. That's what separated him from Dickson, who was gold-mad and couldn't trust another mortal, and couldn't trust himself.

"All right," he said. "Two hours a day on my claim, with my rocker. I reckon I'll be gone seven or eight days unless I run into trouble. If there's a gold rush I may not come back with what you want, and it may cost more than you figure."

"We understand that, Stephen," Bidwell said.

"I want to use your rocker whiles you're gone," Dickson said.

Jarvis waited for an offer, a rental, a proposition. It didn't come. "It's taken some hard use; I'm planning on getting some screws and some sawn wood to repair it. I think not, Dickson, unless you make it worth my while."

"I knew you wouldn't. You're all against me."

Jarvis paused, choosing words carefully. "Not against you, no, sir. I didn't hear an offer. Dust or a share. I went to some work and expense to build that machine. It's worth a lot now."

"Just get me my goods, damn you—I'll give you a list—and don't pad the prices with that crook Sutter. I'll pan gold on my own rather than sell out to some bloodsucker like you."

Jarvis sighed. "You can use my rocker if you want, for an ounce a day."

"No," snapped Dickson.

Jarvis swallowed back what he itched to say.

Bidwell swiftly intervened. "Stephen, we'll help Dickson here, rock some dirt for him. He's been a good neighbor for nigh on a year, and I'll look after him. We'll find a way to pay you back for what you bring him. We must all work together."

Dickson's pugnaciousness faded a little.

Bidwell talked with natural authority, quieting the surly man with the ordinary affection that Dickson seemed unable to return. After that, Bidwell drew up a formidable list: flour, cornmeal, sidepork, tinned or dried fruits, salt, sugar, soda, coffee, tea, oats, ready-made flannel shirts if available—if not, a bolt of red or blue flannel—needles and thread, and twenty yards of duck so they could sew up their own duds; sole leather, any newspaper or book he could find, and anything else he could think of.

"You're going to pay with dust?" Bidwell asked.

"Yes, and find out what to do with it. I don't much like leaving it about—but I don't know who'll buy it or what to ask for it."

"We'll find out," Bidwell said.

He and Northfield and Jarvis pooled their gold and loaded it into a stout poke. The three would split their purchases. Jarvis carried a separate poke to purchase Dickson's supplies, and one for his own private purchases.

At dawn, they helped Jarvis load three fat and yawning mules with the empty packsaddles. He saddled his dun, tied down his bedroll and kit behind the cantle, and put a packsaddle on the burro. He took a two-day supply of parched corn, hoping to find more vittles en route. Then he rode up a steep, pine-scraggly trail and into rough country that only occasionally let him glimpse the churning river below. The mules followed behind on a picket line, reluctant at first but soon settling into the journey.

It felt odd to be alone after many weeks of easy camaraderie. He was carrying over thirty pounds of gold, mostly his own, all of it in a saddlebag. He intended to sell it or trade it for coin, or at least store it in Sutter's iron strongbox.

All morning he rode silently, seeing no signs of mortal life except once in a huge oak-grove where a recent campsite told him one tribe or another had gathered acorns. The flour they made from the acorn was their staple food. They leached the tannic acid from the acorn meal by soaking it, and after that it made a tolerable flour. He nooned at a gushing spring, wolfed down some corn mush while the mules grazed, and then started downriver again. Thus did he pass a long and silent day, alone with his thoughts of Rita.

Late that day the tumbled country surrendered into gentle swales and ridges, and he could approach the Rio de los Plumas again. Just when he began looking for a campsite at one of the places they had prospected as they worked upstream, he discovered a gravelly flat swarming with miners. They all looked alike, with red or blue flannel shirts, hand-sewn trousers of cotton duck or jean cloth, and broad-brimmed slouch hats. Most were growing luxuriant beards, and probably luxuriant gray-backs, too. Jarvis squinted against the low sun and counted thirty or so. He discovered snappy new tents, brush arbors and lean-tos, campfires, racks where washed clothes were drying, bedrolls opened to the sun to air out.

The gold rush was on. Here would be news and some vittles.

He descended a long slope, the mules balking at the frightful sight below, but eventually he paused in the midst, as the burly fellows crowded around.

"Who be ye?" asked one giant.

"Stephen Jarvis—discharged New York Regiment man. I'm with a party upstream, and heading to Sutter's place for some provisions."

"Ah! A Stevenson, eh? Well, we've a half dozen here. We thought we were the vanguard, but there's always a few smart dodgers ahead," the fellow said. "How's the digging up above?"

"We're mining gold," Jarvis said neutrally. "We're working. Right now we're about starved out. I'll give a pinch for some food. Fact is, I'll give a pinch for some news."

"Well, spend the night, Jarvis. We've vittles aplenty and no one's gonna put a pinch on you for it. Now it's news you want, is it?"

One of the young fellows handed Jarvis a plate with boiled beef on it, a real potato, and a mess of red beans. The aroma made Jarvis faint. Then another fellow handed him a cup of scalding coffee, and Jarvis sipped gratefully.

He learned a lot that next twilight hour. The Mormon elder Sam Brannan, that Yerba Buena newspaperman and mercantile operator at Sutterville, had decided to drum up some business, so he went out to Sutter's mill, bought a few ounces from Marshall and Sutter, sailed back to the little port village they were renaming San Francisco, and howled like a coyote right down the middle of town, yelling, "Gold, gold, gold!" And that started the avalanche.

"Why," said one fellow, "there's hardly a salaried man left in California. Monterey's half deserted, and those Californios, they've got to do for themselves because the help's all vamoosed. To hold a man at his job it takes sixteen dollars—an ounce of gold—a day, and even then precious few take it. As for the rest, look us over. They say there's some four thousand crawling the Sierra, and more rushing in from Sonora. And getting plumb rich, too. Why, we're making a hundred a day. Heard of one outfit, three fellows, they took out eighty thousand—yes, that's eighty thousand—in three weeks over on an American River fork. Mostly we're independents, or partners, or a small company here—one's got a rocker, the rest are panning . . ."

On and on it went, precious news, the world opening up minute by minute. Jarvis listened, and learned about soaring prices, acute shortages, bags of flour going for two hundred dollars, an egg or an onion for a dollar each . . . and empty towns along the coast, populated only by the Californios, who scorned the grubbing even if it yielded a fortune.

CHAPTER 27

The prices at Sutter's Fort and Brannan's store stunned Jarvis. A dollar a pound for flour and everything else in proportion. He wandered through both stores, unbelieving. A needle cost a dollar. A small crock of pickles five. Molasses a dollar a bottle. Vinegar the same. Potatoes, melons, onions, eggs, a dollar each. Saleratus, six dollars. Barley for horses a dollar a quart. Lumber a dollar and a half a square foot. Candles a dollar each. An ordinary dollar-shovel cost ten. He could find no blankets at all.

"You're making a killing," he grumbled at the Mormon clerk in Brannan's store.

"No, sir, we're not," the young man retorted. "Let me tell you a few things. To keep me here, managing this place, Brannan pays me twenty dollars a day, and the clerks sixteen—one ounce of dust. If he didn't pay me twenty, I'd be off in the mountains myself. But twenty's fine with me. I get it every day, except the Sabbath. Five hundred a month. I don't sleep on the ground or in the open. I don't break my back or take sick. I don't worry when the gravel doesn't pan out."

"It's still an outrage," Jarvis said.

"No, sir, it isn't. Brannan, he's got sloops bringing goods up from the bay. Every sloop has a crew, and every man and every mechanic and every teamster requires sixteen a day—one ounce of dust—or off he goes. It's hard to get any crew or any mechanic. Most of the crews are Kanakas. You want commerce, you got to hold the help to it. If you won't pay my price, a dozen others will—they'll bid it up and pay because they need the goods."

Jarvis glared, adjusting to harsh realities.

The pale clerk grinned and pushed up his gold-rimmed spectacles. "And yes, you're right about one thing. Old Brannan, he's making a killing."

They laughed.

"I don't see blankets. You got any?"

"Nary a one. That's the first thing these gold bugs want is a pair of blankets. And none coming. All the sheepherders are panning gold. No one's shearing, spinning yarn, weaving blankets or carding the wool. And Boston blankets are six months around the Horn."

"I guess I need some flour. I've got a list here. . . ."

"That's Oregon flour. Rushed down here from the Willamette when the news broke. Merchants know what a gold rush's about. They're shipping flour, lumber, apples, you name it. I hear there's a thousand men from Oregon here already. Sutter'd have flour if he had anyone to harvest his wheat. He's got a few hundred acres, and its going to rot because he won't pay the going wage. Same with his cattle; they're scattered to the moon and back, and not a herder to keep them." The clerk eyed Jarvis's list. "I got people waiting here. Let's get this filled. You paying in dust?"

"Yes."

"Clean or dirty? We give sixteen for clean, twelve or thirteen for dirty. Pour it out on that piece of velvet there and look it over. Weigh it on the scales. We pay highest for amalgam gold."

"Is that the quicksilver process?"

"Yeah. Give me a hand here, and I'll tell you about it." He hoisted cotton sacks of flour and beans to the rough plank counter, and worked through the pungent shelves, grabbing item after item to fill the list. "How much molasses?" he asked.

Jarvis hesitated, the price biting him. But then he shrugged; they needed the sweetener. "Six bottles," he said.

"We've got the quicksilver. Ten dollars a flask. There's a cinnabar mine at New Almaden, south of San Francisco. You just add a little quicksilver after you've washed the gold good. It makes an amalgam. The mercury combines with gold, but ignores the bits of sand and grit and rock. So you take out the pasty stuff and throw away the grit. Then you heat up the amalgam. The mercury evaporates, and you get coarse spongy gold. That's pure, and we'll pay eighteen for it. That's as high as we go."

"I'll take a couple of flasks," Jarvis said.

The clerk pulled two heavy metal flasks off a shelf. "Now remember, it's poisonous. When you boil it, stay upwind. And if you do it in a skillet or Dutch oven, scrape the residue real good before you cook in it."

"There's no way to recover the mercury?"

"Sure, if you've got a retort and condenser and can cool it down and run it back into your flasks. Brannan's got some tin-smiths and glassblowers in San Francisco making some, but they ain't here yet."

"Reserve me one."

"Sorry, fella. They'll sell out ten minutes after we unpack them."

"Anyone building rockers?" Jarvis asked, his mind blooming with possibilities.

"Few mechanics are; but they have to pirate lumber and hunt down sheet metal. Cradles go for two or three hundred, and sell as fast as a fellow can build one. One fellow, at the fort, he's getting rich at it. Makes two a day, pays Sutter half for the smithy and tools and wood. You want one?"

"No, I have one."

"Worth three, four hundred in the diggings."

Jarvis's mind reeled. He helped the clerk load the bags of flour and beans and cornmeal into panniers on the mules, and then all the rest.

"That comes to five hundred seventy and six bits," the clerk said.

"Five hundred seventy . . ." Jarvis felt as if he'd had the wind knocked out of him. "For that?"

The clerk looked testy, and fiddled with his white apron.

"I've got customers," he grumbled. "And they don't complain, at least to my face."

Jarvis pulled out the big poke and handed it to the clerk, who poured dust into a gold scale and added balances. Then the clerk studied the gold closely.

"This is pretty clean," he said. "You should see some of the stuff I accept. I'll give fifteen an ounce." Deftly he measured thirty-eight troy ounces and added a pinch. "Do you want a receipt?"

"Yes, and I have a separate list for another fellow."

The clerk sighed. Three waiting miners glowered. Jarvis bought Dickson's order—as much as he could, anyway—and wondered whether he would be paid for it. Dickson would howl at the prices and feel conspired against. But that didn't bother Jarvis; he'd have no trouble selling the goods in the camps if Dickson resisted. Then Jarvis bought random supplies on his own account to sell at the diggings: spare cornmeal, a tanned half-hide, nails, duck cloth, axes, some tinned luxuries such as sardines and oysters, and a jug of whiskey. High as the prices were here, he could sell still higher in the camps. He was limited to what his burro could carry, and wished he had more pack animals.

Supplied at last, to the relief of an irritable crowd of gold-seeking riffraff, Jarvis loaded his burro and headed over to Sutter's Fort, thinking to buy a few more items and perhaps store his own poke in Johann Sutter's strongbox. He found the fort mobbed with people, but the grandee was not among them. He found Sutter closeted in his office, poring over a ledger.

"Ah! It is my friend Jarvis," Sutter exclaimed, as affable as ever. "You are a sun-blackened scarecrow. Are you rich?"

"I thought I was until I bought supplies," Jarvis said ruefully.

"And how is my friend John Bidwell?"

"We have good dirt, and if we don't starve, we'll all come out fine."

Sutter sighed. "I'm almost ruined. This gold rush . . . I thought it would make me rich, too, but now I can hire no one, hardly even an Indian. Look at me. A poor man, in debt."

"But you've land and cattle . . ."

"Cattle. My brand is on thousands of cattle, and they drift

everywhere, sometimes into the bellies of all these madmen. And my wheat, soon it will be ripe and rot in the fields. My tannery, my bakery, my vegetable gardens, my sawmill—ruins. But my debts don't go away. I owe this and that everywhere."

"But your store. There's a mob out there in the yard."

"My store has nothing to sell. I can't keep the shelves stocked. I can't keep a crew on my sloop. I can't fill my orders."

A glimmering came to Jarvis, a thought so large and luminous he could barely stand it. "Mr. Sutter, these people out there—they're all heading up to the mines?"

"Every day, every day, and it gets worse. If I had something to sell, I'd get rich."

"You have cattle."

"But no one to gather them."

"What are they worth?"

Sutter shrugged. "It used to be they brought a few dollars. Now—who knows?"

"If I were to gather and buy some, what would you charge me?"

A swift calculating mask slid over Sutter's dark face. He sighed. "If I charge you fifty, you will get two hundred in the camps."

"If I pay fifty, you're that much ahead. Where are they?"

Sutter stared. "Some are on my northern land. Maybe the miners have stolen them. The rest—east of here. They can't cross the American River."

"They have your mark on them?"

Sutter said, "The older ones. The calves, the newborns—who knows?"

Jarvis plunged. "Write me a bill of sale for twenty head, and I'll give you the dust. Fifty apiece."

Sutter didn't answer, but scavenged a sheet of used paper from an old ledger book. Paper was scarce in California. Silently he dipped his nib into the inkpot, scratched, blotted, and smiled sourly at Jarvis. "Now, let's see your dust," he said.

A few minutes later, Stephen Jarvis was nominally the owner of twenty adult beeves, to be taken from Sutter's vast rancho. Out in the hot yard of the great post, he approached likely looking young men. Some probably were deserters from the regular army or ship-jumping sailors. Some were Mormons who had come with Brannan or with the Mormon Battalion. Some were adventurers. A few were swart Sonorans.

He approached one cluster. "If you're looking for a grubstake, maybe I can help," he said. That certainly won their attention.

In the space of an hour he made different arrangements with different men, but soon had a party of six. Three he simply outfitted in exchange for their help in gathering the beeves and driving them up the Feather. With two others he exchanged labor for one beef. In the camps, they could sell their own beef for whatever they could get. And he simply hired another man at an ounce a day to help drive the cattle to the diggings.

When these fellows had outfitted, they gathered at the bank of the American and took a cutter across. The ferrying of men and horses and mules cost Jarvis still more dust. But as Jarvis and his crew trudged north, guided by a map Sutter drew, he began to feel grand. He'd collect his twenty head and take his pick, too. And he had enough herders to drive them.

This was California, the land of fortunes. This was his future. He would sell cattle at each bar, and he would make a profit from this trip. The time away from the diggings hadn't hurt him after all. There were lots of ways to get gold. Someday the gold at Bidwell's Bar and other sites would run out, and he should look to the future. He had discovered this fateful day that he had a knack for business. He could become a merchant in this new land, supplying the miners with necessaries. It would certainly be more comfortable than grubbing gold out of icy streams and living in shacks and tents.

Yes, he thought, this trip had broadened his vision. Someday he would be a businessman, with a Californio wife he adored.

CHAPTER 28

S utter's cattle had scattered over a vast savanna, so Jarvis decided not to be very choosy. He would take what he found rather than waste time sorting animals. He and his crew found a bunch of forty or fifty long-horned animals chewing their cud near a grove of sycamore a half dozen miles beyond the American River. He and Adam Botts, the only other of his company on horse, managed to separate twenty from the bawling bunch and looked them over. None were steers. Some were bony old cows and bulls. It would cost some time, but he could do better.

With hard riding, Jarvis and Botts improved their pick, choosing young animals Botts said were two-year-old heifers and bull calves. Then Jarvis spotted a black-and-white Californio dairy cow with a calf at her side, and cut out the pair from the restless herd, delighted by the opportunity he saw in them. That pair he would keep.

After that, the party toiled toward the Sierra, the men on foot leading mules while the two mounted men herded the unruly cattle. Jarvis figured the whole venture had cost a day and a half, and hoped Bidwell, Northfield and Dickson wouldn't mind. And if they did, a taste of rib roast and some fresh milk might change their opinion.

The cattle proved to be a bonanza beyond Jarvis's imagining. At each camp on the Feather River, the kine drew a milling mob. He had supposed he would ask two hundred for each beast—but his shyness tongue-tied him. How could he ask so much for an ordinary heifer or two-year-old bull? But his reticence only served to pour gold into his purse. Wherever the party stopped at some scraggly collection of tents and brush arbors, bearded miners began bidding, sometimes feverishly. In one newly named camp after another—Thompson Flat, Potter's Bar, Adamstown, Stringtown, Long's Bar—Jarvis sold cattle at prices bid up to three or four hundred dollars. Dust and nuggets poured into his pokes. By the time he had reached Long's Bar, the last place before the steep hike up to Bidwell's diggings, he had sold out, except for his dairy pair, and had paid off two of the herders with a beef each, as he had agreed to do. The men he outfitted drifted off, their obligation complete, and he wished them well. Only Adam Botts stayed on, wanting to try his luck alongside Jarvis, upstream. Together they herded the laden mules, Jarvis's burro, and milk cow the final hilly miles.

When they rounded the last high bend, Jarvis halted, stunned by what he saw below at his own diggings. Instead of three men toiling in the late-afternoon sun, there were scores of them, their bright red-and-blue flannel shirts polka-dotting the dusky grays and greens of the flat. A tent town had sprung up, alongside huts, half shelters, and brush wickiups. Trousers and shirts flapped from lines, or lay drying over chaparral. Smoke hung in the valley. A quick survey told him there must be fifty men there. So John Bidwell's bonanza was no longer the secret it had been eleven days earlier.

"I hope there's a claim left for you, Adam," he said to Botts. "If not, maybe we can work something out. I've two claims, as one of the discoverers, and maybe we can partner on one."

Botts eyed him almost truculently. "I reckon I'll make my own way," he said, his voice taut. "You outfitted me; I herded for it, and we're square. I think maybe there's gold enough down there for me to find some. Nary a man's digging into the hills. Might be dry diggings anywhere. Riverbeds change over time, you know. I'll just wander around here and see."

Botts' attitude surprised Jarvis. Gold did odd things to a man. "Suit yourself, Adam," he said, gently, as Botts rode ahead.

One thing alarmed Jarvis as he descended. It looked like a dozen men were working his ground. Had he lost his claims? Rage roared through him. He'd been suckered into going for supplies, and now he was being robbed! It was *his gold* and they were on *his claims*.

By the time he crossed the flat, he was boiling. Men were crawling all over his claims, digging and panning. He found Bidwell and Northfield toiling at their rocker, just as before. And Dickson, the loner, was panning gold as he always had, glowering at every man around him.

"Stephen!" Bidwell exclaimed. "Thank God you're back. Look at those packs. We've been waiting."

Jarvis ignored the greeting. "Men are all over my claims!"

Bidwell lifted a hand. "Slow up, Stephen. There's been a rush here."

"So I see. I want them off my gravel. Help me get them off. You've let them mine my gold."

"I'm glad you're back safely. We've a lot to talk about," Bidwell said quietly. He turned to Northfield. "Let's take a break." He motioned to Jarvis. "If you've any coffee in those packs, we'll brew some. I ache so much for a cup of java, I'd pay an ounce for it."

Dickson came storming over, and Jarvis braced for more trouble. These men he had trusted had let him down. Sullenly, he dug through the loads until he found a small sack of ground and roasted coffee.

"They poured in four days after you left," Bidwell said. "More each day. Oregon men, some French sailors, a lot of Mormons from the regiment. We read our rules to them, and they didn't like it. Said our claims were too large; twenty feet bank-to-bank, and discovery claims too, that was a whole acre of gravel for each of us."

Bidwell sighed. "Upshot was, they held a miners' meeting three nights ago—sixty-three attending—and voted to cut the claim-size down to twenty feet by twenty. They said the gravel's so rich we shouldn't mind. And fair was fair. We'd made our pile. Now it was their turn. That vote went sixty-to-three, Stephen. And they meant business. A lot of 'em packed sidearms. They might've driven us out."

"But we found it!"

Bidwell shook his head. "We were plain lucky to get here first. None of the other gravel's yielded what we dug out those first days. They're all doing fine, some of them making two hundred a day. But we hit the best of it. We skimmed the cream, Stephen."

"What are my claims now?" Jarvis asked acidly.

"It's your best gravel. We put up corners for you and recorded it for you. Those other fellows, they're all recorded in the claim book."

"On my gravel."

Bidwell grinned. Northfield busied himself at a fire, heating up silty water and ground coffee in a smoke-stained, speckled blue pot hanging by its bail over the blaze.

"Where's my goods?" Dickson demanded without a greeting.

"On that last mule," Jarvis said.

"It's high time. I had to buy flour and coffee from these crooks." Dickson stormed away to fetch his load.

Anger slid through Jarvis. Dickson was as sour as ever. No thanks from Bidwell or Northfield for a two-hundred-mile trip.

Everything had fallen apart. Grimly, he watched Bidwell wander to a brush arbor and return heaving a heavy leather sack, almost too weighty to handle.

"Here," Bidwell said. "This dust is yours. It comes to several pounds."

Jarvis gawked.

"We worked your claim two hours a day, as we promised. You did well. About ten troy pounds. Then, when the mob flowed in, man after man begged to use your cradle. They all saw it sitting there. I finally struck up a deal with one, a fellow yonder called Joseph Laird. He's got a rich claim right there. Laird's using your rocker for a quarter of his take, except for the two hours a day Northfield and I dug for you. It was worth about four and a half thousand to you."

Jarvis gaped. In that heavy leather sack was about six thousand in gold dust and nuggets, all of it mined for him.

"Is that all right?" Bidwell asked.

Jarvis nodded, still absorbing it.

"Laird knows he's got to surrender the cradle when you return. And part of the deal was, he had to keep it in perfect shape for you. He whittled a new rocker for it and bolted it on. He's been a good and faithful man, Stephen. You got a quarter of a rich strike. We'll go meet him in a bit. But first we've some book-keeping to do."

"Thank you, John," Jarvis said, searching for words. His anger had drained away. "I've got most everything we wanted except spare blankets. The prices—you can't imagine."

"I can. I've been hearing nothing but howls in the camp about prices."

Jarvis dug the invoices out of his saddlebags, along with the big poke of pooled dust, and settled up with them. They studied the invoices, but made no protest. Then the three pulled the loads off the mules and burro.

Dickson returned, looking sour. "Things I asked for, you didn't get. Things I didn't ask for, you put in."

"I got what I could at Sutter's store and a new one run by Sam Brannan. They were out of most things. I tried to fill in with some substitutes for you."

"What's the tariff, Jarvis?"

"It comes to a hundred ninety-five. Here's the invoice from

Brannan's store. And you were going to add ten percent for my services. Make it two-ten. That comes out less than you offered."

"What? That's robbery. Did you and the clerks jack up the price on me?"

Jarvis said nothing; a question like that didn't deserve an answer.

"Lots of miners and not many supplies," Bidwell said levelly. "It was mighty fine of Stephen to go fetch all that truck for you. He didn't have to."

Dickson grunted impatiently. "I'll pay you half. That's all you get for bungling an order."

Rage flared in Jarvis. "Pay the price or return the goods."

"I'll pay half or nothing."

"He deserves two hundred fifty from you," Northfield said. "Going all that way, getting your supplies, leaving his claims for eleven days."

"He's rich. Why should I pay him anything? All the while he was gone his rocker made him a fortune."

"He had the foresight to build the cradle, Dickson," Bidwell said quietly. "Too bad you didn't think of it before you started. Or rent it from him."

Jarvis had become so tongue-tied he didn't trust himself to speak, but Bidwell was making the case for him.

Dickson wouldn't budge, and ended up refusing to pay anything. "And don't you try to take it back," he said. "I shoot camp robbers. You or some crooked clerks tried to bilk me, and you'll suffer for it."

"I guess I'll call a miners' meeting tonight," Bidwell said. "They'll decide, and also decide on punishments. If they think you should pay, you'll pay. If you resist, they'll use force. They have the power to banish a man from camp."

"Over my dead body," Dickson snapped, retreating to his claim.

Jarvis watched him go, wondering if he would ever see the dust Dickson owed him. He'd let it rest for now, but it wasn't over, and he'd fight if he had to.

"I've never seen a man so transformed by gold and greed," Bidwell said. "He could've rented your cradle while you were gone, but he refused to. You offered him a fair deal. Better than the one I offered Laird. He has no one but himself to blame."

Jarvis spent the rest of the afternoon stowing his new goods in his tent and putting his animals out on pasture. From now on he would need to move his animals frequently because dozens more were cropping grass.

"Is that a fresh milch cow before my eyes?" asked a blond man, eyeing Jarvis's dairy pair. "And might you sell some holy, precious, unseen, unheard-of milk and cream?"

"I was coming to it. Just got in."

"I'll pay you half an ounce for a milking."

"Half an ounce?" The amount startled Jarvis. Everything seemed so wildly overpriced. Was it only a few months ago he was earning eight dollars—half an ounce—a month soldiering? And only two years ago he was working for nothing but board as an apprentice?

"I could sell the milk for a good profit. Has she been milked today?"

"Only by the calf. Well, all right. You get a pail. But I want a quart along with the half ounce."

"It's a deal. My name's Sven Pedersen. Any chance I could milk her daily for half an ounce—and you get a quart, yes? I'd make a little on it, a pinch or two a cup."

"Let's try it, Mr. Pedersen. I'll want a quart a day and half an ounce of dust. We'll need to find more grass soon. And wean that calf. It's old enough. And watch out for the Indians—Miwaks, I guess. They'd make off with her if they could."

"I'll do all that, sir. I have a dairy farm in Wisconsin. I've been familiar with a three-legged milking stool since I was a boy. . . . They tell me you're one of the discovering party."

"Stephen Jarvis. Yes, I was with Bidwell."

Thus, almost before he was settled again, Jarvis found himself earning a half an ounce a day from the cow. The camp would devour every drop of milk and cream and butter.

Late in that July day, just before most of the motley bearded men on the bar began to ignite their cookfires, Dickson stalked over to Jarvis and dropped a small poke into Jarvis's hand.

"There's thirteen ounces," he said. "Take it or be damned."

Jarvis thought a moment. Thirteen ounces probably came to a hundred ninety-five dollars if the gold was fairly clean and worth fifteen an ounce. "All right," he said. "I'll take it."

Dickson dropped the pouch in Jarvis's hand and walked off.

Bidwell slipped over. "I'm glad you took it. I hated to call a miners' meeting, but I was just getting set to spread the word. You didn't earn a dime fetching his truck for him, but I hope you'll forgive him. I've known Dickson for a while. He was a good-enough neighbor, and I think that after this madness passes, he'll be good enough again. And someday he'll even be embarrassed by what he's said and done here."

"This poke covers my expenses, anyway," Jarvis said. "And I made enough out of the trip. Better than I hoped. I can forget what Dickson agreed to. It's not the owing that bothers me, it's his attitude."

"You meet all kinds, Stephen. I'm learning something myself. This gold rush brings out hidden things in a man, what laid inside of him all the while. A bad actor turns worse out here; a good man becomes all the better. And a few men have sides to them I never expected. Dickson's one like that."

But Jarvis wasn't really listening. He was off in a sunny upland of the mind where a man dreamed. Gold had piled up, but there might be more to make from feeding and outfitting the thousands of men flooding into California. The cattle sales had told him that. Why, if he could build and sell two rockers a day, he'd earn more than most men got from a bonanza claim. He saw the need, saw the future. Someday soon there would be a Jarvis tent-store on all the major bars in the Sierra. And after that, Jarvis and Company mercantiles in the new towns. But before that, there would be Rita Concepción Estrada Jarvis.

CHAPTER 29

I t was as if the very ground had shifted under Rita Concepción's feet. Rancho Estrada no longer gave her joy. She grew restless and impatient. Her brothers, whom she had loved in varying degrees, seemed impossibly callow and foolish. She no longer enjoyed living so deep in the country, so far away from the excitements of Monterey. Even her father, whom she had admired with a bursting heart whenever they traveled, kept evoking her temper.

All this had nothing to do with the *yanqui*, she assured herself. She was a woman poised at adulthood, and her new impatience was nothing more than seeing her family with an adult's eyes. Her child's eyes had not seen her family truly, but her adult eyes saw too much. Perhaps Señor Jarvis had stirred the slumbering woman in the girl's bosom, but that was all. He was gone. She would not think of him. *Nuncá!*—Not ever! The encounter had all been for nothing. *Por nada!*

She patrolled the familiar house restlessly, wishing she had tasks to perform. But the servants saw to everything. The Estradas had Mexican housekeepers, cooks, *mozos*, and Indian field hands. The servants dipped tallow candles, and resurfaced the packed earthen floors with a wash that dried hard and gleamed in lamplight. They scrubbed the clothing, folded it, and put it away in the big rawhide trunks in the bedrooms. They rubbed away the soot on the bright Valencian tiles of the wide fireplace, and trundled in a daily supply of fat pine kindling and seasoned logs. In the evenings they lit the candles in their sconces.

And all the while they produced lavish meals in the steaming kitchen, with its copper pots and crockery jars. Each day they baked bread, made from wheat kept in the jugs, ground to flour and sifted as the need arose. They indented each unbaked loaf with a cross to bless it and assure its rise. These they served to the Estradas at the waxed refractory table, where the family sat erect and proud in gloomy chairs that forbade slouching and reminded them that comfort could erode the soul.

It was Rita's duty, as the sole competent female of the household, to direct the servants. That was the hallowed way of all old families and true Californios. She had few duties other than unquestioning obedience to the iron will of the *jefe de la casa*, and no social obligations but to bring something feminine and lighthearted to the household. One thing her station allowed her was the arranging of flowers, which she did exuberantly, abetted by California's poppies. And she might sew or embroider, and often did, making altar cloths and little gifts for cousins.

On one of her restless rides with Plata, she dismounted beside a purling spring, sipped water from it with cupped hands, and sat back under a eucalyptus tree to study the naked heavens that hid God. The winter rains had soaked the slopes, and now verdant grasses turned the world emerald. She knew what she would do: She would ask her father to permit her to spend the last of the winter in Monterey. She would tell him she was not meeting enough friends here. She was missing the social season and the company of other young women. And she wished to further her schooling and refinements.

She would not tell him, at least not just yet, that she wished to learn English. He would have a dozen arguments against it. Not the least of them would be his reluctance to have her trafficking with the conquerors of Mexico and California. Neither would he want to expose her to radical ideas, and heretical religion, and the uncouthness of the *yanquis*, observed by everyone and condemned by all. No. It was better to proceed one step at a time. She had thought of learning the tongue from Cullum, and decided not to try; his harsh, crude Spanish was all the warning she needed about his English.

She pulled herself over the elaborate, concho-studded saddle, and rode astride back to the casa, knowing she had to do something about her existence. The days had pressed heavily, and her heart sagged. The winter's fog and chill had reached her bones and numbed her spirits.

None of the male Estradas had pushed her toward marriage, though her father had eyed young men of her age, one by one, with a considering and weighty gaze. But her brothers had examined her potential husbands with squinted eyes and surly questions, as if to protect her from unworthy and unwanted men.

Ah, if only her mama lived. Women would arrange a good match. If only she had a mother or aunt or sister in the casa. They would talk of marriage and its beauties and duties. They would invite the caballeros and see to it that Rita Concepción attended every *baile* and was gowned in silks and velvets and gold-threaded satins from China, bejeweled and slippered until she glowed in the candlelight. But Mama had been in her grave for a long time; Papa's sister, Maria, lived in Monterey; Mama's sisters and mother lived far, far away in Santa Barbara. And Grandmother Estrada, while alive and present there at the casa, had slipped away into her own holy world, and knew only God.

Plata seemed entirely rebellious this February day, and Rita Concepción thought to discipline the mare. Imagine such a thing. Plata had never been rebellious, defying the bit and heels, and Rita wondered what *bruja* had caused this strange thing to happen. But it would not matter. She loved Plata, but soon Plata would return to the *ganados*, the herds, and she would go to Monterey. Her papa couldn't refuse her, especially when Tía Maria had a large home and Indians to care for any guests.

She brushed Plata, feeling the muscles bunch under her hand, and then led the mare to her paddock. She knew her father would be in his *cuarto* off the *sala,* a male place she rarely entered. He would be enjoying a crisp pine fire, a glass of claret, and a *cigarro*, probably talking to one of his sons, or dozing away another day.

She entered without knocking, and discovered Hector there, too. She didn't want that, but couldn't help it.

"Papa, I hope you had a good siesta. It is a fine afternoon for a fire."

Juan Carlos seemed surprised to see her, and grunted something unintelligible as she settled herself across from him in this semiforbidden place. Hector looked about to say something acid, but she cut him off.

"Papa, I would like to go to Monterey, and live with Tía Maria awhile. I would like to go to the *bailes* and meet people my age."

"Meet city fops and *yanqui* barbarians," Hector said.

"I am of age," she said, ignoring him. "I wish to learn new graces from my aunts and cousins."

Juan Carlos eyed her amiably, his brown eyes taking in her tasseled woolen rebozo. The casa was not warm this chill day. "It is colder there than here, *mi querida*," he said.

She didn't argue that. "The season is almost over, and I haven't been to one *baile.*"

"The *yanquis* are going to them. You will learn bad manners, lewdness, and how to spit on the floor," Hector said.

"You do not know any," she shot at him.

"I do not wish to. What I hear about them is bad enough. They will not be around long, though. They're so undisciplined that General Vallejo could run them out anytime he chooses."

"Then why does he not?"

"They are amusing," Hector said.

"I wish to meet some. I wish to learn *inglés*." She enjoyed shocking them, even if it would defeat her plan.

"Rita, you would not want to meet one. Your honor would be compromised," rumbled her papa. "And the less you learn of that barbaric tongue, the better. It is impossible. It is a bastard tongue, welded together of a dozen ancient ones. Now, any tongue that comes from the Latin is better. Ours is spiced by the Moorish. We are logical people and think intelligently because we speak a logical tongue that inspires good order. No, not even as a novelty should you learn that barbaric *lengua*."

"But it would be good to speak to our new masters, would it not?"

"Masters. There are not but a few hundred of them here, and California is too far away from their capital. Soon they will slink away, defeated by distance and our proud spirit and the knowledge that they are unwelcome."

She sighed, a certain irrepressible merriment building in her. *"Pues, ya me voy.* I will leave in the morning. Cullum can drive me. I shall have my trunks packed."

"If you go, I must go," Hector said. "Someone must protect your honor."

"No es necesario, Hector. Tía Maria will protect me. She is of age and married. A perfect duenna."

He sniffed. *"Yanquis!* I would rather send you into a den of rattlesnakes."

"Their *capitáns* are smartly dressed," she said. "Perhaps I can teach them a dance step. If we have barbarians governing us, then we must civilize them." She laughed lightly.

Hector took offense. *"No me escucha.* You are not hearing me. These *norteamericanos* will compromise you. They have no beliefs and will not submit to God or the church. They are scheming to steal our estates from us. *Es verdad.* You can count on it."

"That is better than our caballeros, who have no ambition beyond stealing each other's wives," she retorted.

They gaped at her.

The next morning she climbed into the big, clumsy Victoria and tucked a thick robe about her. Cullum dragged her leather trunk to the carriage and deposited it in the front seat, beside himself. Tía Maria had not been informed, but Rita knew her aunt would welcome her heartily, and consider the visit to be the best thing to happen in the winter social season.

Her papa and annoying brothers lined the gallery of the casa, like ravens in a row.

"I did not say yes," her father said. "But you are headstrong. I pity the caballero who wins you."

"We should pick one, before she embarrasses the Estradas," said Hector.

"That is what they say in Monterey about you," she shot back.

"You will be sorry for that," he threatened. He didn't take it as a joke. She examined him. Twenty-three years old. A caballero with a richly caparisoned mount, a silver-gauded black hat, fine velvet pantaloons, a red sash, a vest of China brocade, and a great rancho, but no señorita ever encouraged him. He was too sour and arrogant for them. She suddenly felt a rush of pity for him, and her other rural brothers.

"I do not want to leave with hard words hanging between us, Hector. You come to Monterey, and I will introduce you to young ladies with sparkling eyes, good Catholic girls who would make an Estrada man very happy."

His face softened, though he said nothing. She was weary of his criticisms of everyone and everything, especially the *yanquis*. According to his version, they lacked the manliness even to conquer a village, and fell upon California and raised the Bear Flag like opera singers rather than true men.

"Write some more pamphlets," she said, alluding to the fiery diatribes he wrote and circulated among the Californios. "Maybe then you can inspire your *compañeros*, gather an army, and go chase away the invaders, who will surely run at the sight of your bayonets and rifles."

"I pray that I may receive the task; it would be sacred to me," he said gravely.

"Adiós, mi queridos," she said gaily.

Cullum snapped the lines lightly, and the lurch of the carriage threw her back into the plush seat. The creaking Victoria took her away from the rancho, down a long, snaking road. Tomorrow she would arrive in Monterey, begin English lessons, meet *yanquis* galore, study them and learn their ways, go to dances, invite them to Tía Maria's parlor for bloodred wine, and find out what she could about this one, the discharged private Stephen Jarvis, whose adoring gaze filled her life with something new and untried and dangerous.

PART III

1849

CHAPTER 30

Virginius Dobbin shot the mule. The worn animal shuddered and then dropped like a rock. The rifle-crack echoed through the somnolent slopes, jarring the peace of the rough country a mile from the Sweetwater River.

Ulysses McQueen watched silently. He had learned to contain his every thought, especially around the captain. Nowadays he gritted back the bile in his throat and said little.

"You cost us a mule, McQueen," Dobbin announced for all to hear, his sulphurous glare on the young man.

It wasn't true. McQueen's only connection to the loss was that he was walking ahead of the mules when it happened. They were descending a steep slope south of Devil's Gate. The heavy wagon had pushed against the harness breeching of the wheelers, an ominous weight jamming the weakened mules forward. If the mules had been in better condition they might have resisted, dug in and refused to let the wagon dislodge them. The wagon wheels had careened against a ledge of rock, twisting the tongue; the opposing wheels hit another rock, lashing the tongue back, this time into the foreleg of the mule, shattering its cannon bone. The wagon instantly rumbled to the bottom, dragging the bleating broken-legged animal. Miraculously, it stopped upright, undamaged, although the cargo had piled up in front.

They had stood around staring, until Dobbin commanded McQueen and Hoke to free the mule. But the animal, lying on its side, writhed and kicked, braying piteously. Its broken leg poked off at a grotesque angle. McQueen unhooked the first two spans, and then Dobbin shot the mule.

"You should've been watching," the captain said to McQueen. "You let us down. Pull the harness off, fix that load, and let's get going."

The company stared at McQueen, suspicions alive on their faces.

He rehearsed what he wanted to say about the entire week, but it would do no good. Virginius Dobbin was blatantly over-riding the majority of his company, and was pushing the mules harder than ever. He did heed the company's wish to recruit the stock one day a week, but the mules weren't benefiting because he was pushing two hours more each day, often not quitting until it was pitch-dark, which sometimes meant a dry camp.

McQueen wondered whether the rest even noticed. They were city people mostly. He wondered whether they cared, even if they did notice. And he wondered whether anyone observed that Dobbin was riding him harder than ever, but more subtly. He was getting twice the night duty of anyone else, which he did stubbornly, without complaint. He was deter-mined to weather whatever the captain threw at him, and tri-umph in the end.

McQueen tugged the harness off the mule, getting help from Will Hoke when he had to slide the surcingle out from under the dead animal. Finally Buck Ramsey crawled into the wagon and began shifting cargo back.

"Could've been worse," Hoke muttered, after Dobbin had stalked away like an angry bull.

"Mules too weak to stop the wagon," McQueen said quietly.

"You're right. We all know that but no one'll say it. We'll see more die now," Hoke said.

The prediction proved to be true that very day. That after-noon, after a ten-hour trek without a nooning over steep ridges, in choking alkali dust, a gaunt mule slumped to the grass and refused to get up. McQueen tried twisting it up by the tail, but he knew it wouldn't move. It had quit and nothing would per-suade it to pull again. Silently he pulled the harness off the sprawled animal. If it were left alone, it might decide to go look for water. But it would be useless to the company.

He became aware that Dobbin and Clappe were watching, and knew there would be more trouble this hot afternoon. McQueen and Hoke pulled the mess-wagon free and stowed the extra harness. Only two span remained to drag the heavy mess-wagon, and those four mules looked ready to collapse.

"You're abusing our mules, McQueen," Dobbin snapped.

"No, you are," McQueen said quietly. "And more'll die in the next few days."

"Getting lippy, are you?" Dobbin asked. The stonemason loomed over McQueen like a towering cliff, his giant fists clenching and unclenching. Dobbin was looking for a brawl.

McQueen stuck to his guns. "They need rest. And you need to lighten this wagon."

"You telling me what to do, farmer?"

"I have experience with harness stock, sir."

"Sure you do, boy," chimed in the Reverend Clappe. "Lost your whole herd to the redskins. And we had to pluck you up."

He meant to win a laugh, but no man in the company joined him. Losing mules to redskins was something that could happen to any of them.

Buck Ramsey braved the storm: "These here mules, they're done in, captain. We lost that lead mule because they didn't have the muscle to stop that wagon. Anyone can see that."

"You're working both watches tonight, Ramsey," Dobbin growled.

"That how you treat a man with a different opinion?" Hoke said. "I guess it's time to call a meeting. Maybe we didn't make ourselves clear last time."

"Get going!" Dobbin roared. "We're not meeting now, and we're not meeting again."

Men stared at him, uncertainly.

Homer Camden cleared his throat. "Maybe we'd best plan it for this evening, after chores," he said.

Dobbin glared sourly at the doctor and then stalked away. He returned a moment later with his rifle, and slid a cap over its nipple. Then he walked to the downed mule.

"What're you doing that for?" McQueen said. "He might recover."

"So no one behind us gets the advantage of him," Dobbin said.

"But there'll be desperate men behind us—once this mule's rested, it might be the salvation of someone."

"McQueen," Dobbin said, "here's my answer." He pulled the trigger. The rifle cracked. Blood bloomed behind the mule's left ear. It sagged into the bunch grass, spasmed, and lay still. The gunpowder smoke drifted into the wind.

McQueen clenched his fists, but Dobbin was grinning, and holding his rifle loosely, poised to use it as a club.

"That wasn't necessary," said Ramsey. "We're not out to hurt the men behind us."

Dobbin smiled and spat, then turned to McQueen. "Boy, you're soft. You just don't know how the world works. Now here's an order. See that creek down there? That's Rush Creek. You and Ramsey and Hoke drag this mule and dump it in. It'll rot in a few days and foul it. That'll slow down the outfits behind us."

"No, sir," said McQueen.

"Ah! Defying the captain. You know the rules, McQueen. You're out. Get your bedroll and quit us."

McQueen stared mutely at Asa Wall, wondering if the gambler might try to help his old traveling companion. But Wall stayed silent and stared at iridescent magpies darting nearby.

"Captain, you're being hasty," Dr. Camden said.

"You want to quit us too, Camden?" He turned to his lieutenant. "Oscar, show these dainties we mean business."

Camden sighed unhappily.

The Reverend Clappe laughed, pulled a rope out of a wagon, and wrapped it around the mule's hind feet. "All right, boys, let's haul," he bawled. Dave Otter and Julius Garwood came to his aid, and began sliding the mule down the slope. A few minutes later the mule sprawled in the creek, and Clappe untied the rope. Then he stood. "If God means for other outfits to pass us by, he'll send a thunderstorm to float the mule away," he said.

All his life Ulysses McQueen had listened to the preaching at Sunday meetings, and had never paid much attention. But now a recollection came to him. "I thought maybe you'd follow the Golden Rule, Mr. Clappe," he said softly. "There's some behind us in need, men who'll welcome sweet water for themselves and their stock, a helping hand from us, and maybe a rested mule. We should treat them the way we'd like to be treated."

Clappe laughed heartily, maybe too heartily. "You learnt sissy religion," he said.

Mutely, McQueen watched the water eddy around the mule, carrying off the blood oozing from it. Soon the carcass would rot, and the water would be undrinkable. It would sicken rabbits and deer and meadowlarks, and mules and oxen and men for good measure. He glanced at this company, who stood uneasily, guilty, determined, amused, rapt. He knew his words had evoked shame in them, but the shame hadn't lasted more than a moment. Some stared flint-eyed at him, condemning him for weakening their will. Julius Garwood looked as if he might like to jab his kitchen knife into McQueen. Dave Otter stared, dark and saturnine, his face impenetrable. But Charley Pyle looked like he might oppose Dobbin.

McQueen turned silently to the mules, appalled at how poorly they looked, their heads hanging, alkali dust whitening their scarecrow frames.

"I guess you didn't hear me, boy. Get your bedroll and get out," Dobbin snapped.

"Just a minute," said Ramsey. "I think we're going to have a meeting, and right now. There's some of us that don't like killing mules and fouling creeks and burning pasture and driving the rest of the stock into the ground. I'm calling for a meeting, and we'll talk this out. If it comes to it, I'll call for a division of the company. If we can't agree, we'll just divide up and go our separate ways."

Dobbin's eyes lit up. "Well, now! It's the old hooraw." His voice turned savage. "All right: Them that won't obey your captain, you fools stand yonder. And them that want to get to the goldfields ahead of the rest and get rich before the mob plunders the good gravel, you stand here beside me."

"We haven't called a meeting to order, captain," said Will Hoke. "Let's do this proper, according to our articles. We'll make motions and vote. We'll decide what's on the table. We've other things to deal with. Every fellow here knows you've defied us since the last meeting. We all know you've driven the stock harder than ever, even after we voted to rest them. We all know you've treated McQueen hard, even though we all voted that the work should be equal."

"I'll call the meeting to order," said Homer Camden, speaking with some authority. "We'll talk this over the way our articles require. There's property involved, and we'll do everything fair and square, here and now."

"You heard me, Camden. We're rolling."

The owlish doctor stared. "No, sir. We've come to a watershed. This company is seriously divided. Your leadership is being questioned. We'll do this properly."

Dobbin fumed, but didn't attempt to bully the group further. The doctor's authority won the day. McQueen stood quietly, wondering about his fate. The temptation to withdraw from this Illinois outfit clapped him. He could go ahead alone. With a bedroll, his kit, and his scattergun, he might just walk to the goldfields ahead of this whole bullheaded crowd of city-bred sharpers. If Asa Wall joined him, all the better.

But McQueen said nothing. He wanted to see the result. He had gathered his courage, protested against brutality and barbarism and greed, and now he would see what speaking up against evil would bring him.

CHAPTER 31

There, south of Devil's Gate on the California Trail, the Illinois company tore itself to pieces before McQueen's eyes. He and Wall weren't charter members so the pair stood to one side and watched. Virginius Dobbin swiftly gathered his clique around him. He transformed himself into an artful politician, witty and forceful, a magnet for men with gold fever. There was no organized opposition; simply a minority of six who couldn't stomach Dobbin's brutality, with Buck Ramsey the most vocal.

Dobbin was, by turn, sarcastic, disdainful, and full of missionary zeal to reach the goldfields first. Ramsey was, of all things, comic, making jokes, answering easily, appealing to the decency of all—but standing firm on several issues: There was no need to be first, no need to brutalize the mules, and no need to try to slow competitors.

A man who could sing, McQueen thought, might well be a man to keep things peaceable.

Then Dobbin surprised them all: "I've got eight men. Maybe nine. I'm inviting Wall. I won't take the crybaby over there. I'm taking twelve mules, the saddle horse, and the five packsaddles. You slowpokes can keep the wagons. You'll have eight mules. We'll divide up the mess, eight parts to six parts."

The packsaddles! No wonder Dobbin had drawn so many men, including the fair-minded doctor, Homer Camden. They were ditching the wagons. They would divide their load among McQueen's and Wall's five packsaddles and would have seven mules to spare, and could rotate them each day. Dobbin's cunning would probably carry that outfit to the goldfields.

"That's not right, cap'in. We'll have us a proper division," Ramsey said. "Your group gets three packsaddles and two wagons. Our outfit gets two packsaddles and one wagon. You should get eleven mules and the saddle horse; we should get nine mules. And we should each get some of the better mules."

Dobbin demanded a vote; Camden polled the company, and the division cut along the two factions. Buck Ramsey and his faction, including Charley Pyle and Will Hoke, found themselves with three wagons, eight mules, and no packsaddles. A brutal decision, McQueen thought.

"That's a raw deal," yelled Hoke. "We get some packsaddles."

Clappe laughed. "God loves a cheerful giver," he said.

The meeting ended sourly, and might have turned into a brawl but for Buck Ramsey's relentless cheer. "It's all right, boys," he said to his men. "We'll rest these critters, cut down our loads, and drive on out to Californy before these hard cases get near the gold."

Brave words, but McQueen didn't believe them. It would take a month of grazing on good grass to recruit the mules, and by then most of the forty-niners, as they were all calling themselves, would pass them by.

Quietly, the dissenting group watched Dobbin's men gather their gear, divvy up the mess, and pack the mules they selected. They were leaving the weakest, lamest, sorriest mules to Ramsey's group, and enjoying their power to do so.

"I guess you'll be eating our dust," Clappe said to Hoke. "Or maybe sampling our ash."

McQueen eyed the cheerful victors warily. Asa Wall had cast his lot with Dobbin, and this would be the end of the partnership. Wall paused in his preparations and walked over to McQueen.

"Well, Ulysses, this is it," he said. "See you out there."

"You made your choice; I've made mine."

"Oh, it's not easy. They're making me carry my faro layout on my back. Dobbin says no mule's gonna carry sin on his packsaddle." Wall laughed softly. "I'll manage. The faro outfit weighs plenty, and it'll be no pleasure. But it's the easy way to mine gold." He stuck out his smooth gambler's hand. "Been a pleasure. Don't stop at my table. I'll skin you good if you do." The warning was as close to friendship as the tinhorn could get. The warning was affectionate in a way.

"I owe you four dollars. Thanks for lending it. I'll pay it when I get there," McQueen said. He shook Wall's hand silently.

An hour later, the Dobbin faction walked out. McQueen watched them go: the captain and Clappe, Julius Garwood, Dave Otter, Homer Camden, Asa Wall, and the rest. They were leaving their troubles behind them, and their consciences also. Their mules and saddle horse carried heavy packs, but they had other mules that carried nothing, and would gain strength along the way, nipping grass and enjoying themselves.

Ramsey watched too, muttering under his breath beside McQueen. Will Hoke and Charley Pyle looked as if they had just swallowed a rattlesnake. Basil Lalique stared mutely.

"They didn't leave us much," Hoke muttered.

"We have one thing," McQueen said stubbornly. "We can look other men in the face. And we can look into a mirror and like what we see."

"Well, boys, what's your pleasure?" asked Ramsey.

"Stay here tonight and rest our mules," said Theodore Bacon. "Pull that dead mule out of the creek. I've been itching to do that for an hour."

The rest agreed silently. Swiftly they roped the dead mule and dragged it fifty yards from the bank. The act made McQueen feel good. The rest felt good, too; he saw some rare smiles.

"They sure cut the deck peculiar," said Pyle.

"That's the past, boys," Ramsey said. "Let's forget it and get ourselves settled into camp. We'll rest these mules. McQueen, you look 'em over and see if you can do any doctoring. Charley, you look over the wagons and pick the one that's the least ruint. Maybe trade wheels or kingpins or tongues. Make one good outfit outa three. Same with the harness. We'll ditch the worst of it. Then we've got to cut down our load and fit it into the one wagon."

But no one moved. They were all watching the other party walk west, growing smaller and smaller until they vanished around a bend. A great quiet settled over the camp.

"I reckon that's what happens when you reach a place called Devil's Gate," said Ramsey. "Some fellers go to the devil."

"I guess I was the cause of this," McQueen said. "I've caused you trouble."

"No, McQueen, all you done is remind us we're decent men and some things are more important than the yeller metal," Ramsey said.

McQueen smiled gratefully at the man who had, by default, become the new leader of the group. Suddenly he felt a vast esteem for these men. Each of them had made a hard decision. Each despised such things as burning pasture, or driving helpless livestock to their doom. Each had clung to some sense of right and wrong.

McQueen studied them. Something had changed their mood. Ramsey was enjoying himself. This evening he'd pull out his banjo and serenade them again. Pyle was an older man, potbellied when McQueen had first seen him but gaunt now, quiet, not bright or talky, but with an honest and open face. Hoke was young, like himself, full of an innate decency and courage. McQueen didn't know Bacon very well, but the compact Illinois man had never shirked, and was keeping a journal, scribbling something each evening. The other men, Sorley Mulligan and Basil and Martin Lalique, McQueen scarcely knew, but he intended to find out what he could. They were all smiling.

McQueen took Mulligan with him to look after the mules, which drooped in their harness. Span by span, they watered the worn animals in the creek, and led them back to the wagons where they stripped off the harness, checked hooves, felt pasterns and hocks, and let them graze in the short grasses of the valley.

Hoke and Pyle started cannibalizing two wagons to make one good one. Martin Lalique and Bacon began packing the scattered remnants of the mess, tallying up what food remained, and what bowls and cutlery had been left to them.

Basil Lalique began loosening a wagon sheet from the bows of an abandoned wagon. Spare sheeting had a dozen uses.

"Throw away everything we don't need," Ramsey said. "And that goes for your own kits, too. Them poor mules, we'll have to nurse 'em every step."

Men nodded and worked. They didn't need direction. Joy permeated the group. McQueen could feel it.

"We'll be camping for a while, maybe down on the Sweetwater where there might be better grass," Ramsey said. "I reckon we'll watch a dozen or two dozen outfits pass us by. They'll get to the gold ahead of us, boys. Beginning tomorrow, you'll be itching to join each outfit coming by."

"I hear tell there's lots of gold," Bacon said quietly. "I'm not worried about finding some. The only thing to worry about is getting through the passes before winter. But we're near the vanguard and not in any danger from that—as long as we don't delay for long."

Dusk brought an unmistakable pungence out of the hazy west: the rank odor of burning grass, soft and elusive on the breeze. Men stared at each other, knowing what lay ahead, and what a pair like Dobbin and Clappe would do, even to old comrades.

Dusk brought something else, as well, a party of seven mounted men, all on lively horses. They bristled with rifles, sidearms, and knives. They rode into camp, surveyed the men one by one, and spread out in a semicircle.

"Welcome, strangers," Ramsey said, rising from the rock he was sitting on.

"You're the ones," snarled a brown-bearded man, swinging the bore of a double-barreled fowling piece at Ramsey. "You're the ones burning pasture behind you. Swine. Scum. We'll show you what we're going to do to bastards like you as soon as we find a tree."

T wo thoughts hit Ulysses McQueen like a fist in the gut. One was that his life might come to a violent end here on the Sweetwater. The other was that he was innocent. He had protested against burning pasture, fought it at risk to himself.

A silence settled in the dusky camp, lit only by the lingering blue of a July twilight, and a wavering cookfire. Every man in camp was helpless. The silence hissed like a lit fuse.

"I think you're mistaken," Ramsey said at last. "Not a man here's started a grass fire, and every man here's opposed."

"So you say," snapped the big man who was leading the hanging party. "So you say." He peered around him. "Where's the rest of your outfit?"

"We're all there are," Ramsey said.

"No, you're not. We've been studying on your leavings. You're the outfit. Three wagons. You have another eight or ten men, a lot more mules, and a horse. Where are they?"

"Go check our wagon," Ramsey said. "We've one. It's loaded. And eight mules we're resting for a few days."

"They're probably out hunting," said another horseman.

The big leader nodded. "Go look," he said. Three of the horsemen rode out, looking for the rest.

Theo Bacon walked straight toward the leader. "You have no evidence. If you caught us setting a fire, that'd be one thing. But unless you've seen any of us set a fire, you might be condemning innocent men."

"Bull!" snarled the big man. He glared about him, his eyes wild, the orange firelight dancing madly in them.

The sight chilled McQueen.

"Where you from?" the leader demanded.

"We're Illinois men," Ramsey said. "Peru, Streator, LaSalle, and thereabouts. One's from Iowa, and he's not with the company."

"Who?"

Ramsey pointed to McQueen.

"How'd you join this outfit?" the leader asked.

"A partner and I lost our stock to some redskins the other side of Fort Laramie. This outfit came along." He gathered his courage and asked: "Who are you?"

"It's no business of yours. We're behind you, trying to feed stock on burnt-over range. There are six ox and two mule outfits on your heels, all needing grass. We're all having to take our animals two or three miles to find some. Burning pasture is the lowest, skunkiest, rottenest, meanest thing we've ever seen. Killing man and animal is a hanging offense."

"What makes you so certain we did it?" McQueen asked.

The leader stared keenly, as if seeing McQueen for the first time. "We've seen you. We saw you a few times on the north bank of the Platte. You got ahead of all of us on the south bank because it took us two days to cross the river. But we knew you were there."

"You have no evidence. If you murder innocent men it'll be on your conscience."

"Shut up," the big one growled. "I won't hear it."

McQueen itched to tell the intruders that the guilty party was ahead. But no one among the Illinoisans was saying it. Despair settled in him, and cold dread. He would never see Susannah again. He would feel the rough hemp circle his neck, feel it jerk tight, and feel himself plunge into eternity. And all because he had been rescued by a party of gold-mad men.

"Hey!" yelled one of the horsemen, from the crest of the ridge to the west. "Jared, come here."

The bearded man responded. "Watch these rats," he said to his remaining men, and cantered away into the gloom.

McQueen could no longer make out what was happening on that distant ridge, which was veiled in murk, but he knew several of the horsemen had gathered there, and that they were engaged in animated talk. Eventually they all rode back.

The big man addressed them. "There's a grass fire far to the west, maybe five or six miles. It's burning some brush, and we could make out the flames. Here's how we read it. That party ahead's some of your bunch. You've split up, probably because you couldn't stomach what they were up to. That's it, and don't deny it."

"That's it," said Ramsey.

"When did you split up?"

"Early afternoon."

"They're packing?"

"Now they are."

"We'll catch up with them someday soon. We can't get around that fire now. But we'll catch them. Maybe we'll try the other bank of the Sweetwater if it's not burned."

"Is it coming this way?" Ramsey asked.

"Not unless the wind comes up. If it does, you'll have to move. Maybe in the night."

"We're fixing to go to the Sweetwater tomorrow. Recruit our mules on the other side. I'm Buck Ramsey. Every man here's square."

The leader glared, as if he hated to find his quarry innocent. "Jared Cain. Missouri outfit here, right on your heels."

"Coffee's on," Ramsey said. "We're gonna sing a little. We'll be a week resting these abused critters. We'd enjoy some palaver."

Cain consulted his men. They elected to have coffee. A pack-mule party five miles ahead with worn-out stock wouldn't escape them. One by one, the Missourians sheathed their weapons and dismounted.

McQueen listened to them, and felt giddy with relief, and not just for himself. He didn't want Asa to hang. He couldn't even stomach the thought of Dobbin hanging. The captain was gold-mad, like Clappe, like Camden, like Otter and Garwood. What sort of darkness had stolen into men who started out merely to seek a fortune?

Basil Lalique dug some tin cups out of the mess gear and poured some java for the horsemen.

"There's gold enough for all, we hear," said Cain. "We just can't fathom men who'd murder those coming along behind. I don't suppose you'd give us the names. There's not a man in any company behind us who'd ever forget those names."

"Rather not," said Ramsey.

Cain surveyed him sharply. "We'll get the names," he said.

"There's two in the party that did most of the burning.

There's others that just want to get to the goldfields fast, and don't scruple how. A just man would leave them alone."

Cain grunted his disagreement. "Who are the two burners?"

"We'll leave that to you."

Cain sipped and sighed. "All right. That's fair enough. . . . But we have our ways," he added.

For the next hour they shared trail-talk. Ramsey never did tune up his banjo. McQueen learned that they were barely ahead of an awesome migration. Tomorrow two Missouri companies would pass by, a Wisconsin company, an Illinois pack-mule outfit, and some Mormon families heading for Salt Lake. A day behind these were half a dozen large companies, some of them with badly worn oxen, but gamely making headway.

He discovered that several parties had lost stock to unseen Indians who had struck at night, but there had been no fights or loss of life. No one had seen very many buffalo so far, but it was believed the legendary herds were drifting north and others along the trail would get their shot at them. Cholera had taken twenty or thirty men so far, but seemed to stop on the high plains well shy of Laramie. The army was now garrisoning the old fur post. There were quitters going east every day.

McQueen learned there was a lot of traffic between the companies; riders rode forward or backward, and knew who was ahead or behind. By taking the route along the north bank of the Platte, he and Asa, and the Peru company, had missed all that.

"If any of you want to send a note back, write 'er quick," said Cain, finally affable. "There's a man in the outfit behind us planning to quit if he can earn his way back with some mail."

Sorrowfully, McQueen declined. He lacked so much as a penny. But when Will Hoke dug into his possibles for paper, nib and ink, McQueen saw a chance.

"Will, I can't afford a letter. But would you ask your folks to write my wife and tell her I'm well as can be expected, just about halfway to the goldfields?"

"Give me her address and consider it done," Hoke said, struggling to find some way to write in the evanescing light.

A while later the Missourians rode back to their outfit and a sudden loneliness descended on the camp. In spite of the frightening beginning, it had been good to palaver with others and gather some news. All the forty-niners were in the rush together, and the outfits were keeping track of each other, cooperating, helping each other when they could.

He slept fitfully that night, the threat of the noose robbing him of peace. He awoke to a crisp, chill dawn, with dew on his bedroll. He stood, seeing before him the aching reaches of a virgin land. In the northwest, snowcapped mountains caught the dazzle of the sun, making them glow eerily, even though gray dusk still clung to the sagebrushed hills. Where had the summer gone? How long would good weather last?

On this day they would descend two or three miles to the valley of the Sweetwater River, find a ford and cross to ungrazed and unburned land away from the Oregon Trail. That would be the only burden on the eight half-dead mules, but it would be more than enough. And then, as they rested the mules, they would watch company after company pass them by, each man in them intending to scrape a fortune out of the legendary gravels of the Sierras. He thought that it would be a test. Within a day or two, the good-natured men in his company would be itching to stampede west, even though the mules wouldn't be rested at all. He surmised that by the end of three days there could be sharp trouble, even among these steady men. They were not yet halfway.

CHAPTER 33

T he enforced rest turned out to be as agonizing as anything Ulysses McQueen had experienced the entire trip. They crossed the Sweetwater half a mile upstream from the point where they struck it after detouring around Devil's Gate, and set up a camp in virgin grass, within yelling distance of the road across the river.

After that they hunted and counted wagon trains passing them by on the other side. With each new arrival, they crowded the banks and exchanged halloos, along with news. The ongoing companies wanted to know if there would be more burned grass ahead. The men from Illinois wanted news about their state. McQueen sought news of Mount Pleasant, cholera, travel information, and whether any company would trade one sound mule for two or three worn ones.

No one would. No one had fresh stock.

That first day, they studied the mules, looking for miracles. One by one the men wandered out to the shrunken animals, willing them to eat, to fatten, to muscle up. No sooner had any mule partially grazed down the patch he could reach from his picket line, than someone moved him to fresh bunchgrass. It didn't seem good pasture to McQueen, not like the lush green fields of thigh-high timothy, brome, and orchard grasses growing promiscuously across Iowa. But he knew tough Indian ponies thrived on the dry bunchgrass. It seemed to offer a power of its own.

If any of them could have willed the mules back to fitness, the eight miserable creatures would have bloomed instantly, so strong was the collective wish. But that first day the stock slept, too weary to eat much. And none of them looked an iota better.

Dobbin's party had not only selected the strongest of them, but had left behind the troublemakers. McQueen spotted two that whirled and kicked; three that refused to work unless spanned with a worker; one that nipped the other mules, one that would work only under the threat of pain from a whip.

Meanwhile the wagon trains rolled by, along with an occasional pack outfit. All the stock looked worn. Buck Ramsey greeted one and all cheerfully, but Pyle and Mulligan eyed each company bitterly, seeing rivals who would snatch away the good gravel and leave the dregs for the slowpokes.

"Devil take the hindmost. That's us," Mulligan muttered.

On the third day, most of the men were growing irritable, and McQueen knew nothing would hold them much longer. He was as restless as the others, having counted forty-seven companies rolling ahead. That came to about fifteen hundred men, and a handful of women, all of them destined to reach the diggings before the Illinoisans.

"Let's go look at the mules, Ulysses," Theo Bacon said that third evening. "We've got eight and we only need six. We can rest two, and rotate."

"They're so poor they'll give in," McQueen replied.

"Well, you're the farmer. Most of us from Peru hardly know the rear end of a mule from the front."

They wandered out to the picketed animals, who stopped their listless grazing to eye them.

"See those caved-in haunches, the ribs, Theo?"

"But they'll still pull, won't they?"

"See that one that limps? He's got a stone bruise that'll take a week to heal—at least a week. Maybe a month. He's not worth keeping. We can't rotate him."

"Well, I've got the itch. I can't stand it here anymore."

"I can't either. But we've no choice. We're not halfway."

Buck Ramsey joined them. "They're still poor, aren't they, Ulysses?"

"Yes. We'll start losing them in a week, sooner if we hit poor pasture—which can happen now, with all those outfits ahead of us. Lots can happen. Everything from snake bites to dry weather or alkali water or a swarm of wasps."

"You're the one knows mules. What do you reckon?"

The answer saddened McQueen. "Two more weeks of rest."

Ramsey winced. "We can't do that. Mulligan's threatening to pull out and join any passing company. Martin Lalique's despairing. Pyle, he's turning downright sour."

"That's how I feel too," Bacon muttered.

"All right. Ask 'em if they'd be willing to move just a few miles a day. No more than half days."

"You think the mules would last?"

"They might. If we hit good pasture, they might even gain a little."

"It's done, then. We'll shove off in the morning. I'll tell the boys."

That afternoon four more big ox-drawn outfits rumbled by across the river, churning up alkali dust, cursing those ahead who burned grass. McQueen watched dourly, knowing that from now on every blade of grass would count, and they would have to take the mules miles away from the trail to find pasture.

"I'll tell the boys to lighten up again," Theodore said.

"That'd help," McQueen said. "Some other things'd help, too. At every hill, I'd like to see us all behind the wagon, pushing. If we pass good feed, I'd like to stop and graze the outfit."

"I'll talk it up. This is sort of a headless bunch, but I'll put out the word," Theo Bacon said.

McQueen liked the man. Bacon was about Ulysses' age and had been a blacksmith's apprentice. He could shoe a mule, carpenter, fix anything that had broken. His wry humor put calamity in perspective. Bacon and McQueen had found good solid ground and Ulysses hoped they could partner at the goldfields, maybe with the silent Basil Lalique and his son.

They pulled out before dawn, exhilarated to be rolling again, but McQueen knew the mules would balk and quit soon. He wished the others could see the animals through a farmer's eyes. They toiled painfully west, passed by companies from all over the Union—Georgia, Tennessee, Ohio, Pennsylvania, and especially Michigan. For some reason, gold fever had swept Michigan, depopulating the state of its sons. Quietly McQueen kept count: One day he calculated three thousand men ahead; then five thousand; then nine. The others were keeping count too, restless and bitter. By the time they had crossed South Pass and were descending the gentle slope toward Big Sandy, all but McQueen and Bacon were demanding full days of travel, and the mules be damned.

Then at Big Sandy events overruled his discipline. They had forty dry miles to cross before hitting the Green River and the only way was to start in the evening and drive straight through, carrying what water they could. They made it by the next afternoon, steering the parched mules down steep slopes into the sunken valley of the Green. But McQueen knew the drive had worn away most of the gains, and the mules had reached death's door.

They lost one in the dry hills the next day. It quit, wouldn't get up, and didn't care whether it was pushed, pulled, twisted or whipped.

"Pull off the harness and let it go," McQueen said gently. "It probably won't live."

Two days later another mule died suddenly on a long slope that was taxing the weak animals. It simply quit and lay down, letting itself be dragged before anyone could stop the outfit. Then they had six.

The company stared bitterly at the dead animal. Life had fled swiftly. This time McQueen didn't have to tell them: They knew the mules were failing. Earlier that day they had come to a sort of signpost, a barrel full of messages for those behind. Many of the companies ahead had taken a new cutoff, called Hudspeth's, that supposedly saved fifty miles. The men had voted to take the new cutoff, which started on level ground only to plunge into steep ascents in a tangle of mountains.

"You thinking what I'm thinking?" Bacon asked McQueen.

"Graze the mules around here for a few days?"

"No, the wagon's got to go."

"But, Theo—"

"Listen, Ulysses. You rest the mules. I'll carpenter some sawbuck saddles out of wagon wood. The rest can stitch up some saddlebags or panniers, or we can diamond-hitch some loads—if you know how. I don't."

"I don't either. But we can make some saddlebags," McQueen said.

The boys bought the plan without a quibble. They found a grassy gulch near water, drove up it a half mile, and set to work. Here, for a change, thick, luxurious grass flourished, and the mules were picketed on it. Bacon unwrapped his tools and began manufacturing some aparejos, or Mexican packsaddles, made of two boards at right angles.

With the whole company furiously sawing, hammering, converting harness, and threading panniers together with thong, the conversion went swiftly. Despair gave way to high spirits and nightly musicales, even though, day by day, one company after another rumbled up the twisted, rocky, plunging trail that men cursed each other for taking. Now ten or twelve thousand men were ahead, but no one could calculate the numbers anymore. It seemed the whole gold rush had passed them by.

McQueen toiled along with the rest, hunted game but found none that close to the trail, checked the scarecrow mules, some of which had started bleeding around their teeth, rasped hooves and reset shoes, and felt less confident that these miserable creatures would get them to California.

He wondered how Dobbin's outfit was faring; whether every mule had died; whether angry companies had caught up with the pasture-burners and hanged the lot. No one knew, and not even the occasional quitters they had encountered had any knowledge of the vanguard, which was now probably in

California. One thing they all agreed on: Hudspeth's Cutoff was a disaster to man and wagon and beast.

McQueen yearned to send a note home to Susannah. Yearned for a letter from her. Yearned to know how she fared during these last weeks of her confinement. Ached for Mount Pleasant. Ached for California. Ached for gold. Ached to justify this dash across a wild land. Ached to be anywhere but stalled in an obscure canyon somewhere north of the Great Salt Lake.

What a tribulation. No flights of imagination could equal what he had seen, and the hardships—cold, pain, thirst, stony beds, drenching cold—he had experienced. All along the trail he had seen fresh graves. The last only a few days ago: "Samuel Peters, D. Aug. 7, 1849," scraped into a board. It was said by passersby that scurvy had struck some outfits. Snakebites, catarrh, heart failure, alkali poisoning, beestings, broken limbs, heat exhaustion, mule kicks, and the ever-present dysentery had taken others. He had stopped at each grave, looking for a name he knew, but saw no Dobbin, Wall, Clappe, Garwood, or anyone else from the Peru Company. Perhaps that doctor, Camden, was pulling them through.

It occurred to him one chalky July evening, when the alkali dust of still another wagon train was filtering down on them, that Susannah's time had come. He might have a son! Or a daughter! Or twins! Or she might be dead. . . .

He walked upstream to a brushy place where he could be alone, and there he pulled out the note Susannah had prepared for the last week of July:

"My darling husband. I am close to the time of my delivery. Wherever you are, be aware that my confinement is at hand, or over, and the child we created in a sacred and beautiful moment is entering the world. Pray with me that all is well. Rejoice with me that we have a son or a daughter. Prepare with me to raise this infant to be a good and devout person, rejoicing in the inheritance we will give him. Wherever you are, whatever you may be to me, our child and I seek your blessings. Love forever, Susannah."

CHAPTER 34

S usannah felt weary, not joyous, this twenty-ninth day of July. She knew it should be the other way around. Her joy in delivering an infant into the world should transcend all else. But all she could summon was relief, and a desire to be left alone, after a brutal eighteen hours of labor.

She stared tearfully at the wizened little girl lying at her breast. Mrs. Gottschalk, the midwife, had cleaned the baby, while Susannah's mother had toweled away the slick residue of Susannah's tribulation.

"It's a perfect child, Susannah," Mrs. Gottschalk said with forceful cheer. "She'll be as beautiful as you. Mark my words. She'll be a feisty girl. I can always tell. I can divine it. No wall-flower, this one. The boys'll be buzzing around her from the time she's ten."

Susannah summoned gratitude, and thanked the bustling little woman. She had eyed the infant cursorily, through tear-fogged eyes, and then shut out the light. She wasn't ready yet to rejoice or be happy. The pain clung in her like a terrible memory, and she could not excise it. Since yesterday noon she had not been in control of her body; waves of anguish had crashed through her like surf on a beach, and she was helpless before the tide. And that was followed by the agony that would not end.

"You're a little torn, Susannah," her mother said. "But Mrs. Gottschalk says you'll be all right in a few days. First babies are hard, and come slow. But that's why we love them all the more. We've much to be thankful for, don't we?"

Susannah nodded, wishing she could feel the joy she was supposed to feel. Maybe it was because Ulysses was so far away, and out of contact. She had heard nothing from him since the note he had written at Kanesville. She had wanted to present this child to him, this child of a sacred moment not long after they were wed. She had known, somehow, in the beauty of that union, that she would measure the months from that moment to this.

The dull ache would not go away, and the slightest movement sharpened it to knife-stabs. She wished she could be dry and clean, instead of lying in her sodden cotton nightdress, on sodden sheets.

"Clean me," she whispered. "Help me."

"Nurse the child now, dear. Bring your milk down, and start her sucking. We'll see to the rest later."

Susannah felt grateful to her mother. The Strawbridges had wanted her to lay-in at the Strawbridge farm, but Susannah refused. She would have her child in her own home, in the bed she had shared with Ulysses.

"I'll stay on a little, Mrs. Strawbridge," the midwife said to Susannah's mother. "With that tear, she'll need watching."

Susannah drifted through a weary sleep, scarcely aware of her child, yet needing to know this little thing with the velvety skin, this creature she would soon love as much as her own flesh. Now, at last, the infant gladdened her. She blinked back her pain, focused her eyes, and studied it. Wispy light hair. An ugly old face. All the proper limbs and digits and toes. A firm chin, and delicate ears. A lump at the navel.

Now this creature would turn Susannah into a mother who would watch over her. For years this little girl would not be much of a person. And then one day she would talk intelligently and be a daughter. If she lived. Susannah sighed. Many families had lost half or more of their babies to colic, dysentery, mysterious diseases. And then there would be swift painful burials.

At last the infant stopped sucking and dozed, a tiny peaceful bundle. Susannah dozed too, scarcely aware of the bustle of the women about her. She knew, vaguely, that they were changing bedclothes, rolling her from one side to the other, and pulling back her drenched nightdress, and slipping on a fresh, cool and dry one. The July heat had made the ordeal all the harder. But it was over, thank heaven.

She opened her eyes once, and at last felt the stab of love. This was her baby girl!

Sometime later she was awakened by a sound, and beheld her father and brother and sisters gazing at her. She felt suddenly naked and shy. Birthing was so intimate, and spoke of such private things that she could not bear their gaze. But they were smiling and rejoicing and cooing, and making odd gestures and strange faces at her and the infant.

"What will you name her, Susannah?" her father asked.

"Margaret. I decided on that."

"Why, that's a beautiful name. We've no Margaret in our family, and one'll be welcome," her mother said. "Have you chosen a middle name?"

"Temperance. I think a name should reflect a virtue," Susannah said, shyly. She was bolting from family tradition.

"Now there's a thought," her father said cheerfully. "Margaret Temperance McQueen. It has a ring. May she be a light unto the world, and may her life be blessed, and may you be rewarded in the raising of her."

"Amen to that," said her brother Tim.

They didn't dally, knowing what eighteen hours of labor meant to Susannah.

She slept through dark and light, cuddled the silken bundle at her breast, felt loss whenever someone placed it in the bedside crib, and finally awakened the next noon feeling much better, filled with love and joy, grateful the ordeal was over, and yearning for Ulysses.

She drifted dreamily through the midday, her mother softly present on butterfly wings, the infant girl sometimes sleeping, sometimes wailing her demands, sometimes hiccuping and in need of simple hugging and motion. Then, as the sun slid lower, Susannah had visitors.

"I'm glad you came, Father and Mother McQueen," she said, uncertainly. She had never conquered her fear of them. And now the elder McQueens, and all her in-laws, had gathered in her bedroom to behold the new child.

"It's a perfect girl," said Henrietta McQueen, holding it gently. "A blessing to the McQueens."

"Yes, a handsome girl. We're delighted. See how she clasps Henrietta's finger," said Stanford McQueen.

Susannah felt invaded, and scolded herself for it. Here were the elder McQueens, as well as Stanford Jr., Sarah, Jonathan and Lucy, and Alexander gathered around her bed, where she lay in disarray. Still, Margaret was their kin too, and Susannah knew she could bear this examination cheerfully.

"Have you heard from Ulysses?" McQueen asked.

She shook her head. "I'd tell you instantly," she replied, the faintest rebuke in her tone.

"Well, we're here to carry on," he said. "You need only call on us. We're a close-knit family, and you're one of us." He paused. "We've some thoughts about a name."

"I've given her one," Susannah said softly. "Margaret. Margaret Temperance."

"Margaret Temperance? Margaret?"

"I've always loved Margaret, and she'll be Peggy."

"Is this what Ulysses chose?"

"He wasn't here to choose with me."

Stanford McQueen cleared his throat. "We have a suggestion, in that respect. Nothing's final until the baptism. As you know, Henrietta and I have a bounty of sons and no daughters. Yes, we've been blessed. And we've named them after their elders and ancestors, of course, to keep family names alive, and passing through the generations."

Susannah began to grasp what this was leading to, and dreaded it.

"We thought it'd be fitting to name the girl after my two grandmothers, Agatha Kerr and Violet McQueen. Agatha Violet, or Violet Agatha, either would be fine with us, and give you a choice. I lean toward Violet, myself. I remember my grandmother kindly. She was a hardworking woman who loved to make bread, and liked to read a Bible verse each evening before supper. Yes, we'd like Violet and Agatha. And so would Ulysses."

"He would?" It astonished her.

"Of course he would. Since he's not here to say so, we're passing his wish along."

"But—did he say so? He never told me . . ."

"Well, he takes pride in family names. Now, Margaret's a fine name, but not a McQueen name, and not even a Strawbridge name, far as I know."

"But Mr. McQueen . . ." She couldn't will herself to resist him. She felt weak, and trapped.

Henrietta smiled. "You need rest, dear. We've overstayed.

Don't you worry about names. The McQueen names'll grow on you, and you'll be proud to keep those names alive in our family."

"Nothing's final until the baptism," said Jonathan.

Only Alexander, among them, seemed uncertain about all this. He smiled at her quietly, sympathy in his gaze.

Guilt flooded her. Here these people were caring for Ulysses' farm, planting, weeding, hoeing, and cutting hay. Soon Stanford Jr. and Jonathan would be harvesting wheat and plucking corn. What right had she to resist?

They filed out, leaving her alone and desolate. She disliked Violet, and just barely tolerated Agatha. Could she love a child with a name she couldn't stand?

None of them except Sara and Lucy had paid much attention to the infant, or coddled it, or exclaimed over it. None of them had asked after Susannah's health, or seemed to care very much. None had asked whether the labor had been hard or long. Perhaps they had been told these things, but she sensed they hadn't been very curious about them.

Her mother, who had been hovering about during the visit, slipped in and perched on Susannah's fourposter. "Now you have a dilemma," she said gently. "You don't have to decide today. But it's your decision, not theirs." She sighed. "It won't go well for you if you resist, I'm afraid. The McQueens are quite a clan."

"I know. Oh, why isn't Ulysses here?"

"Maybe it's best that he isn't, Susannah."

"What would you do, Mama?"

"You might not like my advice."

"Oh, don't say that! Try me."

"The bond between a mother and her child is sacred. If you don't like a name, don't let it be forced on you. It might hurt the child. Many times when husbands and wives don't agree, they choose a name they both like. If Agatha and Violet don't appeal to you, just say no."

"If I weren't so tongue-tied, I'd just say no to them."

"They're taking advantage of you because Ulysses is gone. Well, dear, you choose the name you want, and don't let them stop you. They're fine people, but you're the mother. This child is not theirs, and of course they know that in spite of their expectations. I think you've chosen grand names for the little girl. You know your father and I will always support you."

"It'll be Margaret Temperance," Susannah said. "Ulysses had to cut loose of them, and I will too."

CHAPTER 35

D ay by day the ragged argonauts hiked westward, dragging their weary packmules. They had started in the vanguard, but now they were somewhere in the middle of the migration.

At every hand McQueen saw abandoned gear. The sinuous, tortured Hudspeth's cutoff, which had been pioneered only days before, had taken a terrible toll. He passed abandoned wagons, bloated oxen and mules that stank in the hot sun of early August, chests, bedsteads, trunks, crates, clothing, even barrels of flour.

At least they didn't lack for food. McQueen had worried about the shrinking larder, since Dobbin's party had made off with so much of it. But the trail offered its own bounty. He salvaged bacon, buckwheat flour, a cask of molasses, salt, a crock of pickles, dried apples, saleratus, and even coffee beans. Neither did they lack for clothing. Fresh shirts and britches and stockings lay about, for the taking. The men festooned themselves in slouch hats, gaiters to hold up their pants on their scarecrow bodies, and bright-colored flannel shirts. McQueen found some hobnailed boots that fit, and set about repairing them with his awl.

The mules seemed no worse off, carrying light loads on the crude packsaddles, and wended their weary way through waterless hills denuded of grass. When at last the trails came together at Cassia Creek near its confluence with Raft River, McQueen learned they had saved only a few miles, perhaps one day. When they reached the junction with the Salt Lake Trail near Cathedral Rocks, they found scores of beggared men, many of them sick and injured, bargaining with wagon trains for passage. But few of the big wagon companies could help them, and the packmule outfits could do nothing at all except supply a little food.

McQueen spotted fresh graves almost daily, some of them dated the day before he came upon them. Men had died of heart failure, mountain fever, scurvy, weak constitutions, mule kicks, gorings, tramplings, wagon wrecks, and unknown causes. Scarcely any grave recorded death at the hands of Indians, and men grew careless. But one grave, containing the remains of two men, served warning: These arrow-victims had been traveling alone instead of in a strong party. McQueen spotted only one woman's grave, but it was silent about the cause of her death. None of the marked graves held men he knew. Dobbin's relentless march, weeks ahead, had apparently not killed anyone.

But he saw Dobbin's hand in other things. Some wagons had been burned so those behind couldn't use them for spare parts. Flour and sugar had been soaked in coal oil and set afire or scattered across the brush. And many of the patches of grass in this arid land had been burned. All these things shocked McQueen. But other things heartened him. Other, finer men had left advice, messages, invitations to those who followed to help themselves. Barrels and cairns along the trail had become veritable fountains of information and help. They contained notices that such and such company had passed by, on such and such a date. He looked in vain for a note from Asa, but found nothing. The Dobbin faction had left no word behind them.

They reached Goose Creek after a terrible descent out of the mountains. After that they had adequate water, but not much grass. A mule came up lame one morning and had to be abandoned. The rest had shrunk to bone and rawhide, looking more and more grotesque. McQueen marveled that the mules could still tote packs, and that they could still walk on hooves that had lost their shoes and were worn down almost to the quick.

On August 5 they reached the Humboldt, a stream so small they could nearly jump over it, with brackish water that tasted foul. No wonder the forty-niners were calling it the Humbug River. It had been Mary's River or Ogden's River until Frémont renamed it. It seemed such a putrid little creek that it didn't deserve a name. The sluggish stream would take them west through pitched and parched country that could scarcely support a snake. But it did support another sort of danger, the varmints the parties ahead were calling Diggers, or Paiutes.

"BEWEAR!" the messages warned. "SEVERAL MULES BE WOUNDED BY ARROWS HEAR. MAN INJURED STAY ARMED WATCH YUR STOCK. DONT LET DIGGERS INTO CAMP. TRADE WELL AWAY."

And now, McQueen was finding headboards with more ominous markings, painted with grease mixed with ash. "Mr. Eastman died here of Digger arrow." The arrow had been jabbed deep into the headboard for all to see.

"We'd better stay armed," Buck Ramsey said. "And we'll have to start a night watch. We're a small party and we'll try to camp with other outfits."

No one disagreed. They toiled down the Humboldt, through a relentless heat that showed no sign of diminishing, through choking alkali dust, squinting against the glare until their eyes tortured them, scaring up lizards, drinking vile water that did not quench the raging drouth within the body. This was the place of miseries, and the elusive little Diggers were only one more torment.

More and more, these tortured, hot days, McQueen walked with Theodore Bacon, the jowly, black-haired young man from Streator who had kept his own counsel during the troubles.

"You thinking much about the goldfields?" McQueen asked him.

"Every moment. I suppose Dobbin's there already—if he kept his mules alive."

"Lots of men there by now. Just this last desert to go, and then the east slope of the Sierras. They say it's a hundred miles."

"Don't believe it," Bacon said. "Maybe three hundred. Believe it when we get there."

McQueen grunted. Bacon had a way of bringing reality home, which was why McQueen liked him. "You partnering with anyone in the goldfields?" McQueen asked.

"No . . . you interested?"

"Yes. I think you and me, we could hit it good. You could build a rocker—a smith like you. I can carpenter a little. We could start now, cutting parts from these wrecked wagons. The ones with rockers take out a lot more dust than ones with pans."

"We're partners, then. I was thinking of asking you. I was thinking of making it a foursome, for protection and doing some serious digging and fluming together."

"Who else?"

"The Laliques."

"A mute? And a boy?" The proposition startled McQueen. "But why?"

"Never saw harder workers. That boy's adult for his age."

"What's the old man's story? Do you know?"

Theo Bacon shook his head. "Some of it. All of us out of Peru and LaSalle and that country heard most of it."

They paused on a ridge to let the mules rest. McQueen had never seen country so desolate. It drove him to melancholy just to see this rock-ribbed, ferocious desert.

"Lalique and his wife, Minnie, and their children—Martin's the oldest, but there's two young ones—settled on the river—that's the Illinois River—right after the war," Bacon began. "Basil Lalique never said a word, and looked so—I don't know, desolate—that he aroused a lot of curiosity. The missus jabbered at him all the time, but he paid her no heed, though he was hearing good enough.

"We got the story, a few pieces of it, anyway. They're upstate New York people. He fought in Mexico under Quitman, clear to Chapultepec. Then he quit talking. He hasn't said a word since then. The boy, Martin, sort of communicates with him some, like they have sign language."

"I've noticed. Serious young fellow. You know why the old man quit talking?"

"They say he was sickened by the battle for Chapultepec. That's when we stormed in and shot all those cadets from the military school, those boys of twelve and eleven. They say Lalique shot his share, watched the rest of them commit suicide by jumping off the walls, and then he cried. After that he never said a word, almost like he's a deaf-mute, or had his tongue cut out. But he's got a tongue and he's got all his faculties. The rest is simple. He settled in Illinois early in 'forty-eight. His wife left him and took the young 'uns, saying she couldn't stand it. The older boy, Martin, stayed with his pa. We don't know whose idea it was to join the company, but they did."

"You talk to Martin yet?"

"No, I was thinking to have it out with you first. You think we could make a foursome and get at the gold?"

"I do," McQueen said.

"Then I'll put it to them both. We won't hear for a day or two. Basil may not talk, but he thinks a lot."

That all seemed good to McQueen. Now he would have partners, a man who could build the equipment, others who never slacked and who seemed tough and honest. It wouldn't be long now. Maybe three weeks, maybe a month. Then he'd be shoveling gravel and collecting his share each evening after the washing.

He wished he could send a letter to Susannah telling about his new partners. They had passed numerous eastbound men, some of them army couriers. All full of news about the goldfields. If only he had two bits he'd send a letter along with them.

He ached to hear from her. He was a father now—or was he? Had her labor gone well? Was his baby a boy or girl? Would there be letters at Sutter's Fort? Was she well? Had the cholera come to Mount Pleasant? He would not know for a long time.

They found a patch of grass far south of the Humbug that evening, and chose to camp there even though they would be over a mile off the trail. One good thing about this wasteland, and this time of the year: The heat didn't linger. As fast as the sun plummeted, the air chilled and the company slept soundly.

They washed the mules carefully, as they had disciplined themselves to do. Some of the creatures were galled now, and these running wounds needed nightly attention. McQueen slipped a halter over one of the weaker critters, intending to lead it to the best of the thin grasses.

An arrow struck, a hard thump, and the mule grunted, drooled, fought to keep standing on all fours, surrendered, and collapsed in a heap of curling dust. McQueen stared, not comprehending until he spotted the thin shaft, made of reed, poking out of the mule's ribs.

"Hey!" he cried, racing toward camp. An arrow seared his left arm.

"Diggers!" he cried.

CHAPTER 36

B uck Ramsey fired at something behind McQueen, and Will Hoke followed. McQueen dived into camp, hunted for his fowling piece and powder flask, and turned to meet his assailants. Sharp pain lanced his upper arm. Just below, Basil Lalique stared, frozen, jeopardizing the remaining mules.

Charley Pyle knelt, sighted down the barrel of his old rifle, and shot at a whirling brown form. Swiftly, he pried the copper cap off the nipple and cleaned the hole with a wire to clear it of fouling. He measured a charge from his powder flask and poured it down the barrel, patched a soft lead ball with a disk of old flannel and pressed it into the muzzle, driving it home with the hickory ramrod that clipped under the barrel. Lastly, he pressed a new cap home while looking for a target.

But the elusive Diggers had vanished.

"Must of been thirty of those devils," Pyle said. "Up outa the ground like snakes. Waiting for us at a patch of good grass, behind brush and rocks. I hear tell they like mule meat, and they'd sooner put arrows into an ox or mule than steal it. Soon as we're gone, they'll have them a roast."

"I don't think we hit a one," Sorely Mulligan said.

"No, but we gave 'em a fight," said Ramsey.

"We walked right in," McQueen said. "Can't say we weren't warned."

"We were warned, all right," said Ramsey, venturing to stand up now. "Watch out for the Diggers. The Paiutes. The Shoshones. The lizard- and grasshopper-eaters."

There was contempt in Ramsey's voice. Not a man among the forty-niners thought much of these desert dwellers who lived in brush wickiups, wore almost nothing, ate rabbits, lizards, grasshoppers, snakes, and whatever else the arid land offered; and stole or killed anything they could. The story had been told in warnings along the trail: "Beware Diggers. Don't trade. They come in to steal." "Lost two ox here to Diggers. Came in the night." "Man wounded here by

Diggers. He was trading with them when they put an arrow into him."

Near the mules, Basil Lalique stood rigid, locked by a gigantic force within him. But his son held a rifle. McQueen stood and walked over to the youth. "Is your pa all right?"

"No, he's never all right." The youth studied the ground in front of him.

"This reminded him of things."

"Who are you to say?" the boy snapped.

Rebuked, McQueen didn't reply. He stepped toward the frozen man, who stared at some infinity that lay entirely within himself.

"Mr. Lalique, it's over now. We didn't hurt anyone. They attacked us and we chased them off."

McQueen detected not the slightest acknowledgment from the man. The remaining five mules stood wearily, still burdened by their packs. Lalique had not been able to herd them away from the Diggers. An arrow hung from the sawbuck of one. McQueen pulled it free, finding no wound.

"When we get to the goldfields, we'll be all right," McQueen mumbled, not really believing it.

"Pa, time to graze the mules," Martin Lalique said.

The man slowly emerged from his private world and began loosening cinches and lifting packsaddles.

Ramsey paced around the area, studying the slopes that commanded this hanging gulch, and then gathered his meager crew. "We'll graze the mules until dusk, and then camp down on the Humbug," he said. "If we stay here tonight, we'll lose every mule we have left. They want meat. They'll put arrows into the rest."

No one argued. But McQueen knew the mules wouldn't get enough grass in the next two hours.

He spotted Theo Bacon sitting in a natural strong point, protected by rock and slopes, his rifle at the ready. Bacon had seen what to do, set up a defense, and was protecting the rest of them. McQueen hiked up to the spot, and sat down beside his partner.

"You all right?" Bacon asked, eyeing McQueen's bloody sleeve.

"I guess so; don't know. It stings." Gingerly, McQueen

removed his shirt to have a look. He beheld an inch-long shallow furrow, now caking brown as the blood congealed. "I'll be all right if it doesn't mortify," he said.

"Better tie it up," Bacon said, producing a battered red bandanna. McQueen winced when Bacon drew the cloth tight, but then it was over and McQueen slid back into his torn shirt.

"Ramsey's going to pull us out at dusk, and I think he's right," McQueen said. "But we'll give the mules a good lick at this grass—if you could call this stuff grass."

"There's power in this grass," Bacon said. "It doesn't look like much, short and brown and thin, but the mules haven't lost ground on it."

"It takes the humble grass to take us to the gold," McQueen said. "Wheat is grass. So is oats, barley and corn. Grass is more important than gold. We can't eat gold."

Bacon smiled. "No, but gold'll buy me a good life," he said. "I don't expect to stay out here; I want to fill my pockets with rocks, go back East and read law. I lack schooling but I keep working at it. A congressman in the next district, a rough cob named Lincoln, taught himself law, and so can I. A little gold'll pave the way, I reckon."

"I'm going back too," McQueen said. "I've got a wife, a good black-bottom farm, and a little baby now. It should've been born a week or two ago. I don't even know. All I can do is hope."

"There'll be a letter for you at Sutter's Fort."

"I hope so."

"I haven't anyone to go back to, except my folks. I look like a seed potato and didn't have any prospects, and the two or three ladies I set my cap for, well, they didn't take long to decide." He enjoyed his self-deprecating humor. "I've counted up my assets. I work like a devil. I can fix things, carpenter and smith. I'm inclined toward the virtues, as long as I can take a week off from them now and then. But mostly I need a stake, and then a profession. I was always good at arguing, so maybe I can hang up a shingle someday and propose to the sweetest flower in Streator. She might even ignore my potato-face and flappy ears if I could give her some comfort."

"Theo, let me tell you something," McQueen said urgently.

"Proposing is scary. I mean, you're asking a woman to hitch up and have children and live with you and tolerate all your worst qualities, and . . . well, it's scary and the wedding is scarier, and the honeymoon is still scarier. If you don't like your face, you're a goner. You won't ever get up the nerve. The thing is, your face isn't important."

"Well, that's what gold is for," Bacon said. "She might go for the bullion even if I look like something in Barnum's freak museum. I believe in true love, all right, but it's got to be greased a little with cash."

They watched the mules graze and the men prepare some cornmeal cakes over a small fire that consumed greasewood and juniper brush. No Diggers returned, but McQueen didn't doubt they lingered just out of sight, waiting to make meat out of the mules.

"Lalique froze during that fight. He just stood there like a statue," McQueen said. "Are you sure about him?"

"I'm sure. He'll be a good partner. So will Martin. This reminded him of whatever it was in Mexico."

"Hope you're right," McQueen said.

They watched Lalique and Mulligan move the mules to ungrazed grass and drive the picket stakes into the earth.

"Five left, and one lame," said Bacon. "We'll have to ditch some gear again. All of us. You think they'll last?"

"Not all of them—but enough to get our gear over the Sierra Nevada. We've got that bad spot ahead they're all warning about. Forty miles from a spring west of the Humboldt sink to the Carson River or the Truckee, and not a drop of water or blade of grass. That's what they say."

"We can start at night, and carry all the water we can," Bacon said.

"If we only had fresh mules or oxen . . ." McQueen said. "But we don't. Do you think Dobbin and Clappe made it?"

"I think so, but not with mules. They must have walked to the goldfields carrying everything on their backs."

"They had cash; probably bought what they needed from outfits along the way." McQueen felt a moment of gloom. "I don't know why I'm particular. Doing right doesn't get me anywhere."

Bacon didn't reply for a long moment. "Yes it does, Ulysses," he said softly. "You have friends. And you won respect. If justice and good conduct always got rewarded, we'd all be deacons. But it isn't rewarded. We have to do things because they're right, and not for any other reason. Dobbin's a hard man without a friend in the world. Clappe's become a harlot and a traitor to his calling. But you're a *man*."

"They're probably staking claims and raking in the nuggets by now. And we're parked here trying to be good to our stock and risking our necks for grass," McQueen replied.

Bacon clapped him on the back. "You go eat. Someone has to stay up here. They've got the biscuits ready."

"I'll bring you a batch."

At dusk they herded the mules back to the Humboldt River, and settled on a barren flat. They stood guard that night, two hours per man, and had no trouble. The next two weeks they pushed westward through choking heat, often detouring far from the river where it ran through canyons, crossing the Humboldt time and time again as the trail took them from one bank to the other. They made good time, as pack outfits do on level ground, and passed several wagon outfits, all of them suffering from exhaustion, heat, insect bites, and a strange lassitude that reduced cheerful men to black silence. The long walk across a continent had taken its toll.

Debris still littered the trail. They were astonished to find an oak armoire standing majestically in the middle of the desert. The heavy piece must have been greatly loved to have come so far before being abandoned. An awesome amount of wealth had been abandoned along this road by the emigrants.

They arrived at last at the Humboldt Sink, a marshy area where the river vanished into the earth. Except for a meager spring about fifteen miles to the west, there would be no water or grass for fifty-five miles. They would have to cut hay and load up all the water they could manage—and make a crucial decision.

According to all they had learned on the trail from messages and eastbound travelers, they could choose among three routes to the goldfields. One would take them to the Truckee River, which they could follow into the Sierras. Another, the Carson Route farther south, would take them across desert to the Carson River, up its west fork, and over a pass to the southerly gold country. And the last, still vaguely defined, was the new Lassen Route to the north, which supposedly would take them clear around the Sierras on level ground, and bring them into the central valley of California from the Oregon border.

They had no trouble eliminating that route.

"We're not a wagon outfit," Ramsey said. "No need for a level route, and no need to walk an extra few hundred miles."

"Well, it's the Truckee or the Carson, then," Charley Pyle said. "We don't know one from another, but I reckon the farther south we go, the better our chances of digging gold late into the fall. I hear tell gold's as rich in the southern districts as in the north."

That decided it. No one could think of any reason to try the Truckee Route.

"Remember the Donner Party?" asked Bacon. "They went up the Truckee and got snowed in. We're much earlier, and we're packing, but it's a thing to remember. I'd hate to spend a winter gnawing at your ribs."

Men laughed uneasily. The horror of the Donner Party's starvation and cannibalism in the fall and winter of 1846 and '47 had become a national sensation. Without further discussion, the outfit prepared to strike across desert for the Carson River. It would be the worst ordeal of the trip, blistering heat by day, icy cold by night, shifting sands to mire man and animal, a boiling spring gushing water too hot to drink; the only good water and hay to be carried on their backs.

They decided to rest the mules that afternoon while they cut hay and filled what few canteens they possessed. Their passage would be easier than that of ox-drawn wagons, but still a grave matter that could kill them all if they were careless. They worked quietly in the furnace heat, aching for some shade, storing up grass, filling every cask and canteen. And then, when the murderous sun finally dropped behind the shimmering western mountains, they plunged into a living hell where the earth radiated fire to McQueen's boots, and scorched his legs. In places the bottomless sand sucked at his boots and tormented the pack animals. He wondered whether men and mules would drink at the Carson sometime tomorrow, or whether he and the others would give up their bones to the desert.

C H A P T E R   3 7

A gibbous moon shot solemn light over the sloping wastes, supplying the travelers with a lamp. They had no trouble picking out the trail; macabre sights greeted them at every hand. They could scarcely walk a hundred yards without passing the reeking corpse of an ox, or the scattered skeleton of a mule.

McQueen trudged ahead grimly, his mind focused on reaching the Carson River and keeping the weary mule he was leading from quitting every time it sniffed another carcass. He had to tug it, talk to it, coax it along, but sometimes 'it stopped, refusing to go another foot. Then he was forced to detour. It never did any good to drag a mule; they were too contrary, and stronger than a man, even in their weakened state. His only hope was to outsmart the creature.

The ghastly carcasses at every hand had plunged the whole party into weary silence. Sand sucked at their feet, making each step an ordeal. They had walked a continent, and now they were worn, sick of hardship, and melancholic. And they were still two hundred miles from the goldfields.

This awful stretch had become the graveyard of wagons, too. They littered the trail, mired in grasping sand, abandoned because the oxen had died, most of them still burdened with their entire load. A scavenger with fresh teams and plenty of feed and water could harvest a young fortune here. But no wagon had been pillaged. No gold-rusher had any thought but to lighten the burden on his own beasts.

As the night deepened, the temperature plummeted and at first McQueen welcomed the change. The coolness would help man and animal. But by midnight or so, a fierce chill numbed him, and he shivered in his thin clothes.

They reached a place where the trail climbed ruthlessly up a ridge. Buck Ramsey called a halt.

"This slope's a killer," he said quietly. "Let 'em rest a few minutes. Give 'em a lick of water."

A lick was about all anyone had. McQueen unstoppered his canteen, poured a quart into his felt hat, and stuck it under the muzzle of the mule. It nosed about furiously, slurping up the precious water, and then tried to eat the hat. McQueen loosened a bait of the hay they had collected at the sink, and let the mule feed.

They made the crest without losing an animal, but disaster struck on the way down the far side. A weakened mule, gingerly negotiating a stair-step descent, lost footing and tumbled into a rocky hollow. It refused to get up. Mulligan pulled off its pack and saddle while Bacon twisted its tail, all to no avail. They checked its legs and found nothing broken; it had simply given up and would not be budged.

"All right," said Ramsey tightly. "Pitch out more. Carry what you can on your backs. We can't shift very much."

McQueen knew he faced another of those terrible moments when he had to surrender prized possessions. Sadly he examined the few things he had left, knowing that nothing could remain other than the necessaries for sheer survival. He kept the awl and thong and shoe leather. He abandoned the Testament, Frémont's *Report,* and a tattered shirt. He kept the locket with a miniature of Susannah in it. Around him others were making the same agonized choices. Men laid razors, strops, and shaving mugs on the ground; abandoned precious books. Mulligan abandoned a silver flask of brandy. Pyle pulled out a Colt revolver, powder flask, ball mold, and a small bar of lead, and left it in a small heap.

"Maybe someone can use it," he said softly.

Basil Lalique left a chess set.

"Feed out the hay," Ramsey said. "That'll take a little weight off the mules."

But in the end, even after each man had jettisoned all he could of his personal items and they had jointly cut their mess gear in half, which meant feeding themselves in two shifts, the remaining four mules were more heavily burdened than before. McQueen fashioned a strap to carry his bedroll, and slung it over his shoulder. Other men loaded what they could in flour sacks.

They did not kill the downed mule. It might decide to live, and might reach water. More likely, though, it had given up and would simply wait for death, which would come with the morning's murderous heat.

They trudged through the waning night, never far from another macabre spectacle, passing mounds of bones that looked suspiciously like human remains. This ghastly stretch was the burial ground of a thousand dreams, and would kill many thousands more dreams before winter set in.

Weariness plagued McQueen now, and it became harder to take each step. Yet he could not quit. To stop now, and suffer the morning's furnace heat, would kill him and the mule he led. He heard not a word from any of the rest; they were all concentrating on taking one step and then another through sand with no bottom under it.

They struck the boiling springs just before dawn, when shadowy gray light had infiltrated the gloom. To drink this scalding water, it was necessary to let it cool down. A number of barrels had been left there for that purpose, but all were empty.

"Well," said Ramsey, "do we want to wait a couple of hours for a drink, or push on? That sun's going to blister our hides soon."

"Let's go," said Bacon. "We've covered thirty miles, I reckon. Not bad, all things considered. We can make ten more before that heat kills us."

McQueen wondered if he could make two more, much less ten. He swallowed the last of his water, and refilled his canteen with the boiling variety, scalding his hands in the process. The animals nosed around the boiling springs pitifully, trying for a lick and getting burned.

They started westward, but McQueen stopped them. "Let's fill these barrels," he said through his parched throat. "It might save lives behind us."

"I don't see why. No one filled them for us," Will Hoke said.

"I want to. Just because we should do it. Because we decided not to act like Virginius Dobbin and that crowd."

They stared at him. Wearily he dragged a barrel to the springs, and let the water swirl in. When it was half full he wrestled it free. Then he spotted a small cask he could use to fill the big ones, and began ferrying water from the boiling springs to other casks.

"Well, he's right," Bacon said, and joined McQueen.

The next to help with this act of charity were the Laliques. It took ten minutes, but at last seventeen large barrels stood filled, enough to rescue a large outfit with many oxen. This sight of all that water cooling in casks filled McQueen with an odd joy. Around him other men smiled. McQueen felt refreshed, as if this act of charity had renewed his body. And as a bonus, the mules drank some of the cooling water.

They set off in full dawn, somehow as lively as if they had just enjoyed a sound night's sleep, talking with each other, striding with giant steps ever westward, spiritually immune to the ghastly litter of dead animals and abandoned wagons. In two hours they covered six miles. Their high spirits never abandoned them, and McQueen pondered the effect of ordinary kindness on these men. Why had an act of charity turned worn, desperate men into strong ones? This was all a great mystery.

By mid-morning they struck the valley of the Carson, and rushed through grasslands and thickets of brush to the river, whose sweet water tumbled out of the Sierras. There they collapsed bankside, hoorawing, laughing, soaking themselves, drenching the mules, and washing away grime.

"We did it!" yelled Charley Pyle, standing hip-deep in the cold river.

"Reckon we'll stay here today," Ramsey said. "Let's find a campsite and rest."

A mile upstream they found a fine stand of cottonwoods, abundant firewood and pasture. Like most earthly paradises, this one had flaws, in particular, ferocious horseflies that bit man and animal. But that seemed a small price to pay. Other outfits were camping on the Carson too, recovering from the ordeal. Their neighbors included a company from Athens, Ohio, which had lost twenty-three oxen crossing the desert a few hours ahead of McQueen's group. They had abandoned four wagons, and their stock looked so poor that they would probably have to ditch a fifth.

That evening, after buckwheat cakes and some dried apples they had salvaged, Buck Ramsey brought up the topic that was on their minds now.

"We're probably a hundred miles from the goldfields, boys," he said. "Maybe less. We've all been picking partners or wondering whether to go alone. We're all poor as church mice. There's eight of us, four mules, mess gear for four, and our personal items. How are we going to divide it?"

No one felt like venturing a word.

"Now, I'm not blind," he continued. "I know that Bacon, McQueen, and the Laliques want to partner. I know that Pyle and Hoke have made plans to dig together. I haven't heard anything from you, Sorley."

"I don't know yet," Mulligan said.

"Well, how about trying out the goldfields with me?"

Mulligan nodded, tentatively.

"Good. That makes dividing up easier. The party of four gets two mules. Each party of two gets one mule. The party of four gets two sets of mess gear. We each get one set. And we divide up the two kettles, skillet, and so on, one way or another."

"I guess you're saying we'll split up right here," Bacon said.

"Yep. Some want to hightail to the goldfields; others might want to go slow and try to keep their mules in shape. It depends on how you see it. If you think you can stake some good ground fast, you won't worry about the mules. If you think you may be hunting a long time for a good strike, you might want to keep your mules in shape."

"I don't even have cash to buy a goldpan or a pick," McQueen said.

"I hear a man can work for others and get an ounce a day," Bacon said. "That's about sixteen dollars. It won't take long to outfit at that rate."

That sounded like bonanza money to McQueen. A shovel back East cost a dollar. A pan might go for six bits. A mechanic in the East might earn a dollar a day. Here ... sixteen dollars was the worst a man could do if he was willing to pitch in.

"Does that split sound fair?" Ramsey asked.

Each man agreed.

"Then, in the morning, I suppose we'll all go our separate ways."

CHAPTER 38

R amsey and Mulligan left first, loading their share of the stores and shaking hands all around. "We'll see you in the clover, boys," Ramsey said.

"In the clover," Mulligan repeated, sounding as though he doubted it.

McQueen watched them go, wondering if he'd ever see his traveling companions again. The world was such a big place. He and Theo Bacon and the Laliques would follow in an hour or two. They wanted to give their two scrawny mules a good graze first. And Bacon intended to cannibalize wagons for lumber and sheet metal, the raw materials that would make a rocker. In two hours of wandering through the graveyards of wagons and dreams, he collected planks, sheet metal, hoop iron, assorted bolts, and even some dowels. The rested mules could carry all this, and the items would be priceless when the outfit got down to digging.

Hoke and Pyle had made other plans. They decided to camp right there on the Carson for a few weeks, making their fortune.

"Every evening we'll head east and salvage what we can out in that desert," Charley Pyle explained. "Why, I never did see such loot. We'll take hay and water, and rescue a few half-dead mules and oxen, and load up all that loot—I even saw beds and bureaus and sacks of flour out there. We'll just set us up a nice little store and sell stuff to the outfits coming by. They'll all be hurting for tools and chow and whatnot. If we can recruit some oxen, we'll sell livestock, too."

"And that ain't the end of it," Hoke added. "We'll get to the gold a little later, but we'll have full pokes. There's already quitters going home. We've passed fifty, haven't we? With full pokes we can buy good claims. If we're patient now, and collect all that stuff out there, we'll do mighty fine."

That sounded so good to McQueen that he was tempted to join them. Hoke and Pyle could hardly lose, especially if they could nurse some livestock back to usefulness. But Theo and the Laliques itched to get moving. They hadn't walked across a continent just to dally at the pearly gates.

So, with another round of handshakes, the four men parted company with Hoke and Pyle. Once again, sadness filled McQueen. He treasured these men. They had shared hardships, stood up together against the cruelty of Virginius Dobbin, nursed the mules, scared off Injuns, confided their hopes and dreams and fears to each other, and confessed their loneliness for wives and children and parents left far behind.

They trudged south along the Carson, finding grass and water in the riverbottoms, although the surrounding country looked rough. They passed ox-drawn outfits resting their kine or repairing their battered wagons. All of them looked like skeletons: men, oxen, horses, and mules.

Late that day they turned up the west branch of the Carson, following a well-marked trail that ascended slowly into towering, somber mountains that rose, green layer on purple layer, toward distant blue peaks, some patched with snow. They still faced the formidable Sierra Nevada, and it sobered them all. A lot of hard climbing lay ahead, and probably mountain showers, icy nights, and bad footing.

That evening they shared camp with two bearded eastbound travelers, each leading a fat mule. The pair had been reticent to strike up conversation at first, and McQueen supposed they were carrying a lot of gold.

"Where you fellows from?" asked one.

"Illinois and Ioway," replied Bacon.

"What part of Illinois?"

"LaSalle and Peru. Up north."

"And where in Iowa?"

"Mount Pleasant," said McQueen. "I'm Ulysses McQueen. We're heading for the diggings."

Some sort of tension vanished. "I'm Jacob Evans and this here's Josiah Lee," said one. "I guess if you want company, we'll camp here. Grass is good."

"We'd like news of the goldfields," McQueen said. "Where're you headed?"

Lee surveyed them a moment. "Salt Lake City. We're Latter-Day Saints going home. We served in the Mormon Battalion under Kearny. Our leader, Brigham Young, asked us to fetch what we could from the diggings and bring it to Zion before winter." He examined the others sharply, waiting for a hostile reaction that didn't materialize. "We thought you might be Missouri pukes," he said. "There's some old scores . . ."

"You're welcome here," Bacon assured them. "This is Basil Lalique—he served in the war, too; and his son Martin, who does the talking for them both. We'd like news about the diggings, and we've a few things to share about the trail back."

They dug into the best victuals they'd had since leaving Kanesville, thanks to the Mormons, who were carrying fresh sidepork, California plums and grapes, loaves of bread, and new potatoes. McQueen ate wildly, enjoying foods he hadn't tasted for months.

In the chill dusk of the foothills, they got down to trading what they knew. Bacon and McQueen told the Mormons what to expect when they struck across the desert to the Humboldt Sink.

"There's abandoned goods galore there," Bacon said. "A fellow with good livestock and a wagon could harvest a fortune just picking up what's there for the taking."

"It's a thought," Lee said.

"The grass clear to Salt Lake's been grazed down, and it's going to get worse. There's thousands behind us, most of them big ox outfits."

"Good to know," Evans said. "We'll cut grass and carry it when we can. And we'll pick up abandoned flour. We'll cook it into cakes and feed the mules. Same with cornmeal and oatmeal. Mighty strong feed."

McQueen wished he had thought of that. He felt dumb. Just by collecting abandoned flour and frying it, he might have saved some mules.

"Tell us about the diggings," Theo Bacon said. "Do we stand a chance?"

Lee shrugged. "There's good strikes every day. Someone or other's hitting a pocket, cleaning out three, five thousand. Lots of fellows making a hundred a day. Even a bad claim might yield an ounce a day."

"We'll have a chance, then," McQueen said.

"Oh, certainly you do. But it's filling up fast. Thousands coming in each day, a lot of them from the sea. There's gold being washed out of the Sierras for three hundred miles, but the good places are all taken up. Not that many bars, when you figure all the people rushing in."

"I once thought we would be the first, almost," McQueen said. "Until the parade went by."

"Son, this rush is a year and a half old. Started spring of 'forty-eight. That's when every pueblo in California emptied out. Then a few thousand came down from Oregon, and a few thousand Mexicans came up from Sonora. We've got Chileans that sailed up the Pacific coast, and a bunch of toughs from the Australian Penal Colony, Sydney Ducks they're called, and you'd best be careful of them. We've got Kanakas from the Islands, color of taffy and good workers. And sailors. Oh, have we got sailors from all over the world. They jump ship soon as they get to San Francisco or Sacramento, and now they're digging gold. And the whole Panama crowd's in and digging. A lot more coming that way, across the Isthmus, than overland like you. They're flooding in on anything that floats. I'd say twenty, thirty thousand just these last few months."

The figure stunned McQueen, and he felt a tight knot building in his chest. "Be realistic now. Do we have a chance?" he asked.

"It's never too late, McQueen," Lee said. "But the odds aren't so good, and the way to make money is to gang up and build a flume and a long tom—that's a long trough with riffles in it. Not much chance to make it just by panning anymore."

"We can do that," Bacon said. "We're partnered up. But we don't have a nickel amongst us."

"You can always find work. Lots of men own several claims and hire fellows to work them on shares, or pay them at least half an ounce a day, sometimes an ounce if it's good dirt. Some are working the local Indians, getting cheap labor. But you can mostly find work that pays half an ounce—that's eight dollars."

"That's good money."

Lee paused, shaking his head. "No, not in the diggings. It's bare survival money. You keep body and soul together, but you don't get ahead. Flour costs fifty cents a pound—used to be worse. Eggs and potatoes cost a pinch. A shovel costs ten dollars—if you can find one. Coffee—I don't touch the stuff myself—but coffee's just as high. And half the time you can't find what you need."

"We'll find a way. Even if we come in last, and everything's staked out, we'll find a way," McQueen said. "If a fellow has the right attitude, and some faith, he can move mountains."

"Never too late," Evans agreed. "Son, it's all luck. Virtue hasn't a thing to do with it. One fellow works hard on a claim and gets five dollars a day. The next fellow, one claim over, is lazy but he's on a place where the streambed picked up gold, and he makes five hundred in an afternoon. Just plain luck."

"I'd hate to rely on luck," McQueen muttered. "I can work hard. We all can: every man here knows how to toil. We'll make luck, not fall into it. We'll make our pile."

"Might. Mining's no fun. You'll be digging down to bedrock, freezing your legs in the water, poking coyote holes into gravel, climbing hills, trying dry diggings in an old streambed. But your best bet, like I say, is hydraulics. You get some promising ground, build a flume, set up a long tom with lots of riffles to collect the dust, and you'll prosper."

"It sounds like the storekeepers and teamsters are the ones getting rich," Bacon said.

"They ain't hurting, that's for sure. But they pay high prices too. Stuff coming into the levee at Sacramento City gets bid up the moment it arrives. You can't blame the storekeeps for it all. There's thousands of gold-rushers coming in each day, and they all want victuals and equipment and a few comforts," Evans explained. "The whole world's shipping stuff on speculation, so you can get things cheap when there's a glut. One day lumber's so scarce you can't find a board; next day there's too much. Same with shovels and goldpans and flour."

"You run across a tough character named Dobbin? Or a man named Clappe?" Bacon asked.

"No, we can't say as we have. Do you know them?"

"We do. They had a little too much ambition for our tastes."

"They're probably cleaning up, then," Lee said. "The ones with no scruples, they're the ones making a fortune."

Ruefully, McQueen acknowledged the truth of it.

They talked deep into the evening, and by the time they hit their bedrolls McQueen knew that striking bonanza gold in

California would be much harder than he had ever dreamed. But the Mormons had suggested the Mokelumne district as a good place to start.

The next days they toiled upward along a crude, stump-riddled road hacked through chill forests, awed by giant trees and intoxicated by the scents of mountain evergreens. The towering pines rose taller than any McQueen had ever seen, and dropped cones the size of a loaf of bread. They topped a divide, and beheld layered blue ridges ahead. Two days later they reached the gold country, a land of slopes, mild temperatures, trees with shiny leaves, and tent settlements. They inquired where to go.

"Try the Mokelumne River," said one man. "Biggest strikes anyone's ever heard of, like Big Bar. And plenty of good dirt back from the river—harder to wash, but it bears gold."

Gold! For this McQueen had crossed a continent, endured torments, and discovered that not all men thought highly of him. He thought back upon all that had happened, and knew that it had strengthened and annealed the young man who had left Mount Pleasant in March. That youth had never gone more than fifty miles from home. This man gazing down on the gold-bearing country had met all kinds, and knew himself.

McQueen and his partners headed for the Mokelumne River. They would meet their fate there.

CHAPTER 39

Susannah watched the black buggy wend its way up the lane, knowing who was coming to call, and suspecting that it would be more than a social visit. She hurried to the kitchen to stir up the fire and set some hot water heating for tea. By the time she had doffed her apron, patted her unruly hair into place, shaken flour off her sleeves, and checked the crib where her dear girl slept through the afternoon, she was ready for the Reverend and Mrs. McCracken.

This would be about the baptism. The time had come for that. And there might be some tension in it because the McQueens had not reconciled themselves to her choice of names. Now she would see whether the old patriarch had enlisted the parson in his cause. She wished her mother could be here, but her mother wasn't coming to Old Oak so much now that Susannah was back on her feet and the baby was a lusty imp.

Margaret Temperance McQueen seemed a healthy enough baby, though colicky sometimes. But Susannah had already learned that a child is an innocent tyrant, and that from now on the mother would schedule her life around the infant.

Susannah didn't really mind. Day by day, the child had forced its way into her life and her heart. At first Susannah scarcely cared. Her first birthing had gone hard. After it, she hurt. A great sadness enveloped her. But as night and day passed, and Susannah gained her old strength and her body began to reshape itself, and she could fit into treasured dresses again, the child had stolen her heart away. Nursing it, holding it, washing its velvet skin became moments of joy.

The first weeks, Susannah's mother came daily to Old Oak Farm to help with the tedious things, rinsing diapers and then scrubbing them on the washboard, changing the baby, tending the girl to let Susannah out into the sun for a stroll down the lane. Margaret Temperance McQueen bloomed, although Susannah felt a thousand fears whenever rumor of summer complaint, or cholera, or a thousand other dread diseases drifted to her ears.

She didn't hear from the senior McQueens for a fortnight after the birth, though her farm was next to theirs. But her brother-in-law Jonathan sometimes hoed away weeds that were sprouting between the rows of tall corn. After that, she saw all the McQueens at Sunday meetings, but they seemed reserved.

She could ask for nothing more except the most important thing of all: Ulysses. She had written him the day after the birthing, sending the letter off to Sutter's Fort, hoping he would have the news in two or three months. From him she heard nothing. Each day, as soon as she was up and about again, she walked clear to Mount Pleasant and sought a letter while her mother tended the child. But none came. And then, with heavy heart she walked home again, worried sick. Had Ulysses died? Had he abandoned her?

She opened to the McCrackens as they stepped onto her broad veranda, and bid them into her lovely parlor, with its fine horsehair sofa and stuffed chairs. The cadaverous jut-jawed minister stepped lightly and settled in the largest wingback, sighing his pleasure. His dignity always touched some wellspring of respect in her, and she felt herself in the presence of a spiritually powerful man.

"I'm so glad you came. We haven't visited," she said, trying hard to feel what she said she was feeling.

"And how's our lovely young mother?" the parson asked.

"Tell us about the child, dear," added Philomena McCracken, carefully choosing the smallest chair and perching wrenlike in it.

"She's a dear. Rarely fusses now, but she did at first. And she's already gained a pound. Would you care to see her?"

"Oh, when we leave, we'd enjoy it," McCracken said. "We might offer a blessing over her."

"That would be lovely. Let me pour you some tea. I've heated the water."

She fled to the kitchen, ashamed that she really didn't want this visit. She hurried through her preparations, and soon reappeared in the parlor bearing the Haviland teapot and three cups and saucers, along with a sugar bowl. The tea would surely civilize all this.

"Now then, Susannah," said the reverend. "What's the news from Ulysses?"

"I have none," she said. "The mail's so slow. It goes around the Isthmus, you know."

"But surely you would've heard something . . ."

"I'd hoped to," she said.

"He's a brave lad, going out there to that papist place. I hear it's a handsome country, though riddled with temptations for a single man. You must be lonesome for him."

She smiled, concealing the hollowness. "Yes," she said.

"A home needs a strong man to give direction and protect a woman. I hope he returns soon, with or without the, ah, pocketful of rocks, as they say. The farm goes untended, the future ignored, the well-being of a tender wife and mother neglected."

"Ulysses isn't ignoring me. . . . I know he's building our future. Not one man in a thousand had the grit to go west. And of course I have my family here. My mother comes over. And there's Mr. and Mrs. McQueen, of course."

"You're most fortunate," said Philomena. "Many a young mother lacks the comforts of two strong families."

They sipped and sugared and poured and sipped and stirred.

"A pleasant visit," said the reverend. "But of course, we in the ministry are always upon a mission. We've come to have a word about the baby."

Susannah nodded.

"You know, the McQueens had their hearts set on other names. And now, as baptism approaches, they've asked my dear Philomena and me to come counsel with you. We do that often, helping young men and women find their proper and most rewarding roles within our community of faith."

Susannah nodded and folded her hands tightly. Perhaps Margaret would start to yowl for her afternoon feeding at her breast, and rescue her. But the perfidious girl slumbered on.

"One of the things I like to point out is that the community of saints is continuous from generation to generation, an ongoing village that includes the dead, the living, young and old, and those yet to come. It's an unbroken line stretching back to Saint Peter, and to the Good Lord Himself."

"Yes, that's true," she said.

"Ah! You see, then. It is a godly thing to honor those who've gone before, to preserve their memories, to continue names sacred to families from generation to generation. You know, Stanford McQueen has been deprived of the opportunity . . . with sons, you know . . . to remember his beloved grandmothers, saintly women whose memories should be preserved forever. He feels very deeply about it. So much so that he's gone into mourning because he can't persuade you."

"I understand." She gathered her courage and plunged ahead. "Of course he has other sons and daughters-in-law who'll have more children, and he can ask them. I just don't like either name. I'm sure some people love Violet and Agatha, but I'm afraid I couldn't bear to call a child of mine by those names."

"Well, I can understand that. I deplore some names myself. Always had an aversion to Richard. Show me a Richard and I'll show you a man with the soul of a squid and the habits of an orangutan. It's all I can do not to purge the church rolls of all Richards."

"But what about Richard the Lionhearted?"

"A garden-variety butcher, tricked out with a halo by our cousins across the sea."

"Then you know what I mean. I'd have trouble with a girl named Agatha or Violet. It'd affect me, and hurt the child. I don't want my girl to suffer any slights. . . . I mean, it'd affect me. And her."

"Well, I do understand. But there're larger issues here. The community. The McQueens. In a way, this lovely infant isn't really yours. She descends from a long line of beloved ancestors. And two sainted women whose spirits must be hovering here now, aching to melt your heart."

Susannah resisted the impulse to surrender. "She's my child, Mr. McCracken. I've given her names I love. Her middle name's a virtue, an instruction to her."

She thought she spotted the faintest impatience flash across his corded face.

"The child belongs to both of you, Ulysses and yourself," he said. "He and the McQueens have a say in it. Consider him present here. Surely he would swiftly side with his beloved father, and name the child after his great-grandmothers. A man is the head of the home, and ultimately the choice is his. And in his absence, his father and mother are providing this direction for you."

She chose her words carefully. Resisting her minister and spiritual counselor could not be done lightly. "Sir, if Ulysses were here, he'd support me. He's chosen to govern his life as he will, and I approve, and he'd support me."

"But you don't know that for a fact."

"I'm his wife."

He sighed, and summoned up a offhand smile. "Forgive me. I feel so strongly about family unity and our obligations to one another I perhaps overstated the case."

"Thank you for your counsel, then. I'm committed to other names, and sorry they don't please Father and Mother McQueen."

Philomena intervened intensively. "Think on it. Pray on it. We'll all seek illumination."

"My baby is Margaret Temperance, Mrs. McCracken."

The minister stared out upon the green cornfields, and finally turned to her. "You've graciously asked the McQueens to be sponsors, godparents. Stanford confided to me, brokenhearted, that he just couldn't manage it. He said he couldn't be a proper godparent, doing his Christian duty to a child that wasn't named Violet Agatha. I fear you've pierced something very tender in him, broken his heart."

That seemed highly unlikely to Susannah. Nothing could break Stanford McQueen's heart. "I'm sorry he won't sponsor my girl. I asked them expressly so that we might be reconciled. Maybe I can ask Jonathan or—"

The reverend waved a bony hand. "No, no. Your in-laws all feel this way. And Stanford told me frankly he wouldn't sit still at Sunday meeting and watch you rip the child from him."

That astonished Susannah. "Rip *his* child from him? Not come to Sunday meeting? I've offered my child to him; asked him and Mother McQueen to be the godparents."

"Well, yes. Oh, my dear, these are the moments ministers of the gospel dread. There's no way out. I think we'd best plan a little baptism ceremony midweek, say next Wednesday, in the chapel. And of course your parents, or whoever you choose can be the sponsors. Fine people, blessed members of our congregation. Yes, we'll do that. I'll plan on it for eleven in the morning Wednesday next."

"Please invite the McQueens," she said tautly. "They'll want to come. Margaret is their grandchild. And their niece."

"Of course, of course, but I'd better warn you . . ."

The rest of the visit went lamely. At last, having allotted a decent time to visit about other things, the McCrackens begged leave. They paused at the cradle, stared dutifully upon a slumbering child slowly closing her tiny fists, and hastened away.

But he smiled at the door. "I like your pluck," he said, the faintest glitter in his eyes. "I'm partial to Margaret myself. It's Philly's middle name. Whenever I call her Peggy, she chases me with a rolling pin. Come visit us any time, Susannah. And bring that delightful Peggy with you."

She smiled back, with understanding. The man had done what he'd promised Father McQueen.

Susannah returned to the cradle and gazed at her lovely

Margaret. Somehow all this had become important. The minor business of naming an infant had burgeoned into a sinister and vaguely frightening issue. She could not help feeling that Stanford McQueen would begin the process of disowning her—for the terrible sin of defying his authority. She smiled tenderly at her infant, wondering what Fate would bring. She had surprised herself this day, and discovered strength she didn't know she had.

PART IV

1848

A sharp chill one September dawn reminded Stephen Jarvis that he could no longer put off some decisions. Rita Concepción Estrada had given him a year. At least he thought she had. October was looming. Almost a year had elapsed since he had encountered her. Should he abandon Bidwell's Bar and seek her?

Common sense decreed otherwise. It had been a passing infatuation, romantic imaginings whirling around a lovely young woman he had yet to know. To leave Bidwell's Bar was to surrender his claims there. A miner held his claim by leaving his tools on it; if he left it for a month, he had abandoned it and anyone could claim it. These were rules adapted by various miners' meetings at Bidwell's Bar. Jarvis could only abide by them or lose his claims.

His recollection of Rita Concepción had grown hazy after so long a time. He couldn't remember the timbre of her voice. What remained to him was the flash of her brown eyes, her grace on horseback, her ready smile, and those soulful looks she had exchanged with him. Now he must either chase that chimera, traveling to Monterey and then the Estrada Rancho to press his suit, or let it go and concentrate on the fabulous gold he was extracting from the rich gravels of the Feather River.

Common sense ruled, but his soul protested. Grimly he toiled at his rocker. Digging gold from gravel hadn't grown any easier, even though his body was now inured to the backbreaking labor, bending, lifting, shoveling, working in snowmelt water, rain, blistering sun, clouds of mosquitos, and chill dawns.

The daily yields hadn't dwindled though some areas of his two claims produced far less than others. He had formed a working partnership with Joseph Laird, an Oregon man who'd left his Willamette Valley farm for a crack at a bonanza the very day he'd heard of the strike in California. But Laird was no

flighty opportunist. He was simply a man with his eye on the
main chance. He had staked the claim next to Jarvis's and built
up a small fortune in pea-sized nuggets and coarse dust. Jarvis
and Laird toiled together because two men working a cradle
could move five or six yards of gravel a day. They shoveled and
rocked and poured and cleaned from dawn to dusk, usually
twelve hours, seven hours on Jarvis's claims because he owned
the rocker, and five on Laird's, and both did better than if they
had worked alone.

The number of men working Bidwell's Bar actually diminished, and now only forty-odd toiled there. No woman had ever
settled, though one or two had come through, en route to some
other fabled place. Men had come and gone, lured away by the
scents of bonanza perfuming the breeze; here the North Fork of
the American, there the Mokelumne, yonder the Yuba River.
These were fabulous. Almost daily, Jarvis heard that miners
were picking up acorn-sized nuggets right from the surface up
on the American; that a fifty-pound nugget had been unearthed
over on such a creek; that a man with a rocker could gather two
thousand a day, here, there, everywhere. So the population at
Bidwell's Bar, an aging strike now, dwindled day by day. But
Jarvis toiled on, and so did John Bidwell, and so did half a
dozen cheery Miwak Indians Bidwell had induced to labor on
his other claim for trinkets and a glass of spirits each eve.

There had not been a single case of theft at the bar all that
summer of 1848. Men left their gold dust in glass jars, or tin
cans, or crockery mugs, or leather pokes, knowing it would be
safe in their tents or brush arbors. A few buried it under their
bedrolls or under their firepits, but none was stolen. Perhaps
that was because the goldfields were huge, news of awesome
strikes arrived almost daily, and it didn't make sense to steal
when gold could be plucked up without risk. Or perhaps
because it made no sense to steal when a miners' court could
impose its own harsh justice: confiscation of claims, banish-
ment, thirty lashes, even hanging. In the absence of formal law,
the miners' own swift and relentless version served admirably.

These men—mostly former New York Volunteer soldiers like
himself, a few Regular Army and Navy deserters, Sam
Brannan's Mormon settlers, the poorer classes of Californios,
the handful of Yank settlers who had drifted in, Oregonians,

merchant sailors, and Sandwich Island Kanakas—weren't any more honest than any other motley crowd, but something checked their thievery.

Still, Jarvis worried. He had collected a fortune in gold and didn't know what to do with it. Bidwell was worried, too. Some gossipy miners whispered that John Bidwell had close to a hundred thousand dollars of dust and nuggets in tough leather pokes in his tent, several hundred pounds of gold. Jarvis wasn't sure how much he had reaped, but he guessed it might be seventy thousand dollars. A fortune.

He had experimented with the quicksilver, amalgamating the dust and nuggets and then boiling off the mercury over a fire. The result was a spongy gold, largely free of impurities, and also easy to detect if it were stolen because no one else in camp had any sponge or quicksilver. But Jarvis knew that would not stop a determined thief.

That chill September morning he tried to take stock. He shaved himself, as he had done once a week all summer, dressed in his usual duck-cloth trousers, flannel shirt, brogans and slouch hat, and wandered across the broad flat, through dew-laden stubble. Bidwell's Bar had bloomed into a rag town. Some miners were erecting log cabins against the looming winter. Pack trains operated by entrepreneurs out of Sacramento City had regularly visited the camp, charging astronomical prices but nonetheless supplying it with its needs. Not just the miners were reaping a harvest of gold.

Serious mining at this bar had scarcely begun. Around him lay virgin gravel, all of it gold-bearing but much of it yielding less than the fabled claims, including his own, which had enriched a few men. The place had a future for those who operated long toms. He could stay on and multiply his riches. The news of gold in California had yet to reach the world. He had heard that no one back in the States knew anything about it, although a military express, carrying a tea canister of nuggets and dust as proof, was on its way east. Except for military expresses along the southern route, there was no reliable communication with the States. Someday, when the news finally broke in all those papers back there, a lot of Yanks would flood in. If he held on to his claims this winter and worked them next year and sold them to the incoming mobs, he would probably earn several times his seventy thousand, and be a truly rich man.

He peered at the awakening camp. Cookfire smoke hung in the air, redolent with the smells of sizzling sidepork, flapjacks, beans or biscuits. Some men were already panning and shoveling in the deep lavender shade. Dickson was among them, still panning gold, still a sour loner, still obsessed with the unfairness of it all. Men said that Dickson buried every ounce he panned, and hid his gold in so many odd corners that he probably wouldn't remember where it all was. Jarvis had long since stopped talking with the man, but sometimes Dickson's bright bitter glare turned toward him like a shaft of blackness.

The Feather ran at its seasonal lows, exposing gravel that had been inundated until recently, and those exposed bars were yielding the richest diggings now. But when the winter rains came, they would be underwater again until next summer when the last of the Sierra snows melted away. He had come to know this place. He had explored the hills around it while moving his stock. His cow prospered, and the calf had grown to the size of a good chunk of veal. He was still making milk money. This place had become home. It could be his future. He had no reason to quit it.

Except for one. Two, really. He was sick of mining. He had other dreams.

He found Bidwell up and trimming his beard before a looking glass dangling from a tent pole.

"An omen of winter," Bidwell said.

"What're you going to do—build a cabin?"

"I imagine. I'll try to weather it right here. Get some supplies in. The Miwaks are coining money for me. I just figure I'll stay warm and let 'em work. Northfield and I'll share, and keep on going."

"I figure I'll sell out."

"But why? We've hardly tapped this bar. I'm thinking my claims'll net me half a million dollars if they don't peter out. Half a million."

"If no one steals your gold. Have you figured what to do with it?"

"I heard there's some home-grown smelters in Sacramento City. You bring them your dust and they'll amalgamate it, retort the quicksilver, and then smelt it in their charcoal furnaces. They cast it into fifty-dollar octagonal slugs, two and a half ounces of pure gold with a fifty stamped on it. You can transport that. Take it east to a mint if you want. I'm going to take a load down there, see Sutter. Northfield'll keep this work humming."

"Don't you worry about leaving so much around here unguarded?"

"More and more. Next year there'll be a real rush. This strike'll stir them up back there—and when it does, watch out."

"I'll go with you to Sacramento City. I'm going to sell out."

"Sell out? You've got two of the richest claims in the Sierra Nevada."

"I'm going to be a merchant. I'm worn out. Bad food, bad weather, endless hard work. What good is it if I take sick? I've a fortune and I'll put it to use. If there's a rush next year, I'll be ready for it. We've seen a few Oregon men and a bunch of sailors and some Sonorans up from Mexico, but when the world finds out . . . I'll be able to sell anything to anyone, and make a real fortune."

Bidwell smiled. "Suit yourself. You put a price on those claims yet?"

"I'm still thinking it over. Maybe tomorrow I'll take bids. You want to buy the milch cow? She's still fresh, but she should be bred."

"Sell it to Pedersen. I'm a miner, not a dairyman."

"For almost three months that cow's brought me half an ounce of dust a day. She's as good as a claim. And Bidwell Bar's had milk and cream and butter."

They laughed, the easy camaraderie of men who had shared ordeals and toil and hopes for a long time. "Sure, let's go to Sacramento City," Bidwell said. "If you really want to sell those claims, let me know."

"I want Laird to get one if he wants it. He's been a good partner. We've worked like demons for months. He might want to send some of his dust along with us."

"You armed, Stephen? We'll be carrying a lot of gold. It's those merchant sailors I worry about. Not the Oregon men or the Kanakas. Sailors are a rough lot. They won't stop at anything including murder. And they all deserted their ships to come to the goldfields."

"You wonder what's kept them at bay all these months."

Bidwell shrugged. "There's gold everywhere. Why, we've only scratched the surface. The Sierra's a treasure chest of gold never seen before in history. There's enough gold here to make the United States the richest country on earth. Enough to make a Spanish king sour as buttermilk. Enough so that as long as this country lives, generations of Americans'll be talking about this gold. Aren't you glad we got here ahead of the mob? Imagine what's coming. Think about next year. Eighteen forty-nine's going to be one of the most amazing years in history."

"Guess so. I'd like to be the outfitter ready for 'em, too. Picks and shovels and pans. Shirts and boots and flour and beef. Coffee and tea and sugar and molasses. I'm going to get ready for them, and then I'll coin gold faster'n I can dig it, even with a rocker. Even with a long tom. Even if I leased my claims."

Jarvis paused, suddenly realizing he'd made up his mind after all. "John, I'll be back on Bidwell's Bar, but not as a miner. I'll be wearing a shirt and a vest and standing behind a counter. Maybe here, maybe somewhere else. Maybe with branches all over the Sierra."

And maybe with a wife, but he didn't tell John Bidwell that.

That day he sold one claim to Joseph Laird for eight thousand in dust, and the other claim to Bidwell for nine thousand. He traded Laird the venerable rocker for a revolver and two sound mules and packsaddles. By afternoon he had sold his milch cow and calf, peddled his tent and mining gear to eager buyers, gathered his horse and burro from a distant canyon, and prepared to leave. He had in his bags ninety-three thousand dollars in spongy gold concentrate, nuggets and dust, and in his mind a dream worth even more.

He had come a long way from his private's eight dollars a month. The gold might make him comfortable and a man of parts. But she would be his happiness.

CHAPTER 41

R ita Concepción Estrada's discontent deepened each day. She had come to Monterey for its bright social life, and for a few months she had found it. But now the pueblo was a sleepy, empty husk, without young men, without servants and clerks in the *mercados*, without people on the streets taking their *paseos*. Abandoned sloops and brigantines rocked and creaked in the bay. Grumbling shopkeepers kept their stores open without clerks. The barracks at the presidio, now occupied by the *yanqui* conquerors, was three-quarters empty.

Her social life consisted of consoling other young women, or helping Tía Maria with the endless work now that her aunt had no servants. Where had the caballeros gone? They had all professed to disdain the gold, and swore holy vows not to grub for the disgusting metal by shoveling in icy creeks like some common *trabajadero*. But they had vanished too, called back to their ranchos to help with the ordinary labor there. For all of California's manhood had rushed madly to the distant Sierra Nevada in search of gold.

When the tidings flooded in from Yerba Buena—the *yanquis* were calling it San Francisco now after laying out stiff streets in dreary rectangles—in the spring, no one paid much attention. Or at least the *ricos*, people of means, didn't. She went to several *bailes* in April, but only one in May, and that was the last. One couldn't even hire a fiddler, much less a band. And who would serve the refreshments? Monterey had emptied itself out, until now it was a husk of a city thrust into the bitter blue bay, and too cold for comfort.

She didn't know what to do with herself in a city of women and children and *viejos*. But she stayed. The rancho would be worse. In *diciembre* Juan Carlos had married a rich widow, the doña Socorro Valenzuela of Sonoma, notoriously stern and excessively dignified, and Rita Concepción dreaded life there more than ever. The famous widow and her brothers deserved each other, she decided. But that was callous. She confessed this hardness to God, before Padre Tecolote, so she might be forgiven. She adored her brothers, most of the time, and wished they would marry.

Tía Maria, at least, bubbled with life and mad plans to marry her off, and sometimes ventured into topics she could never discuss at the casa Estrada, while Tío José Jesús puffed his *cigarros* and consigned casks of sour wine to outlying customers, and absently patted her on the head as he passed. Rita doubted that Tío José Jesús was even aware she was now a woman.

But that didn't give her a life. Desolately, she had waited for news of her *yanqui*, Estéban Harvis, but nothing washed up on her shore. Well, yes, she had a glimmer of *noticias* once. She had met Thomas Larkin, once the consul of *los Estados Unidos* in California, and now a prominent, bilingual citizen and merchant in Monterey. Yes, said Señor Larkin at a fiesta one day, yes, he knew the young man. Studious, quiet, alone. The señor had lent him some books, and instructed him about this great province, and befriended him. Yes, he was different from the ordinary *soldados*, that one. He always had his eyes upon distant horizons, beyond the edge of the sea, or someplace far to the east of the Sierra de Salinas.

That was all. No one else among the *yanquis* she had met in Monterey had ever heard of the obscure *soldado raso*. But it was enough. Thomas O. Larkin's esteem for the young man fevered her dreams through the winter, then the spring of 1848, and even into the dreary summer when the city had emptied out. And then her dream faded. She would never see the *americano* again.

For a while she had wrestled with the *inglés*, studying each day with a pale *yanqui* hombre who styled himself a teacher of children, and taught Spanish to the families of the conquerors. Mr. Josiah Bullfinch, that was his name. A burly, lantern-jawed youth who made daily rounds, teaching in the casas of his clients. Tía Maria had surveyed the grotesque man and concluded no *dueña* would be required for these lessons and had left the pair alone each forenoon in the *sala*.

Thus had Rita stabbed at the ungainly tongue, with all its thick dissonants and wild irregularities. What a *lengua loca*!

No wonder it made *yanquis* mad. That tongue gave no peace for the soul. She had paid particular attention to the words for love, and rolled them over on her tongue. They tasted like ash in her mouth. What would the word be for *querido*? Darling. Dear Stephen, my darling. That sounded like sheep talking.

Then one May day the bulky professor with the great jaw sent his regrets. He would teach the tongue no more. And no one in Monterey saw him again, though it was bruited about that he had purchased a pick and shovel from Castellana, the ironsmith, the day before.

She had tried out her awful *inglés* on Señor Larkin, but he had shaken his head, puzzled. What she could do now was listen. She could catch the drift of the conversations of the *yanquis*, and often translated while she sat quietly at their tea parties, some of them in the home of their military governor, the *coronel*, Richard B. Mason. She had learned much more from Mason's aide, the *lugarteniente* William Tecumseh Sherman, a sad-eyed, reserved, but attentive young man who quietly paid her court over teacups or punch, and enjoyed bridging the gulf between them. Together they played word games, pointing and naming, pronouncing and correcting.

"Señorita," he once said. "I've been offered a lot in San Francisco for sixteen dollars. I've turned it down. Do you think that was a mistake?"

"No, Señor Sherman, it was very wise. Speculations go bad. Or is it badly? Ah, endings, conjugations, I never get them right," she replied.

The last time she saw the *lugarteniente*, he reminded her of that exchange. "That lot is worth a thousand dollars now," he said wistfully. "West Point does not train officers in business or in gold rushes."

She supposed she learned more in her social encounters with the melancholic young officer than she did with her instructor. Sometimes, when she studied him furtively in the Larkin home where they usually met for afternoon tea, she wondered if this young officer would bear life's burdens well. He was *católico*, which surprised her, but the Holy Faith obviously offered him no solace.

From Sherman she had learnt conversational English. If ever

she saw Stephen Jarvis again, she could understand him and even reply slowly.

But she wouldn't see him.

She busied herself caring for her cousins, Tía Maria's parade of children, which had issued regularly for years. It amazed her that her aunt's house could expand to include her in it without the slightest difficulty. She even had a room of her own, and her impish cousins Fernanda and Isabel had gleefully shared a room. At least the bosom of this family was merrier than the one on the rancho Estrada.

Tía Maria had probed a little, her curiosity sometimes getting the better of her discretion, but Rita Concepción never confided what she wanted from Monterey life, what her plans might be, or why she had dallied around the *americanos* so much and was learning their tongue.

"You have a secret *yanqui* lover," her aunt had ventured once, when Rita had turned evasive. "You never keep anything from me, but this one thing. I think Padre Tecolote knows a lot more than I do. Priests know everything, but an aunt is the last to learn. Take my advice, Rita Concepción, and do not pine, and do not wait for a man."

"I do not want any man. I had too much of them *allá en el país,* out in the country."

"Ah! You do not fool me. *Tiene la cara.* You have the look."

Rita could not imagine what look. In the glass, she seemed exactly the same. She did not even look like an adult; just a girl. But soon she would be twenty—more than an adult; a spinster. Life had stopped. Monterey had died. She considered returning to the rancho and riding Plata again.

Then one somnolent October day in the fall of 1848, she rose from her blessed siesta around the hour of four, dressed, and wandered into the *sala.* There the faithful *indio* Salina handed her a card. Thomas O. Larkin had called and left it for her. "See me when you can," he had written on its back in Spanish: *Ven cuando puede Vd.*

She knew she would find him at his large two-story home with the double gallery around it that offered shade to every window, upstairs and down. She might, by day, venture to his home alone, and enter his offices where clerks labored. She might attend the teas and salons Mr. and Mrs. Larkin offered to Monterey society many afternoons, also alone. But evenings her honor would require a *dueña*, and she hated to impose on Tía Maria, who had so much to do, and so many *niños* to tend. That meant she must hurry, before the hours of business ended.

She wore her canary-yellow twill dress this day, against the chill of the waning sun, and tied a canary ribbon into her brown hair to complete the ensemble. It was a dress she had sewn for Estéban Harvis, but no Estéban had come to her.

"Ah, señorita, you got my card," Larkin said, welcoming her into his cluttered offices, where he labored at a rolltop desk. *"Siéntase usted.* Seat yourself," he said. Larkin was a restless, balding man who wore his hair long at the sides. He rose and swung the door almost shut behind her, but carefully did not close it, which would create a scandal.

"Now then, we can talk privately. I have been asked to pursue a delicate matter. A gentleman and an officer simply wishes to know whether you are open to his honorable advances. He tells me he is smitten, knows you a little, and would seek your hand if encouraged. He is of your faith."

Sherman. And as swiftly as she recognized her suitor, she knew the answer.

"I am fond of the lieutenant, Mr. Larkin. But I fear . . ." She left the rest unsaid. "Tell him I am honored, but I would discourage him."

Larkin nodded. "I thought it might come to that. I hope you did not mind my asking, or his inquiry."

"I am honored. He is esteemed in my thoughts. A true caballcro and a scholar."

Larkin leaned back in his swivel chair, and she thought something vital radiated from him. Like so many *yanquis*, he burst with energy and was happiest when engaged in great enterprises. Now he eyed her shrewdly. She sensed he had more to say.

"Once you inquired after a young private, Jarvis, who interested you. I have news of him I have been meaning to pass along."

Her pulse lifted, but she masked the leap of her heart. *"Sí,"* she said tautly. "I am curious."

"I talked to John Sutter recently. He mentioned Jarvis. That young fellow has made a fortune."

"*Un rico?*"

Larkin nodded. "And not just in gold, either. He has a head for business. He sees what is needed and tries to supply the need. Sutter thinks Jarvis will be one of the great men of California soon."

"Estéban Harvis?"

"You know, some men are in the right place at the right time. Jarvis went to work for Tom Marshall. He was there when Marshall found the gold in the tailrace. He built a rocker, one of the first gold-washing devices in the province, and built another for John Bidwell. Then Jarvis joined Bidwell's party and found gold on the Rio de las Plumas."

"What else?" she asked tightly. "Is the Señor Jarvis still on the river harvesting his gold?"

"No, señorita, he left a while ago, sold out, commissioned the erection of offices and a warehouse in Sacramento City on the levee, and the last Sutter knew, was headed on a schooner for San Francisco to find a tailor. He said he couldn't find in Sacramento City the kind of black cutaway suit and white shirts he needed to seek the hand of an unnamed lady."

Rita Concepción lost her composure, but didn't care what Thomas O. Larkin thought of her tears.

Almost a year had passed.

CHAPTER 42

In Sacramento City, the tent-town blooming a mile or two from Sutter's Fort, Stephen Jarvis staked out a river lot, three hundred feet on the levee, and then headed over to the fort to pay Johann August Sutter for it.

The gesture astonished the Swiss. "Jarvis, you are the first one to walk in here and offer me a *real*. I haff no rights. This is occupied Mexican territory. Nothing protects property. I haff no way of driving these usurpers off."

He stared at Jarvis's fifty dollars of gold dust. "You will not be forgotten, my friend. When this becomes a territory, and I haff my rights, you will be remembered." Something misty formed in the man's eyes. For months he had watched an empire of land, cattle, and crops fall into ruin, all his cheerful succor and kindness to so many instantly forgotten.

"I am only repaying you for hiring me," Jarvis said gently, still in awe of this grandee who had carved a kingdom out of a wilderness. "You helped many men."

The saturnine Swiss stared through a window upon a brilliant day. "Let me give you some advice," he said softly, in his usual precise and formal English. "Soon the whole world will rush in. There will be shortages. Men will want for food and blankets, or picks and shovels and pans, and no doubt lumber and clothing. That will excite speculators. A speculator in New York will think ahead, hire a vessel and send ten thousand shovels or blankets or casks of salt pork around the Horn. Even now, the Chileans are shipping flour and Oregon's sending lumber."

Jarvis nodded. Sutter's advice was something to weigh carefully.

"Think about it: One moment we will famish for blankets here and sell them for ten dollars; the next moment there will be too many blankets and we will sell them for one dollar and take a loss. My advice is, don't speculate. Don't try to corner a market. Stock your shelves as best you can, but never for a killing. Then you haff a sure profit. Speculators will come and go, rich one day and in rags the next. But you haff a good head and a sound manner."

Jarvis thanked the man, wondering whether Sutter's herds, crops, rose gardens, and great adobe post would survive. The Swiss was adamantly refusing to pay his field hands and mechanics the new going wage, an ounce a day, which he considered outrageous. And for that stubbornness he might pay a terrible price.

"Captain Sutter, could you store some dust for me? I need a safe place, and I'll pay you something for it."

"Ah, you miners and your nuggets. Always looking to Johann Sutter for something. There's not much room left in my strongbox, Jarvis. It scares me, all the gold in it. But I'll store all you want. I haff a smith building a bigger box."

"I'll store two hundred pounds of dust. It's in leather pokes. I'm going to turn my amalgam into bullion and sell it."

Jarvis collected a deposit receipt, and hiked back to the river-front. There, in the space of an hour, he purchased a grimy fore-and-aft sloop that had been abandoned by its crew and lay helplessly alongside the levee. He didn't much like the owner, Ham Breyer, a rough buccaneer lacking four fingers and several teeth, but making up for them with a dozen body odors.

"I should get three thousand for it, but the scurvy lot mutinied. That's what you get for hiring Kanakas," Breyer grumbled. "All right, a thousand in gold."

Jarvis wrote up the sale papers, since the man didn't seem to know how, and weighed out some clean gold nuggets he was valuing at sixteen dollars an ounce.

"There you are, Breyer. If you want to earn a little, stay on board and guard this ship while I'm gone. It'll be a warehouse until I can build one. I'll be back in a few weeks, and pay you two ounces a week just for keeping watch. There'll be goods coming aboard to guard."

"That's not even a wage," the man grumbled. "I'm a master, not a hireling."

"I'm only asking you to stay on board and keep watch. Maybe I'll employ you at full pay to shuttle between here and San Francisco. I'll be looking for a master as soon as I start buying goods in San Francisco and shipping them here."

The man grinned suddenly, and shook hands on the deal.

Next, Jarvis hired a shrewd Mormon clerk away from Brannan and made him a purchasing agent to bid on whatever items he thought might sell in the goldfields, especially shovels, picks, pans, flour, sugar, molasses, coffee beans, and bolts of duck cloth and muslin. These were to be stored in the sloop, and paid for through Sutter. Then he hunted down a tailor. He could find none in a blow-away tent town, and hoped he would do better when he reached San Francisco.

Later he supped with John Bidwell who had spent the day searching Sacramento City for a factor who would buy gold dust and nuggets, or arrange for dust to be smelted into bullion.

"Didn't have much luck," Bidwell said. "I bought some bank notes and some eagles and double eagles. One fellow reduced a little dust, and made some fifty-dollar slugs for me, but he couldn't handle much of my gold in his little charcoal furnace."

"California needs a bank. Maybe I should start one," Jarvis said.

"That'd help. I'm taking my gold home to Rancho Chico and store it there. That's the best I can do until things improve."

"John, what're you going to do with it? You're rich. You can have anything you want."

"Oh, I've some dreams, all right. Almost embarrassed to tell you. I'm going to build a handsome home with vistas of snowy mountains from the windows, and it'll be the domain of my sweetheart. I love gardens and lawns, and I'm going to have flowers that bloom in every bed. What's California for, if not to have flowers? And I'll have parks with great spreading oaks. And fields planted to grains, and some good riding and carriage horses. Oh, it'll be a beauty spot, but it'll also be practical, too, returning an income."

"That's a good dream, John. You've always had a dream."

It was painful to say good-bye to the man who had included him on his gold-hunting venture, and whose kindness resulted in a fortune. They had become fast friends those months on Bidwell's Bar. But at last they shook hands, and Jarvis faced the world alone again.

The next day Jarvis caught a San Francisco–bound sloop, and distrustfully loaded a fortune in gold aboard her, and a mule to carry it. But the sullen journey down the Sacramento and across the vast bay turned out to be uneventful. The bearded master deposited him and other passengers on the tidal flats below a chaotic tent-town lining a cove. Jarvis's flesh chilled. He had never in his life seen such a motley crowd of villainous men, each more sinister than the last. Half bore wounds of some sort, missing fingers, eyes, ears, or feet. A few wore penal-colony brands on their cheeks. Most were ragged or diseased. Some plainly were cutpurses or scheming guttersnipes. But peppering the gaudy crowd were merchants in ordinary business attire, most of them speculating wildly for any cargo that reached the new Gomorrah.

He trekked the mucky streets, dodging manure, recoiling from reeking garbage, the swill of tent beaneries, and even more offensive offal. No one had paused to build an outhouse. The new burg stank.

He discovered half a dozen shops advertising various services, such as assaying, gold reduction and smelting. After several attempts, he found a man he trusted, largely because the man invited him to stay and watch the whole two-day process. The fellow, Hiram Long, wanted two hundred dollars to reduce Jarvis's sponge gold to bullion in his bellows-operated furnace. By the next noon, Jarvis's gold had been transformed into one-pound bars of pure bullion.

"Where can I store this safely?" Jarvis asked Long, after they were done.

"Not with me. On a ship, with a master you trust," Long said. "They all have strongboxes and a few still have officers aboard."

"There are lots of abandoned ships in the harbor. Is it possible to buy one—for a warehouse or a mercantile?"

Long smiled. "Half the ships lack even a master. And the other half'll have a master begging you to buy."

Jarvis knew at once what he would do. His mercantile company would need a warehouse in this port city. He would buy a ship.

At the waterfront he hailed several solemn ships and got no reply. A proud clipper swung silently on its chain, desolate and abandoned. A squat, fat-bellied vessel bobbed beside, this one with a man on it.

"What can I do for ye?" the man yelled.

"A berth for the night; store my mule and gear."

"Oh, I can do that. One pinch it'll cost ye. You supply the feed. You'll be on your own. Your vittles. Bloody damned crew. I have six and a half thousand in this bark, a fortune to make at sea, and not a whelp to sail it. Maybe you'll be my crew, eh? I'll be master, you'll be mate. And we'll send ghosts into the rigging when the wind comes up."

"I'll need a lighter."

"Naw, lad. There's a gangway on the starboard; a jury-rigged jetty across three barks that ye can use, if your dainty beast'll walk the plank." He laughed. "After ye claim a bunk, I'll break out the brandy."

Something engaging radiated from the master, and Jarvis

decided to accept. He coaxed his mule up wobbly scaffolding, across decks, and stepped onto a dark teak deck redolent with the briny sea.

A gray-bearded scarecrow fitted out in flapping blue serge and brass buttons met him. The man had been bleached by weather until his face looked like sun-checkered white paint. "Marble," said the master. "Caleb Marble, of Dilbert and Marble, Boston and Gloucester, shippers before our fat ended up in this infernal fire. This bottom's for sale, I'm for sale. We're both old and semi-sound, but the rot's not far away. Stow the beast forward, there's a ketchpen there, and throw your gear in the fo'castle."

"Maybe I'll buy. I'm Stephen Jarvis. A merchant."

Marble eyed him sharply. "Merchant? A skinny whelp is what you are, hardly off the teat. Get stowed away and meet me in my cabin, aft. A buyer, are ye? A boy wonder. Maybe I'll find some salt pork and a few biscuits and some java I picked up from the pirates of Portsmouth Square, and we'll have us a dicker."

Thus did a young man and an old salt square off over a battered galley table that exuded the aromas of tobacco and fish.

"Now, Jarvis, ye've no count to trust me, and if ye do, ye're a kangaroo's whelp. But here's how it is. My partners and I built a fat profit on this run, bringing Spanish sherry and Lowell unbleached muslin to the Californios. But we lost the damned crew. Gold! This old scow, the *Gloucester*, she's for sale, and at a loss. I've a third interest and the power to transfer title. She's on the block for three thousand Yankee dollars, and ye can send two thousand directly to my partners in Massachusetts. I'll take mine in gold. Buy 'er for three, and we're profitable, even selling the bark for half its worth. But I'll not sell at a ruin. My partners, the Dilberts, are my mast and sail and I'll not give them the worst of it. If I don't get my price I'll camp in her for a year, two years, whatever it takes to shanghai a crew and sail out. That's my offer; three thousand and no less, or I'm not a man worthy of my ship."

"I'll buy it," Jarvis said. "And I'm looking for a partner with your habits."

"Ye don't fathom all my habits. I'm fond of spirits, and sometimes they rule me." He squinted. "And that's just the tip of the iceberg."

"Would you damage your new partner?"

"I might, Jarvis. That's your bloody risk."

"Marble, I don't believe you. I'll bet the bank."

That was how Stephen Jarvis bought his second vessel, a sound, seaworthy tub capable of warehousing many tons of merchandise destined for the mining districts. And ultimately how Jarvis acquired a rancid, proud old master as his junior partner. Marble knew merchandise, knew how to fashion a ransom out of alert buying and selling, knew what gold miners would need in the camps, knew how to barter whole cargoes for better cargoes, knew how to report regularly via informal sea mail to his former partners, the Dilbert brothers of Gloucester, Massachusetts, and knew how to handle men—except when gold madness consumed them and left him beached. Thus the ambitious new California mercantile firm, Jarvis and Marble, was born over a bottle of fiery brandy, in a stout old scow that creaked and complained with the tide, that October twentieth of eighteen forty-eight.

When the grays of twilight permeated the ship's galley, the weary, stubble-jawed young man and the grizzled sea wolf had hammered out a mercantile company. The old ship would be beached for a warehouse and general offices. Jarvis would buy the sea lot where the ship would be beached, and eventually build a warehouse on it. Marble would manage from San Francisco, making opportune purchases as supplies poured in, but always with Jarvis's general plan in mind: don't speculate; obtain a wide variety of goods in demand in the mining camps, including some luxuries. Jarvis would work from Sacramento and supply the stores he would set up in the camps.

Marble's partners, the Dilbert brothers, would be reimbursed two thousand for their two-thirds share of the old ship. Marble would get a thousand clear, and work as Jarvis's partner for one-quarter of the profits. For now, the master's cabin would be the heart of an unborn empire that would acquire freight wagons, teamsters, schooners running between the Bay and Sacramento City, inventories, banking facilities, and numerous junior partners, each managing a fine tent-store in the mushrooming mining camps from the Feather River to Mariposa.

The weakness in all this, they realized, was manpower. How did you keep fickle employees in a gold rush?

"We'll keep 'em the way Sam Brannan keeps 'em," Jarvis said. "By paying them enough. That's the only way. It'll mean we'll charge high prices in the camps to cover ounce-a-day labor, but if we're on the ground floor, we'll get the trade anyway. We'll have a tent-store in place within days of every new gold strike."

But Marble had fallen asleep.

Jarvis studied the weathered man carefully. He had a ghastly pallor about him. But he seemed alive and forceful. Let him sleep.

Jarvis left him and sought out a tailor. He knew just what he wanted. He had become a man of substance, and now he would dress the part.

He found a young man working in a loft on Montgomery Street.

"I need a suit and some shirts fast. Can you do it?"

"In a week."

"I need them faster."

"It'll cost extra. I'll have to hire out some of it."

"That's not important. Fit me up in a black suit, the best, stiffest, finest wool you have. I want this suit to say something to the world. I'm going to wear this suit at my marriage, and I'll wear it in my business life. Give it a conservative cut. Make it so perfect that it draws the eye. And three white shirts, the best you can make. I want perfection."

The tailor grinned. "Clothes make the man," he said.

"Do it well and I'll order some more."

"Well, let's get some measurements," the tailor said. "And maybe we'll be fitting it on you in three days."

"That's perfect."

After that, he headed for a barber where he got himself shaved and shorn, and bought a hot-water bath, his first in years.

When he returned to the *Gloucester* that evening, Marble took one look at him and grinned. "Look at ye. I smell witch hazel. I reckon you're an ambitious man. Either that or you're going to get married."

"Both," said Stephen Jarvis.

M onterey!
Stephen Jarvis stepped from the bobbing lighter to a shaky pier. Crewmen toted his three heavy valises and a humpbacked trunk.

He felt a cramping in his chest, almost as if his heart were failing him. Behind him the bay glittered like dancing sapphires. Ahead of him stood the sleepy white village, as chill now as it was when he was a private in the presidio.

Had anything changed? Nothing within him. He was still the shy youth, the lovestruck suitor, the awkward and lonely soldier. But he wore a new suit of stiff black gabardine that announced he was a successful man. He knew he was an impostor. A year plucking gold from the gravels of the Sierra didn't make him a man of substance.

Monterey, above the rocky coast, slumbered through its siesta hours, too ancient and haughty to attend the arrival of a nouveau riche youth. Behind him, the crewmen vanished, and the lighter bobbed toward the sloop that had brought him down the cold hard coast of California.

She would not be far away; a few leagues east. The thought of Rita Concepción tripped his heart again. He wondered if he could summon the courage to visit her. How would he do it? What would he say? Who would translate for him? How would he present himself to her family? Was he presentable? And what would those haughty rancheros think of him? He knew the costly black suit wouldn't cloak his awkward ways.

But even as those desolating thoughts swarmed him like wasps, the yearning that had drawn him here flooded him anew. He was mad for her. No matter if she laughed at him, or had forgotten that galvanizing moment; no matter if her father and brothers drove him away ... no matter if she had found another. Thus did his hopes and dreams inspire a boldness he didn't normally possess.

"Ah! Señor! Qué linda día."

Jarvis beheld an ancient and bent Californio, perhaps part Indian, the color of old saddle leather.

"Qué desea usted?"

The man had a cart hooked to a pair of sorry burros. He looked guilty, as if seeking trade during the siesta hour violated the Ten Commandments.

"Uh, a hotel?"

"Sí," the old man said, hefting Jarvis's bag and trunk into his ancient cart.

Jarvis was duly deposited at Barberry House for one-half of one *real*. The *viejo* worried the bags and the trunk into a small parlor, and won himself the other half of the *real*. Then he bowed, creaking almost to the clay floor, and backed out into the chilly glare of the seaport. A melancholy mutt in a corner measured Jarvis sternly, and returned to his afternoon séance. Somehow it made Jarvis ponder his own insignificance. The dog had seen a cooper's apprentice.

In spite of the name of the hostelry, the prim proprietress spoke little English. But she managed to give him a seaview room without a lock on its door, and summon help from a scullery man to tote Jarvis's luggage up a narrow, creaky stair to his alcove.

The man muttered, no doubt at the imposition and at the weight. It was bad enough to be summoned from siesta; worse to haul bags that felt like pigs of lead.

The small room would do.

He was only a moment's walk from Thomas O. Larkin's gracious home and headquarters. In spite of his weariness, he would go there at once, driven by a need beyond reason. Who could explain what Rita Concepción meant to him? He couldn't explain it to himself. Why didn't he go east and marry some dimpled dumpling who could at least speak his tongue and share a jest? But he had long ago abandoned reason. The yearning for Rita could not be denied. The longing for her became so strong at times that he didn't know how he endured the separation. This matter wasn't complex after all; it was primeval. She was all that life offered him; for her he would give everything, do anything. Life without her wouldn't be life.

He poured water from a pitcher into a basin and splashed his face. He eyed the lockless door doubtfully. No one stole so much as a penny in Monterey, but still, all that weight must have told the porter something. It didn't matter. He had no choice. He had a quarter of his gold with him; the rest was in the *Gloucester*'s strongbox.

He stepped out of the slumbering inn and paced the familiar cocked streets, past frowning adobe walls, until he reached the home of the former American consul, now an important importer and exporter. He remembered Monterey's odd seagirt chill that made it uncomfortable every season except summer and wondered why sane people lived there when they could never get warm.

His rap wasn't answered and he wondered if Larkin slumbered away the camel's hump of each day too. But eventually Thomas O. Larkin himself opened, staring blankly at Jarvis. He ran a hand over his balding crown. "I'm my own servant from noon to four," he said.

"Mr. Larkin, I'm—"

"If you're a tradesman, come back in an hour. Better yet, don't come back unless you sell window glass. There's not a pane in California."

"I'm Stephen Jarvis. Remember me?"

Larkin peered at him. "Private Jarvis? The presidio?"

"Yes, sir. The same, but I'm, ah, in business. I want a word with you, if possible."

"Jarvis, is it? Gad, yes, that's who it is. The bookworm. Your getup confused me. I thought you were selling funeral wreaths. Yes. Come back to my lair with me. I've heard a thing or two from Sutter about you. You've got a fortune."

Hurriedly Jarvis followed his host to the bright, airy room where clipper ships were commissioned, cargoes ordered, captains sent to sea, silks from Asia and Araby purchased, and men of consequence formed alliances and levered governments.

"A lady inquires about you," Larkin said.

A flame bloomed in Jarvis. "Rita Concepción?"

"The Señorita Estrada, yes. Why on earth does she inquire? The last I knew you were a private, borrowing dull treatises from me, haunting the customs house, gleaning politics and economics, and asking astonishing questions."

"I met her when I tried to buy a horse. I—"

Larkin looked amused.

"We— Well . . ." Jarvis knew suddenly he couldn't explain himself. "We love each other," he said weakly, tossing it away as a useless bit of foolery.

Larkin smiled, swallowed back a reply, and waited for more.

Jarvis was grateful that Larkin hadn't joked away something so sacred.

"Let me pour you some port. You've obviously come in on the coaster anchored out there. Tell me. I'll listen. You no doubt want something from me that I can't give."

"Just advice, sir. And later I've some business matters. I'm in business now."

Larkin handed Jarvis a goblet of ruby fluid. "So I've heard," he said.

Stephen Jarvis sipped and talked, pulling words out of himself. The former consul took him seriously, listening to a strange story of love born of glances and yearnings and imaginings and misty promises, a love plighted between two mortals who could not even talk to each other.

"I've lived by this dream for a year, sir. If you look at it from a practical sense, it is nothing but a foolish fancy. But, sir, there comes into a man's life the mysterious, the strange and sacred. Rita is that to me, sir, beyond explaining, beyond reason."

Jarvis stumbled along, aware of his lame words, yet desperate to convey the vision that had gripped him so long.

"I fathom you want my help now. How to approach her family. What Mexican tradition requires. How to do this. Is that it?"

"Yes, sir."

"Ah, I wish I had loved like that. It's a love that other men can only envy. How can I resist helping all I can?" Larkin smiled broadly.

The warmth of that response made Jarvis dizzy. "Yes, please help me. I'll be forever in your debt."

"Your lady's here in Monterey, living with her aunt."

"Here? *Here?*"

"Two hundred yards from where we stand. She attends every Yankee affair, the balls and salons . . . my afternoon soirees. We've been busy here, you know. The constitutional convention. The November ballot. Statehood. Señorita Estrada's turned down every advance—she professes to scorn the caballeros, and she rejected a suit from Lieutenant Sherman—Mason's aide, you know. And yes, Jarvis, she's asked me about you. A word, a rumor, anything. Once I did have a bit of news from Sutter, and I passed it along. She fell into a strange silence, almost a trance. . . . Why do you peer at me like a lost puppy, Jarvis? Is this Romeo and Juliet?"

"It's more, sir. Love is not an adequate word for what we feel for each other." *She had asked after him. She had waited.*

"You're floating over the Pacific, and I'm duty-bound to bring you down to earth," Larkin said briskly. "I'll arrange the meeting but I won't guarantee the results. It needn't even be public. I'll arrange for you to see her here. I'll chaperone you, of course. I want no dishonor upon her, you, or me. And I'll translate, since you were more interested in winning gold than learning her tongue."

"Whatever you say, sir. I put first things first: I needed to offer her something more than a life as a mechanic's wife. She comes from a family . . ."

"She comes from a proud ranching family with vast riches in cattle and land, and hardly a dime in cash."

That seemed strange to Jarvis, but he nodded.

"She also comes from a Californio family that's a hotbed of anti-Yankee sentiment, a family that hatches conspiracies to free California from the United States. Her brothers write ferocious tracts and drill rancheros into cavalry dragoons even while we Yankees write a constitution and apply to Congress for admission to the Union. You'll face their opposition. And Señorita Estrada is a traditional, dutiful daughter, if I read her right. And a devout Catholic, close to a powerful clergyman here."

"What we have between us will triumph over that, sir," Jarvis said, believing it down in his bones.

"Perhaps if you elope. But if you do, the brothers'll hunt you down and take her back."

"I'll win them over . . . somehow, sir."

Larkin peered out upon the horizons that stretched to Asia. "A man bursting with a dream can do anything," he said gently. "I hope the señorita's dream is as magical as yours."

CHAPTER 44

Rita Concepción shivered. She had done that ever since she received the note from the powerful señor, Thomas O. Larkin, inviting her to his offices at four, there to meet Señor Jarvis.

That was yesterday. Now the hour approached.

"Válgame Dios!" she cried. *"Virgen santísima! Ay qué pena!"*

"What troubles you so much, *mi niña?*" asked Tía Maria. "You have been fevered all day. Perhaps we should put you to bed and spoon some soup into you."

"I am well, there is nothing wrong; I am going out," she cried.

Her aunt studied her gravely, unbelieving. "Is there something you wish to tell me?"

"He is here."

Her aunt absorbed that. "You have never talked about this one. But you have waited for him a long time. You will want a chaperone, yes?"

"I will be chaperoned."

"Will you tell me about him?"

"No, not yet. Soon. Just let me—see him."

Let me see Estéban Harvis, let me see whether this Yankee who filled my dreams for a year is the man I have waited for. Let me see whether there is any truth in my memories, whether I have invented a man who does not exist, whether his gaze, his voice, his manner, his eyes, his awkward smile are as I remember them. See whether his spirit, that ineffable thing that drew me to him long ago, is the spirit I remember, whether I was only a girl, whether he is the same, a *rico* now, once a common soldier; whether I love this real man so much my heart bursts as I loved the boy who came to the ranch to buy a horse, and who stared at me as if he had known me in a hundred past lives. *Ay de mí!* I cannot bear it. I am fevered and icy all at once.

"You are ill, Rita Concepción," her aunt said. "I will go in your place and receive this young man, whose name I do not know. He is a *yanqui*, of that I'm sure. Maybe this is not such a good thing."

"No! *Déjame.* I must go."

Her aunt laughed. "I cannot stop you."

"I am in rags. *Mira!* Look at me."

Tía Maria stared solemnly. "You have never looked so beautiful. The white dress becomes you. Your hair glows. Only your eyes show fever." She smiled softly. "Maybe this is good but your papa will not like it. You know what he thinks of the foreign devils."

Rita nodded. How well she knew.

"A protestant, I suppose. I hope you've talked to Padre Tecolote."

Rita Concepción didn't reply. She held up the tiny looking glass, aching for a full-length mirror so she might examine every faulty stitch, or adjust her hair. But her aunt had no such luxury. Maybe it was just as well. Rita stared at her face and despaired. Jarvis would not be drawn to such a plain face, with such wide lips and big eyes. Why had she ever been born?

"I will be waiting for you, little one. If you are not back when the bells ring the hour, I will come for you."

"*Ay de mí! No dame la vergüenza,* do not embarrass me." She plucked up her final garment, a tasseled rebozo of shantung, and whirled it over her bodice and then whirled it back upon her shoulders, and then over her head, and then around her honey-eyed bare arms.

She hurried past her amused aunt, down the gloomy corridor, through the salon and into the bright cold street. She was already late. Ah, Stephen Jarvis. How could you come to me like this, with no warning? She hurried along the dusty twisted alleys, arriving eventually at the noble house of the American trader and friend of the military governor. There she froze.

Within, somewhere, Stephen Jarvis, her Estéban, awaited her. Woodenly she forced herself forward, pace upon pace. Then she retreated, wild anguish welling through her. So much for Harvis. *Basta!* Then the dim image of a lonely, adoring youth came to her, and she trembled. She retraced her steps, encouraged by the vision, and knocked.

Blessedly the great trader, Larkin, opened to her, smiled, his eyes studying her until she was sure they read her every secret.

"Ah, Señorita Estrada. I feared you might not come. Your young friend paces in anguish. Come and comfort him. He needs you."

"He needs me?"

Larkin smiled softly. "It does an old man good to play the matchmaker," he said.

He led her through his airy house, with real glass windows that flooded rooms with sunlight, and into his tobacco-scented study.

Estéban stood there, solemn, unsmiling, perhaps frightened, and looking as vulnerable as tissue. She barely remembered him. This bronzed lean man in black gabardine and a stiff collar and a cravat wasn't the youth she had met and loved on the rancho a year earlier. *Estaba vestido de luto.* He seemed to be dressed in mourning.

"Rita?" he said.

"Stephen?"

Then the light rose in his eyes, and the fear left them, and she felt the light bloom in her own eyes, and the fear leave her. She felt nervous, but safe. He stepped gently to her and lifted her two hands into his own. The touch of his hard hands upon her own delighted her.

She saw in his face the things she remembered: his courtesy, his gentleness, his sadness, his awkwardness, his solitude—and his unconditional, unbridled love. *Gracias a Diós!*

"I've waited forever for this moment," he whispered. "Mr. Larkin says you know a little English."

She nodded. She had to think about the words, but she could understand. She felt his two hands holding hers, and ached to reach for him. *Ah, qué alegría!* What happiness!

She glanced about the room and discovered Mr. Larkin staring discreetly out of his window, present but granting them their privacy.

"Say to me what you think," she managed in English.

"Only that I love you. Now more than ever. I loved you from the moment we met. I love you now a thousand times more. I've spent a year preparing for this. I offer you my love, my life, my substance, my future, my prayers . . ." He stopped suddenly and glanced at Larkin, who pretended not to hear.

"*Amor mio,* you have all those things from me," she said.

"I'm not a pauper. I—I can give you the life you've enjoyed. I found gold, and now I'm starting a mercantile company. If your family opposes me, I'll do whatever's required. I'll convert to your faith if that's necessary. I'll give you half of all I possess. I'll esteem your father and your family. I'll—"

His words bewildered her. They flooded over her too fast, and she reached to fathom them, sensing what they meant, but not really knowing.

As if by magic, Larkin was translating. Estéban looked wildly frustrated, as if the translator violated something so personal that it seemed almost obscene to change it from one tongue to another. She felt it too, grateful as she was for the quiet man's help.

"Ah, Estéban," she whispered, "*querido mío.*"

"Have a seat, you two," said Larkin. "I'll sit here at my desk and translate. Don't mind me. Nothing you say to each other will ever leave this room. Your affections light candles in me, and remind me of my first moments with Mrs. Larkin." He slid gracefully around his desk and into his stiff highbacked chair, somehow making himself invisible.

"Thank you," she said.

They sat, making a stiff ritual of it, self-consciously finding postures that might convey their yearnings to each other, crossing feet, discovering they had unruly hands that had no home. She smiled suddenly, at Estéban's embarrassment and hers. He returned her smile, and sunlight rimmed the clouds on his face.

Jarvis spoke again, but she wasn't listening. She was gazing into his soul and seeing the joy and courage in it. She watched his rough hands, tradesmen's hands that had wrested gold from the gravels and had fired a musket and had fashioned staves. She watched his lips and felt an overwhelming need to press hers to them. She listened to the timbre of his voice, and found fiestas and funerals in it. She stared at his ungainly ears, and repressed a giggle. She felt the need to touch him; worse, God forgive her, to slip her hand under his stiff black suitcoat to the muscle and warmth of his back; to reach out and press herself to him . . . *Santa María!* What would she confess before Padre Tecolote?

"He is saying," said Larkin gently, "that he knows love is more than this; it is the caring and befriending and sacrificing. It is the respect. It is the sharing of decisions together. It is putting himself into the yoke of an oxen so that he may bring you comforts. This attraction he calls the passion; he will give you *amor, cariños.*"

She nodded, barely listening. She was thinking of the curly brown hair that would be on his chest, and the lightly freckled skin of this fair man, and the lean hardness of him, and the honesty of his embrace, its simple power.

Then he was speaking again, and she loved the soft rough gutturals of his voice, in that unruly tongue of his. She made herself listen this time; she desperately needed to fathom his every word. But she only caught the gist.

"He says he is going to provision the gold camps," Larkin translated. "Next year there will be a great rush, when word reaches the whole world, and he will be ready. He is done with mining now. He will throw up *mercados* in the camps, supply the miners with flour and beans and coffee and molasses and blankets and picks and cloth. He will build you a handsome home, give you your heart's desire . . ."

"I do not need anything but Estéban," she whispered weakly.

Jarvis understood that. "Tell me what I must do, then, Rita Concepción. They tell me your family might be opposed."

"Ay de mí!" she groaned. "I must persuade them that this is good for the family, and for me."

"But isn't it your choice?" he asked.

She could not answer through the tears.

CHAPTER 45

S tephen Jarvis couldn't sit still the following afternoon. He paced Larkin's office, adjusted his cravat, dusted minute flecks of dust off his stiff black suitcoat, rubbed his jaw to make sure he had scraped away the beard, and worried about how his clammy, cold hands would feel to Rita's aunt and uncle.

Larkin eyed him patiently, perhaps remembering the long-ago pangs of courtship. "Stephen," he said gently, "you also came here to do some business with me, and we've hardly had a moment to talk of it."

Jarvis paused, sensing that the change of focus might quiet his spirit. He settled into the chair across from Larkin's commodious desk, but couldn't stop his boot from tapping on the plank floor, or his knee from bouncing. The forthcoming meeting with Rita's aunt and uncle and cousins would be the first rung on the ladder.

"Yes, sir," he said. "I'm going to be a merchant to the gold camps. My year on Bidwell's Bar netted me about ninety-three thousand. But mining's not for me, sir. It's grueling, mindless work. I want to use whatever ingenuity I possess."

"You possess considerable. But business requires schooling, timing, shrewdness, and an ability to gauge the private nature of those you trade with."

"Yes, sir. I've worried about that. I've a partner I trust, a master of a charter vessel from Massachusetts. I've bought the ship for an office and warehouse in San Francisco. I bought another, a sloop, for a warehouse in Sacramento City. And paid the fellow a little to watch over it."

"That's a start. I presume you have reasons to trust the partner?"

Briefly Jarvis described what he knew of Marble, and why he brought him into the company.

Larkin nodded. "And what do you want of me?"

"Simply to purchase your imports, sir. I'll make a market for whatever you bring to California."

Larkin gazed skeptically at the young man. "Markets are not a problem for me. I've always sold everything I've imported. The Californios don't manufacture much of anything, you see. It's not in their blood. The place abounds in grapes but they import their wine. They ship out hides by the ton, but import shoes made in New England. There's not a bank in the province. They scorn banking—it's beneath them. And no proper Californio works at anything as long as he can employ an Indian or a *peón*."

"Then they're lazy, sir."

"No. The humbler classes toil themselves into an early grave. It's a matter of pride. Grubbing for money, enterprise, that's all contemptible to them. It dirties their hands."

"But why?"

"I've spent decades trying to find out. I just don't know. They depend on foreigners like me for almost everything."

"How can they be rich if they don't do business?"

"Oh, they're rich in land and cattle, but poor when it comes to cash. I trade through barter, hides mostly. They won't even operate shops if they can help it. The ones here in Monterey are largely run by foreign interests, usually Americans."

"But that's going to change, sir. There's a future in the gold camps."

"Indeed there is. Right about now, or at least in the next few weeks, word of the gold must be reaching the States. Last July, Commodore Jones—Thomas ap Catcsby Jones—sent Lieutenant Beale and a strong party across Mexico with a sample of California gold. In August, Governor Mason sent Lieutenant Loesser around the Horn with a tea caddy filled with two hundred thirty ounces of nuggets and dust—worth about thirty-five hundred dollars. They'll report to President Polk, of course. A few private letters have surely gotten through by now but no one puts much stock in letters. What I'm saying, Stephen, is that there'll be a rush soon. I won't particularly need you as a market."

That didn't discourage Jarvis. "Well, sir, what if I pay you more than my competitors? I've learned one thing: miners in remote camps'll pay any price, any price at all, for things they need. Even for things they merely fancy, like a tin of sardines or a straw hat. If they lack a shovel or a pan or a pick, or a blanket or a shirt, or boots, it doesn't matter what the price is: they can always make the price by panning more gold."

Larkin swiveled around, peering out the window awhile, steepling his hands. "Very well. You've been in the camps long enough to know what miners want. You know them better than I do. As soon as I was certain the gold strike amounted to something, I chartered several bottoms, seven I believe, and commissioned their masters to barter on my account. The States, you know, are farther from California than other sources. My best suppliers are Chile, for foodstuffs, and various areas of Mexico—especially Durango and the Federal District—for various manufactures. And I sent one vessel up to Oregon for whatever could be gotten. I don't rightly know what'll come in, but my list includes flour, coffee, sugar, tea, and so on; knives, picks, shovels, pans, pitchers, basins, duck cloth, chambray and other cotton fabrics, blankets, flannels, ready-made clothes, needles and thread—you name it."

"You chose well, sir. I'd add luxuries. And spirits. There's many a miner who strikes a pocket, puts a few ounces in his poke, and wants a good whiskey, or a book, or a glass of buttermilk, or something to send to his wife."

Larkin reached across his desk for a quill, dipped it into an inkpot, and scratched a note to himself. "It's time to go," he said. "But I'll tell you now, Jarvis, you've a head on you, and we'll do business. If you can actually put goods into the gold camps next year, ahead of the pack—and you've hardly begun to build a system to do it—we'll both profit." He stood. "Let's go woo the señorita and her relatives. I'll translate and keep out of the way."

Jarvis stood, feeling a flood of anxiety again. Larkin led him across the plaza, toward the low, whitewashed casa of the tobacco and wine merchant José Jesús Chávez and his wife Maria Guadalupe, and innumerable children, younger cousins of Rita Concepción. The afternoon sun heated Jarvis's black suit. He felt out of control. He had come to court the girl of his heart, and now this quest had fallen into the maw of an extended family.

"Let me tell you a bit about the Mexicans," Larkin said as

they paced. "The first thing a Yank should know is that they're a modest people, in spite of rumors to the contrary about fandangos and wild times. They live according to the spiritual precepts of the Roman church. Not like New England puritans, mind you, but with a keen sense of morality and propriety—which barely contains their Latin passions. All this is necessary. If you court a Mexican maid, you court her family. And the outcome is a family decision."

"I hadn't thought of that, sir. I just want her. I've wanted her ever since we met. That's all I've wanted since I came here."

The older man eyed the younger one, and stopped in the middle of the plaza. Polite children, posturing as adults, stared at them; they seemed so unlike the scampering ones Jarvis knew from his youth in the States. "Stephen, I'll be candid. Love at first sight happens, and it's one of life's mysteries and miracles. But it hardly seems the basis for marriage. You've never even talked to one another except through a translator."

"I know that, sir. But I conceive of all this as prelude. We'll become friends. We'll share dreams. We'll be partners. That's what marriage comes to, friends and partners."

"Stephen, it's not you I'm worrying about. You've shown me a maturity, an understanding. It's Rita Concepción I worry about. She's had no mother to guide her in these matters. She's very vulnerable. She's fashioned an adolescent passion out of a chance meeting with a romantic stranger, a foreigner. She lived in a womanless house, except for her poor daft grandmother. In a Mexican home a daughter learns certain things from a mother. How to separate worthy men from the goats. Things like that. But neither her father nor her brothers have ever perceived her as a woman, or granted her a life. I think maybe this girlish passion might vanish in a cloud of dust, Stephen."

The older man's gravity gave Jarvis pause. "I hope not, sir," Jarvis mumbled.

"Just remember she's lacked a mother, and she's an innocent. There may be no love at all—real love—in her." He smiled wryly. "Ah, now I've dampened your spirits. It's an older man's vice. There's one other thing I'd better warn you about. They won't approve of your grubbing for gold. That sort of thing's beneath them. You would have been better off presenting yourself to the family as a discharged soldier with no prospects and mad for their daughter, than as a laborer, a *trabajador*, who slaved in the goldfields."

That stunned Jarvis. "But I can offer her everything. Comfort. Position."

"All of that's meaningless to them, Stephen, because in their minds it's ill-gotten. They're a peculiar people."

A bleakness grew in Jarvis's soul as they reached the casa across the plaza. Larkin rapped sharply on a heavy door hung on ornate iron hinges.

An older woman opened and rattled on in Spanish, eyeing Jarvis intensely even as she welcomed Larkin. She wore what must have been church clothes, a black silk dress with voluminous skirts and a high neckline. On her bosom rested a silver crucifix. A gossamer rebozo wrapped her shoulders. A mother-of-pearl comb lifted her glossy jet hair. She nodded again, her liquid brown eyes gravely measuring Jarvis, and Larkin led him into a salon, bristling with formality; obviously a place rarely visited except when guests were being entertained.

He saw no sign of Rita Concepción there. Only a blocky graying man, dressed in black cutaway, his stiff collar digging cruelly into his weathered neck, his face puffy. Jarvis had the sinking sensation that this was already going badly; that he would be the subject of a formal examination that would cover his whole life, even if the questions were polite and indirect.

"Will Miss Estrada join us?" he asked tightly.

Larkin explained. "She's indisposed, they tell me. But they wish to make the acquaintance of the gentleman who wants her hand in the sacrament of marriage."

She wouldn't even be there. These strangers would entertain him. Jarvis perched gingerly on a stiff chair, one of those straight-backed Mexican ones intended to impose penance on slouching bodies. No wonder these people had such marvelous carriage: proud, erect, dignified, commanding. They could do no less, after being raised upon such furniture.

The señora produced some tea, which she wheeled in on an ornate tea cart inlaid with ivory. With studied formality she poured cups for each and handed them out. Jarvis took his as one takes the sacrament.

They sipped. A salt breeze slid through the salon.

Thomas O. Larkin, man of affairs, set down his cup, nodded amiably at Jarvis, and addressed his hosts in Spanish for a long time. He turned to Jarvis. "I've simply told them about you; that you've done well in the goldfields, and you're becoming a man of parts in California."

Chávez spoke at length, while Larkin nodded.

"He says he wasn't always a wine and tobacco merchant. Before the conquest, he was an inspector at the customshouse, for the colonial administration of Governor Pio Pico—an important post, with high honor—and now is much reduced to being a merchant, but that is the hardship of the affairs of nations that grind up men. He says his blood is purest Castilian, his family comes from Avila and he counts the great saint, Teresa of Avila, in his family tree. He says the Estrada blood is mostly Castilian, though there is a mad strain of Andalusian in it that he suspects is gypsy, though he is sure his wife would deny it, which is why the daughters of that line are impulsive and hard to control. He says the wine business is a temporary expedient until he can work out something with the Republic of Mexico. He hopes to become a consul here, representing his former nation, as I represented the United States to the Californios. He wishes to learn about your blood."

"Well, I'm just a regular American, English mostly but a little Dutch, like all those people in New York, and I set out to make something of myself—Mr. Larkin, just tell him I'm a sincere admirer of Rita Concepción, and I'll give her a good home and don't need a dowry—"

Larkin lifted a hand. "Not yet, Stephen. These are not her parents. Consider this an exchange of credentials. Your pedigree, their pedigree."

"The last thing I have is a pedigree, Mr. Larkin."

"I understand that. But they want to know everything to know."

"Just tell them I love her. I saw her and loved her and never stopped. Just tell them I've wrestled gold out of cold streams for a year for her. She loves me, too. She's the woman of my heart, my one and only love, and I'll become whatever I must become, if I may win her."

Reluctantly, Larkin did, while Rita's aunt and uncle listened solemnly.

Then Larkin translated. "He can't understand why you would do that, dig in the goldfields, a laborer. Such things must be done by those whose calling it is. Grubbing out gold does not mean anything to an old Californio family. Surely it was a mistake, but probably one that can be forgiven in a man so young and inexperienced, especially after common service as a soldier. Now, if your father had been an official, a man under the seal of service to the government . . ."

"He died when I was a child."

They whiled away another half hour, the Chávezes turning the conversation this way and that, but never again toward Stephen and Rita.

"When may I see her?" he asked hoarsely, at the moment of parting.

"Young lovers are kept apart for the good of their souls," Larkin translated. "It is necessary, so that they may form a sure and Christian perception of each other. She will consult with her priest about all such matters, because the Catholic Church offers counsel beyond the wisdom of mere mortals."

"I must see her."

"Perhaps you will. Abide in their ways, Stephen, and perhaps the blessings you seek will come."

CHAPTER 46

T he note, in Spanish, invited Rita Concepción to join Stephen for a *paseo*, a stroll, that evening. He would be waiting at the plaza at the hour of eight.

Tía Maria handed it to Rita in her room, and waited. "It came from Larkin's clerk, but it is from the man," she said. She had been referring to Jarvis as "the man." She waited for Rita to read it and didn't budge. Reluctantly, Rita handed it to her. There could be no secrets where a suitor was involved.

She sniffed. "You will need a *dueña*. I suppose I can find the time. Do not walk too fast, now. I cannot keep up anymore. And not too long. I will be worn out. *Y yo no hablo inglés.*"

"He does not understand the Spanish," Rita replied.

"Well, do not cause a scandal. You must pray to your name-saint, Rita of Cascia, for counsel. Or to the Virgin. Maybe it is not so bad, but *Dios mío!* What a trial you put on us."

Rita smiled. Her aunt was sorely divided by all this, and had become rather grouchy. Maria was her father's youngest sister, and had never really been close to Juan Carlos because of the difference in their ages. One moment, Maria's eyes would light up at the thought of Rita's *yanqui* swain; the next moment all the duties and prohibitions of family and church would overwhelm her, and she'd frown disapprovingly at Rita and "the whole mad business."

"The note says no answer is required," Rita said. *"Con su permiso*, I will enjoy the stroll."

Her heart leapt at the prospect. The introduction of Estéban Harvis to her aunt and uncle had been draped in black crepe, and she despaired that she would ever hear from Jarvis again. Why were things so difficult? Why did custom make her so helpless? Why could she not choose her mate? She knew the answer, of course. Marriages, especially of daughters, were political and social alliances, measures of status and honor, matters that required the approval of the church, bonds that demanded the finest moral scruples. These things had wrought many a tear in many a Mexican maiden, but they were all for the good. Wise counsel was superior to momentary passions. And many a maiden who had wept for a forbidden beau had come to understand the wisdom of her elders who had arranged a good marriage to someone more suitable.

Maybe this would be her fate, too, Rita thought. She felt so helpless. What if they drove him away with all their funereal disdain? She couldn't bear the thought of not having Jarvis, her sweet, beautiful man. And if they all said it was not love, but just a girl's frivolous passion, she would scorn them. She would even laugh at Padre Tecolote if he told her such a thing, God forgive her for such a thought. She did not mean to resist; surely she could be a good daughter of the family Estrada, and see heaven and God someday safe within the church. *Ay qué pena!*

That sleepy afternoon she dressed nervously for the *paseo*, unhappy with her wardrobe, and unhappy with her face and form. She was so plain. Her hair was the color of a mouse. And it ricked up where it should lie smooth. And her emerald silk rebozo had a stain she'd never seen before. How could that happen?

She found Tía Maria waiting for her at the door, wreathed in black and white lace, as formidable as the Empress Victoria of the *ingléses*. She had costumed herself to terrify Jarvis, and no doubt would. He was a shy man, not timid but reserved and tongue-tied. Tía Maria would stare imperiously at him, like a queen upon a vassal, and ice crystals would form around the courtship of Señorita Estrada and Señor Jarvis, the American.

They pierced into chill twilight, and found him on the plaza. He wore that stiff black suit again, the suit of deceptions that made him look like a grave old man. It fell like a wall between her and the shy man within it. As usual, many Montereños were out taking the air, gossiping, seeing who was walking with whom, and studying foreigners. Nothing in the life of Rita Estrada would escape their sharp eyes and sharper tongues.

She felt the ache she always did when she saw him, the fear and the meltingness, the yearning to be held, the need to chatter, and somber silences, the helplessness and dread, all at once.

"Ah, you came," he said, looking surprised. "And how good of you to accompany us," he said to Tía Maria, who didn't understand a word but did understand his courtesy. He was holding something wrapped in paper.

"See, I've purchased some chocolates for all of us," he said, offering a treat to the chaperone first.

"He offers me chocolates. How could he know I am a fool for chocolate? *Dios mío!* He is a seducer," Tía Maria rattled.

"She gives you the thanks, Harvis," Rita said.

From within his paper he produced something more: a white camellia for Tía Maria and another for Rita Concepción. "Something for your hair," he said.

"What did that rogue say?" Tía Maria whispered, as if whispering were necessary.

"Para su pelo, Tía," Rita said. "Let me tuck it in."

"Oh, that rogue, *tan scandaloso,*" Tía Maria said. "The Virgin save us."

"She says you have the good taste," Rita Concepción whispered to Jarvis, and wondered why she was whispering.

"May I?" he said, taking the other camellia. She stood numb with eagerness as he gently thrust the stem into a roll of her tightly bound hair. Then he stepped back and studied her. "You are beautiful, Rita Concepción," he said, his voice as tender as the petals of the flowers.

"*Pícaro, pícaro,*" Tía Maria muttered. "Foreign heretic devil. *Sin vergüenza.*"

Amiably they took their stroll, several times about the bustling plaza, past old whitewashed adobes, past a few shops still open, mostly run by foreigners, past the tobacco and wine shop run by Tío José Jesús, past caballeros who eyed Jarvis maliciously, though she was sure he didn't notice. And immediately behind, never yielding a yard, vigilant as the Inquisition, walked her aunt, spreading and shutting her pearl-handled fan, waving it over her face, her fierce gaze upon one and the other, conjuring every English word they spoke to each other into seductions and rapes and knavery—except when Jarvis turned and smiled at Tía Maria, and then she smiled back, as if she were the one being seduced, holding her opened fan to her face.

They could say so little. Rita listened carefully and spoke hesitantly. He talked slowly, but lost her in a sea of confusions.

"I should've learned your language," he said. "I was so busy in the goldfields I plumb didn't have time."

"You must learn. If you love me, you will learn," she said. "*Quiero decir,* I want to say—*como se dice?* It is like in the convent. I am behind the wall." She blinked back tears of frustration.

"I'll start tonight," he said. "Mr. Larkin says that I would have had a better chance if I'd just come to you as a penniless discharged private, but I couldn't. I had to do it this way, you see. . . ."

She barely grasped what he was about, but she gazed up at him, her eyes swimming with love, listening to the timbre of his voice and its tumble of strange words, yearning for him so much she ached, and hating having Tía Maria puffing along behind like a rowboat behind a galleon. Surely if her aunt weren't present, she would hurry him into a darkened street, turn and kiss him madly.

He found her hand with his and grasped it. Rita heard a

shocked clucking from behind, but she clung to his all the more fiercely. It was the first time, except for that mad kiss, he had touched her, and now the warmth of his palm and fingers, so strong and powerful, shot delight through her.

They did one more turn, but the plaza had mostly emptied and the citizens of Monterey were heading to their homes for their usual late supper.

"It is time for the *paseo* to end," Tía Maria announced in a stentorian voice.

"I guess she wants you home," Jarvis said. "I've so many questions, Rita Concepción. What's coming next? I'd just like to get to know you. Can we talk some? In your parlor? Will I meet your father? Your brothers? Can I talk to your padre? I'm willing to do whatever it takes—"

"Ah, Estéban, it is . . . difficult. Word has been sent to the rancho Estrada. Maybe they will come to Monterey. Maybe not. Maybe they will say no. My mama—she is dead long ago. But now I have a—how do you say? New mother. My father, Juan Carlos Estrada y Portola marry now. I do not know her. She is . . . *fuerte, tiene mucha fuerza.*"

"Well, what can I do, Rita? Anything. I don't want a dowry. I just want to win your people. Show them I can be a good husband and provider."

"Suffer my bro . . . bro . . . *hermanos.*"

"Your brothers?"

"*Sí!* They do not like to be under the rule of *yanquis.*"

"What can I do?"

"Do not let them insult you. They will find the ways. To prove you are a bug. Be *muy macho! Muy fuerte.*"

"I don't know how to be that," he said.

"*Andale!*" said Tía Maria.

"I go now, Harvis," she said softly.

She ached for a kiss. She saw uncertainty in his face and stood still, her every fiber crying for him. He looked uncomfortable, all too aware of her aunt who had screwed up her face to look as formidable as possible. Then, as if he had made a decision, he pulled her to him and gently pressed his lips to hers.

"I love you," he whispered.

"*Amor mío,*" she whispered.

"Basta. Basta. Vámanos," said Tía Maria, but not unkindly, and with a tone of sweet patience.

Rita was glad night had fallen so she could kiss Harvis properly without causing a scandal. With that thought to encourage her, she did. And he did.

CHAPTER 47

Jarvis waited impatiently at Barberry House for word from the Estradas, and when it came at last, through Larkin, it dismayed him. The Estradas wished to meet this suitor of their daughter on November twentieth, at the Monterey home of José Jesús Chávez.

That was a long time away. The family was in no hurry to meet him and was not inviting him to the rancho. He didn't know what all that meant, exactly, or whether the family was deliberately making him cool his heels. The Californios lived according to their own rhythms.

He pushed aside his impatience, and saw good in the delay. For one thing, his evening *paseos* with Rita had turned out to be the joy of his life. He never failed to court Tía Maria, offering her chocolates, pastries, and little things he picked up in the *mercados*. And as for Rita, he loved her more each day. When they couldn't converse, they taught each other words and phrases. Jarvis's fund of Spanish words grew daily, and her English kept pace. Tía Maria became a boon companion, enjoying her role as a permissive *dueña*, enjoying even the farewell kiss each evening, and sighing as if such a treasure should be visited more often upon herself.

The long days of waiting turned out to be profitable too, though at times Jarvis chafed to be about his business in San Francisco and Sacramento City. He heard regularly from Marble, and grew to admire the partner's genius. The old vessel was now beached on the waterfront and impervious to the tides. He had cut down the masts and traded the wood for shelving that now lined the hold. He had converted the sails into shelf stock to sell in the camps as tenting. He had acquired large quantities of additional sailcloth cheap from the masters of abandoned ships, and had commissioned some seamstresses to sew stout ready-made tents from it, to sell in the camps. A smith in the area was cobbling together shovels and picks, while a tinsmith was manufacturing goldpans. And he had purchased what he could, including the few blankets available.

All that was heartening Jarvis and yet he wished he could be there, applying his overflowing energies, creating a company that would reach into every gold camp when the real rush began.

He sought out Larkin almost daily, not only to do business with the importer-exporter, but also to fathom what he could of the Californios.

"Why can't a man and a woman just decide for themselves to get married?" he asked the older man on an overcast afternoon.

"Stephen, you must accustom yourself to a different culture, with different values. For Californios, the church comes first. Always. Reaching heaven. Going to God. Reverencing the Virgin. Obeying their spiritual mentors, whose approval not only ensures joy in this life, but the ultimate ascent to God, and being with Him in the next. A natural authority exists among them, running from the bishops and priests to the heads of families. These men, very like Juan Carlos Estrada, have an unquestioned power to decide what is best for their sons and daughters."

"Sons, too?"

"Many a son's marriage is arranged, Stephen. Often the bridegroom doesn't meet the bride until the time when they are to be wed."

"But what about love? What if they break Rita's heart? Is there no recourse?"

"Not for a proper young woman. No. But the system is rarely so . . . rigid. Let a daughter grieve, and her parents may try to make amends. The mothers especially set to work on the fathers and even the priests, and who knows? Remember, too, the Mexicans love a love match, love lovers. So don't despair, Stephen. Be patient. Many a Yank like you has been invited into a Californio family. There must be a dozen right here in Monterey."

It didn't console Stephen that the Estrada men would decide the fate of his suit. He felt helpless. What right did Juan Carlos Estrada have to intervene, anyway? He also found himself razor-edged sensitive to criticism. All the while he waited, the Estradas were examining him like a hanging beef carcass, gently probing his past, listening to Tía Maria, maybe even quietly discovering what they could from Thomas Larkin. Jarvis felt prickly about it.

By the time the family gathering rolled around, Jarvis had slid into a mood that gyrated between the elation of being with Rita, to a dread of the squint-eyed ordeal he faced. But as the hour approached, he resolutely groomed himself, brushed off his severe suit, donned his cravat, combed his unruly hair, wished his ears didn't stick out, and set sail across the square for the forbidding Chávez casa just off of it.

He would be alone. Larkin hadn't been invited. He didn't know who would translate. He stood at the massive door at last, engulfed by his own shyness. Why had he been born tongue-tied and bashful? These proud people would admire a proud man who stood tall, radiated ease and grace, and commanded respect. And what would they see, instead? A homely frightened fellow. But maybe it wouldn't be so bad. They would look him over, he would look them over, and then his fate would be out of his hands.

He knocked.

José Jesús Chávez opened to him. The man of this household had donned his finest finery, including a gray frock coat, red sash, black velvet *pantalones*, and shoes gauded with shining brass buckles. His pomaded black hair gleamed; his observant, intelligent eyes radiated good cheer.

"Bienvenidos, señor," he said, waving Jarvis in.

Jarvis found himself being escorted to the salon again, where a large crowd waited him. There they were, the Estradas, from an elderly vacant-eyed woman to alert young men to an imperious dowager whose gazed sucked in everything there was to know about Stephen Jarvis in a fraction of a second. And there, too, was Rita Concepción, looking radiant in a white dress that reminded Stephen of weddings or maybe first communions or other things sacred. Over her shining brown hair lay a delicate white mantilla that framed her face so beautifully Jarvis wanted to cry out. Rita smiled desperately. Blood was in her cheeks, nervousness in her hands.

"Rita Concepción," he said.

"Estéban, my own Harvis," she said. "Come, meet."

Thus did he meet the family, one by one, the names distinct on Rita's tongue so he would grasp them. Juan Carlos Estrada y Portola, the saturnine patriarch, formidable but with a kindness of eye; Hector, who radiated hauteur and malice and missed nothing; the former doña Socorro Valenzuela, now the new Señora Estrada, inscrutable and reserved and full of mysterious nuances, all in black, including an ebony crucifix, as if life itself were a funeral. The ancient one, Rita's grandmother, her spirit already in heaven according to Rita; her name, the doña Teresa Portola. She alone went beyond greetings, to address him with words he didn't grasp, and fold his hands in her frail ones.

Then the younger brothers, Benito and Santiago, stocky, friendlier of eye than Hector, and bright with curiosity. Both of them had dressed gaudily, with embroidered vests, red sashes, and soft doeskin shoes made by Indians. Jarvis fathomed warmth, even friendship there; certainly not the hostility he had steeled himself to expect. These two seemed to be rustics, more at home on the rancho than in Monterey.

And there was one other. Jarvis found himself being introduced to a formidable man wearing the collar of Rome, a black cassock, a large silver crucifix, and black boots; stocky, middle-aged, gray at the temples, his nose hooked like a beak, his eyes staring. Padre Tecolote. Of course, of course, Jarvis thought: the family priest, whose counsel would be crucial here.

"The Reverend Father Juan Montalvo Pérez," Rita was saying.

"I'm honored to meet you, sir," Jarvis said. The man's hand gripped his in jaws of steel.

The priest smiled, the English beyond him.

Swiftly he was reintroduced to Rita's nieces and nephew, and then Rita was finished. Her gaze, so liquid and melting, cheered him. She was radiating some mysterious joy that made all the light in the room gather about her. She gave out a heady fragrance sweeter than any perfume, now sandalwood, now bayberry, now sagebrush, now orange blossoms, now the smell of the earth after a deluge.

She approached, and slid an arm clad in white silk, a nuptial arm, through his, and led him to a table in the adjoining room laden with sweets and steaming pots of coffee. He wondered what might come next; whether he would be grilled about his background; whether the priest would explore his beliefs, his willingness to convert, his Protestant attitudes toward the Church of Rome. But none of that happened. They nibbled at the mountain of sweets and the light pastries, sampled chocolate and mocha, sipped a spicy punch. They could not address him, but he felt their polite gazes pause and then dart away. Those gazes paused long and frankly upon Rita, perhaps because they had never seen her glow the way she did. But only the old woman, Teresa, seemed to bestow her benevolence on them. She smiled at him and murmured things he desperately wished to understand. She clasped Rita's hands and whispered things to her until they both giggled. The sight made Hector scowl, while the doña Socorro stared with a blankness that exuded enigmas. What was she thinking?

Jarvis wanted especially to talk with the priest, but could find no way to bridge the gulf. Still, for a while he sought the padre's company, and the good father accepted him cheerfully, his thoughtful gaze on Jarvis now and then, the company unbridged by talk the whole time.

Time edged by, conversation lagged, and it occurred to Jarvis that they were waiting for him to leave before they, the collective hosts, went their own way.

He took Rita Concepción away from a lively conversation with Benito. She was so animated her eyes seemed twice their normal size, and he felt her glow warm him.

"I must go now," he said. "I fear I've overstayed."

She nodded, led him through his round of farewells, and saw him to the door. It had turned dark and chill, and as he left, a fierce loneliness engulfed him like a shore wind.

He hoped he would hear from the Estradas soon.

But two weeks slid by like crawling snails, and he heard

nothing. The sun hid in the south, and the winter solstice neared, and still no answer arrived.

"They take their time, Stephen," Larkin said. "Their way is to let nature take its course. Be grateful for the *paseos* with our dear Rita and let the rest come as it will."

But something was going wrong with the evening strolls, too. Rita seemed pale and withdrawn, her gaze upon things beyond his seeing. And Tía Maria seemed a stranger.

Then, as Christmas approached, he received his answer.

CHAPTER 48

The news came to Rita Concepción before the holy feast of Christmas, and during an all-day pilgrimage to San Carlos Borromeo Mission out on the peninsula at Carmel. There the don and doña Chávez, their family and niece, repaired on an Advent sabbath to renew their life in their church.

Rita always had loved this mysterious and sacred place, with its great dome tipped by a melancholy cross, enshrouded so often with mist off the sea. The red-tiled mission lay in a hazy valley that seemed never to warm, and always to hold secrets beyond knowing, kept by the dead. She had been there many times, always to reverence the great Carmelite father Junipero Serra, who had brought the Holy Faith to Alta California and the Indians. She paused before a lovely image of the Virgen de Guadalupe, lovely before her gilded sunburst, to utter a small, desolate plea.

"Blessed Mother," she whispered. "I love Estéban. I can never stop loving him. It is in my soul, this love. Pity me." But somehow she sensed she would not be happy with what was to come.

Her aunt and uncle left her alone with Padre Tecolote, no doubt by some design conceived within the family. She knew even before she set foot in the ebony carriage that she would receive her answer at the mission.

The padre's cheery manner seemed forced this day, she thought as he led her to a lovely bench in the sunlight, where they might escape the December sea-chill and the relentless mist. She had long known this man, and she read the signs. Some things he did naturally and with an ingrained authority. Other duties of his office came hard, and then he was masked. Today, she thought uneasily, the padre wore a cheerful mask.

"Y la familia, como están? And how are your family?" he asked her, as they settled in the stingy sun in a weeping courtyard.

"You should know; you've talked to my father more recently than I have," she retorted.

He laughed. "My dear child, I have at that. And about your future."

She waited, a small, still fist lying in her chest.

"A fine young man, this Jarvis. A young man of piety and courage and honesty and industry, so I am told by the American, Larkin. An opinion I cherish, and so does Juan Carlos Estrada y Portola."

"I am glad you like him," she said softly.

"Yes, I liked him. So do all of your family, or, ah, almost all. Jarvis cuts a respectable figure. No wonder you are infatuated. A foreigner, a man to stir a woman's romantic imagination. Someone different and exotic, and alien, especially to a young señorita on a distant ranch, far from the busy world."

"Do I have my father's blessing?" she asked directly.

"Ah, yes, perhaps. Things are not yet settled. What he said to me was, let her wait awhile. Let a year pass. These sudden lurches of the heart often come to nothing, and she might find herself trapped and bitter, in holy wedlock with a man she cannot even talk to, a prisoner of a girlish fancy."

She shook her head. "No, padre, I am sure. I would like to post the banns. There is no need—"

"Ah, Rita, for the sake of your soul, you will kindly heed the counsel of your loving father, whose decision is tender and merciful. He would prefer you marry a Mexican, of course, one of your own. Yet he has not said nay to you."

"And what if I don't wait?" she cried. "What if I flee to Estéban?"

The padre stared into the mists, as if to distill wisdom from

them. *"Mira,* it is so. When we first talked, child, I told you I
have learned never to resist Cupid but to watch and wait and see
what our Heavenly Father has in mind. So it is now. Surely you
have sought the help of your favorite saint, and all the hosts of
heaven. Surely they would have changed your father's mind if
it were the will of God above. I think perhaps a willful daughter might be putting her soul at risk."

"What does the doña say?"

"Your father's new wife thinks Señor Jarvis is common. He
is a *trabajador* in a fine black suit, a laborer dressed like a professor at the University of Salamanca, that is what she said.
And I know her words count heavily with Juan Carlos."

"What else?" Rita asked tightly.

"The doña thinks that Jarvis has no good blood. What has he
done but grovel in the goldfields, doing demeaning work that
no respectable person would ever do? And now he is taking this
gold and making a business instead of living at his leisure. His
god is wealth, worldly things, and his eyes do not gaze upon the
heavenly rewards. She has a point. You are a Californio of good
family, and she is simply protecting you from an ill-conceived
passion."

So, she thought, it was worse than Padre Tecolote let on at
first. At least he was being candid, even if he did reveal things
layer by layer, as if he were peeling an onion.

"Your brother Hector, of course, would not be reconciled at
all. The hardness of his heart disturbs me, and I will speak to
him of it. For him, your Jarvis is not merely a Protestant
heretic, but a fiend incarnate, a conqueror whose boot presses
upon the face of our people."

"That is Hector," she said wearily.

The priest eyed her. "Yes, that is Hector. And as the elder
son, he is not without influence. He has proposed something
that is gaining favor at the rancho Estrada, and perhaps it will
be a difficult moment for you."

"What?" she asked sharply.

"A marriage to one of our own . . ."

"No!"

". . . to a young caballero you have not met, but who is perfectly suited for you, and for the family Estrada."

"Who is this?"

The padre threw up his hands. "It is not for me to say. Your good and gentle father is considering it, but for the moment his word is to wait. If Hector has his way, in a few weeks—surely before Lent—you will be given into a happiness blessed by your entire family."

"No! I will not. I cannot." She leapt to her feet.

The priest blinked owlishly. "You are a spirited young woman," he said gently. "But listen carefully and reverently. They are thinking of you."

"Who is going to tell Estéban?" she shot at him.

He shrugged. "They do not speak his tongue. It is up to you. Or I will do it with the help of Señor Larkin."

"I will not. He will not hear it from my lips. They can tell him themselves."

Padre Tecolote pondered that, smiled, and escorted her back to her aunt and uncle, whose sharp eyes betrayed them. They had obviously been a party to all this.

During the long carriage ride to Monterey, she struggled to hide her feelings from them, but failed. Tears wet her cheeks, making her cousins nudge each other. But she did not care. Let them see her wounds. Like the nails of the Christ.

So, Hector and Socorro had done this, she thought. They had rejected Jarvis without a second thought, and worked on her father. Their real intent was to marry her off to some caballero, and doom her love of Jarvis in a spider's web of family interests, the authority of the church, and a simmering hatred of the Americans. She despised the stepmother she scarcely knew, and her brother, too. So that was what they thought of Jarvis. A *trabajador* in a fancy suit. He didn't stand a chance. They had rejected him before they had met him. He was a *yanqui*.

She drew her black angora rebozo about her to ward off the damp sea-chill, but it did no good. She had no heat within her; her heart had gone cold and her blood had congealed.

For two days she declined to take her evening *paseo* with Stephen Jarvis. She scarcely ate, and spent her hours staring at the mysterious and meaningless sea. Some caballero, off on some rancho somewhere, would be her husband, and she would submit her body and will and soul to him. She fasted, looked for ways out, examined the hold that the Holy Church and her father and stepmother had over her, knowing she must surrender. But mostly she slept, the darkness of the season matching the darkness of her soul.

Then, at Tía Maria's prompting, she met her beloved Jarvis, knowing she would relent and tell him. She didn't want Padre Tecolote to do it.

He peered at her in the chill of the early twilight. "My dear Rita," he said, as she took his arm. "I thought I'd die if I didn't see you soon." He stared sharply, seeing the darkness in her face. "Where's your aunt?"

"I am alone."

His face lit. "Could it be? We don't need a chaperone? Have your people given us their blessing?"

"Ah, Estéban," she sighed. She could not say anything. They walked solemnly through the December gloom, the chill salt air pinching her cheeks red.

"It doesn't sound good," he said softly.

"Ah, Virgen Santísima!"

He drew her closer, and she felt his strength and warmth through her scratchy black cape. She couldn't yet bear to let him know. Nor could she tell him the whole of it. They rounded the plaza two or three times, and then, freed of Tía Maria, he steered her past the old customshouse and down the narrow path to the bay, where the cold black water lapped hollowly on the rocky strand. A band of blue still lingered in the southwest.

"Tell me, Rita," he said.

"They want us to wait."

He pulled back so he could peer into her eyes. "That's not so bad. I feared I'd lost you."

"It is bad, *querido mío*."

"But we can wait. And I understand. They want us to make sure."

"No, they want us to lose interest."

He laughed softly. "Nothing on earth could make me lose interest in you. You are present when the sun rises and when it sets, and in my nights, and in my thoughts all day. No, Rita, we have nothing to worry about."

"Yes, we do."

"How long do they want us to wait?"

"A year."

"Who are you speaking of? Who brought this to you?"

"Father Montalvo. The family is divided."

"I can understand that, too. Well, Rita, I'll show them I can be a worthy suitor. I don't want to wait; I want to meet you at the altar and pledge myself to you forever, and hear the words from your lips. . . . But if we must wait, I'll put my company together, visit here as often as I can, and make the time pass. Then you can tell them we are certain. Mark my words. In the spring we'll hear the mission bells ring."

She began to sob. He tried to comfort her, but couldn't.

CHAPTER 49

A fter spending the first hours of 1849 with Thomas Larkin and his family, Stephen met Rita Concepción for a last *paseo*.

She looked pale when she joined him on the plaza, and she kept gazing at him from eyes rimmed with pain. New Year's Day proved to be mild and sunny, but she wisely wore her cape against the chill of the sea. He led her in taut silence in a new direction, out the peninsula, along a rough livestock trail marked by black rock and stunted pines and sharp, eddying air. She clung tightly to his arm, her grip desperate, her eyes often seeking his as they left Monterey behind them.

They reached a prospect where the sea glittered beneath, and green slopes loomed at their rear and bristling copses of pines guarded their privacy. He stopped there and faced her. She turned to him as he took her into his arms and pressed his lips to her soft, eager ones. They clung desperately, while chill and hostile winds blew around them, as if to cool their ardor. Then she pushed herself free, her face torn between joy and despair.

"Válgame Dios!" she cried. Tears spilled down her wind-reddened cheeks. *"Querido, querido mío,* Stephen Jarvis." She rubbed her tears away.

She held him before her, her luminous eyes absorbing everything about him, while the wind rippled her hair.

"I love you even more than the day we met, and that day I loved you forever," he said.

"Amor tan precioso, tan caro," she replied. "Such a precious love, so dear."

From a pocket in her black skirts she extracted a small paper-wrapped packet and pressed it into his hand. He pulled the paper loose and discovered an ornate silver locket. He slid a thumbnail under the lid and lifted it, discovering a breathtaking miniature of her within. The artist had caught her pride, her great brown eyes, the luster of sun upon her deep brown hair, and her imperious gaze.

"Rita," he whispered. "I will carry it with me always."

"Yes! *Siempre!* " she cried. *"No me olvida usted.* Do not forget me."

He puzzled at that. "I'll be back soon," he said gently. "As soon as your family's satisfied about your feelings."

"Vaya con Dios," she whispered. "Go with God."

"I will, and may He watch over you every moment I'm away."

"Ah, Estéban!" she cried. He could not fathom her mood. This would only be a temporary parting; in the spring the mission bells would ring.

They clung again, gently and fiercely, but no matter how tightly they clung, the bitter wind blew between them, and soon Jarvis led her away from that exposed place.

At the doorstep of the casa Chávez he smiled, she smiled, they clasped hands over hands, and then she was gone. Not a word had been spoken.

The next day he abandoned Barberry House and caught the coaster for San Francisco, a chill and choppy trip in which he never grew warm. Something about that last meeting troubled him; something desperate in her face.

The coaster anchored within sight of Yerba Buena Cove and the water lot where his own warehouse ship was now beached. He studied it happily as a lighter carried him to shore. San Francisco astonished him. Even in the brief period he had been away, it had burgeoned. Helter-skelter tent-cities covered the teeming beaches, while inland, carpenters and masons—no doubt working for fabulous wages—had thrown up trim commercial buildings that were doing a bustling trade. One of these had the words CALIFORNIA STAR painted on its front, and he knew that one to be the site of Sam Brannan's weekly newspaper. San Francisco already had two, ever since Long Bob Semple had moved the *Californian* up from Monterey. And off on the slopes behind the waterfront, he spotted a scattering of houses, mostly unpainted raw wood. The place had bloomed into a great entrepôt for the gold rush—raw, ugly, temporary, cruel, but exuding animal energies.

On the beach he paused to admire Caleb Marble's handiwork. The old potbellied ship lay mostly on land at low tide, and a solid ramp led to a door sawn amidships. A sign said JARVIS AND MARBLE, MERCHANTS. Abovedecks, the ship looked naked, its masts gone and much of the topside gear sold off.

He found the old seadog in the hull, overseeing some Kanakas shelving crates.

"Ah, Jarvis, so 'tis you!" Marble exclaimed. "Here, have a peek at our inventory. She grows by the day, but so do the sales. It's already paying its way. I've picked up whatever catches me eye, whatever a man up in the Sierras might hanker for. Look yonder, aft, and you'll see the bones of a sawmill, blade and carriage and all. I paid a hundred, and I reckon we'll make a thousand percent."

"Good. How're you doing, Caleb?"

"Well, look about while I get these fellows started, and I'll meet you up in the galley."

Jarvis did look, pleased at what he saw. Everything on those shelves would go for a fine price in the gold camps—if he could get the goods to the camps. He needed to find reliable men who would run the tent-stores on a partnership basis, find men who'd rather drive oxen, load wagons, or run pack strings than stand knee-deep in icy streams and toil for gold. He knew there would be some; not everyone took to mining.

The seadog joined him a few minutes later, brimming with rancid cheer, squinting even in the gloom of his cabin because he had squinted in the blinding sea all his life. He seemed as pale and raw-skinned as ever.

"Well, Jarvis, now we'll talk. But first, there's a thing I'm worrying about. I've tried to contact that fellow, Breyer, in

Sacramento City, the one on the sloop you bought. And they tell me he's gone. Plumb vanished, sloop and all, with some inventory in its belly, and your lot's as empty as a parson's wallet."

"Who told you this?"

"Why, Johann Sutter himself. I sent him word I was partnered with you, and to put that bloody Breyer in touch so we can start moving goods up to the mines. And Sutter sent word back, the fellow's gone. The sloop's gone. Off to Tahiti or someplace—with our cargo. Some said he'd gotten up a crew of Peruvians, bribed a-plenty with that gold you paid 'im. If I see him around this bay, I'll stretch his neck from the nearest yardarm, and don't think I won't."

Jarvis stared bitterly out a small porthole. "I ignored my instincts. I knew better. Everything about the man told me what to expect. But I was eager and I had a pocketful of gold. I think if he knew how much, he'd have killed me on the spot. Well, maybe I've learned something."

"You'll learn it over and over, Jarvis. There's a lot of men who give no outward sign of weakness, and they'll do you in. How much, might I ask, did it cost ye?"

"A thousand for the sloop. And whatever the consignment man bought and put in it. I'll know better when I get there. And Breyer's wage for watching the ship . . . and the delay we face getting goods up to Sacramento City."

"Well, draw me a picture of that sloop, Jarvis, and if she floats into this bay, I'll clamp her." He stared at Jarvis. "I've strung up a pirate more than once, and I'll do it again."

"How could you do that? This province has no regular law, and won't have until Congress gets busy."

"It's called main force, Jarvis, and you're talking to an old seadog who spent his life where there's no law, and dog-eat-dog is the rule, and pirates run with the sharks." He smiled, radiating secrets, and stirred up a fire in the tiny stove, intending to reheat some ancient java. "But it's not that bad, Jarvis. We've some alcaldes now, appointed by Governor Mason—Washington Bartlett, Edwin Bryant. They're law in San Francisco. No one's waiting for the United States Congress."

Jarvis scarcely heard. His own folly sickened him. It wasn't the loss, bad as it was; it was his stupidity, his naive trust. He was nothing but a raw miner in a black suit after all.

"You're looking like a drowned rat, Jarvis."

"I haven't learned to take the measure of a man, Caleb."

"A sharp lesson teaches fast, man."

He stared at Marble. "I'm lucky," he said.

"No, there's more than luck in it. You've a head on you. I've worked with all manner of men, from brute animal that needed cuffing or whipping because he understood pain and nothing else, to devious monkeys that whistled hymns while doing the devil's business. I liked what I saw of you from the start. Call this a mistake. Don't call it worse."

Jarvis nodded solemnly. Over the next hour he described his sojourn in Monterey, saying little about Rita Estrada, and a lot about the understandings he had come to with the principal importer and exporter in the province.

"Larkin's already scouring the Pacific from Oregon to Chile for items needed in the mining camps. According to the best estimates of Governor Mason, there're ten thousand in the camps already, and that's only the beginning. Kanakas, Chileans, Peruvians, a few Australians, some settlers down from the Willamette Valley, and plenty of Mexicans. In addition the camps are full of army deserters and merchant seamen off the ships—"

"Ah! I'd be under sail for Chile right now if I had a damned crew."

Jarvis grinned. "Your loss is my gain. I've got you and this beached tub. And soon enough we'll be profiting from your crew and a lot of others like them."

Marble bawled his sour joy at that. "True enough, Jarvis, but I'd rather feel the teak deck roll under my feet, and listen to the breeze whip the sails, and hear the masts creak and the lines hum, and smell the salt in my nostrils. . . . A master's a dread lord sovereign, friend Jarvis, beholden to no one."

They got along famously, though Jarvis found the man's sourness alien. Before they lit the lamps that January day, Jarvis learned that most of the sailcloth had already been sold to miners desperate for winter shelters, and at tenfold profits; that a number of jackleg packing outfits were carrying goods to the camps, often over country without wagon roads; that Marble had purchased half a dozen freight wagons, and had leased them to teamsters; and he had some prospects, men who might set up tent-stores and sell in the camps, for a share.

Marble, in turn, learned that the news of the gold had no doubt reached Washington, carried by the military; that Larkin would sell to Jarvis and Marble; that this new year would be memorable, with the province likely to absorb several tens of thousands of gold-mad men and a few women, all in need of supplies.

Together they decided to hunt for scales and strongboxes. They would be taking in dust and nuggets, and each store-keeper was going to need to weigh and secure his gold.

"I'm going to Sacramento City and start over, Caleb. We need to ship everything we can and store it there. I imagine that ere long, everything we've bought'll walk off our shelves. In a year or two, with a little luck and a little shrewdness, we could retire at ease."

"Who'd want to do that?" asked Marble. "It's the game, not the gold, that counts."

"For me it's the dream that counts," Jarvis said.

CHAPTER 50

Enero, the first month of 1849, slid somnolently by, but Rita Concepción knew that things lay hidden from her, and the mild days, when Monterey Bay glittered in the low sun, shrouded Fate.

There had been an effort to draw Rita back to the rancho and come to know her stepmother, Socorro. But Tía Maria, God forever bless her, had resisted. What Rita Concepción needed, in her cheerful estimation, was the Monterey social season, with its bright *bailes* and fiestas.

But what Rita needed was much simpler: a life with Stephen Jarvis, their children, their dreams. She missed the rancho, and the freedom of its lands, and her great silver mare, Plata, and the rough humor of the *vaqueros*. But her father's marriage changed everything. Socorro would be an alien presence in her life, forever disapproving, finding fault with the simplest and most innocent hopes, wallpapering her imperious rule with religion and piety. No, not the rancho. Her aunt and uncle offered a warm, lively home.

But the Estradas had other plans. On the feast day of Saint Valentine, Tía Maria directed Rita to wear her white ballgown, and cover her hair with her white Brussels lace mantilla. Something glorious would happen this holy day.

The Estradas arrived en masse at the Chávez home, and brought with them several guests who had traveled a great distance by packet and coaster clear from Sonoma, where the northernmost mission, San Francisco Solano, brought the Holy Faith to Alta California. Present as well was the formidable Padre Tecolote.

Rita Concepción knew at once what this was about. The young, sandy-haired caballero studied her curiously. He didn't wear the bright clothing of the rest, but garbed himself in brown, rather like Stephen, though somehow more ascetic. His skeletal face spoke of piety and spirituality. His austere manner hammered at her senses. Still, she saw kindness in his gray eyes, and lively nature.

These, she learned, were the family Zamora, holders of several ranchos north and east of Sonoma, a land of great lush valleys and mild climate. The Zamoras, she swiftly learned, were cousins of Socorro, her new stepmother, and cousins also of the Altamiras, a name known throughout the province. Thus was Rita introduced to Francisco Zamora, the patriarch; Luz, his consort; Mercedes, a wiry, bright-eyed daughter married to a son, Ramón Zamora; Manuel, a married brother whose pregnant wife did not come; and Salvador, he of the smoldering eyes and ascetic cast.

Rita sensed that everyone in that *sala* knew the thing she had not been told. It screamed at her from the way they conducted themselves. Especially this Salvador, whose gaze never strayed far from her, and who avoided contact after their brief introduction by Rita's father.

It fell to her father to deliver the news. In a tone appropriately ornate, if not baroque, he lifted a wineglass in a toast:

"It has come to pass in this year of our Lord," he began, "that the distinguished families Estrada and Zamora should deepen the bonds of their esteem. Our beloved friend, Francisco

Zamora, and my lady and I have therefore arranged the betrothal of our beloved daughter, Rita Concepción, and their beloved son, Salvador . . .''

Rita stood stock-still, her body too leaden to move.

"The dowry has been accepted, our dear padre, Juan Montalvo Pérez, has agreed to our designs and will post the banns, and the date, immediately after the Holy Day of Easter, will be settled upon."

Her father turned to her, gently. "The holy sacrament of matrimony will bond two families as well as two young Mexicans who know and understand the traditions of the fathers. Such arrangements as these turn out better than those temporary infatuations that last a little while and then leave strangers staring at one another. Even as our Lord governs us for our own blessing, so do those at the head of families govern their own, for their blessings. . . ."

Rita said nothing. She endured the remaining hours of the visit without disgracing herself. She did not speak to Salvador Zamora, nor did he speak to her. That was the custom. Sometimes, when parents arranged marriages, the bride and groom didn't meet each other until they approached the altar. On other occasions they met briefly just beforehand. It was a blessing, really. What would she say to this man?

The hours ached by, they drank and ate—all but Rita, who had no appetite—and then the guests departed for rancho Estrada in two great, creaking coaches.

On the way out the door, Father Owl paused before her. "Come talk with me, child," he said.

She did not respond.

Afterward, when Tía Maria was industriously cleaning up, Rita slid to her room and died a little there. She did not like this man Salvador, who smoldered like a pile of rags and looked all too much like Stephen. How could she endure him for a husband? What sort of man would he be? Would they even be friends? Could she take this man into her arms?

That afternoon she had seen Hector study her also, smug, satisfied, arrogant, triumphant in the designs he and his stepmother, Socorro, had fostered. And in the face of her mysterious stepmother she spotted the faintest malice, cloaked in layer upon layer of virtue.

None of it came as a shock to her. Arranged matches were common. She could name a dozen young women whose parents had negotiated their marriages and paid the dowries. Usually, though, the future husband and wife at least knew each other, had met at *bailes* or fiestas, or at great family gatherings, and that way a daughter could resist someone she found unbearable, usually with her mother's support. But in this case, seething Hector, hating the *yanquis*, and the scheming doña had not consulted her.

Dear Tía Maria left her alone with her thoughts that night, so she sat at the unshuttered and glassless window and stared into an aching void, a star-strewn heaven beyond understanding. She found nothing in the sky but lost dreams. There, one small tear welled from each eye, and slid reluctantly down her cheeks, and vanished into her white skirts. She rubbed her eyes and went to her thin pallet.

The next morning she donned her one black dress, the one with dozens of little buttons, which she slowly fastened. Ever more, she would wear black, the only suitable color. She would wear black to church, black in her daily rounds, black at fiestas, black upon black in her bedroom, black at her wedding. Black she would wear; black linen, black velvet, black satin, black silk, black lace, black wool, black cotton, black ribbons, black slippers, and upon her bosom a black crucifix that might tell the world of more than one death. Let them call her the woman in black. She drew her black lace mantilla over her, and plunged into the sun, ignoring her aunt's stare.

She found the priest in his parish rectory office preparing his monthly report to his provincial. He paused, set down his quill, and smiled.

"Let us walk in the gardens," he said, surveying her as he rose. Silently she accompanied him into the warm courtyard, embraced by a low adobe wall. "You are dressed in mourning," he said.

"Yo soy muerta. I am dead."

"Perhaps you will enjoy a resurrection."

"My heart has stopped beating."

"We are fencing, playing with words. You grieve. It is not what you want."

She nodded.

"You wonder how this could be. You love the American; your spirit rejoices in him. You dream of love ever after, laughter, a growing family, sweet tendernesses, and the look of adoration in Stephen's eyes—I saw that. He loves you."

"*Sí.*"

"And you wonder why this vision of Eden lies dead and why your beloved father has chosen another destiny for you."

"No, I do not wonder about that. He did not want me to marry the American. It is simple. He has his reasons."

The priest pondered her brusque response as they rounded the path through the rose gardens. "You wonder what authority he has to do this, and whether you must obey. And whether you might choose your own destiny."

She nodded.

"I do not suppose all the usual reasons interest you."

She glanced at him quizzically, and he took it as a signal to continue.

"He is the head of the family. And you are a grown woman."

"Yes."

"In the church we learn obedience. For our own sake. So that we might be spared hell. So we might do the work of the church. And if that is not enough of an answer, then there is the pragmatic one. There are older and wiser heads above us, those who have lived long enough to understand impulse, impetuosity, folly. They yearn for our happiness. They wish to spare us the errors they made and suffered for. Juan Carlos—"

"My father would have obliged me and welcomed Stephen Jarvis. There are many such matches among the Californios. This was not really his idea."

The padre nodded, and walked quietly awhile. "I am always short on wisdom when I need it," he said. "But when I lack understanding, I find I have something else, sweeter and more sublime. It is faith. It is the power of God. It is the love of Jesucristo. Now there is the mystery. That is the way of the Holy Spirit, to take a wound and use it to make a life sweet. Shall I tell you not to suffer? No. Shall I tell you to rebel? No. But I shall tell you that all things shall work for the good, for those with faith. Eh?"

"And if I cannot bear Salvador Zamora, and if things do not

get better, and if my spirit shrivels under this burden instead of growing through adversity, and if I end up wanting death and release, then what? If I grow bitter, and this is sin, then what? If I do not love, then what?"

"Carry your cross," said the priest. "And find good in your husband. You have not given him a chance. He will grow in your favor, I think. All it will require is patience and charity. Each day, find something to esteem in him, and soon you will have a good marriage."

"And what if he finds little to esteem in me?"

"Bear your burden with courage and joy, for the grace with which you bear your wounds will bring you glory. If you love when you are not loved, you will give the world a gift. If you are kind to the unkind, then you are better than the unkind."

"I have no choice," she said.

"There is one. A life as a religious. Your name-saint, Rita of Cascia, was forced into marriage by her parents while all the while she yearned only for the convent, so she might serve God. You were named for her. It seems fitting. I could arrange it."

She laughed softly. "It is not my calling. Perhaps that is why I do not honor my name-saint as much as I should. Say the sacrament and the blessing over Salvador Zamora and me, then," she said. "I will wear the black of mourning."

CHAPTER 51

S tephen Jarvis left San Francisco one January day in 1849 on a river packet so shorthanded that the master required service from his passengers. Jarvis found himself awkwardly setting sail, along with assorted teamsters, deserting soldiers, Oregonian farmers, and gold-mad adventurers. Their inexperience didn't seem to impede the brig any; they docked two days later amidst the hurly-burly of the Sacramento City waterfront.

He found himself staring bleakly at his own riverfront lot,

now occupied by two strange vessels—one a proud four-mast clipper—and overrun by strangers who had appropriated his land and were storing a mountain of supplies on it. He had no time to lose, and there was no point in wasting tears over Breyer. The whole waterfront seethed with frantic energy, fueled by men whose vision was the same as Jarvis's: the real money lay in supplying the gold camps.

Angrily he approached one of vessels and yelled up to its young master. "This is a private lot, sir. You'll have to vacate."

"I will, will I?" the man retorted. "And who'll make me?"

"I will, sir. I have the title to this property."

The ship's master laughed. "Go ahead," he said.

That interview had been short and brutal. Jarvis did no better with the master of the other vessel, a sloop not unlike Breyer's. That old master was discharging a cargo of Oregon planks and timbers, which would command wild prices up in the gold camps, especially during these winter months. The lumber sprawled over much of Jarvis's lot.

It dawned on him that there might be opportunity in this. "Have you sold this load?" he shouted up to the bearded owner of the sloop.

"Not yet, fella. I'm accepting bids."

"How many board feet?"

"Oh, eighteen thousand five hundred, give or take." The man eyed him. "Cash or gold. If ye'll bid, and if ye'll pay gold, and I can turn me around for Oregon, we'll deal."

An hour later Jarvis owned the lumber that covered his own water lot. He returned to the master of the clipper and bought eighteen tons of merchandise lying on his land, ranging from Durango iron to Chilean flour, hating the prices but knowing he'd triple them in the camps even after all his costs getting the goods into the mountains.

Then he hiked the three miles out to Johann Sutter's fort to pick up some of the gold Sutter was storing for him and pay for his purchases. He felt better, if only because his lot was now covered with his own goods.

He had found Sutter in a bleak mood. "Ah, it's you, is it, Jarvis? Well, they stole your lot, and there's not a thing a man can do. They've stolen my businesses, my land and livestock, and what recourse do I have? There's no law. Your government hasn't acted. We're not even a territory. Where can a man find the police or a court, eh? So we both suffer. I am selling this place and going up to my rancho. In a week we'll be gone. My son will look after it until it's sold."

Jarvis kept a discreet silence. The difference between the Swiss grandee and himself, he thought, was that Sutter was trying to restore the past, and losing more of it each day, while Jarvis had turned a disaster into an opportunity, recovering his waterlot by buying the goods on it. If only Sutter had instantly put everything he owned up for sale when the gold rush washed over him. Or had been willing to pay the going wages, no matter how high . . .

"Ach!" Sutter exclaimed. "That villain with the sloop. Breyer. He took your gold. Loaded in everything your factor bought. And sailed off."

"Where did he go?"

Sutter shrugged. "Who knows? There are no police. Your army and navy don't govern." He paused. "Breyer went to the southern mines, up the San Joaquin River. He had to; he couldn't go up the Sacramento without being caught coming back. He wouldn't go to sea with a holdful of goods worth a king's ransom in the camps. He would go down the San Joaquin, yes, and then past the tules, and unload at Captain Weber's ranch, eh? Tulesburg. They're calling it Stockton now. And it feeds the southern camps. Sonora, Mokelumne, Angel's Camp. He'll sell the sloop there, and escape with a fortune—your fortune."

"I'll hire someone to look for him there," Jarvis said. "Maybe go myself. I've papers for that sloop, and the goods in it. Maybe I can get something back."

Sutter laughed sardonically.

Jarvis collected the gold he needed, traced his way back to the waterfront, paid off both masters, and stood upon his lot, examining four thousand dollars' worth of goods. The entire business had consumed less than six hours.

He contemplated a meal in one of the tent-beaneries that abounded in Sacramento City, and then he would hunt for a place to roost for the night, as close to his unprotected goods as he could get. He surveyed the heavens nervously, hoping the next monsoons would hold off until he got his flour under cover.

But rest eluded him. A half a dozen freighting men were hunting for the owner of the goods on his lot. They had gotten his name from the masters, and were waiting for him. He found himself dealing with a wagon outfit and two pack outfits servicing the northern camps. By the time winter's early dusk settled upon that memorable day, Jarvis had sold everything for double what he had paid, holding back enough posts and beams and planks to build a canvas warehouse on his water lot. He had made enough to pay for the theft of his sloop and all the goods in its hold. What's more, he had forged alliances with the teamsters and found a man who might want to run a store in a camp. All that astonished him. It happened too fast, before he could think about what he was doing; before he could be wary. This was only the beginning. Right now, no doubt, people back in the States were chartering steamers and organizing parties to come overland. It wouldn't be long before a frenzied new mob arrived—and every man would need to be outfitted. The first of those who were coming by sea might arrive in a few weeks. The realization dizzied him.

Instead of staying in Sacramento City, he had himself and his luggage carted out to Sutter's post, put his new gold dust in Sutter's strongbox, and fell into an exhausted sleep.

The next weeks whirled by so fast that Jarvis lost track of time. He erected his board and canvas warehouse, using sailcloth shipped upriver by Marble. His carpenters cost him twenty dollars a day, but he didn't mind. At the same time he bought and sold, bidding on every cargo that arrived in Sacramento City, and often selling it in days. Marble began shipping goods upriver and these sold also. Both partners wished they had their own river transportation. Abandoned ships were plentiful but masters and crews could not be found.

Jarvis paid no heed to his personal comfort, sometimes sleeping at Sutter's post, but as often as not in storerooms as in one of the quarters there. Neither did he eat regularly. His life had become a frenzied round of building and trading, and gauging what the camps might want. He grew desperate for reliable men, especially a good factor who could run his business. He finally promoted his Mormon clerk, Oliver Lee, and made him an overseer of the whole waterfront operation for three ounces of dust a day. Lee didn't plan to stay long; like his brethren who stayed in California after the war, he was collecting resources for the new Zion at Salt Lake and would soon return. But for the moment, he was a godsend.

Larkin wrote regularly, and Jarvis always made time to reply, usually enclosing a note to Rita Concepción in English, which she could now read. Soon Lent would pass, and the Pascua de Resurrección, and then, then, then Jarvis would sail to Monterey and claim his bride. That dream, that candle burning through his lonely nights, lit his way each day and solaced his worst moments and harshest encounters with speculators, thieves, confidence men, and frauds.

He sent word out, via every pack and wagon outfit he dealt with, that he was looking for his stolen sloop, especially on the San Joaquin. Then one day in March the operator of a mule train, one Sorley Grant, reported that he'd seen the sloop and it was heading downriver. Swiftly, Jarvis hired a ketch with an armed crew and overhauled his boat near Benicia.

The sloop's new master explained he had bought it for fifteen hundred, his papers were valid, and he'd be damned if he'd surrender the ship to pirates like Jarvis. Let them shoot it out; let them meet in court. He discovered that the master, Robert Graves, was a competent man of good repute who'd prised some gold out of the Mokelumne, and had merely been looking for other opportunities.

"Graves, we could fight this until we're both broke," Jarvis said. "The fact is, I'm looking for a sloop and the right sort of man to operate it. I paid once for this, and I'm not inclined to pay again, but if you'll join my company and ship goods up from San Francisco, you keep the sloop and maybe we can work something out."

It ended up a deal. Once again, Stephen Jarvis had turned a catastrophe into an opportunity. With Graves and the sloop, he could now ship to points well up the Sacramento and up the San Joaquin. It would all turn to gold if Graves was the man Jarvis believed him to be. Joyfully, Jarvis sent Graves on down to San Francisco with a letter to Marble, explaining what had happened, and to welcome the new man into the firm.

*   *   *

Spring came early, and Jarvis's spirit soared. He had formed his company; he had good men running it. He would soon go to Monterey. Easter came and went, and in its aftermath a letter arrived at Sutter's Fort from Thomas Larkin.

In it was a brief, brusque note, and a clipping from the *Alta California* about the marriage of Rita Concepción Estrada and Salvador Zamora of Sonoma, at the Mission San Carlos Borromeo, officiated by Father Juan Montalvo Pérez. The bride and groom would live at the *estancia* of the groom near Sonoma.

The note confirmed it; said that the family had made the decision, the wedding had drawn most of the Californios in the whole area; and that Rita had insisted on a strange black silk wedding dress that had shocked all of Monterey with its somberness. She had never smiled.

"You've become like a son to me," Larkin concluded. "I grieve as much as you do."

Jarvis spent that whole sunny spring day meandering through Sutter's endless fields, surrounded by the red poppies dancing in the zephyrs, staring westward toward the black-wreathed horizon. Somewhere beyond lay Sonoma, the mission town, the place where she would be spinning out her life.

He didn't know what to do, or why to do anything, or whether it mattered. Maybe he would go back to Troy and see his family. Maybe some of them were dead. Maybe he would reenlist. He thought maybe he would turn it all over to Marble and catch the first ship heading toward Panama City.

What did he need gold for? An empty house? Who would inherit it? What would he want land for? Or a business? Maybe he could give it to Larkin. There was nothing for him in California.

PART V

1850

CHAPTER 5 2

On New Year's Day, 1850, Ulysses McQueen discovered he was the father of a healthy girl. The news reached him at Mokelumne Hill, where he and his partners had several claims.

The expressman found him in town, and demanded two ounces for the four letters from Susannah. That was more than McQueen carried, but he swiftly borrowed dust from Theo and paid the man. With trembling hands, he sorted the four by postmark, and then read them in order.

Most of her letters hadn't gotten through: that was plain. But these had. The news of the child, Margaret Temperance, filled the third letter, along with assurances that the baby was perfect, and healthy except for occasional colic, and that Susannah was well enough, though desperately lonely for him, and weary beyond words of their separation.

The fourth and most recent letter contained bleak news. The naming of the child had alienated McQueen's family. McQueen read and reread the miserable news, the pressures that his father had put on her to name the child Violet Agatha; and now the shocking isolation Susannah was experiencing. Jonathan and sometimes Junior still worked the fields of Old Oak Farm but no McQueen came to her door. Only the Strawbridges were family now.

She begged him to write. She had heard nothing since Kanesville. She feared he was dead or ill or in trouble. Surely she would have received some sort of news by now? What was wrong? Why had he not written?

The desperate and lonely tone shot guilt through McQueen. He hadn't tried to write since Fort Laramie. He couldn't say why; he just hadn't gotten around to it. And now his neglect was eroding Susannah's faith and dreams, along with her troubles with his family. He choked back anger at his imperious father and his slavish brothers and their families, who had ostracized his wife for the high crime of choosing her own names for her own child. Would the penalties ever end? Could he and Susannah ever live independently in Mount Pleasant?

He needed to write to her. But the expressman, Silas Tagg, had already vanished. These entrepreneurs had found a way to make a good living in the gold country by delivering letters to news-hungry miners who couldn't get down to Sacramento City or San Francisco to see what mail might be waiting. The expressmen reached each camp and bar and diggings once a month or so, taking names and delivering mail. Then they traveled down to Sacramento City and Stockton, and even San Francisco, signed for letters addressed to any names they had on their lists, and charged as much as an ounce for each delivery to men in the camps.

He could write her now. Transportation was getting better daily. Steam packets plied the great rivers. Stagecoaches operated from Sacramento City into the mountains. Big oceangoing steamers were shuttling thousands of passengers and tons of mail and goods to and fro, at the Isthmus of Panama. But rumor had it that the post offices were swamped; mail languished in them for months or got lost in them; letters were stacked from floor to ceiling, and no postmaster had been given the authority to hire more clerks. The whole system had collapsed under the pressure and was impossibly snarled.

Well, what good would it do to write her? What good news did he have for her? He knew why he hadn't penned a letter as soon as he got to the diggings: he didn't want to confess how penniless he was, and how grim were his prospects. No, he couldn't bear to let her know. Just give him a few more weeks, a chance to put that cradle to use on good dirt. Just let him put five hundred dollars of dust and nuggets in his poke. Then he'd write her the most glowing letter he could dream up.

He sighed, unhappily. He should write just to let her know he had arrived in California; just to rejoice in the news of their baby; just to say that some, at least, of her letters had miraculously wended their way into his hands. He promised himself he would do that just as soon as his outfit settled down in one place and began earning more than eating-money. That day would come.

Restlessly he headed south out of Mok Hill to some dry diggings in Chili Gulch, where he and Theo Bacon and the Laliques had finally alighted after restless weeks along the Mokelumne River trying to find a claim that might yield some gold. They had lingered at Poverty Bar, Middle Bar, Big Bar, French Hill and Rattlesnake Gulch, barely making enough to keep body and soul together, even though McQueen and Bacon had built a rocker. It turned out that owning a rocker wasn't enough. It took skills to operate it, and good dirt.

Everywhere they encountered men toiling in the emerald valleys, under green hills shot with oak groves. If it was winter in the Sierra, no one noticed it in the southern diggings, except when a storm blew over and the temperatures plunged and they huddled miserably in their brush shanties and ragtowns.

In all this McQueen's party had experienced only one thing: disappointment. Where was all the gold? They found almost none. The strike at Sutter's Mill had happened almost two years earlier. Most of the forty-niners were simply too late. And now forty thousand newcomers scratched new ground, froze, dug, sluiced and scrambled for what was left. And the first thing they learned was that solitary panning no longer could earn a man a living. Rockers and long toms and hydraulic flumes might still yield a fortune, but those required companies and capital and major construction.

Thousands of these rootless men wandered along the rivers, looking for good dirt. The riverbottom claims were all tightly held, and even when apparently exhausted, garnered a good sale price. Each mining district, each bar, had its own rules and specifications, but most of the rules were similar. A man held his claim by keeping his tools on it. If he was absent more than a specified period, he forfeited it. McQueen and his colleagues didn't have the cash to buy a good claim on a gravel bar, so they had to buy dry claims, often a hundred or two hundred feet from the river. But every bucket of water they needed to wash the dirt had to be hauled from the river. It took all four of them to do the work of two men operating a cradle on the river gravels. So they wrestled with poor claims, earned five or six dollars apiece each day, and spent almost as much on necessaries.

California wasn't the bonanza that McQueen had imagined long before. Unless his outfit hit a good pocket—and many outfits did—they wouldn't go back to the States with their pockets full of rocks. The foursome had observed countless men who were wandering the hills and gulches, prospecting rather than toiling for gold. These drifters were dreaming of the next big strike, the undiscovered gravel where they could pluck up nuggets and earn five hundred a day. They were the poorest of the lot, starving because they were chasing chimeras rather than getting what could be gotten. McQueen, Bacon, and the Laliques chose a moderate course, working at what they had while keeping an eye out for something better. If they kept at it, they might earn enough to buy a good claim.

Restlessly he hiked back to the gulch and found Bacon there. "I'm a father!" he cried. "I've a girl. And everything's all right!"

Bacon set down the shovel, which had cost them an awesome ten dollars, and grinned. "Now you'll have to support her," he said. "We'd better find some nuggets."

"She's my nugget. My wife named her Margaret Temperance McQueen. I like it. Never would of thought of names like that."

"Mrs. McQueen must miss you," Theo said softly. "Alone with a baby; you a half a year away."

"She does. She's gotten no news. This so-called postal system—"

"The Jarvis store in Mok Hill has paper and envelopes, Ulysses."

"Well, they're pirates. I won't pay three bits for a sheet of paper. Then it's another half ounce to the expressman."

Bacon eyed him thoughtfully. "She would like to hear from you, good news or bad, I imagine."

"I guess I'll wait a little, Theo. I'm going to send her a letter one of these days, and it'll say, 'Susannah, we're rich. You trusted me to come out to California and I made good on it. I'll be home in a few months.'"

Bacon smiled suddenly. "You've got a patient wife, Ulysses."

McQueen took it as criticism and set off angrily toward their rocker, where the Laliques quietly labored. The claims they had staked were well upslope of the ones worked by some Chileans, who had fiercely driven off various Yanks who had tried to horn in lower down. Several times matters had almost come to bloodshed.

But a dry claim that far above the riverbed meant bucketing water a hundred yards. They were collecting about an ounce a day. After every few loads, they patiently scraped the cloth behind the riffles of its burden of gold dust and black sand. At the end of each day Bacon, who had a gentle hand, whirled this mixture in a goldpan until he washed out the black sand. Most of what was left went for food. They couldn't afford even to replace the rags they wore, and a broken tool would be a catastrophe.

"Maybe we should look again, Theo," McQueen said, after he had plunged back into the work. "We're losing ground here."

"Maybe we should start a store, or hire on with a freight outfit," Bacon said. "Those teamsters are getting an ounce a day each."

McQueen shoveled another load of dirt into the hopper and pawed through it for oversized rocks, while Bacon poured water at a steady pace, slowly washing the muck through the perforated sheet-metal barrier. They had performed this grim, thankless, bone-tiring task for almost two months.

"Wish I had a piece of that Jarvis outfit," McQueen said. "They plumb monopolize the whole shebang. I hear he made his pile in the spring of 'forty-eight and then set up a whole company with stores in the camps, just to milk us. When I pay half a dollar a pound for some moldy flour, I'd like to wring his neck."

"Well, if it's not the Jarvis Company, it'd be another, I suppose," Bacon said. "They're all charging the same."

Below, some Chileans had paused to glare at the Laliques, who were carrying pails up from the river across their claims. Then one big man blocked the way, forcing the silent Basil Lalique to detour. McQueen watched, disturbed.

"I guess maybe we'd better find some other dirt," he said to Bacon. "This is trouble, and it'd just cost us time. And if they wreck our rocker, we're done for."

"Where?"

"Maybe we should just rent this rocker to someone who's on good gravel and needs one. Or go on shares. Or find some part of the river where we could run a long tom."

"Dreams," Theo said. "But I have an idea. Let's go back to Big Bar and watch for a claim right on the river that's been abandoned. Last I knew, men were pulling out of there. It's supposed to be exhausted. None of us shies from work. I think maybe some coyote holes down to bedrock might rejuvenate our fortunes."

The Laliques swiftly agreed. No one wanted to wait for trouble in Chili Gulch. The whole of the Mok Hill area had been divided up by various groups. Some black runaway slaves mined one gulch; some Frenchmen another. Chileans and Mexicans each had their enclaves and defended them with fists.

Wearily they retreated to Big Bar, half a mile away, passing toiling men in flannel shirts and canvas britches, worn boots, hickory shirts, battered slouch hats. Almost all looked thin and ragged, some were sick, most desperate. At the legendary Big Bar, where fortunes had been prised from the gravel flats, men looked a little more prosperous.

At Big Bar their luck turned. They found three adjoining claims on the north bank of the Mokelumne River, all abandoned, there for the taking.

They claimed the three by setting tools on them and recording the claims with the camp clerk, and then inquired among the many neighboring miners why the claims were available.

"Fellows never got more than two or three dollars a day," said one gravel-voiced man. "Breaks a man's heart to pan all day for two pinches. You'll be the ninth or tenth to work 'em."

"Well, we'll try," McQueen said, optimism welling up in him. "We have some ideas that might work."

CHAPTER 53

Susannah McQueen fairly burst with joy every time she paused to behold her little girl. Those blue eyes had deepened into midnight, and focused up at Susannah from unplumbed depths. Now, as the child approached her first birthday, she clearly resembled her strong-limbed father. The baby crawled, then toddled, and often squirmed recklessly when Susannah held her.

And the girl had discovered her own delights, stalking the

tabbies, which dodged her and never clawed the child. She was too young—so far—to miss her father or grasp the sadness that increasingly pervaded the white house, or understand her mother's tears. Susannah never lacked work, especially now that she was so alone. At harvest time there had been all the preserving to do, a task she undertook alone. Jonathan and Stanford Jr. had dutifully harvested the crops according to their agreement with Ulysses, putting the field corn into cribs to dry, and taking the wheat to the mill. But they never paused to talk, or entered her house, nor did their wives. They took their share of the bountiful crops, and she received hers. But then, after Thanksgiving, Jonathan had stood solemnly on the porch—he wouldn't come in and announced that next spring, she would have to find someone else to sharecrop Old Oak Farm.

That had been a frightful blow. It would not be easy to find others. The Strawbridges lived miles away and other neighbors had their hands full. Ulysses had counted on his brothers to run his place on shares until he returned from California.

Her subsistence would fade, other than what she might garner from her gardens and what she might sell to the mill of her stored grains, and what she might get for her fattened cattle, hogs, and sheep. That would last for a while.

Was all this because she had named her baby as she chose, instead of knuckling under to Stanford McQueen? The question lay bitter as quinine on her mind. Yes, that was a part of it. But it went deeper. The McQueen family was punishing Ulysses, ostracizing him—for being himself. In the moments when these sharp-edged truths welled through her, she had to curb her own disgust. Could something so innocuous—naming her child—yield such a vile harvest? The answer was yes—if you were the looming old patriarch and frontiersman Stanford Constable McQueen, surveying the one corner of his world that hadn't knuckled under.

Oh, Ulysses! She nursed a hundred wobbly explanations that would account for his silence, and talked endlessly to her daughter about the man she had married—who was off somewhere, God knows where, his time apart from her so lengthy that her marriage now seemed a small island in the river of her life.

She haunted the post office each week, becoming a byword,

even a sad joke, around Mount Pleasant. At each visit, old Eli Peters, the postmaster and grocery operator, anticipated her question with a grave shake of his head. "Sorry, Miz McQueen. The California mail's a bit slow. Maybe next week."

But the mail wasn't, really. She heard constantly of wives in Iowa and Illinois who had received letters from California. Many of these had been reprinted in local weeklies, and these in turn were reprinted by other papers. She had a thin but growing knowledge of what the goldfields must be like—the hard work, the disappointments, the wild successes, the awful prices, the cold and heat and insects and the dysentery that swept through the mountain camps, disemboweling shivering miners and sometimes taking lives.

She took comfort from a morbid understanding: When a miner died, either on the trail or in the gold camps, others made a serious effort to inform the family back in the States. All over the country, bereaved women were receiving word, generously mailed by other miners from some lonely diggings up a Sierra gulch. No such word had ever come about Ulysses.

Then one gloomy frostbitten morning, a week after Valentine's Day, she did receive word. The postmaster handed her a letter addressed to Mrs. Ulysses McQueen, Mount Pleasant, Iowa. Within the envelope she found a note, written in a bold hand. It was dated December 11, 1849, written from Salt Lake City, Territory of Deseret, and signed by one Josiah Lee.

"Madam," it said. "Permit me to pass along word of your husband, Ulysses, whom we met while traveling eastward on the Carson Branch, en route to Salt Lake City. He kindly entertained my colleague and me in camp, while warning us of certain perils we must face along the Humboldt. That timely warning helped us negotiate a cruel desert and a trail so overgrazed it would ruin our stock. While he didn't ask us to write you, I am taking the liberty of doing so, knowing the extreme perils and slowness of the California mail, and the relative ease of communicating to the States from Deseret. I wish to assure you that he is in good health, and the worst of his ordeal has passed. He was heading toward the southern mines, viz the Mokelumne River, and he and his colleagues would have arrived in the goldfields no later than mid-November, and are no doubt enjoying the bounty thereof.

Respectfully, Jos. Lee, Bishop, Church of Jesus Christ of Latter-Day Saints."

"Oh! Ulysses!" she cried aloud in the post office. This good man had talked with him. And that was only four months ago. She raced home, her child bouncing on her arm, and then she nestled beside the woodstove, there to read and reread this kindhearted note, until at last she wept and couldn't stop weeping. "Somewhere, over the horizon, you are there, my darling, my darling . . ."

She bundled up again and stumbled across corn-stubbled fields to Jonathan's farm, gulping ice crystals in the air, to show them the letter. Ulysses' brother read it calmly and handed it back. "I hope he returns in time to put in the crops," Jonathan said.

"But it's news! We have news."

"It's not news to the McQueens," Jonathan said.

She stared at him in horror, and backed off the wide porch. The trip across the fields, against a sharp north wind, chilled her. What had Ulysses done? What had she done? The clan had disowned their own flesh and blood. For what?

She did not yield. Instead, she wrapped the scarf over Margaret Temperance's ruddy face, and trudged through the snow, striping the rutted fields to the solid home of Stanford McQueen, Senior.

"I have news of Ulysses," she said to Mother McQueen, at the door. "Here." She thrust the letter at her mother-in-law, who took it silently, read it, and returned it with a nod.

"Thank you for sharing it," she said. "But Mr. McQueen has washed his hands of him."

"What's this, Mother?" asked McQueen, looming up behind her.

"Ulysses is well." Susannah thrust the letter at her father-in-law. He didn't take it. The letter zigzagged to the planks. She bent to retrieve it, understanding his act and hers.

"Is he coming back?" he asked.

"No, he just arrived. I'm sure—"

"Old Oak Farm has no one to farm it."

"Ulysses' brothers agreed to."

"And they did. All last year. Now there's no one. I can't let a productive farm lie idle in the hands of a wastrel son."

"But it's his farm."

"No, it's mine. I gave it to him to use, for his prosperity, just as I gave all my sons their farms. But I own it and I pay the taxes on it."

Icy air eddied about her, as she registered that. She had thought that the farm was Ulysses'. But *of course* it wouldn't be. Stanford McQueen could not surrender anything, including the black earth. Least of all a son.

"If he isn't back by March, when the work begins, I'll take it back."

"He won't be, Father McQueen. He's just starting in California."

"Then you must leave. I won't have idle land. I'm sure the Strawbridges will care for you. I'll turn Old Oak over to Jonathan, my most reliable boy."

She could scarcely speak, and where her next words came from, she didn't know. "I'll go to California," she said.

He stared at her for so long that she wondered whether he was going to speak at all. "Let me know when you depart," he said at last. "The sooner the better."

"Oh, dear," said Mother McQueen. "My heart aches so. I will miss you."

That was how it ended. Or how the earth split between them. Susannah trudged back across stubblefields rimed with snow in the furrows, and retreated to the rowdy radiance of her stove. She pulled off her mittens, her scratchy scarf, and then her woolen coat, knowing that something large had just happened, though she couldn't quite sort it all out. California! She would leave this bitter soil behind her, and make a new life with her beloved.

Her news wrought dismay among the Strawbridges. Her mother and father arrived on a Sabbath afternoon for a Sunday supper of popovers swimming in butter, and that's when Susannah told them about the letter, the McQueens' response to it, and her decision to go to Ulysses.

"But Susannah," her mother cried. "Not California. Not all alone."

"I won't be alone," Susannah replied. She snuggled her blanket-wrapped Margaret Temperance to her. "It'll always be clear that I'm traveling to meet my husband."

"That's a rather innocent assumption," said her father.

"But Susannah, you'd leave everything behind?" her mother asked.

"I love Ulysses. I know he's doing all right there, trying to build a future for us. He has a bold spirit, and he'll need a woman to match. I'll find him and help him."

"But how would you pay? A trip to New Orleans on a river packet. Steamship passage to Chagres. The cost of getting to Panama City. The cost of passage on a Pacific ship. The cost of tracking Ulysses down in California . . ."

Susannah had thought long about this. She looked around her at all her possessions, many of them wedding gifts. The golden oak furniture, McQueen heirlooms, the Haviland wedding china, the wedding silver.

She and Ulysses owned the wheat in the granary, the corn in the cribs, the six shorthorn milking cows and eleven Poland China hogs and a dozen Merino sheep. All of it would yield enough at auction. These weren't hard times. She could get something for their possessions, but there would be nothing to spare.

"Mother, I can sell this. I hate to part with any of it—these lovely things given to us to get us started. But oh, I haven't a choice. I'm evicted."

Her mother sighed. "Evicting you. I'll never forgive Stanford McQueen as long as I live."

"Oh, now, don't carry on so," her father interrupted. He turned to Susannah. "You know, this magical California's caught my fancy for a year now. It's a bright new land of milk and honey. After the mining's over, why, it'll be settled by good people, maybe by you and Ulysses, until it's a proud new state in the Union. From sea to sea, that's what the Republic'll be. You go out there, and I'll be walking beside you in spirit."

But her mother was weeping. "I'll never see you again if you go. California? How could old people ever get there? You'd be gone forever; our dear Margaret'd be gone. . . ."

"It's not forever, Mama," Susannah said.

But her mother had subsided into soft sadness that permitted no consolation.

"Yes, Susannah, it'd be forever, most likely," her father said quietly. "Someday they'll build a railroad clear out there, but we won't live to see it. If you go, we won't see you again." He paused. "But you go anyway. You go settle that country and make your way out there, and enter into it the way we entered into Ioway. When we left for the West, our parents in Delaware said the same thing: They'd never see us again. But we chose it, and we don't regret it, and we kept in touch, and exchanged tintypes, so they knew all about us. Oh, there're bad moments, all right. When my father died, and I had no way to go all the way back East, up the canals, I had a hard time of it. Couldn't say good-bye properly. But—correct me if I'm wrong, Mrs. Strawbridge, my dear—the regrets've been small, and the rewards have been grand."

"But I'll miss them so. . . ." Susannah's mother whispered, not really answering.

"I have to go," Susannah said. "Or else just wither away."

CHAPTER 54

At Burlington, a long day's carriage ride from Mount Pleasant, Susannah's family put her on the City of Cairo, a Mississippi River packet bound for New Orleans. The gingerbreaded white vessel bobbed on slate waters under an overcast sky, primed to head south where the waters contained no dangerous ice floes, and mild weather lifted the hearts of riverboat men.

Her mother and father wept. She wept. They would probably never see each other again. She would always remember this twelfth day of March, 1850, as the end of one life and the beginning of something uncertain—and exciting. She had funds enough and some to spare, because old Stanford McQueen had given her cash for the grain, livestock, and all the McQueen family heirlooms.

"He wanted the McQueen furniture more than he wants you and Ulysses," Susannah's mother had observed drily.

But it came to over six hundred, a fair price, and the offer had saved Susannah a painful auction. The very day she had abandoned Old Oak Farm to spend her final hours with the

Strawbridges, McQueen and his sons were busily moving Jonathan's family into its commodious house.

The packet shivered as the boilers shot steam into the giant cylinders, and the paddles cranked. A shrill whistle shattered the sullen morning, and then the packet eased away from the levee, its twin chimneys belching black smoke that rained cinders. She felt the packet gather up its muscle, heard the paddles thrash the Father of Waters, and watched her family grow smaller and smaller, until they blurred in her wet eyes.

She gulped back her sorrow and threaded her way to her small stateroom, her baby in her arms. The cold had numbed her. The stateroom wasn't much warmer, but she supposed that with the steam up, she would discover the heat soon enough. She sat on the edge of the hard bunk and clutched Margaret Temperance to her. The child was all the company she would have for many months.

Through a small porthole, she watched the banks of the mighty river grow distant, and then slowly slide by. She felt utterly alone. Had she made the right choice? The more she questioned, the more all those fears that lay buried within her rose to her consciousness. Foremost among them was the one thing that tortured her. Did Ulysses really care? Was he really an adventurer, for whom a wife was a ball and chain, and a baby a barred prison? If he cared, why hadn't any letters reached her?

She couldn't endure these thoughts, and pushed them aside. Margaret needed changing. She wondered how she would manage, with only a few diapers and no way to clean them, and not so much as a diaper pail to contain them. She would ask a cabin boy. Maybe the one who had helped her brothers drag the trunk and the portmanteau into her cabin.

The ritual of changing her daughter comforted her, if only by its familiarity. She had set her mind on California. Three letters preceded her, each notifying Ulysses she was coming: one to general delivery at San Francisco, another to Sacramento City, another to "Mokelumne River"—where she supposed he would be. Somehow, Ulysses would find her. Or she would find him. But it clawed at her that they might never connect. The world was such a huge and alien place.

She opened her door, looking for the cabin boy. Her state-room opened on the central saloon, the area that ran down the center of the ship where passengers could visit with each other, buy spirits, and eat their meals at plush tables. The gilt and glit-ter, the glass chandeliers, the gingerbread, the shining white enamel, all dazzled her. This was a floating palace, but appar-ently a half-empty one. Not many people sailed in winter.

She found the acned boy, who was settling another woman passenger, and asked what to do about diapers.

"I'll take 'em—we wash 'em in the river, put 'em in a net over the side for a few hours, and dry 'em in the engine room. Just give me your messed ones each evening, and you'll have dry ones at your door in the morning."

That was good news. The packet's crew knew all about the needs of young mothers. She vowed to tip the youth. Margaret Temperance was a docile child, but the trip might upset her. Susannah hoped the child wouldn't keep everyone up at night.

The next days she prowled the packet, climbing clear to the hurricane deck, exploring the main deck, watching the bleak black river draw the packet along on its sinister currents. Often they pierced through fog and haze so heavy she could barely see a shore, and during the worst moments the riverboat inched along, its crew alert, men at the bow dropping poles to fathom the depths.

The packet nosed its duckbilled prow into every port of call along the way, discharging a few people—mostly drummers in gaudy attire, men who had looked her over too alertly at meals—and sometimes taking on a few new people. At each stop the burly crew loaded cordwood, which came to rest in square piles on the main deck to feed the hungry firebox. The master paid for the wood on the spot, usually with a letter of credit redeemable at the company office in New Orleans. She met several men who were headed for California, but she was the only woman going there. They were all young. One of them told her the rush of 1850 would exceed the rush of 1849. Many men had returned from the goldfields carrying wealth with them, concrete evidence in the form of octagonal gold slugs, which only excited thousands of others.

One young man with a cowlick and a cast eye befriended her, and announced that he and his pals would look after her clear to Sacramento, and look up her husband for her if they could. He and three others had boarded at St. Louis, the first major stopping place, where, at last, the ship had filled up, largely with California-bound passengers.

"Ah'm Jasper Cotton, and ah'll make mighty sure a pretty little lady like yo'self gets taken care of proper," he said, smiling shyly.

"I couldn't be more grateful. I hope you and your friends'll join me for meals—if you can put up with a baby," she said.

"Put up? Why, I come from a family that made a lot of babies, and I'd be half bored without three tuggin' at me."

The weather suddenly warmed near Memphis and Susannah saw strange foliage, some of it in spring bloom. The *City of Cairo* had reached the South. Now she haunted the sunny main deck, or walked the hurricane deck where she could see far up and down the sparkling blue river, or talk to the officers in the texas above her, or enjoy the exciting moments when they met upriver traffic, including some big white palaces rather like her own. As they passed, the officers would exchange news through their megaphones, and always salute with some shrill blasts of the whistles.

She began to call Jasper and his friends, Amos and Jubal, her guard of honor because they always managed to be on hand whenever other men approached. Drummers invited her to have a drink, but she told them she never imbibed. At St. Louis the vessel had picked up a new type of passenger: suave men dressed like deacons, who ran card games in the saloon amidst clouds of cigar smoke. Some of these gentlemen, many of whom had gaudy headlight diamonds poking from their cravats, eyed her contemplatively, their gaze resting at last on Margaret Temperance. The child had become a lively attraction in her own right.

The debonair gamblers fascinated Susannah. Day by day they somehow drew passengers to their tables, usually cleaning them out. Paper banknotes, silver Mexican royals, gold quarter eagles, half eagles, and eagles, and even IOUs decorated the tables. She gawked, never having seen such open sin in all her days in Mount Pleasant. But the one who intrigued her the most didn't seem to be a gambler at all, and had quietly announced himself as a plantation owner and cotton commission agent returning home after a business trip to St. Louis. He always played poker apologetically, blundering now and then, laughing at his own mistakes—and raking in the pots. Once their eyes met and he winked.

Then, as they approached New Orleans and the ship wound through strange bayous and she could see no shore at all, talk turned toward the next leg. Coal-burning ocean steamers were hauling passengers to Chagres as fast as they could, scarcely stopping to refuel and reprovision. "We'll get you on board a good 'un," said Jasper Cotton. "There's sometimes a wrestle for tickets, but I reckon a lady has an advantage."

Even before they reached New Orleans, agents boarded the ship and circulated flyers promoting their lines, all of them making broad and cynical promises of comfort, fine provender, low prices, fast service, safe vessels, shipboard comforts, and good connections at Chagres for the trip over the Isthmus.

Steamships were charging a hundred fifty and up, two hundred for a stateroom. The slower sailing ships were charging seventy or eighty. Susannah thought she could manage the price of the faster steamers; she couldn't bear delay any longer.

New Orleans fascinated her. It squatted low and moist and oppressive at the base of the great river, staring out upon misty seas. She saw black slaves, slick with sweat, manhandling bales of cotton and casks and crates along the brick-paved riverfront. She wondered what it must be like to endure that living death. Two towering steamers rocked on the tides, each the focus of frantic loading. All along the levee crowds of sweaty people mobbed the shipping-company offices, clamoring for passage to Chagres. They looked to be a vile lot, and she suddenly felt fearful for her money, most of which had been sewn into a canvas money belt she wore around her waist. Not that such a ruse would stop a desperate man.

But those were the risks. One could shear away from all danger, or one could face it. She put aside her worries, left her portmanteau and trunk in the care of her young friends, and penetrated the sour-smelling offices of the Atlantic and Southern Company, owners of the *Star of Louisiana*.

"Ah!" the clerk exclaimed. "A woman alone. We've a state-room."

That astonished her. "But I thought—"

"There's another, of course, and we can't put a man in with her. We're departing at four; better hurry. Steam's up. It'll be a hundred fifty-nine."

Furtively, hoping the mob of males behind her wasn't studying her too hard, she slid banknotes from an inner pocket in her cotton skirt across the sticky marble counter.

An hour later she was ensconced in her cabin. Whoever she was rooming with was no doubt touring one or another of the decks. With a shrill blast of its whistles, the steamer edged away from the levee and into the misty Gulf of Mexico, off to New Grenada and a jungle port.

When Susannah's cabinmate finally did materialize, Susannah studied her and wondered how she would get along with this seductive brunette lady in a straw hat and skimpy white dress that clung like a wet sheet. She knew that New Orleans boasted a demimonde.

"Ah'm Belle, sweetheart, and you're?"

"Susannah McQueen . . ."

"Well, happy sailin'. I'm heading for Portsmouth Square in San Francisco. Gonna join my man; he's got a club with six faro tables, three monte, and four poker games. Ah'm gonna be the main attraction." She whickered.

"I'm going to join my husband," Susannah replied in measured tones.

"That's a cute little brat," Belle said.

Susannah paused. "I hope Margaret won't trouble you. She's a very good baby, most of the time."

"That's how I was until the age of thirteen," Belle said. "We'll get along just fine, dear."

Susannah smiled agreeably, hoping it was true.

When Susannah looked out the porthole, she beheld a hot blue sea, empty and featureless, and nothing that might connect her with her past life. The ship sailed toward a destination, but she was adrift.

G old at last.

McQueen and the Laliques watched as Theo Bacon swirled the day's take in his pan, deftly washing away the black sand until a gleaming mass of fine flakes and pinhead nuggets remained. In a single day they had accumulated over three ounces, which came to twelve dollars apiece.

"We did it!" Martin Lalique cried. He had been the most discouraged of them, perhaps because he was the youngest.

Bacon sighed. "It'll take work," he said.

He was alluding to the frightful toil that had gone into this small harvest. They had paired up and started two coyote holes, shafts sunk through barren gravels to get at the gold resting on bedrock. The Laliques had hit bedrock at five feet on one claim, and McQueen and Theo had struck it at seven on another claim. Except to sample the gravel now and then, they hadn't bothered to wash the material they excavated. But the last foot before they struck solid rock yielded plenty of gold, and the final inch of compact aggregate was loaded with it.

"All we have to do is work ourselves to death and we'll get ahead," McQueen said. This was a bitter harvest. Down in those coyote holes a man gouging out the gold-bearing gravels would undermine the walls and increase the danger of a cave-in with every spoonful. The only alternatives were hydraulic washing of the overburden, or digging innumerable coyote holes all over their claims.

"We aren't afraid of work," Bacon said quietly. That had been the watchword among them. "But let's all work the claim where the bedrock is closest to the surface. The best first."

Bearded old Will Sykes on the next claim wandered over in the twilight to congratulate them. "Well, you finally done it," he said. "Lots of jaspers tackled that gravel, and none had your grit. Big Bar's mostly cleaned out. Them forty-niners sure skimmed the easy gold."

"We made over twelve apiece today," Martin Lalique said proudly, "and just you wait and see how we'll do when we get this down pat."

Sykes eyed the water shrewdly. "Lucky for you, you've got a few months before the spring rise. This old Mok River roars when the Sierra snows melt."

"We'll be done by then," McQueen said, hopefully.

The next weeks they slaved as they never had before, rising in starlight, cooking biscuits and sidepork before dawn, and digging new coyote holes day by day. But slowly the dust in their pokes grew heavy, and the fat pokes felt good in the hand. They refined their techniques, learning to dig their shafts close enough so they could easily chop out the material in between them, saving labor.

In spite of mining-camp prices, McQueen found himself with two hundred dollars of gold, valued at sixteen an ounce, in his poke two weeks later. Twice in those days expressmen brought him letters from Susannah, one written in October, the other in November. Gladly, McQueen let the expressmen raise a pinch from his poke, the assumption everywhere in the goldfields being that a pinch equaled a dollar.

Joyfully, he read of Margaret Temperance's growth and rosy cheeks and eyes that reminded people of his own. But he found word of trouble: his family had shut out Susannah. She no longer saw her sisters-in-law. Now that the crops were safely in and the shares divided, she never saw her brothers-in-law. All she saw was her own family. Each of the two letters begged him to write. She was frantic from the lack of news. Just tell her he was in good health, that's all she asked.

Guiltily, he contemplated his delinquencies. At first he couldn't write because he couldn't afford to send a letter. And then, through the early failures, he didn't want to write and admit he had fallen into desperate straits. But now he could. He hurried to the store in Mok Hill one rainy day and bought a sheet of paper, an envelope, and a stamp at the Jarvis and Marble store there.

"I'm pleased as punch about the girl, and I'm doing right well," he bragged. "I'm gaining about ten dollars a day even after expenses, and my poke's looking fat. It takes some doing, Susannah, but it sure beats plowing a field and getting a few bushels of wheat or barley out of it. Pretty soon I'll be buying you a mansion, and anything your heart desires. It's not easy to take gold out of these streams, but we—my partners and me—have found the way to do it without investing a lot of capital. I now own a half interest in three productive claims, and you can bet they will steadily assure us a future of comfort and ease.

"Give my love to my little daughter, and of course to all the Strawbridges, and the Reverend and Mrs. McCracken, and all my friends in Mount Pleasant. They all wondered whether I'd make it, and now you can tell them that I did. Putting rocks in my pocket. Pretty soon I'll have a stake, and then I'll return to your loving arms. Your adoring husband, Ulysses McQueen."

He left it at the store for an expressman, along with a pinch. Then he studied the shelves of goods. This outfit, Jarvis and Marble, had become famous in the camps for meeting every need imaginable, and charging uniform prices. Everything was costly in the mountains, but usually these stores had, or could swiftly supply, any commodity. Some miners despised the outfit, calling it "the octopus." Other, more thoughtful miners considered it a blessing. McQueen treated himself to some dried apples, a ready-made chambray shirt, and two eggs. He hadn't eaten an egg in a year.

Mok Hill was wilder than some of the camps he'd been hearing about. It stretched over the crowns of several hills south of the river. New businesses, most of them with a covered porch or gallery facing the dirt road, were rising everywhere. There had been some trouble between the Chileans and the Yanks, but nothing like the trouble between the Mexicans and Yanks down in Sonora, a few miles south, or the troubles with the Chinese all over the southern mining districts. No group drew more ire than the Celestials, and every time any of them found gold, a mob of Yank miners drove the Chinese off.

These dark events troubled him, along with the occasional reports of theft or murder, and the rough justice of the miners' courts, which usually banished a man from a district, or whipped him, or in one or two cases, hanged him. And in most instances, the one suffering the punishment wasn't a white man. But California lacked legal government even though it had set itself up as a state, and the miners would do what they had to do.

Trouble came to Big Bar that March when two swart Mexicans from Sonora began to work dry claims, bucketing water up the verdant slopes to their diggings. Some of those in the camp, especially a big red-faced man, didn't take kindly to the "foreigners" and rumbled loudly about knifings and theft and whatever else came to mind. Then one morning the man, Hod Pope, bawled that his poke had vanished, and he knew exactly who'd done it—the two Sonorans. Grimly the miners marched on the Sonoran camp, pushed the frightened young men aside, and probed their tent, even digging up the ground under the ashes of the fire. They found nothing, but that didn't stop Pope from demanding punishment.

"I'm out a pretty penny, and they bleddy well took it. Give 'em a whipping they'll not forget," he growled.

That offended McQueen. "We've found nothing. Who knows who stole your poke? Let them go."

Pope loomed over him, his pale blue eyes glittering with malice. "Maybe you're in with them."

McQueen stood his ground. "I'm against punishing men without evidence that they did something wrong."

Pope poked a fat finger into McQueen's chest. "They're Mexicans." That seemed argument enough for most of the miners.

"Let them go. Or call a miners' meeting and hold a trial. They deserve a trial like anyone else. There's so many lawyers in these camps we can find a dozen to defend and prosecute." McQueen thought his ideas made sense, were the normal sentiment of Americans everywhere.

But he discovered he was naive. The ideals of his neighbors and family at Mount Pleasant were not the ideals of these hard men. They solidified into a mob that morning, and dragged the frightened youths, each of whom scarcely weighed a hundred-twenty pounds, away from their claim, down to the bar, where a thick, mean Texan snapped a bullwhip with a tasseled popper on it. There the hapless pair were tied to posts, their backs naked to white men's justice, and there the burly Texan gave each boy ten lashes, each crack of the whip evoking wild writhing and screeching sobs. When the blood ran freely, sheeting down their backs, the pair were cut loose and driven out.

"Now they larned not to steal," Pope said.

McQueen peered at the miners, finding all too much pleasure in some faces. "Now it's a white men's bar agin," said one full-bearded man, speaking for them all.

McQueen pushed back the bile in his throat. As the mob dispersed he discovered Basil Lalique staring, rigid, and Martin trying to console him.

"Let's go to work, Basil," McQueen said, tugging at the veteran's arm. But Lalique didn't budge.

"It stirred him up," Martin said. "I thought he was plumb over all that."

Basil Lalique didn't work that day or the next. McQueen and Theo toiled steadily, and shared the day's cleanup, which was much reduced.

Then, at supper one night, Martin announced that he and his father were leaving. "He can't work here, that's for certain. Not after that. We'd like to sell out our half of the claims."

"We don't have much cash to pay for them," Theo Bacon said, troubled by this turn of events.

"We'd like two hundred each—four hundred," the youth said. "That's fair. Lots of gold under there."

That evening, McQueen and Theo agreed to the deal. Not that they had much choice. They walked over to the Jarvis store in Mok Hill and weighed out two hundred from each of their pokes, and got a quitclaim in return. The purchase took most of McQueen's gold. It left him with only five or six ounces, including a walnut-size nugget he'd kept for a good-luck charm.

"We didn't do so bad," Martin said. "We got us a thousand or so out of it, Pa and me."

"Where are you going now, Martin?"

The youth shrugged. "I don't know. Pa's not fit for mining. Can't stay in California. It's all Mexican country and reminds him of what war was all about. He can't take it. We've no ties left back in the States. We think maybe Oregon. Maybe there's some land in the Willamette Valley a thousand dollars might buy, and a plow and a mule."

Much to McQueen's surprise, the Laliques left that night, on foot, heading for Stockton where they might catch a schooner or even a steam packet. He watched them provision at the lamp-lit store, which kept long hours to cater to the whims of miners whose tastes and hungers were powerfully immediate.

McQueen had rarely been in Mokelumne Hill at night, and now the lamp-lit buildings intrigued him. "I guess I'll stick around here, Theo," he said. "Maybe have a sarsaparilla somewhere."

"Suit yourself. We're going to be cleaning up a lot less gold, working by ourselves," he said. "But we won't be dividing it four ways, either. See you later."

McQueen watched his partner fade into the night, along a steep downhill trail to the river. There weren't many men about, though the night was pleasant. Miners worked until they dropped, and began their next day before dawn. McQueen discovered that Mok Hill at night wasn't the same as Mok Hill by day. The place needed women. He knew of only one in camp, a gray-haired matron with vast dignity, who cooked and mended clothing while her husband panned gold over on Stockton Hill. It was said that she would mend a miner's duds for a pinch or two of gold.

He pushed into a dimly lit new emporium, and found that diversions had arrived in Mok Hill. At a plank bar were various miners, soaking up corn liquor or draft beer drawn from a keg. And at one side he saw two tables, each under an oil-lamp chandelier, one empty, the other with an oilcloth faro layout. And behind the layout, welcoming all comers, sat Asa Wall.

C H A P T E R   5 6

S usannah wished she had a proper lady for a cabinmate, but that was not possible. The ship teemed with people, and she should be grateful she had a cabin, and wasn't camping on the main deck, like so many. The mob worried her. She saw only four lifeboats, and knew they wouldn't hold half those aboard this vessel.

Belle surveyed her cheerfully as Susannah slipped a light cotton dress over Margaret Temperance. That afternoon the cabinmates had said little, and both had explored the vessel, though not together. The ship was a three-masted side-wheeler, capable of hoisting sail if the steam engine should fail.

But the moment came when the dinner bell sounded, and she and Belle smiled tentatively at each other.

"I guess you don't approve of me, do you, honey?" Belle asked.

"I hadn't thought about it," Susannah replied awkwardly.

Belle looked amused. "Try that one again," she said. "Most women don't cotton to a gambler's lady. Fact is, I deal myself and I make a point of using my female charms to draw gents to my table. Well, what's it going to be?"

"What do you mean?"

"You can snub me, befriend me, or give me the cold shoulder. The icy silence usually works."

"Oh, I'm sure we'll get along."

Belle eyed her cynically. "Well, if you can't manage it, just figure it's only a few days and then you'll be rid of the hussy. Where're you from, honey?"

"Mountain Pleasant, Iowa. That's where Iowa Wesleyan is."

"Who's that? Some politician?"

"No, a Methodist college. My family—"

"Oh, Methodists. Don't touch spirits, don't gamble, don't waltz a lady, and don't play cards. But I guess you enjoy box-lunch socials."

"Yes," said Susannah, meekly.

"Well, I touch spirits, I deal cards, my man isn't my husband, and I can whirl a good waltz or mazurka. If you don't want me to sample spirits in the cabin, why, honey, say the word and I'll do my sampling at the rail, watching porpoises."

"No, no, that's all right."

"Booze's good for the bad water. A little brandy, a little wine, that's what you need in the tropics. Any southern lady knows that. Don't sample water, just sip a little bottled stuff, and you won't fetch the cholera, or the Chagres fever."

"Oh, I'd never heard of that. And my religious—my convictions prevent it, of course. We're quite strict, but it's for our own moral and spiritual benefit."

Belle chuckled. "I like you, honey," she said. "You want to make the first sitting—if that's how they do it on this tub? I guess cabin passengers get sittings. Down in steerage, they'll just set out pails of slop."

"Oh!" Susannah cried. Belle could have used politer words, she thought.

"Don't stand there disapproving, sweetheart, grab the little lady and we'll dig in."

Cabin class or not, the food was abominable, and eaten only with spoons from greasy bowls because the ship lacked utensils. They nibbled at a tasteless stew, tackled hard rolls, and were served thick black coffee, which Susannah politely declined.

"Guess coffee's on the Methodist list too, eh?" Belle asked cheerfully. She uncorked a brandy bottle and laced her coffee with it. "Rotten meal. The brochures said French cuisine. Well, I'm French and I haven't seen one onion or truffle or mushroom yet."

"I don't believe I know your name," Susannah said, slowly feeding broth into Margaret Temperance, who was making faces and spitting it out.

"Look at that little thing. She's honest. Spits the stuff out, and no nonsense about it. . . . Call me the Yellow Rose. That's what I'm called in the Quarter."

"I like Belle better."

"Well, my young Methodist friend, it strikes me that we should travel together for our mutual comfort. You know nothing about males, so I'll be the expert. And I know nothing about children, except how to prevent them, so you be the expert."

Susannah blushed. Thus did she come to enjoy her first acquaintance with a demimondaine. They walked the ship together as it plowed through glittering tropical seas, hovered in their shadowed cabin during the oppressive heat of midday, and took the air together in the tropical twilights when the sun plunged under the sea and darkness fell like a curtain. They worried together when a youthful passenger died of cholera and was instantly buried at sea wrapped in sailcloth. And worried more when two others died the next day.

"Have a little brandy, honey; it'll hold off the fevers. I promise you it will," Belle said.

But Susannah firmly shook her head. "It's the road to perdition—ah, I mean, it might be," she stammered.

Belle whickered affectionately.

The next dawn they anchored at a sea road a mile off Chagres, which appeared as a green wall on the ocean, with misted verdant slopes rising behind it. The river split the town in two.

A swarm of small craft, some rowed, some sailed, and one of them a steam launch, descended on the *Atlantic Star,* but only the little launch tied up. It turned out to be New Granada officials, health inspectors, who would not permit any sick person off the ship. There were several of those, all survivors of cholera, duly quarantined. But at last the officials debarked and the swarm of little lighters and dugouts edged in, banging and bobbing against the iron hull.

"You want to stick together?" Belle asked.

"Yes, please yes," Susannah said, relieved. Belle was much more worldly, spoke some Spanish and French, and had been protective during the whole trip.

The bedlam proved to be too much for two women, and they waited while gold-crazed passengers negotiated their passage to shore with a variety of half-naked men, none of whom spoke English, but understood what a dollar or a shilling were. An ocean swell careened the bobbing boats into each other, and tossed descending passengers about like dolls. Trunks and portmanteaus bounced and burst, each mishap yielding a babel of profanity in three or four tongues, which made Susannah blush. But at last, for two dollars apiece, and one for the baby, the women were ushered into a wobbling craft propelled by two oarsmen who looked like some mixture of Spaniard, Indian, and African. When at last the bobbing craft approached the beach surf, the passengers were given their choice of stepping into the ocean, along with their trunks—or being carried to shore, for another dollar apiece.

Belle laughed and forked over. A burly boatman lifted her bodily, stepped into the breaking waves and deposited her on the sand beach. Susannah, determined not to permit a man to take such familiarities, primly lowered herself into the furious water, felt a wave lift her, screamed, changed her mind, dug in her reticule for some bills, and found herself and her infant deposited on the warm beach. She dripped water from her heavy skirts, which clung all too close to her body. Belle laughed.

"Now we hire some more of these pirates to take our trunks to a hotel—if they have hotels here—and then we hire someone to take us up the river and down the Pacific side," Belle said. "I don't suppose any of these gentlemen would care to help us." She said it loud enough to rattle the consciences of a dozen American males, but it yielded no results.

After that Susannah left matters to Belle, who conducted lively negotiations in some sort of fractured Spanish with various native gents, most of whom smoked cigars and laughed at everything she said.

"All right, honey, they're taking us to the United States Hotel, run by some American. And that big buzzard there, he'll fix us up on a bungee in the morning."

"What's a bungee?"

"Little flat-bottomed scow with a canopy over it for passengers. Some native boys'll pole it up the Chagres River, two or three days, until we get to Gorgona. From there we walk twenty-two miles—or hire some impossible mules that buck at every chance—down to Panama City on the Pacific. And there we wait."

Chagres disturbed Susannah, partly because it was so alien, but also because it felt hot and unhealthy. Across the river was the native section, or old Chagres, a mottled collection of cane huts, scabrous wooden buildings, and a few stone edifices clustered under a formidable crumbling fort on a brooding hill. On the newer side, jerry-built plank buildings, looking wet and cancerous, rose out of filthy streets that stank of every foul odor given off by animal or man. Half-naked men, their bodies glistening with sweat, walked the streets, many of them hawking fruits and sweets, coffee and trinkets.

She felt afraid, and pulled a cotton crib-cloth about Margaret Temperance to hold off the sultry air. She could barely breathe in the oppressive heat. In spite of its name, the United States Hotel turned out to be a vile building whose rooms were narrow slots containing two cots, separated by muslin partitions. The price was five dollars a person, including the baby. Helplessly, the women paid, and found themselves and their possessions in a cubicle. For not the first time, Susannah feared robbers, any one of whom could walk in and take all she owned.

She felt trapped, out of air, desperate to escape the place, but there was nothing she could do. Belle had started some serious swilling of brandy, and warned Susannah to do likewise for her health. But Susannah primly refused. She would not stoop, just because she was in a foreign land.

Nothing untoward happened that night. They downed mushy meat of unknown provenance—Belle suspected stewed monkey—and the next morning the gent who had negotiated the bungee trip escorted the women to the river where the little vessel bobbed on oily waters. This would cost six dollars, plus two more for the factor. Belle was enjoying herself, talking a raucous Spanish with these wiry, near-naked males, whose sweaty bodies drew Susannah's gaze more than she wished to admit.

All that day the natives poled the bungee up the Chagres, often in the company of two or three others of the little craft. The river shrank, its gloomy banks a solid wall of foliage, vines, lush palms, towering trees, gaudy tropical flowers. Alligators slithered into the murky water, shooting up bubbles. Monkeys swung from limbs, and gossiped about the intruders. Susannah gaped at a world she had never dreamed of, a world somehow sinister though she couldn't say why.

That night they were taken to a cane hut with a roof of thatched palm leaves, and left to themselves. There were no beds, only the gritty earth, crawling with God knew what, and open to poisonous serpents. Mosquitoes whined and swarmed, biting poor Margaret Temperance until she cried. Belle bargained for some food, and eventually the guides presented various tropical fruits, some coffee beans, and some whitish meat that Susannah feared might be snake. She couldn't eat much. The child didn't eat, either, and had grown restless. They spent that long night on the ground, suffering a surprising chill before dawn, never sleeping and never at ease.

The next day their boatmen poled as far as their native village, a compound of thatched huts, and refused to go farther that day because they were visiting their families. Susannah tried to make herself at home among these people, but felt ill at ease. Belle tried to bribe their boatmen to carry on, to no avail.

"We're stuck, honey," she said, unhappily. But they weren't alone. Half a dozen other Americans, all males, were trapped that night in the village.

By the time they reached Gorgona, the head of the river,

Susannah was weary of jungle, which now arched almost over the small stream. Gorgona consisted of some cane huts, a few white plank warehouses thrown up by enterprising Americans, a stand where one could buy a small cup of coffee from a Yank for a shilling, and a mob of New Granadians eager to guide travelers the final twenty-two miles to the Pacific, either on mules or on foot. Politely she declined the coffee, but Belle drank three cups, each laced with brandy. "You'd better take some for medicinal purposes. It neutralizes bad water. I've got so much brandy in me that the mosquitoes that bite me get drunk. Take some. You look peaked, honey. Look at me, healthy as a horse."

"No, I mustn't do that," Susannah said.

Wearily, she slid into a filthy hut Belle had rented for the night. She felt sick. Worse, the baby was feverish, her cheeks unnaturally rosy, her little lungs working too hard. Frantically, Susannah sought help from several whiskey-sotted Americans, sought a doctor. But there could be no help in the middle of the Panamanian jungles. All that weary night she applied cold compresses to her miserable child, and prayed.

CHAPTER 57

By dawn Susannah felt as leaden as the rain forest around her. Fever consumed her and her head ached. The baby lay quietly. She had not whimpered for hours. Outside of the thatched hut, mules brayed and men stirred. Belle sat up, studied Susannah, and reached for her brandy bottle.

"There's breakfast," Belle said, swallowing a mouthful. "You look like the devil."

"I'm all right," Susannah insisted.

"No you're not. You're sick. The child's sick. Do you want to stay here?"

"I don't know."

Belle laced up the white high-topped shoes she had worn ever since debarking. "Let me see what I can arrange," she said.

A half hour later, in the company of two guides, they set off for the Pacific Ocean, each on a sullen mule, their baggage on others.

Susannah slumped in her cruel saddle, scarcely aware of her surroundings. The narrow road tunneled through rain forest and immersed her in gloom. She cuddled her quiet baby, watched gaudy parrots, heard the strange screeching of wild creatures, and surrendered to the sultry heat that oiled her brow. The air was so oppressive it was hard to breathe.

They nooned in a grassy clearing. Susannah slid off her mule, clutching her uncomplaining baby, and sat on the earth, feeling desperately sick. Belle eyed her sharply, knelt beside her and felt her forehead.

"You're burning up," she said.

"I'm all right, I'm all right!"

Without being bidden, Belle dragged Margaret Temperance from Susannah's arms and lifted the white cotton sheeting away from the child's face. Belle stared, touched the girl, and sighed.

"We'd better bury her now, Susannah. The tropics don't permit much time before—"

"What?"

"We'd better bury your girl now, honey. Yellow fever. Chagres fever."

"I'm taking her to Ulysses."

"Susannah—"

"He's never seen her. His heart'll melt. She's such a dear girl . . ."

"Susannah. I don't think . . . Honey, she's dead."

"No, she's just sleeping. Let me have her."

Reluctantly, Belle handed the small still bundle to Susannah, who clutched the girl to her and rocked her in her arms.

The two guides watched. Belle spoke in Spanish to them, and one approached.

"Honey, you've got to let go, now. We've got to get you to the coast, and a doctor."

But Susannah was crooning a lullaby she remembered, "Rockabye Baby." *When the bough breaks, the cradle will fall.* She saw the native man holding out his arms. He wanted her baby.

"No! You can't have her!" she cried.

Belle sighed and said something to the guides. A moment later they started off again. They traveled nonstop all that day, and plunged into the tropical dark, made all the more inky by the leafy cover overhead. But a fevered yellow moon glared, and eventually the guides led them down a steep descent and out on a plain. They passed thatched-roof shacks, some with howling curs, and then more formidable homes of white-washed plank, ghostly under a pale and eerie moon. A towering stone wall loomed before them, and they passed through an arch into a crowded, rank city, its weary buildings jammed together.

All this she barely observed, having sunk into a strange lassitude. She knew that Belle and the guides were consulting, and finally the mules halted before a stone building incarnadined by the moonlight. A guide shouted its owner awake.

"This is an inn run by an American—a black man from New York," Belle said. "We can stay here. A constable is coming for your child. A sanitary inspector. In Panama City a person dead of an infectious disease must be buried within an hour. You— that child's . . ." She couldn't finish what she had started to say. Susannah peeked at her baby.

"Margaret's all swollen up," she said.

The innkeeper held his candle lantern and examined them solemnly. "I've got a place for the ladies, but not that." He gestured toward the small bundle. "We'll wait a moment, when all this gets fixed up. You each, five dollars a night."

Belle prodded Susannah. "You'd better pay up now, honey. And you owe me for the guides and all. It's twenty dollars, more or less."

Numbly, Susannah dug into a small purse. "Will they take American money?"

"They've got money changers all over the city, honey. Now we'll wait for the inspector. I'll hold the baby and you go on in with Mr. Smiley."

"No," said Susannah, but she couldn't stand up anymore. She stood swaying, clutching Margaret Temperance, and then the child vanished from her arms—as if to heaven—and someone was carrying her into the gloomy place, which exuded bleak, sad odors, and someone was settling her on a canvas cot and unlacing her scuffed shoes, and drawing a grubby sheet over her. She felt a hand on her forehead.

"Gone before dawn, I imagine," someone said. "She'll be yellow as a squash."

She didn't care. She wanted Ulysses to walk in and bathe her with cool water.

She knew light and dark rotated regularly, and she ached and she always felt parched, and it was an ordeal to sit up, and when she opened her eyes pain lanced her head. She kept hearing bells, night and day, some sweet, some sour as vinegar, as if the clappers had broken them to bits. Someone—that woman Belle, she guessed—lifted her head and pressed a glass to it. The liquid was medicinal.

"Hope Margaret's not a trouble," Susannah said.

"You sleep, honey, and when you get better, we'll get tickets. It's a fright, getting tickets. Our names are down. We're in the queue. Might be here a month."

"Take me to Ulysses," Susannah said.

More light and dark smote her, kaleidoscopically tumbled together, and then one evening she woke up to the cracked bells. She lay in a cot in a room with cloth walls. She could hear others moving about beyond the cloth. She had a raging thirst, but when she tried to crawl out of the cot, she couldn't. She drifted back to a gauzy world around Mount Pleasant.

Then she saw Belle, who stood over her holding a candle-lantern.

"You made it, honey."

"My baby's dead."

"Ten days ago. There's a place full of new graves, none marked, ten or fifteen a day they say. She's there. I stuck a stick in, so I can show it to you."

"Ulysses will never see her."

"He'll see you, honey. And you can start over."

"I don't know if I want to."

"You'll feel better in a few days."

"Why do I keep hearing bells?"

"Because that's all they do in Panama City. They ring bells for every mass. Cathedral bells, parish church bells. For mass, for holy days, morning, noon and vespers, and just for the hell of it."

"You took care of me all this time?"

"It wasn't so much. We were stuck anyway. All those nice notions about picking up a ship on the Pacific side in a few days—well, there aren't any. Everyone waits. There're two Pacific Mail Company steamers making the run, and a few clippers and a few old tubs, but they can't handle the mob here. It takes six weeks to catch a ship." She surveyed Susannah. "And you'll need it. They won't take sick people aboard."

Susannah stared numbly at her benefactor. "I owe you a lot," she whispered.

"Fact is, I helped myself from your money belt. We're square. I paid your rent and paid for a doctor—a gold-rush man from Connecticut—and made a deposit on a cabin-class ticket at Zachrisson, Nelson and Company—the booking agents for the steamship companies. We'll share a cabin again, if we get one. They overbook. There's a receipt in your money belt. I have it; didn't think it'd be safe with you when you didn't even know when anyone was in here."

Tears came to Susannah's eyes. "Did they bury Margaret properly?"

"It was the middle of the night. They don't let the dead wait a minute here."

"What was she buried in?"

"Just the things she wore, with a sheet around her."

"Did anyone say anything—a service?"

"All they said was 'Chagres fever.' "

"Is there a minister who'd say a prayer here?"

"Ministers are out of my line, honey."

"I loved her so. I almost went with her. I wish I had."

"You have Ulysses."

"I'm not sure I want him. If he'd stayed home . . ." Her thoughts shocked her.

"We'll see. Now I want you to drink this medicine. The doctor wants you to have it."

"What is it—extract of chinchona bark?"

"No, that's for malaria. It's brandy and water. The water's no good here. You have to put spirits into it or you'll relapse."

"I wouldn't think of it. I've never taken a drop."

Belle laughed softly. "You've taken a quart," she said, amusement playing around her lips.

"I have? Oh . . . well, then, I suppose I must. I will have to talk to Reverend McCracken about it."

Belle handed her the glass. The contents tasted vile. "I don't know how anyone can stand spirits," she said, "when they could have apple cider."

Belle laughed again, almost unkindly.

For the next week Susannah rested in her miserable cot and ached for her baby. Then Belle hired a carriage for a small drive each twilight, after the oppressive heat of the day had lifted. Susannah gazed at a crumbling old city built of stone, with a crumbling cathedral and crumbling mercantiles cheek-by-jowl, the streets jammed with peddlers of every imaginable fruit and vegetable, coffee vendors, pastry vendors, men and women alike smoking cigarillos, the women sultry and vivacious, the men grave and proud. Meat vendors peddled fly-blown monkey and anteater carcasses, along with chicken and things she couldn't identify. Americans wandered everywhere, hundreds, thousands, all awaiting passage. Rotting sheds lined the wharfs. She couldn't see the true Pacific, which lay around a headland, but only the debris-strewn bay, teeming with small craft, all as cancerous as the city.

One day a four-mast clipper glided in, and the city fairly exploded with joy. Americans materialized as if by magic, and mobbed the ship, clambering aboard, most of them to camp on its main deck clear to San Francisco.

"They'll be miserable," Belle said. "It takes forever by sail, and there's no tradewinds here, they tell me. Sometimes it takes weeks just to get west enough to pick up a breeze. They'll eat garbage, live in filth, and half'll croak. Every one of those boats, steam and sail, is overcrowded, the food is rotten, the latrines unspeakable, and they carry more diseases than I can name."

"You put it very plainly," said Susannah, who sometimes wished her companion would use the polite euphemisms she had grown up with at Mount Pleasant. But mostly she loved this frank, hearty woman, who took care of her simply because she cared.

They squandered another ten days waiting for the steamship, and Susannah feared her funds—never very much—would run out. Then, at last, a grimy side-wheeler, *California,* glided in, to the sound of cannon firing, bells clamoring, and the rattle of carriages and wagons in a mad scramble to the wharf.

With a little luck—if the tickets were good—she would soon be off to San Francisco, and Ulysses.

CHAPTER 5 8

The gaunt woman who stood at the rail, watching San Francisco draw nigh, was not the woman who had left Mount Pleasant more than three months earlier. The woman watching a swarm of lighters sail out to her ship doubted that she loved her husband; saw neglect and selfishness in him, and didn't really believe that he had come to California to give her anything. Her comfort had been his excuse. His intent had been adventure, a skylark, being among brash and carefree men, even if he had honeyed it over with the syrup of duty and love.

Susannah would find him and weigh him. She might divorce him. When Margaret Temperance died, so had her love for Ulysses. She was girded for the possibility that his love of her had taken flight—if he had ever really loved her. He could have written. Other men wrote their wives and families and their mail got through. A part of her wanted to blame him for Margaret's death, but she resisted that. She had chosen to make the risky, dangerous trip, and any blame was hers alone.

The trip aboard the overcrowded, malodorous Pacific Mail Company steamer had repeated the horrors of Panama City. Tropical diseases crouched like panthers: malaria, yellow fever, cholera, dysentery, scurvy, and a dozen more without names. Every day until they reached cooler waters passengers had been buried at sea, shrouded in sailcloth, the incantations of half a dozen gold-mad divines committing their souls to the deeps. Each day had reprised her own loss until she grew indifferent to death.

She had followed Belle's example this time, mixing brandy with her drinking water, and neither of them had been scratched by the claws of death. But even as she drank the brandied water, she wondered why she bothered to live. The hollow at her breast, the still-yellow arms and hands that found nothing to hold, all eroded the former self but gave her no new one. If she found nothing to admire and love in Ulysses, she would surrender herself to whatever tides washed over her in California.

"Well, we made it," Belle said, as the great anchor rattled into the waters of the dazzling bay. "Pretty good for a pair of brandy-tipplers."

"A part of me did," Susannah said.

Belle studied her. "Have you enough money left?"

"A hundred something."

"In a place like this, honey, that won't last a week. If you need help—"

"I'll manage."

But Belle would not be put off. "Susannah, in Portsmouth Square there'll be work for any woman—not respectable by your standards, but work that won't violate your beliefs. Like serving spirits or selling cigars. Good tips. I can help."

"Thank you, Belle. I must go to Sacramento City. I don't know how I'll find him, but that's the place to start. It's so big. . . ."

Belle eyed her affectionately. "Susannah," she said softly, "we've come a long way. We've shared the worst. Between us, we survived."

Susannah turned to the cheerful woman who had helped her through grave illness, loss and mourning, and could not come up with adequate words. She clasped Belle to her and wept, loving this woman who had loved her.

The upstart gomorrah lay beyond a forest of masts, a horde of forlorn barks that forced arriving vessels to anchor far out in the bay, and unload expensively by lighter. Susannah beheld a bright city that hadn't existed two years earlier, but now looked as if it had been there for generations, its greedy hand out, plucking at every sojourner. Quietly she watched raucous boatmen bargain for passengers and freight, shouting, bidding, demanding, while passengers grimly dug into their depleted purses for still more coin of the realm.

"Is your gentleman meeting you?" Susannah asked Belle.

"I don't suppose so. He's wedded to the ace of spades, and the turn of a card's obviously more important."

That puzzled Susannah.

"Your face is sure a question mark," Belle said. "It's not love we have, if that's what you're wondering. It's— We're kindred spirits. Friends and allies. We understand each other. Life's better together. We'll make a lot of money and blow it, and make more. When I'm around, his faro bank's never broke. When he's around, I've a shoulder to cry on."

Patiently they watched the maddest of the gold-mad depart, paying more for being first off the ship.

It turned out that they would take different lighters, Belle to shore, and Susannah to a river packet that would weigh anchor within the hour for Sacramento City.

They hugged. "You've got a lot of courage, honey," Belle said softly. "You'll be fine because you're strong."

"Oh, Belle, thank you for everything," Susannah cried.

"All I did was dose you with brandy," Belle said. "Led you down the old primrose path." She laughed heartily, like a female Falstaff. "'Bye, hon."

Susannah watched her cabinmate clamber down a gangway and into a bobbing sailing craft. A minute later Susannah found herself in a lighter lurching across a quarter mile of heaving water to the *Senator,* a glistening packet with side paddles.

No cabins were available. Deck passage and her trunk cost nineteen dollars. She would have to sit up all night, maybe in the saloon. Once she wouldn't have done that; now it didn't bother her much, though she knew she would be fending off men. The air was chill, and the chill matched the ice in her heart. She wrapped her black shawl around her, settled on a bench near the boilers, and watched as the crew at the capstan hoisted the anchor and the packet shuddered to life. Rough, cheerful men, most of them bearded, wearing slouch hats, hickory shirts and home-made trousers, examined her respectfully.

One approached, managed a yard-wide smile, doffed his battered hat, and said, "Good afternoon, ma'am."

She nodded.

"We don't often see a woman, least a white woman," the man said. "Just want you to know, we're all admiring you."

She didn't quite know how to take that. "I'm joining my husband. . . ." she said, tentatively.

"Well, that's a good thing to do. Lucky fellow. Most of us've left our sweethearts back in the States and we pine for them pretty regular. A letter is like a thousand ounces to us."

"Yes, a letter's all that to me, too."

"You know where your fellow's mining?"

She faltered. "No, not exactly. I—I was going to put out word. Last I knew, he was going to the Mokelumne River."

"Oh, the southern diggings. Well, you'll find him. It's easier than it sounds."

"But how?"

"Expressmen. Just about every miner gives his name to the expressmen, so they can pick up mail at Sacramento City and deliver the letters in the diggings. It's a fine old racket. You just go to the post office when we get in and talk to all the expressmen. Pretty soon you'll find one that knows exactly where your husband is."

She smiled. "That does sound better than I'd imagined. Then what do I do?"

"There's coaches now to some places. We're getting organized right smart. Catch a stage. Most of 'em run by Jarvis and Marble, biggest outfit around, regular Concord stages out of New England. What's your man's name? Maybe I know him. I've mostly been in the northern diggings but I moseyed into Angel's Camp for a few weeks."

"Ulysses McQueen?"

"Nope, that's not one I've met. But we've sort of a telegraph system out here, and I'll put word out. You'll want a stage to Mokelumne Hill, and I'll put out the word."

"Why—thank you."

"It's sure nice to talk with a fine woman," he said. "I'm Preston Bean. You need anything, or someone to look after you betwixt here and Sacramento City, just holler for Bean."

"I'm obliged, Mr. Bean."

She couldn't find a dining room, and discovered she should have bought a box lunch from a candy butcher. But the miners rushed to her comfort, plying her with so much sourdough bread she couldn't eat more than a little. Truly, these big, awkward, gallant men, who had braved a continent or an ocean to dig for gold, had a tender side. It comforted her to know they had so many sweethearts waiting for them. She had feared she was plunging into vile company, but now she sensed the goldfields wouldn't be like that. Maybe she had been too hard on Ulysses. They were all Ulysses, in a way.

She studied the distant shores, discovering grassy brown slopes, rather barren for her tastes. The chill of the ocean penetrated far inland, and she could find no place in the packet that felt warm. The vessel tied up at a woodyard near Benicia and took on cords of firewood, the crew forming a human chain to pass the logs aboard. After that, the captain waited for moonrise before building up steam and plunging into the oily waters again.

The packet arrived at the Sacramento levee just after dawn, and Susannah beheld a drab row of warehouses squatting on a flat barely above the river. Mountains of crates and barrels rose from the levee in wild disarray, apparently unguarded. The odors of rot and waste hit her nostrils, making her dislike this ugly place. The gangway dropped to the levee, and the mob on board elbowed its way to the ground.

Preston Bean approached her. "You got a trunk or something? Me and the boys'll save you a drayman's fee. You want to put it in that express office over there?"

"That would be kind of you," she said, pointing to her trunk and portmanteau.

"Well, you tell your fella he's a lucky cuss, and all the miners say so. Now, the post office, it's yonder, just back from the levee. Opens at nine, and you just stand there and ask the customers if they're expressmen."

"Thank you, Mr. Boun, but if I don't get some rest soon—"

"Oh, you can manage that. Not a decent hotel in town, but if you don't mind a little intimacy—"

"Whatever do you mean?"

"Ah, canvas hotels, one big room. You get to sleep on the floor, if it's got a floor. Maybe fifty men in a room and nine thousand bedbugs."

"But there must be a place—an inn. . . . I've been sick. I need . . ."

He scratched at a cowlick. "Well, I tell you what you do—if you can afford it. There's boats all over here, abandoned tubs, live ones with crews. You go deal with the masters for a cabin overnight."

"Thank you again, Mr. Bean."

Wearily she bargained for a cabin in a Jarvis and Marble Company sloop that was laying over and then dragged herself to the post office, where fifty men had already queued up in the early light of day.

"I'm looking for expressmen," she said.

"Most of us are, ma'am," said one. "What can we do for you?"

"Do any of you know where I might find my husband, Ulysses McQueen?"

"Oh, sure," said one. "He's at Mok Hill. Big Bar, just below town. Three McQueens in the southern digs, but only one Ulysses."

"Is he well?"

"Well enough to buy his mail from me."

"How do I get there, sir?"

"By coach, Mondays, Thursdays, and Saturdays. You can get passage back on the waterfront, Jarvis and Marble Store and Express office."

"Why, that's where I have my trunk. Thank you, sir," she said.

"Glad to help a lady," he replied. "But I guess I'll lose business. No more letters from his sweetheart."

Men laughed wistfully.

Now she was so close to Ulysses—and so uncertain she wanted to see him. She had a day to wait, a day to sleep. Then she would see what Fate brought her.

CHAPTER 59

A sa Wall paid off a coppered bet on the king, pushing three chips next to the wagered three, and turned to McQueen. "Well, McQueen, you're looking prosperous," he said.

"I'm all right. I see you made it."

"Just barely." Wall drew two cards, loser and winner, from the faro box with the Bengal tiger on it, glanced at the bets, saw that none of the miners had won or lost that round, and waited for them to lay down more bets.

"You working some gravel here?" Wall asked.

"Big Bar."

"We've some catching up to do, but not now. Wait until I shut down."

"I could play, and we could talk."

"You could, but you won't."

Hotly, McQueen thought of pushing some coins onto the layout, but wrestled back the urge. "I'll come in tomorrow afternoon," he muttered.

"I won't be up."

McQueen retreated into the night, worked doggedly with Bacon the next day sinking a new coyote hole, and didn't reach gold-bearing gravels until late in the day. They divided half an ounce between them. Gouging gold from under six or seven feet of overlying gravel wasn't going to be easy with two of the partners gone.

Early that evening, feeling weary and out of sorts, McQueen found Wall alone at his table, shuffling a stack of chips single-handed.

"Here's what I owe you," he said. "It's five pinches." He pushed some dust, in waxed paper, across the table.

"You're as good as your word," Wall said, adding the dust to a fat poke beside him.

"Tell me what happened after the company split up," Ulysses said.

"Well, Ulysses, it was like this. Dobbin and Clappe were hell on the mules, and just like you said, they didn't last. We were hardly three days ahead of you when those beasts croaked, one by one. Dobbin's a cruel devil. I kept mine alive longer than the others by finding feed for it, rubbing it down, lifting off the packs whenever we stopped. But Dobbin and Clappe took it from me, and the next day it croaked, too. Just quit and laid down. So there we were. And no outfit would help, either. But by God, that didn't slow Dobbin down."

"You didn't save time after all, destroying the mules."

"Oh, we saved a few days. But we arrived in the diggings with nothing. We ditched everything, save for what we could load on our backs. For me that meant the layout. You wouldn't think this stuff'd be so heavy, but it near killed me. We begged food, or paid for it if we had to, walked across the

Humboldt Sink at night, up the Truckee, and over the Sierra to the northern mines. Ended up on the south fork of the American ahead of most of the overlanders, but the Panama crowd had beaten us. The rest had to work for others so they could buy shovels and goldpans. I set up shop under a live oak."

McQueen almost burst with virtue. Dobbin and Clappe and all that vicious, greedy crowd had ended up worse off. But Asa Wall wasn't done with his tale.

"The outfit spent a miserable month, barely making enough to keep body and soul together, Dobbin in a rage. I didn't make much either. Miners were too tired for cards. Dobbin was getting madder and madder, hating the ones who'd gotten there ahead of him, especially the ones who'd cleaned up in 'forty-eight. There wasn't any good ground left, except maybe some dry digs, fifty or a hundred yards from water, where you had to bucket water, or bucket gravel, and take three or four dollars a day out of it if you were lucky. Dobbin and Clappe whined about prices, too. There were rag stores, mostly Jarvis and Marble Company, and they wanted so much dust for flour and beans and coffee that Dobbin was talking of burning 'em down."

"They're here, too, Asa. I might work for one if I had to. They pay enough to lure men away from the gravel."

"Well, Ulysses, it's a long story, the rest of it. We drifted to all those bars up north—Long Bar, Rattlesnake Bar, Whiskey Bar, Deadman, Mormon, Murderer's . . . and the story was the same. Frozen out. Skunked. Busted. Now here's where Dobbin and Clappe are a pair of jokers. The run of men would've gone prospecting for new gravel, or tried to form companies to work with a long tom, or just contented themselves with dry diggings—or quit. But not that pair. Half starved, and hating working for others, ready to slit throats, they took to politics. Clappe's got a silver tongue, and he used it. They simply stirred up the malcontents; demanded a miners' meeting to reduce the size of the claims. They had it all schemed out; wanted to cut all claims in half and raffle off the new ones. Well, that's when things got mean."

McQueen well remembered Dobbin, the former army corporal, with big fists and a way about him. "They must've fought."

"There was fresh blood on the ground, and some fingers busted and some noses mashed. And things got bad. Every man in those camps had a sidearm and was ready to use it. But then, at Deadman's Bar, they won. Dobbin's mob had the votes, the miners' meeting voted to cut the claims in half and parcel out the new ones. Dobbin's toughs—he recruited twenty or thirty more and drilled them into a gang—drove off a lot of angry miners who'd staked there earlier. But by then I'd pulled out."

"You left?"

Wall sighed. "Sporting men aren't welcome sometimes, especially when they come with a party of troublemakers. A man with a gambling layout looks pretty soberly at torchlight parades, armed gangs, and men carrying hemp neckties. I vamoosed, as they say around here. Mok Hill's a hundred miles south of trouble."

"Dobbin and Clappe—they're making money now?"

Wall shrugged. "Who knows? But I'll tell you this. They found it's easier to make money chasing miners off good claims and reselling them than it is to scratch gravel all day. I'd say they're minting gold. They'll do well using their fists—unless some serious law gets organized in the goldfields."

"I'm glad I'm not a part of it," McQueen said.

Wall grinned cynically. "I think maybe old Virginius Dobbin'll be heading east with his pocketful of rocks—one way or another."

"Well, I'm not doing so bad. Theo Bacon and I partnered. We've a cradle, a shack, and a mule fattening up in the hills. It's hard going, because the gold's under a lot of dirt, but we're making our keep and our pokes are getting heavier. We just bought out the Laliques."

"Well, stay out of trouble, Ulysses, and don't blow your dust on this layout. You've got the temptation. I saw it out there on the Platte, you eager as a pup to break the bank. You put down dust on those cards, and friendship stops. That's when you try to get your paw in my pockets, and I try to empty your poke. It's war; it's my living. I take my living seriously. Understand?"

Wall spoke with such menace in his tone that McQueen flinched. But he nodded.

"All right, it's understood," Wall said, blowing a smoke ring.

McQueen spent the next weeks toiling with Bacon. They dug four new coyote holes, looking for the nearest and richest gravels at the bottoms, with inconclusive results. By shoveling from first light to dark, and cleaning up the sand by lamplight, they managed to make eight or ten dollars a day, which they split. They weren't getting rich. Neither were they falling behind. There were always rumors, and every time one swept the camp, a few miners—usually the ones with the worst claims—would take off. The rumor of a fabulous place called Gold Lake, where nuggets lay on the beaches as thick as a carpet of acorns, drew a few men away from Big Bar.

"I hope I'm never that dumb," McQueen said. "If there's one thing I've seen around the diggings, it's how the rumors gobble up fools, and they end up building flumes for some rich outfit for four dollars a day."

"There's some abandoned claims around here. Maybe we should look 'em over," Bacon said.

They lost three days trying to prise dust out of claims men had quit, and ended up back on their own. Then one day, when the spring flood had edged over most of their three claims, Theo Bacon caught McQueen after a pot of beans.

"Partner, I've about had my fill," Bacon said. "Water's up. The Mok drains a lot of high country. I'm not earning much, and neither are you. I'm thinking of pulling out."

"Where'd we go, Theo?"

"I mean selling out to you. I've had my fill. Standing in ice water until my legs go numb. I'm worn down, and likely to take some disease. I'm tired of sand in my pancakes and grit in my teeth and the smell of dung around the camp. Tired of woodsmoke hurting my eyes. Tired of gold-camp prices and never getting enough rest sleeping on the ground. Tired of having no privacy, and worrying about my poke being stolen. Got a cough. I've come close to sickness and so've you. Like when dysentery came through here and we buried three good men, just like us. Like when that coyote hole caved, me half buried and you trying to shovel me loose. Like when the fights started and we couldn't stay out of them. I'll sell you my share for only a hundred."

"But I can't coyote alone. It's a two-man deal."

"Find another partner, Ulysses. You've been a good partner

to work with. We've both worked hard. We got what we could out of California. I've got enough in my poke to get me home over the Isthmus, and maybe a lot of stories to tell a few pretty girls I know back there."

"We could just ditch these and go find some other claims, Theo. We've got enough between us to buy one or two—and the cradle and the mule, and plenty of tools."

· But Bacon shook his head. "No sense in it. Most gravel's going to be underwater until late summer and we'd just be waiting around, wasting what we've got. No, it's a big lottery. Some fellows struck it rich, most didn't."

McQueen nodded. He didn't want to buy Theo's share but he didn't have much choice. "All right," he said. "Hundred dollars for the three claims, your half of the mule, and your half of the tools and stuff."

They walked up the slope to Mok Hill, weighed out the gold at Jarvis and Marble, and shook hands on the deal. McQueen's poke was pretty light in his hand. He hefted it sadly, figuring it contained maybe fifty dollars. He had that much cash, and three claims.

An odd sadness pervaded the parting. Bacon pulled out the next day, catching a ride with an ox-team outfit for a dollar a day. McQueen watched him go. Of all the men who'd come west with him, Bacon had been the one he had trusted and admired the most. Suddenly Mok Hill seemed an alien place, filled with ruthless men, the crowd shifting every day so it hardly paid to get to know any of them. He thought back, remembering all the men he'd met since leaving Iowa, temporary alliances, temporary friends, self-interest dictating whether they work together or split apart. The diggings were the loneliest place on earth. It didn't matter which bar, what town, what mine. No one was there permanently. No one liked the country much. Too brown and dry much of the year, not enough change of season to refresh a man.

Pierced by loneliness, he worked what little dry gravel he still had above the cold torrent of the Mokelumne River, making barely enough to sustain himself. His heart wasn't in it. Maybe in July, when the waters ebbed, he could start in again with a new partner. Maybe he would make a good bundle and go back to Susannah.

He hadn't thought much about her in recent days, when everything seemed to be changing. The expressmen hadn't brought a new letter for weeks. She was probably back there, bouncing the baby on her knee, watching his brothers plow and harrow and plant the fields, patiently waiting for him to bring her what he said he would. He missed her badly.

The thought hurt. Unless he got lucky, he wasn't going to bring her much. He'd end up sneaking back there like a whipped dog. The thought tortured him. He couldn't do that. He had to go back there with his pile and show his folks and Susannah he'd succeeded. Otherwise . . . The vision of returning with nothing, facing his mocking father and brothers, facing a disappointed Susannah, appalled him.

He fooled around on his bar for another day. A lot of men whose claims were underwater were idling in Mok Hill, or taking a jaunt to Sacramento City to blow their pokes on wild women and wild times. A few had quit. Most were just waiting it out.

He just couldn't stand it anymore. That evening, he'd take his dust and try his luck on Asa's faro layout. Maybe he'd win his way out.

CHAPTER 60

A sa Wall set aside the battered issue of the *California Star* that had wended its way from San Francisco to Mok Hill, and surveyed McQueen as he settled himself at the faro layout, laying his poke on the table.

"You've been warned," Wall said.

"Play."

"Whatever's in your head, get it out. If you want to bring Susannah something, go into business. It doesn't take much. Become an expressman. You've got a mule."

"Play."

Wall ground the stub of a cigarillo into the planks, plucked up McQueen's poke, poured the contents onto his gold scale and added brass weights until the balance needle pointed at zero. "At sixteen, it comes to forty-seven and a fraction."

"Put two pinches back and give me forty-five."

Wall counted forty-five grubby white chips and put two pinches back in the poke. Then he shuffled the deck, turned over the soda, a five of spades, and dropped the deck into the casebox.

"You want me to keep cases?"

"Yes."

Wall slid black beads along wires on a contraption that resembled an abacus. The device now told an observer that the five of spades was out of play. Wall squinted, grinned, and drew.

McQueen bet to win. The first three turns yielded no winners or losers. Then he lost ten dollars on the jack. It hurt. At the rate he was mining, that was three days' hard work. Wall watched him, his eyes glowing with feral delight.

Ulysses felt his courage wilt, and cursed his own stupidity. He laid ten chips on the jack again, and coppered it, placing a Chinese copper coin on top of his chips, betting the jack to lose. Three remained unplayed. Wall drew the first card of the turn. A jack. He pulled the second card. A jack. Wall beamed. A tie went to the house. The jacks had lost and won. Ulysses lost. Wall smiled, savoring the victory. The stack of grubby whites before him bulged like a pregnant bride.

Ulysses' heart hammered. He could cash in and walk away with twenty-five dollars. But he hated that devil across the table, his old friend oozing amusement like hot tar. Ulysses would show him who was a man. He edged all twenty-five chips out, betting the nine to win. Delight filtered through Wall's face, the look one might see on a rich man's face when he stole a newspaper.

"I've built my bank from two hundred twelve to nine thousand, McQueen. Maybe you'll break it. We both like nines."

"Maybe I will."

Wall drew the turn, a queen and four. The bet rode. He drew another turn, a king and eight. The bet rode. He drew a nine, loser, and ten, winner. Ulysses watched his twenty-five white hopes snug up to Wall's belly. The gambler kept a quiet silence, but Ulysses loathed him anyway. It had been too easy.

"You have three claims," Wall said, softly.

Ulysses peered around the crude wooden saloon. Two boozy miners imbibed sour beer from battered tin cups at a plank bar. The barkeep, his black hair parted at the middle as if cleaved by an ax, leaned on the planks, puffing blue smoke. Outside the swinging batwing doors, spring light was fading. Over on Big Bar, or French Bar, or Chile Gulch, miners were cleaning up their take or starting cookfires or seining flies out of the soup.

"Two hundred a claim. That's fair."

Wall smiled. "What did you pay Theo Bacon for his half of the three?"

"A hundred." Ulysses choked on the words.

Wall cocked an eyebrow, and politely refrained from saying anything.

"Three hundred for the three, double or nothing on the turn of a card, aces high, suits in order, spades, hearts, diamonds, clubs," Ulysses snapped. His heart was galloping. Six hundred would take him home in triumph.

"Inflation," said Wall. "All right. Three claims for three hundred on the turn of a card." He summoned the keep with a wave of the hand. "Witness," Wall said. "These arrangements require a witness."

The keep wandered over. So did the two mining stiffs.

"Mr. McQueen is putting up three claims on Big Bar, at a hundred apiece, on the cut of the deck. Is that right, McQueen?"

"Yes."

"And it's aces high, suits in order?"

"Yes."

Wall cut a ten of hearts. McQueen cut a nine of spades. Wall reached into his portfolio and withdrew a steel-nibbed pen, a bottle of India, and some foolscap, and pushed them to Ulysses.

Ulysses wrote out a bill of sale: "May 3, 1850. Herewith sold to Asa Wall, three claims, registered to Ulysses McQueen in Big Bar Claim Book, and numbered 47, 48, 49." He signed it, and pushed it to Wall, who read it carefully and handed it to his three witnesses, who signed it.

"It will teach you virtue," Wall said cheerfully. "A good man can profit from his mistakes."

"You enjoyed it."

"Adversity refines a man."

"You're a bloodsucker."

"I warned you away from my table."

Ulysses had no answer, and whirled into the gathering dark, aware of the gazes on his back. He would leave Big Bar. Somewhere, up some unexplored gulch, he would dig up a bonanza, maybe under the mother lode. He'd show them.

By the time he reached Big Bar, darkness lay thick. He saw no stars. They had been obscured by one of those mean mists out of the mountains. The stars would not reveal what direction he was going. He wondered if a compass would. The chill had turned sharp-edged and penetrating. He slipped into the blackness of his tent-roofed shanty and collapsed on his bunk.

So it had come to this.

Who was he? What had he been? Who would he be? What lay in the mysterious future? Why? How?

For a while he let his thoughts tumble through his mind but everything in his head seemed oddly trivial. He needed to cobble one of his boots. His new flannel shirt had a rip in it.

He had spent only ten minutes at Wall's table, but the seasoned gambler cleaned him out. Wall knew how to make use of weaknesses. It was Wall who had suggested the bet on the claims, the double-or-nothing that would let Ulysses walk away with a modest gain, enough to save face. He didn't blame Wall. He could only blame himself. He was a boy, after all.

The boy had found all the justifications to abandon his wife, and adventure into the wild West. The boy had hurt Susannah, left her alone and pregnant early in their marriage. The boy had told her he was doing it for her and had studiously ignored her response that all she wanted was him at her side. The boy had said he was going to find wealth and make her happy, but what the boy had really meant was that he wanted to adventure. The boy hadn't been ready for marriage or the sober business of being a father and a provider.

He wondered whether Susannah loved him now. How would she feel when he returned with nothing—a year later than he had planned to return? How would his family respond when he walked into Old Oak and took up his plowing again—this time using borrowed mules?

He lay quietly, his thoughts adrift, aware of the sharpness of the air. Maybe some good had come of it. Tonight the skylarking boy had vanished. Fifteen months after he had walked down the lane and out of his family's life, he had come to manhood. It was not what he had been that counted, but what he could be now, and would be if he acted with determination and courage.

His thoughts turned to his father, who had been the bane of the boy in Mount Pleasant, his iron will dominating every decision in Ulysses' life. In spite of that, he found himself admiring and respecting his father. At a young age Stanford McQueen had built a cabin there, plowed virgin prairie, fought off the Sauk and Fox, watched civilization creep in around him, protected and nurtured his wife, attended to the spiritual needs of his family, and had lived to see the fulfillment of all his youthful dreams—save for one rebel boy. For the first time in his life, Ulysses didn't resent his ham-fisted father, and for the first time in his life, Ulysses found merit in his father's counsel, endlessly repeated and embedded in the souls of each of the sons.

There came to him a marvelous insight: A boy becomes a man when he finally can befriend his father. He becomes a strong man when he can accept at least some of his father's wisdom. And a boy becomes a man when he follows his own star. He neither disdained his father and his father's wisdom, nor surrendered to his father, as his brothers had. He had reached independence; his brothers never had and would go through life as echoes of the patriarch, not as whole men.

"Well, Pa," he said into the jet of the night, "here I am. I'm Stanford McQueen's son, and most of the things you wanted me to do and believe are what I am and what I want. And the things you warned me against turned out to be things to avoid. Like gambling. I found out the hard way. When I get back to Mount Pleasant, there'll be things to talk over. . . ."

If his father would listen. If he ever got back. He had two pinches of dust in his poke, no claims, and bleak prospects ahead. Things had gone sour for Susannah in Mount Pleasant, according to the last letters. He wanted her here, he wanted his baby girl. Maybe he should leave Mount Pleasant behind him.

Ulysses sighed, knowing he could not resolve these things, or even fathom them, without information. He knew also that he had more immediate decisions to make. Would they be so hard? Whatever the gulf between him and his father, he was a

McQueen. He valued hard work, honesty, courage. And unlike his father, he valued love and independence. He knew suddenly he wasn't a miner, and he wouldn't mine again. All his life he had grown grains and other foodstuffs—wheat, barley, corn, oats, squash and other vegetables. He had raised hogs and sheep and cattle. He had kept milk cows. All these things were in his bones and blood, as easy to him as gambling was to Asa Wall.

He would find satisfaction in them. There would be more pleasure in selling a wheat crop to a miller than in striking a vein of pure gold. He wondered if crops could be grown in the great central valley of California, in spite of the long dry summers. It might require irrigation, or certain good bottomland close to underground water. They were saying in the camps that an incredible hundred thousand people had come in the rush of 'forty-nine, and this year there would be an even larger horde. They all needed to be fed, and yet there was scarcely a farmer in California, and not much of a cattle business either, except for the Californios, who were few in number. Most of the foods that sustained these mobs of miners had come from elsewhere, as far south as Chile. A man could prosper in California, raising foods for this hungry crowd.

All he needed was land. He had a mule, a cradle he could trade for a plow and harness, and a few tools. Then he would feel the moldboard turn the good earth, furrow upon furrow, and feel the harrow break up the clods until his land lay ready, and then he would broadcast his wheat until the land lay pregnant with it. He would hoe and weed until the fields turned golden, and then he would scythe the grain and winnow its fat kernels, warm and heavy in his hand.

He didn't know how he would get land, but the province wasn't really settled. Maybe he could squat, as his father had done, until he could claim the land he worked. He would find a way.

Tomorrow he would leave the gold country. If he worked fast, he could put in a crop this year and earn enough from it to pay for Susannah's passage west.

He felt calm. Asa Wall was right, he thought. A man could learn from his mistakes.

CHAPTER 61

T he stagecoach wound through gorgeous emerald hills but Susannah didn't notice them. The landscape of her heart held her attention, not the exuberant slopes, riotous with spring blossoms. She could not fathom herself. The woman sitting with her back to the future and watching the past roll by wasn't herself; she was a stranger who hurt with every lurch of the wine-enameled coach on its thorough-braces.

She rather liked to sit facing the rear. She was more interested in where she had been than in what lay ahead. Let the other passengers, all men, peer forward. They would not see a dead child ahead, but she could see the very place outside of Panama City where her baby lay under a mound of yellow earth. Belle had reluctantly taken her there, when she had recovered enough to be driven out to a pestilential place hacked out of the forests. Now, in the lurching coach, she could renew the images of her Isthmus passage, the groaning Atlantic steamer, the gaudy river-boat, and her exile from the comfortable farm where she had tried to put down roots in poisoned soil.

She ached for meaning, but nothing came to her. Now she was being carried backfirst toward Ulysses, toward some sort of blank future in an alien land she didn't know or care about. Spiritually it was much the same. She was approaching Ulysses backfirst, not with open arms.

She had married a boy. A beautiful boy with an infectious glow about him, but not an adult ready to assume the responsi-bilities of caring for her and the children of their union. Perhaps it wasn't all Ulysses' fault; no son of old Stanford McQueen had ever been allowed to reach adult independence, and all the brothers had been marked for life by the old iron-willed man. She had to give Ulysses some credit: he alone among Stanford's pups had resisted.

She remembered her wedding day, when she was nervously

dressing in the ivory silk-and-lace gown she and her mother had sewn, and her mother was feverishly tugging and tucking and chattering in a way she never had.

"Well, Susannah, it won't be easy. You're not just marrying Ulysses; you're marrying Stanford McQueen," her mother had said.

Susannah had laughed nervously. "We'll have our own home, and I intend to be mistress of it," she replied. "And when I'm a McQueen, I get to live forever."

Her mother had paused. "Stanford McQueen's luck won't last forever. Someday soon, death will cut down that family. I pray God it won't be you or Ulysses first into the earth."

But Stanford McQueen's defiance of death still held, and she had never been mistress of Old Oak Farm. Invisible cords ran from everything in the house, including the McQueen furniture, to the deathless old man.

That was one of the strands of thought her restless mind plucked at that morning as the rocking coach penetrated deeper into the majestic foothills on the western slope of the Sierra Nevada. She heard the thrum of hoofbeats, the rumble of the iron-tired wheels grinding over rock, the groan and protest of leather, and salty conversation of the Jehu above her head as he talked with the passengers beside him. She smelled sweat and tobacco, though the day remained cool and the glassless windows let balmy air percolate through the cramped interior.

She knew her presence in the coach had stifled conversation. These men weren't used to a lady, and kept ogling her furtively, scarcely believing they had the real article among them. Some had tried hours earlier to make polite talk and she had replied absently, her mind not on society but on the haunting dilemma she faced: whether to stay married to a skylarking youth or undergo the pain of a divorce, which would mark her for life. And plunge into whatever lay beyond that. Those in the coach watched the emerald world slide by, waiting for release from the politeness required by the proximity of a woman.

The time drew close when she would arrive in Mokelumne Hill and she was unprepared. Her ear told her this final six-horse team had wearied; the coach had climbed steadily for a dozen miles, and the brutes would suffer another five before they were halted at a Jarvis and Marble station there. She had maybe an hour to make sense of the future, make sense of her feelings about Ulysses. But she knew she could not do it. When she found him, and experienced that golden grin and glowing cheer, she might forgive him everything and then hate herself for it. Or if she forgave him nothing and told him of the death of their baby, and taxed him with his failure to write, and stood bitterly before him—she would hate herself for that, too.

The weary hour slid by. She was hungry and needed to stop for her comfort, but said nothing. Then, after a long hard pull and passage along a hogback, she found herself passing amiable buildings. Most were board and batten, the rest were framed tent-structures, and all of these were perched on slopes. Mok Hill's commercial area rested on ridges and dropped into residential gulches. The town slept in the sun, and not even a dog met the coach as it drew up before a wooden building with a galleried porch offering shade to several onlookers.

"Whoa, whoa," bawled the Jehu, and the team readily complied, blowing and snorting. The passengers sat politely, until she realized they were waiting for her to debark. She pushed open the veneer door and stepped into hot sun, feeling begrimed as she always did during her travels. The acrid smell of horse sweat drifted in the air. It seemed a benign place, yet she felt fear. She noticed the men in the shade, rough fellows in mining duds, illogically looking for Ulysses, as if he should somehow know of her arrival and meet her. But she was alone, among strange males, and the cynosure of their eyes. Being a respectable woman in a womanless society would take getting used to.

She watched the Jehu and a man from the station pull her trunk and portmanteau from the boot.

"What would you like us to do with these, ma'am?" asked the clerk.

"Just hold them inside for now," she said. "Perhaps you'd tell me how to go to Big Bar."

The thin mustachioed clerk smiled. "That's easy. Just take that long downhill path until you hit the river and walk beside it a piece. You looking for someone in particular?"

"I'm Mrs. McQueen."

"Ah, indeed, Mrs. McQueen. Ulysses, he's got a reg'lar tenthouse there. I reckon Ulysses, he's gonna be a lucky man today."

"You know him, then?"

"Well, everyone knows everyone, at least if they stick around awhile. Some come and go. Now, don't ask me the names of them Chileans, or the Frenchies, but I know the Americans."

She felt ravenous but ignored her hunger and set off, walking a dusty path through thick brush, until she found herself at the river, which raced angrily out of the mountains. Odd panics afflicted her. She couldn't even imagine what she would say to her husband, or how he would react to her unannounced arrival. The path took her to a broad flat where the river widened into braided channels. A shanty city arose there, mostly tents but also crude shacks, dugouts cut into banks, smoke from cookfires hanging over the valley, and innumerable men, mostly bearded, toiling over wooden things she knew were rockers or cradles, while others were shoveling dirt into long wooden troughs she had learned were long toms, their duck-cloth trousers and colorful flannel shirts soaked with river water or sweat.

Somewhere here would be Ulysses! She examined the toilers one by one, aching to discover him. Which one would he be? Big Bar was so large, and she spotted so many.

The presence of a gray-clad lady walking through the diggings halted the work. Men stared at the apparition, tucked shirts into britches, and stood awestruck. All this embarrassed her, though she had come to understand it. She saw no sign of Ulysses, and at last approached a group of four of the miners.

"Pardon me, gentlemen," she said. "Could you direct me to Ulysses McQueen?"

"Ulysses? Ulysses, ma'am?"

"Yes, my husband."

"Why, ah, he left the bar two days ago."

"Left the bar . . . ? But surely you must know where he went."

"Well, we don't rightly. He mined over there. . . ." The man pointed toward an area that looked to be in the river. "Had three claims, but he upped and lost them to Asa Wall and pulled out."

"Asa Wall?"

"Ah . . . in Mok Hill, ma'am."

The name sounded vaguely familiar. Asa Wall. Was there something in Ulysses' letter about the man? "Maybe you could take me to Ulysses' cabin," she said. "Maybe he left a message. Surely he didn't leave the area for good."

"I'm afraid he did, ma'am."

The miners took her to an oak grove back from the water, where a framed canvas structure stood. Ulysses' home. She entered it curiously, seeing abandoned bunks in the soft light filtering through the cloth roof. She found nothing in it that reminded her of him.

"Did he do well, here?"

A cheerful giant with ruddy, sunburnt features responded. "Why, he and his partners had three claims, but the gold lay under a lot of gravel. They coyoted it."

"What does that mean?"

"To get to the good gravel, down on the bedrock, they had to dig holes, maybe five or six feet. Hard work, ma'am, but Ulysses, he was a bear for work. Him and Theo Bacon, they did good enough. At least, while they partnered . . ."

She sensed that the miner wasn't telling all, and wouldn't. "How can I find him?" she asked.

The miners stared at each other. "Ulysses sold his cradle when he pulled out the other morning. That's a sure sign he isn't planning to mine anymore. Cradles are plumb valuable. And scarce. These days, you can hardly make it without one."

"But where would he go?"

"Beats me," said one. "He didn't leave word. You might try Wall. He knew Wall from way back. Come over the Platte River Road together."

The gambler. She remembered now. "I'll talk to him," she said.

She hiked desolately up the long grade to Mok Hill. She found the saloon, and hesitated at the door. It would not be proper to enter it. Over the batwing doors she saw men leaning into the plank bar, and others sitting at tables. At the rear, a middle-aged man presided over a gambling table beneath an oil lamp.

Gathering courage, she swung open the doors, and approached the barkeep. She had never been in a saloon before; no proper woman would enter one. She addressed the surprised keep, who wore a dingy white apron.

"Would you tell Mr. Wall that Mrs. Ulysses McQueen wishes to speak to him on the street, please?"

"You Ulysses' old lady, eh?" the man said, curiosity leaking from him. "All right."

She fled outside, and waited in the late-afternoon light, which cast long shadows across the gulches.

The man who emerged from the saloon had glowing, feral eyes and was darkly handsome. His dress stopped short of flashy, but exuded a certain luxury.

"Mrs. McQueen? I'm Asa Wall," he said, his gaze missing nothing about her.

"Mr. Wall, I'm looking for my husband. I believe you know him. They told me you might know where he went. You bought his claims."

Wall considered that, while enjoying the moment. "It's not often I get to meet a lovely lady," he said. "I haven't the faintest idea where he went. He came in here four nights ago, threw away his last dust and put his claims up on the turn of a card. He lost them. He wanted to go back to the States with something in his pocket. It meant a lot to him, going back with something."

Her pulse leapt. "Are you telling me he's gone east? To Iowa?"

Wall shook his head, amused. "No. He's going to have to earn his passage now. I suggested he become an expressman."

"You took money from him."

"I tried not to, ma'am. You might say he tried to take money from me and failed." He shrugged. "Call it volition. It wasn't my volition."

"I must find him."

"California's a big place, Mrs. McQueen."

"Where can I stay? I thought I'd be staying with him."

"Not much by way of hotels here—unless you want to share a flop on a straw tick with fifty men in a canvas room."

"Could I stay in his cabin on Big Bar? Is it safe?"

"Stay there. It's safe. You'd have two hundred miners looking out for you. . . . Ah, Mrs. McQueen, I've people at my table."

"Thank you for your time. When you have an hour, I'd like to hear the whole story. You and Ulysses traveled out the Platte, didn't you?"

He smiled. "It's quite a story, ma'am. I'll stop by and tell it. And good luck. You start asking, and maybe someone'll know where he is. Word floats around these camps like it was carried by carrier pigeons."

She watched the man who had cleaned out Ulysses' poke vanish through those batwing doors. Why did she like him? How innocent Ulysses was, making a travel partner of a wicked man like that.

At last, hunger overwhelmed her. She discovered a beanery, which she would patronize shortly. She needed to have her luggage hauled to Big Bar. She needed to make a respectable living. The next days would test her mettle. She had a dead-broke husband in California, a man who'd thrown away all he had on the turn of a card. She held the deuce of clubs when she needed an ace.

CHAPTER 62

All that night Susannah wrestled her dilemma. She barely even dozed. Ulysses' canvas cot wasn't comfortable, her shawl was no match for the chill, and she lacked a pillow. Occasionally she heard footsteps outside the thin canvas, and gulped back fear.

But all these were mere annoyances compared to the wrenching reality of being alone, almost penniless, and looking for a penniless husband in an unorganized province. Whatever she did, she would do on her own, with only her own counsel to guide her. By the time the long night faded, she had no answers and no sleep.

When she first detected dull light penetrating the sailcloth over her, she walked into the gray mists, needing a moment's privacy in the bushes. Instead, she found the whole camp awake; cookfires laying smoke over the bar, and men washing at the river. Miners, it seemed, made use of every bit of daylight. She would have no privacy. She didn't like this place. As soon as possible she would hike up the path to Mok Hill and find something there. Hesitantly, she scrubbed at the icy river, but she yearned for a hot bath, and didn't feel cleansed by the shocking ice water.

They all let her alone. Feeling achy and unhappy, she repacked her trunk. She hoped a café would be open up the hill. If not, she would just have to wait. Oh, why wasn't Ulysses here to help her?

"Ma'am?"

Someone was outside. She pulled aside the flap that made a door, and beheld the big bearded miner who had spoken for them all the day before.

"Thought you might like some biscuits," he said, proffering a tin plate laden with them.

"Oh! You're so kind."

"Well, the gents here, we know you haven't got a skillet or a fork or any vittles, and we thought maybe you might welcome a bite."

"Oh, I do. I don't believe I know your name. . . ."

"Jericho Mannion, ma'am, from Delaware. Call me Jerry. Did you get any rest?"

"I'm afraid not."

"That's how we pegged it. You're not fitted out for a camp. But I hope you weren't worried about being a lone woman here. There's some two hundred men here who'd shoot the first devil that misbehaved in your company."

"Thank you. That was one of the things on my mind."

"You just tackle those biscuits and gravy and let me talk a moment," he said.

She did, finding them delicious except for the grit or sand or something she kept biting into. The bracing air made her ravenous.

"We sat around trying to think how we can rope old McQueen and get him back here for you. One thing every man in camp agrees on, it's that you shouldn't go chasing. The thing to do, if you don't mind us saying it, is to get word out. We've got ways around here. You know about the expressmen, and that's a start. But not a day goes by but we don't get a few new fellows, and a few take off for some other place where the gravel's going to be richer. And that's just a part of it. Almost every day, we get freight outfits into Mok Hill, ox-teams, packmules, stagecoaches. All we have to do is put the word out. We'll give the word to the store-keepers. Why, the Jarvis and Marble outfit can find anyone.

You give us a fortnight and we'll snag old Ulysses back here."

"But he might be leaving the country."

"No, ma'am, he didn't have the means—at least, far as anyone knows. He's plumb sick of mining—he told us that when he sold me the rocker. He's going to find work of some sort."

She nodded, polishing off the last of the biscuits. "Those were perfect, Mr. Mannion." She handed him the plate. "I must owe you something."

"No, ma'am, that's a gift from the men here. There's not a fellow who isn't happy to have you here. You're the first woman on the bar, and pretty near the first woman in the district, except the Frenchies and Chilies have one or two. It's, well, you're a sight for sore eyes. You remind us of our sweethearts, if you'll forgive me for saying so."

She enjoyed the affection from these woman-starved miners, but staying here posed problems.

"Mr. Mannion, if I can find a means to support myself . . ."

"Mrs. McQueen, you'll be making out handsome here if you can cook, or sew, or look after the sick. Why, we hear of a woman up on the American River, she runs a regular bakery and makes pies right there in a shanty, and sells 'em for a dollar apiece and profits five hundred dollars a month. She's selling pies to men that haven't seen a pie for two years."

Susannah smiled. "Making pies, sir, requires a stove, a kitchen table, rolling pin, pans and utensils, and all the necessaries, including the fruits—apples, or peaches, or cherries, or what have you. Not to mention a lot of stove wood and pie tins."

Mannion was clearly enjoying himself, almost hopping from foot to foot. "We've got all that. We'll fix you up with a stove, too. You make pies and sell 'em for a pinch, and you won't have to worry about that."

"A pinch?"

"A pinch of gold, ma'am. A dollar. They'll just open their pokes and you see how much you can raise in a pinch. Usually, it's fifteen or sixteen pinches to an ounce of dust, so it comes out fine. That's all we've got for a measure."

She pondered that. "I'm not sure about cooking. Ulysses might return tomorrow. . . . But I'd sew. If the miners need sewing, I'm good at it, a fine stitch—"

"Oh, we need that. But pies . . . every man on Big Bar aches for a pie."

"Well, all right! And I'll take in sewing. I've all the things in my trunk, even spare buttons. But I might not be here long."

"Well, ma'am, as long as you're here, Big Bar'll rejoice."

"You'll help me get word out?"

"Any miner'd help a lady in distress."

That was how Susannah found a toehold. That day she hiked up to Mok Hill, sent brief letters to Ulysses for general delivery at Sacramento City and San Francisco, talked to the man in the express office, asked the shopkeepers to talk to the teamsters and packers about Ulysses, timidly left word in the saloons, and caught the Jehu of the outgoing stagecoach just before he climbed up to his perch.

He heard her request, and tipped his broad-rimmed slouch hat. "We'll scare him up, Mrs. McQueen," he said, cheerfully. "At one time or another, most everyone in California boards a Jarvis and Marble coach or walks into a company store. The company likes to help folks. Goodwill. We'll track him down."

"Oh, thank you," she said.

She had done what she could. The miners on Big Bar would spread the word among their restless brethren. She bravely spent the last of her banknotes at the Jarvis and Marble store, buying small quantities of flour, sugar, salt, dried apples, a crock of shortening, and sundry other things. She hunted for a rolling pin, didn't see one, and wondered if the miners' dreams would crash on the rocks of that humble reality.

She needn't have worried. When she returned, she discovered a simple sheet-metal camp stove set up, a stack of kindling, a plank counter to work on, some pie tins, bowls and utensils—and a heap of torn clothing in a wicker basket. Someone had manufactured a rolling pin out of a piece of barked treelimb.

She looked it over, especially the stove. The oven, with the stovepipe poking through it, wasn't very large. It was going to be tricky to operate, and she would probably burn a few crusts. But this was a camp, after all. In spite of her weariness, she pulled an apron from her trunk and set to work. All that day rough miners managed to amble by, study her and her miraculous kitchen, and smile shyly. The poor fellows hadn't seen a woman for so long they were acting peculiar. She enjoyed the attention. Not a one of those rough men, most of whom wore sidearms, said or did anything that wasn't entirely acceptable to her.

That day she managed eight dried-apple pies. They didn't please her much. The crusts weren't up to snuff; the two on the bottom of the oven had burnt; the top two weren't quite golden; and the apple filling wasn't sweet enough and too runny. But it didn't seem to matter to these yearning young men. When the first batch was cooling on the plank table, miners moseyed by, examining them as if they were gold dust. She didn't know how she would sell them fairly, but it turned out the miners had worked that out. Each pie was to go to four men, and each party of four had drawn a number. She discovered she had been booked up for two weeks.

"I don't know what to charge for these," she said to the first foursome. "What do you think?"

"Two pinches, ma'am. That's what we figured. You'll make about one pinch a pie after you take off the costs."

"Eight dollars in one day?"

"A lot of men here fetch several times that, so don't you worry about it."

Timidly, she pushed her fingers into the proffered pokes and pinched out as much as she could, stowing the gold dust in her kidskin purse. The first four pies vanished, and when the next four sent their aromas wafting across Big Bar, those vanished too. And in her purse was something like an ounce of gold.

The day had whirled by. She scrubbed all the borrowed kitchenware, and then sank onto her cot, bone tired. She would tackle the mending later. She lay quietly, trying to sum up what this day had brought her. She had a livelihood, at least. She never had dreamed what a woman and a woman's skills might mean to miners. She could wait here awhile, especially with summer coming on. But if she didn't find Ulysses? How long before she could settle into a tub of heated water, and luxuriate in it for a while? How long before she could have a home of her own—not as comfortable and grand as Old Oak, but a real home?

She couldn't answer that. She drew her shawl around her again, and wished she had a real bed, and could wear a real nightgown of flannel, and could pull Margaret Temperance to her breast and hold her peacefully, feeling the tug of life and love.

The days rolled by and she barely noticed their passage. She learned the names of the men and their natures. She enjoyed all of them, though some seemed almost surly, and a few were bitter because the gods of fortune hadn't touched them. They were certainly a boisterous, bright, educated lot. Many had books and offered them to her, but after her daily sewing of shirts and britches she didn't feel like reading them. These men were much like Ulysses, she thought, adventuresome and young, well schooled and mannered, not the ruffians she had imagined she would find. They had left sweethearts behind, just like Ulysses. They loved their wives, wrote them, pounced on the mail brought by the expressmen, whooped at the news, studied the occasional newspaper that reached the bar, debated the world's great affairs with passion. California had formed a government and petitioned Congress to admit it as a state, not a territory. But the Southerners didn't like the antislavery clause in the California constitution, and Congress had been in an uproar ever since. There were only two or three Southern men in camp, and they became silent and withdrawn in the face of such vehemence.

June slid into July and July into August, and one day they learned that President Taylor had died of cholera morbus. And Congress still held the fate of California, and the territories of New Mexico and Deseret—now called Utah—in its deadlocked hand.

Ulysses seemed to have vanished from the face of the earth. Where had he gone? Then one day early in August, when new men fresh from the East were arriving in camp, she received word.

PART VI

1850

T here are ways to bury one's self alive, but none of them helped Stephen Jarvis much. The best was work. He toiled obsessively at his business, often burning lamp oil before dawn and after dusk. Over in San Francisco, Caleb Marble bought shrewdly, right off ships that had plowed the Golden Gate. He warehoused some goods and shipped the rest to Sacramento, where Jarvis ran the retailing and transportation ends of their expanding company. To an outsider it might seem that Jarvis and Marble Company had a throat-hold on the gold-rush business, but Jarvis knew otherwise. He competed ferociously with dozens of other large companies and independents, whose managers often had better ideas than his own.

Rita was married, living near Sonoma, and out of his life. Part of him had become resigned to it and knew he was helpless to change it no matter what his dreams might be. But another part resisted his fate bitterly and would not let it go. It didn't matter that Jarvis was still a young man, with prospects, and was often the cynosure of admiring female eyes. He did not lack for the acquaintance of eligible young women, even in woman-starved California.

But love has its own mysteries, and his love for Rita Concepción persisted, even grew, in the midst of sheer futility. He could not answer his own accusations—that he was behaving in a destructive manner; that he would be better off with an American. All those wise things he considered, embraced as his own, even as they withered in his heart.

Rita was the Señora Zamora, faithful wife of Salvador, a ranchero north of San Francisco. So, in the weariness of his defeat and in his unrelenting loneliness, he turned to his ledgers and payments, his inventory and sales, his sometimes unreliable help, his wise old partner, and these things consumed his waking hours so that the hurt returned only at night when he could no longer evade it. That was as good a living death as he could manage.

Out of all this there evolved a strange idiosyncrasy in him. He considered most of his customers, toiling in the distant camps of the Sierra, to be men who had thrown away their one true treasure—their beloved and loving wives—for gold. What good lay in grubbing for metal when they could be with their wives? None of them knew the secret of life, the secret he had stumbled upon in his misery. He voiced this opinion often and acidly, and it was bruited around the camps, generating a lot of gossip. But he didn't care. Miners still spent their dust at his stores, no matter what they thought of him.

On Thursday afternoons he received salesmen, dealmakers, brokers, and occasional malcontents determined to give him a tongue-lashing for the prices he charged in the camps. Good always came from these sessions. He picked up merchandise at distressed prices, learned of surly storekeepers or cheats, discovered ways to improve his operations, added products to his lines, picked up gossip about new strikes or bars that were fading fast, and found himself quietly helping miners in distress, broken men who needed a ticket or a job or a friend. He had become a major employer in California, a place where broken men could earn a ticket to the States.

He had become the man to see with a business proposal; around Sacramento they alluded to him as "the man in the black suit," a phrase laden with connotations: it meant power, cash, and mystery, too, because the private life of the awkward young man who didn't belong in suits was curtained from public view, which generated much curiosity.

On one July Thursday the usual crowd gathered in the anteroom of his office suite in his newly built redbrick building on the waterfront, one of the first permanent buildings in Sacramento. His aide and factotum, Piers Gran, kept the crowd orderly and in proper queue, gave each five minutes before interrupting, and got things done. Stephen Jarvis had become the legendary factor who could help a man swiftly.

One of those who approached him that afternoon was an out-of-luck miner. There were plenty of those, far more than the successful ones. Jarvis surveyed the big, sunny young man and suspected he would be asking for a handout.

But that was not the case.

"I'm Ulysses McQueen. I guess I've got five minutes. I went busted in the goldfields, Big Bar, and want to stay in California. I was a farmer in Iowa—corn, wheat, oats, and some livestock. I notice your stores are always short of fresh fruits and vegetables, and even the flour comes from Chile and places like that."

"You want to import food?"

"No, raise it. There's hardly an apple or an egg to be had in California. Not many melons or squash. Chilean wheat, half moldy after coming thousands of miles."

"That's true. What's your proposition?"

"I'd like land to farm, pay you back with crops. You get everything I raise, and spare me enough to keep going until I get the land proved up."

"What's my advantage?"

"Food. Last year a hundred thousand miners arrived. More coming this year. You're hard put to feed 'em. I've been wandering around the central valley for a few weeks—it could be good cropland if a man learned to irrigate, and planted to take advantage of the fall rains."

"How do I know you'll stay, see it through? Are you married?"

"I've a wife in Iowa, and a girl I've never seen. I'll have to talk them into coming here."

"She expects you back."

The young man's hands clamped his ancient hat, and Jarvis knew he had struck the weakness in this. "Yes, sir. We've a nice farm there, Mount Pleasant, and she likes it."

"And if she won't agree to come here?"

"Mr. Jarvis, I'd like two years. You'd have the title to the land anyway. Just two years to make it work. I can get part of a crop in this year, have produce or grain by late fall."

Jarvis liked the man. They were about the same age. All that separated them was the California lottery, as it was being called. Jarvis had landed on good gravel; this fellow hadn't. "Tell me about yourself," he said.

McQueen started to, but Gran poked his head in the door, announcing the end of the appointment.

"Give us another five minutes, Piers."

Swiftly, Jarvis learned about a life lived in a farming complex in eastern Iowa, of years behind a plow, of serious commitment, of the moral and ethical and spiritual beliefs bred into the fellow—and of his new wife.

"It must have been hard on her—your leaving."

"I—didn't think enough about that, sir."

"Tell me—what does she mean to you?" The sore point again. Was he the only man in California who valued a woman? Didn't any of them know what sort of treasures they were abandoning? An old bitterness slid through Jarvis.

"I have some fence-mending to do, and I intend to do it," McQueen said.

"Not the answer I'd hoped for," Jarvis said sharply. "I'd hoped you would say you love her beyond all else in this world."

McQueen stood silently, defeat filtering into his face.

"A few months ago I would've said this couldn't be done. There was no way to get clear title. Now that's changed. We've a state government, even if Congress hasn't recognized it. They'll come around in Washington, and ratify what we've done here. Where do you want to ranch, and how much do you need?"

"I'd like a section, and in the lowlands along the San Joaquin, back from the tules. There's moisture there even now, when it's been dry. I've been poking around with a spade."

Jarvis liked that, and surveyed the fellow once again. "All right. I'll leave the details to my man, Piers Gran. I bought a lot of land from Captain Weber—he has an old Mexican grant over there. Stockton sits on some of it. I bought some riverfront for a levee. I'll give you your section. You sell me your crops the next two years at the going price and pay me off. If this makes no economic sense after a year, we'll reconsider. Fact is, I've been looking for a way to start some crops here—waiting for the right man."

McQueen stood, amazed. "You mean, you accept?"

Jarvis was growing impatient. "Piers," he yelled.

When Gran entered, Jarvis swiftly explained the transaction.
"Go plow. Draw on my warehouse for your tools and supplies. We've a few one-bottom plows and a harrow somewhere, and I'll send you a pair of mules and harness. And you'll need seed, a wagon, a scythe, and all the rest. We'll get it for you. I'll have seed down there before you're done plowing."

"Thank you, thank you . . ."

"It's not charity, McQueen. Everything I do is for gain."

"You'll gain, sir. I'll see to it."

As Gran was ushering McQueen out, Jarvis poked his nib into the ink bottle and wrote a few notes to himself. He had so much business to do these days that he had to remind himself of his commitments. This might be a good one. He liked McQueen. But the joker in this deck would have the face of the man's wife. The deal would cost two or three hundred plus the land, which lay idle. He had bought San Joaquin riverfront from Weber and had gotten unwanted hinterland as well. McQueen's proposition could turn a good profit in a few years—apples, melons, pears were scarce in the camps. The Californios supplied a few of these things, along with some beef and eggs, but much of it came around the Horn, the eggs pickled in brine, the dried apples and pears in casks. The melons and beans came up from Mexico, half rotted by the time they reached the miners.

He had taken lickings. His speculations in lumber had been almost ruinous. Whole shiploads of lumber had arrived, sent by canny speculators who figured it would be a scarce commodity, driving prices down from four hundred a thousand board feet to almost nothing. The same with picks, shovels, and goldpans, items shipped by speculators in Boston or New Orleans offices who fathomed what was needed and took the risk. He had taken a licking in tobacco, but made a killing in the tacks miners used to make rag houses. But in spite of those sudden hemorrhages, he and Marble were floating, as if on a wild sea.

That tiresome afternoon, he listened to a man who wanted to start a brewery because of the insatiable thirsts in the camps but hadn't thought about where he would get barley and hops, a man who wanted a job as a Jehu, a man who wanted to build rockers and long toms but lacked the means, a man who complained of being cheated by a company store at Campo Seco, and a dozen more. When Gran finally shut off the flow, Jarvis trimmed the wick, lit the lamp and made orderly notes out of all his scribbles. He had become a stickler for record-keeping, and found that his reports saved him money and embarrassment.

He stepped into a hot twilight, his nose offended as always by the filth of the streets of Sacramento City, which had no system of removing refuse. Spoiled goods lay everywhere, drawing rats and insects. The city had bloomed overnight into a muscular metropolis, hard down on the river that was its lifeblood, lying so low that any flooding endangered its commerce. The previous winter the swollen river had washed into his new waterfront warehouse, ruining stock on its lower floor. Jarvis walked up the stairs to his tiny apartment atop the warehouse, his monk's cell.

He might have lived a more luxurious life if he had felt like it. But luxury would be hollow with no wife to share it. So he continued to live in austere surroundings, not caring much about who he was, what he wanted to be, or why he walked the planet.

Only one thing separated this anonymous apartment from other anonymous dwellings: on his bedside table rested a lovely locket of ornate silver, containing the image of a young Californio woman. Every time Jarvis gazed at it, he knew he wasn't rich at all. Not like that fellow Ulysses McQueen, who was truly rich without even knowing it.

CHAPTER 64

Rita Concepción was not unhappy. She devoted herself to being a true and faithful spouse to Salvador Zamora, in all the ways that won the approval of her people. She could not change her life; what would be, would be.

She ran the rancho with diligence, making sure the *indios* kept the great adobe ranch house immaculate, the tiled floors clean, the food generous and well seasoned, the linens washed and bleached, the gardens blooming, the real glass windows washed, the pots and pans scoured, the good Venetian glass-ware shining, and the chapel dusted always. She had done all this at the casa Estrada, and needed no instruction from the señor here. She did not overspend, and marketed frugally on her occasional forays into Sonoma.

In all matters save one she bent to the will of the master of this rancho, but the one was a sore point with him. He hated her black clothing and demanded that she wear other colors. But this she refused to do. Whatever touched her body would be black, from now until the day they laid her in her coffin, and since this was a private matter, and not within his province, he could do nothing about it, though he had spent many *reales* employing dressmakers to produce light-colored frocks, all of which hung untouched in her armoire.

She entertained dutifully as well, a perfect hostess, often providing a feast for Salvador's parents, Don Francisco and Doña Isabel, who lived only a day's carriage journey to the north, or having her brother-in-law Ramón and his wife, Mercedes, out from Sonoma for an evening, or a Sunday afternoon after Mass. No one could fault her. She engaged in light conversation with the women, let the men argue their politics and rage against the Americans, and she agreed with all they said. She never gossiped, never behaved frivolously, and became known among the Zamoras for her genuine piety, her loving attention to all the obligations of her faith, keeping the feast days and holy days, often inviting the priest, the gaunt Reverend Father Emiliano Narváez, to her table.

When she shopped in Sonoma, walking from merchant to merchant around its generous square, she never failed to stop at the gracious mission at the corner, San Francisco Solano de Sonoma, there to light a taper before the image of Our Lady of Guadalupe, or pay her respects to Padre Narváez. A perfect wife, a wonder. The family Zamora openly said so, even if Salvador seemed sullen and withdrawn. She knew that if one looked closely, one would discover almost no communication between Rita Concepción and Salvador, but these things were veiled from even the powerful ranching family.

She sometimes felt his liquid brown eyes glaring at her, his bitterness barely concealed beneath that tranquil face. She could not help that. Whatever he had demanded, she had done for him, in all the facets of their married life. There was no talk of love, except the holy sort of love, *agape*, spiritual in nature and without selfish or sensual qualities. But there did not need to be. Romantic love wasn't considered important in arranged marriages. And if he had secretly expected it, he could say nothing, nor complain to anyone.

They had no children, and would not, and for this she was grateful, though she yearned to the bottom of her soul for several, to nurse and hold and adore and bathe and advise; children to be baptized into the Holy Faith, children to shepherd, in white satin, through their first Holy Communion; children to raise to adulthood. In many ways it was a great relief, even if she saw the hurt in Salvador every time their gazes met.

Late in 1850, not long after California became a state, their new senator, William Gwin, introduced legislation in the United States Senate that stirred fear and anger among the Californios. This powerful man, whose constituents were the gold-rush Americans, proposed to create a board of land commissioners to determine whether the Mexican land grants, given to Californios and a few outsiders like Johann Sutter, were valid. Even though the Treaty of Guadalupe Hidalgo had guaranteed that private property would be "inviolably respected," the greedy Americans would find ways to steal it. They were plotting these things at their new capital, San Jose, where their new governor, Peter Burnett, and his cabal were making laws against Mexicans and foreigners. Had not the new legislature already enacted the Foreign Miners' Tax of twenty dollars a month upon all miners who were not native-born Americans? Soon they would take everything away from Mexicans who were in California first.

It would not be difficult, and at the supper tables, she learned how it would happen. These grants, given to her people, had been casually described, without the usual metes and bounds used by the Americans. After all, there was so much land in California, what did it matter? The descriptions rested on a *deseño*, or hand-drawn map, and each grant had been claimed through a rite of walking the land with witnesses, uprooting grasses, digging up earth and scattering it, and thus possessing it according to ancient Hispanic custom. But these traditions would not satisfy the Americans, and from that day talk at the Zamora table turned dark, and the men of the family spoke blackly of injustice and poverty and rebellion. The news frightened Rita Concepción. What would become of the Zamoras? And the Estradas? And all the old Californio families? Foreboding clouded the life on the ranchos, as if a great storm crouched on the horizon.

But for the moment the Californios continued as they always had; nothing changed save for the presence of so many *yanquis* on the streets, some of them rich and arrogant. What concerned her more was her life with Salvador, this handsome husband, brimming over with passions that spilled like water boiling over the lip of a pot on a stove, vaporizing into steam. He would brood, so she talked to him—almost anything would do, since he didn't seem to care what was said. She talked about her stepmother, who was giving too much Estrada money to the church; and about the Americans in Monterey, whose *bailes* she had attended; and the new cook, Señora Gómez, from Sonoma, whose big fists and coarse threats frightened the servant boys who split kindling for her. But all Salvador did was stare, neither laughing nor nodding.

Thus the first year of her marriage passed. She was resigned to this, and foresaw no other life, until one day, a year and a day after her wedding, the padre, Emiliano Narváez, asked her to come at four bells of the afternoon to the mission church.

She appeared as required and was escorted into his offices, where he sat down, plainly ill at ease, twisting restlessly in his straight-backed chair.

"Peace be with you, sister," he said. "We have painful matters before us."

An odd beginning to whatever lay before them, she thought.

He studied some documents. She hadn't the faintest idea what they might be. He fussed so long that she felt nervous.

"Your husband, Salvador, has petitioned the Holy Church, seeking an annulment of marriage," he said suddenly.

The words stunned her, but on reflection did not surprise her. The reason was perfectly obvious and had been from the beginning.

"It is necessary to ask some questions. They will be painful and embarrassing. It is necessary that you answer truly. Only with absolute truth will you avoid the wrath of God, and the possibility of never seeing Him."

She nodded. It would be difficult. She had never talked of these things to anyone.

He smiled gently, as if to allay her dread. "These matters will go before the ecclesiastical court at the see of Durango, and will be dealt with through canonical law. It takes time; a year or so, because delay is proper, lest circumstances change, and the church must be in full possession of the facts. It is not necessary for you to go to Durango; all this can be done by proxies. Your husband has made the arrangements, along with his family."

Rita Concepción felt a certain bittersweet sadness. It would be too late to help her, if indeed she were given her freedom, a document announcing that she had never been married in the eyes of God.

"I will record your responses exactly, señora," he said, lifting a quill. "Now, first and most important, was your marriage ever consummated?"

"No."

"And was this because you resisted him?"

"No."

"Was there an attempt? Forgive me; was there a . . . coming together?"

"Yes."

"But no penetration, no loss of maidenhood?"

"He tried. But always failed."

"This is a most delicate matter, but I cannot offer you the confidentiality of the confessional. What is said here will be weighed by canonical lawyers and certain learned priests empowered by the Holy Father to perform this mission of the church. But please describe what happened. Of course you need not describe every detail."

It would be so hard to talk about this. She felt more naked than if she had nothing on. Now it would all be known. It must already be known to the Zamoras, but not the Estradas. She could just imagine Hector's leering contempt, or the averted gazes of her father, her brothers, her stepmother. Nor could she imagine what lay ahead. Surely she would be *desgraciada*, disgraced.

She did not need to summon back memories. They had always been fresh in her mind, and had been renewed every time Salvador had stared bitterly at her. He had not come to her that wedding night, nor the next nights when they had traveled by ship and coach to Sonoma, where he had shown her the rancho, and the room she would call her own. Salvador was sensitive, she had thought; he knew of her love for the *yanqui*, and was biding his time as a good man should. Like most well-off Californio couples, they had separate rooms.

At last he did come to her in his robe, toasted their marriage, and hugged her, peeling back her black cotton gown. She had not responded, nor had she resisted. She would always be the dutiful wife, heeding his will.

"Embrace me!" he cried.

She did.

"Make love to me," he begged.

She made the effort. Whatever he begged, she tried to do. And yet, without soul, the act of love lay mortally wounded. He had not succeeded that night; nor the next nights. His manhood always died before her indifference.

"You are tormenting me!" he had cried. *"Tu eres mi esposa.* You are my wife. Be my wife, Rita."

"I have done all you ask," she had said. "Have I failed in anything?"

"Yes! You wear black for mourning, and my body dies and yours never awakes. I come to you with desire, and I leave you with sadness."

Then came the months when he no longer tried, the months

of bitter silences, the months when she turned herself into a perfect, compliant, dutiful wife.

All this she stammered out to her examiner.

"Was Salvador potent?" he asked.

"Yes," she said, embarrassed.

"That is important," he said. "Did you, by any chance, enter this marriage without fully intending to be Salvador's wife in every respect the church considers important?"

"I did not love him."

"Ah, romantic love, that is not important. Tell me this truly now. Did you give your vows and promises honestly? Before God?"

"Yes, padre."

"Upon closest examination of your soul, your intent, your attitude, you can say you did not intend to defraud Salvador of his marital rights; that you intended to be the mother of his children, and a true wife?"

"Yes," she said softly. "It was not my choice, but it was my fate, and I was obedient to my fate."

He nodded. "Would you say that this lack of consummation is the result of your conduct?"

"*Yo no sé.* I do not know. Perhaps. But I have never resisted him. I presented myself to him—whenever he wished."

"Ah. I see no blame in any of this, and I will say so." He wrote for a while. "If all that you have told me before God is true, then you may put your mark here. If you wish to resist these proceedings, you must engage a canonical lawyer in Durango. I can supply names."

"I will sign my name. I will not fight Salvador."

She signed the document without reading it.

"It will take a long time," he said. "At least a year. If anything changes . . ."

"It will be difficult to stay in his home for a year."

He smiled. "It is a cross to bear, my daughter."

N umbly, she unhooked the carriage weight from the bridle and turned her gig home. Not home, really. Salvador's rancho could never be home again. She drove through a mild fall day, but the green-clad ridges and cultivated valleys around Sonoma didn't lift her spirits. She dreaded what she would find at the rancho. Something told her that Salvador would be *un salvaje*, a savage.

What would she do? How could she survive a year or more there? Those aching questions were too terrible to answer for now, but maybe soon she would have some answers. She drove down the long lane, past the gardens, to the red-tiled hacienda, and there a man waited to take her horse and gig away as soon as she alighted. She had come to cherish this gracious place, with the long, shaded veranda and the thick adobe walls, and the pastoral view from every window.

She found Salvador waiting for her, his eyes burning, his face as savage as she had feared. He motioned her imperiously to his library.

"*Pues, es hecho*. Well, now it is done," he said. "Now I will be free of you, and all the suffering you have caused me. Now you know. Now we must go through this disgrace. People will whisper and stare."

She elected to say nothing, knowing that any word would only enflame him.

"Why don't you speak? *Vaya, vaya!* You have shamed me and the family."

"Salvador, I tried to be a good wife—"

"No! You never did. You tried? *Dios mío!*"

"Did I ever resist you—in anything?"

"Yes, in everything. Oh, you made a show of being a wife, but you never were. *Oígame!* You were no more a Christian wife than *una cabra,* a goat."

She regretted saying anything and wished she might escape,

but he stood between her and the door and he was going to have his say.

"Do you know how it feels to have a wife who does not wish to make love? Who will not take a husband in her arms, or kiss him or smile at him, or caress him? Who lies like a log when he wishes to be united with her in joy? Who knows no passion, no desire? Who wilts a man and wounds his manhood? *Ay qué pena!* Now they will whisper—Salvador Zamora is not a whole man and his marriage was annulled. But I am a whole man. A man!"

"Salvador, Salvador . . ." Guilt flooded her. Yes, she had resisted him a thousand ways, just as he said. She had given him nothing, not so much as a smile or a caress. She felt miserable.

She discovered tears in his eyes, tears that welled hotly and coursed down his cheeks.

"I married you full of dreams, Rita Concepción. You are a passionate woman, a woman to grace this rancho with your beauty and joy. I dreamed you would desire me, and conceive children with me in the peace of the night, moments so sacred and happy that they would live in us. I dreamed that during the days we would smile secrets at each other; that when we were at fiestas, or dances, or at dinners, we would smile at each other, and that your smile would kindle flames in my heart. I dreamed we would grow old together—not without our share of troubles, but with an old, comfortable love. I dreamed we would solace each other in the days of aches and pains and feebleness and age. I dreamed that when one of us went to God, the other would soon go too, and then we would lie in the earth side by side, a happy memory to our children and grandchildren. All this I dreamed. . . ."

She did not know what to say. She knew she had cheated Salvador, and yet she could not help it. She had entered the marriage honestly, intending to make it work. She had no other choice. "I have not been a good wife to you, Salvador," she said.

"You love that American."

"It is nothing I can help. He is long gone from my life."

"You should have refused to marry me."

"What choice did I have?"

"The convent."

"That is not for me."

His cheeks glistened with his tears. He was a good and honorable Californio ranchero, and she pitied him.

"Now I must endure a year or more, while the slow priests make up their minds and my youth dries up. How will I live here with you in the same casa?"

She had been wondering the same thing. She did not know how she could endure it. Every day she would stare into his stricken face, and feel her guilt, and sometimes her anger. She had not asked for this marriage—*este matrimonio amargo;* that sometimes made her bitter.

"*Con permiso ya me voy.* I should leave here," she whispered.

"*Sí!* You must go. I cannot bear to see you here. Every glance of you destroys me."

"I will go, then. *Diga los otros lo que deseas.* Tell others what you wish."

He glared. "I will tell them I have applied for annulment."

"*Está bien.* I will say the same. It will be understood."

"Make sure that you say that *I* am the one who seeks it."

She smiled. "I will say that, Salvador."

"Someday I will marry and have many children and a happy life."

"I hope you do. Please make the arrangements. I will go to Monterey."

In the next days, they rarely saw each other. They ate separately, and she stayed in her room or moved about when she sensed he was away. No Zamora visited his hacienda. Painfully she traced out the letters and words of a letter to Tía Maria and Tío José Jesús, asking to stay there again. She gave no reason. They would know. At least, as a married woman, she would not be required to return to the hacienda Estrada and live under the thumb of her stepmother. The marriage had invested her with certain rights and privileges. But she had no idea how she would live; she had no means.

One chill December day of 1850 the Zamora carriage carried her and several trunks down the long camino to the bay. Two days later the coastal vessel dropped anchor in Monterey Bay, and she peered anxiously across its cold waters, wondering what her future would hold. She could see only bleakness ahead. First an endless wait for the millstones of the church to grind out the annulment. Then the scandal and finger-pointing. Then the isolation. She would not be welcome at many Californio homes. Then the scorn of her family—or at least Hector and probably Socorro. And then the struggle to make ends meet, maybe in ordinary service, her status as a daughter of a great ranchero family gone forever. And then endless days and nights without the man she loved.

Later, in the tiny room Tía Maria afforded her after clearing out two impish cousins, her aunt stared, hands on hips. "What is this? Why have you left Sonoma? You are a Zamora. What am I to tell José Jesús? What will I tell my brother? What will I tell the world?"

Rita Concepción could find no way to soften it. "Salvador is seeking an annulment. He was glad to see me leave."

"Dios mío! Verdad? An annulment. *Pero, que has hecho?* But what have you done? Did you not let him sleep with you?"

"Siempre. He tried."

"He tried. But if this is so, *you* should seek the annulment. *Que más hay que hacer.* What else is there?"

"There could be fraudulent intent; saying vows before God and one's future *esposo* that one did not mean. There could be physical inadequacy. Some are born unable to unite with a spouse, for God has given them other purposes. Consanguinity that is too close—first cousins. Incest. Planning never to have children. Many things. The padre explained them all."

Her aunt glared. "I do not know what all those laws are about. The church has laws I never heard of. But saying vows you did not mean? Is this his case? Is this what Salvador says? Is this what you did?"

"I do not know his case. But the padre questioned me closely about it. I said my vows sincerely and I told him so. No, if the annulment is granted it is because I am still a virgin."

"Virgin! A beautiful woman like you, so sweet and bright. Men go mad looking at you. I see lust whenever you walk into a room. Virgin! Ah!" She absorbed that like a Torquemada. "Is Salvador—not a man?"

"That is a very intimate question. You should not ask such things. He is still my husband and I revere him. But I know he is a man, and no one must think otherwise. He loved me, and wanted me. I wish I could have given him all that he wanted. I tried but I could not. But I was a good wife in all the ways I knew how. *No hay falta de mí.* No one can fault me for that."

"Ah, I think I understand now. Jarvis. This is all about Jarvis."

"Stephen Jarvis is long gone, and I will never see him again. That was a year ago. He is a very successful man now, a great merchant."

"Ah, I can tell what all this is. You should never have been made to marry Salvador. It was a mistake your papa will regret. It will embarrass the family Estrada, and you will suffer. *Santa Maria!* How terrible love is. God should never have invented it. It disgraces everyone. Now me, I have never loved José Jesús in my life, but we are friends and do the business of life together and love our children together. That is best."

"Tía Maria!" Weariness stole through Rita. *"No diga usted nada, por favor.* Please say nothing. Just let me sort this out."

"So, *no has dormido con él*, you did not sleep with him. That is it. *Su corazón estaba con Jarvis*—your heart was with Jarvis."

"But I did. I mean, I let him. Whatever he wanted."

"Déjale! Let him!" Her aunt laughed heartily. *"Pobrecito* Salvador. Lying upon a corpse. Trying until his desire died. *Sussureando cosas dulces en su oreja sorda*—whispering sweet things in your deaf ear. *Besando labios muertos*—kissing dead lips. *Ahora, yo sé todo*—now I know everything. You do not have to say another word. But priests are slow, and it will take them a year to think of it."

Against her every inclination, Rita laughed. But it didn't allay the sadness steeping her like leaves of tea.

"Well, you are here and we will all enjoy the scandal."

"No, I will not enjoy the scandal. I have no life now, and may never have one."

CHAPTER 66

S tephen Jarvis caught the *Senator* to San Francisco, delighted with the speed of the side-wheel vessel, the first in service on the Sacramento River. Larkin had asked him to come, along with others, including John Bidwell and John Sutter. Whatever Larkin had in mind, it was obviously important.

Every time Jarvis came to San Francisco, the transformation of the city bewildered him, and this occasion, in the last hours of 1850, was no exception. The city had burned down three times, rebuilt itself in days, and had doubled in size. Nothing looked familiar. The packet could not tie up at a wharf, though one existed at last, projecting from Montgomery Street. It was forced, as usual, to anchor out in the bay, and passengers were compelled to let lightermen take them to shore through a forest of abandoned sailing ships, all for a stiff additional fee.

The tent-buildings of the waterfront had disappeared, along with most of the clapboard buildings, and now the area sported fireproof brick. The lighter deposited him, and other unfortunates, at a dock projecting from a tidal flat, the whole area strewn with crates and casks that leaked noxious fumes. But any mortal in gold-rush California dealt with such discomforts daily, and Jarvis walked to higher ground and waited for his bag to follow.

A few blocks south, his warehouse ship still served as Caleb Marble's headquarters. Caleb would join this conference that Tom Larkin deemed so important. It had to do with politics; Jarvis knew that much. There were troubles afoot. He had studiously avoided politics, but now politics were catching up with him on the wings of statehood. In mid-October, the Panama steamer *Oregon* had boiled through the Golden Gate with its flags flying and cannon booming—a sign that it bore great news. Congress had finally admitted California and recognized its already-functioning state government in San Jose. The legislation being churned out by the new legislature wasn't always pleasing to Jarvis or helpful to his business.

He made his way through miry streets, sometimes stepping on packing crates to carry him over muck, to the plaza, now called Portsmouth Square, where he would stay at the Parker House, the one decent hotel in San Francisco. The sandy square itself grew only weeds, and was now largely surrounded by adobe or frame gambling halls, saloons, and boardinghouses. The Miners' Bank, the only bank in California, stood on the northwest corner. Jarvis and Marble dealt with the bank regularly, selling it gold for sixteen dollars an ounce, which the bank shipped monthly via Panama steamer to the Philadelphia mint, where it was purchased for almost nineteen—a handsome profit even after shipping and insurance.

Men crowded the streets. Most of these were obviously defeated argonauts looking for ways to survive or earn passage back to the States. Every ship brought a new horde of gold-seekers, and every outbound ship carried those who had seen the elephant and hoped to get back to their families with a little profit or at least the clothing on their backs.

Jarvis passed new groceries and meat markets, where beef, grizzly bear, and venison hung in abundance. There seemed to be plenty of flour, most of it sacked, up from Valparaiso, but he could not find vegetables, especially the onions or potatoes so much in demand. This burgeoning population was still being fed from abroad. It had been a good thing to start McQueen on his Stockton farm. Jarvis decided to recommend to Marble that the company buy farm implements and manufacturing machinery of all kinds, and provision other farmers.

He settled himself at the Parker House and then hiked over to the headquarters of Jarvis and Marble Company near Happy Valley on Rincon Point. Larkin's meeting would be held aboard the old beached boat that afternoon, in the quarters where Marble made his home and offices. An additional sheet-metal warehouse stood just above high tide, swallowing the enormous inventories that Marble coolly purchased off incoming barks, often as the highest bidder, it being a company policy that in an economy of scarcity, supply was more important than price.

He arrived at the *Gloucester* barely in time to greet his gray-faced partner and sit down to a catered lunch. This would be an occasion. There was Tom Larkin, John Bidwell, Captain Weber, Johann August Sutter, and a man whom he hadn't expected, his old commander of the New York Volunteers, Jonathan Stevenson. They all greeted Jarvis effusively, but he sensed that he was a junior member of this august group, every one of them an early settler who had arrived before the conquest. It felt odd to eat in the company of his commanding officer, and to be fifty or a hundred times richer than the lieutenant colonel, who himself had prised a fortune out of Mokelumne Hill. Stevenson, in turn, studied his former private with frank curiosity.

Whatever was on their minds, the talk drifted to prices—forty cents a pound for onions, clean gold dust trading for fifteen dollars in San Francisco, tacks and nails now so abundant a man couldn't give them away, and ditto tobacco. Wave after wave of Eastern speculators had sent ships around the Horn, each with a shrewdly considered cargo; each arrival affecting the feast or famine economy of California. Why, a shipload of ice sent around the Horn sold for eighty cents a pound.

When they had finished the crab and oysters and eaten the chocolate mousse, the genial former consul to the Californios stood to address them.

"Gwin's land-grant bill is going to pass," Larkin began, without preamble. "I have it from Thomas Hart Benton in the last Panama mail. This has serious implications for each of us. Every one of us has large land holdings here and every holding is based on a Mexican grant."

Somehow, Jarvis knew it would be about Senator William Gwin's prized legislation, now working its way through the United States Senate.

"Better recap it for us, Tom," said John Bidwell.

"Please do," added Weber. "I've missed some of this."

Jarvis wished he had paid more attention to what had been happening in California and Washington, D.C. He knew that Dr. Gwin was a pro-slavery Southerner who had practiced in Mississippi, and had been a brilliant organizing force behind the state constitution. He had easily won a seat in the Senate, even though California had been settled by adamant antislavery Northerners. The other senator, John Charles Frémont, was an antislavery man, like his famous father-in-law, Missouri's Thomas Hart Benton. The Democratic Party had torn itself to bits on the slavery issue, and the pro-slavery faction dominated it now. Jarvis decided he had better listen closely and ask questions.

"Very well," said Larkin. "After the Mexican government secularized the huge mission land holdings, it granted favored settlers large estates, over eight hundred in all, totaling some thirteen million acres, mostly in coastal regions and along the bay and rivers. Unfortunately, the descriptions of these holdings were crude; often a hand-drawn map. Some overlapped others. No one worried about boundaries in a province so huge. There was always more land. That's become a problem—and an opportunity to certain interests who would like to evict the Californios and grab the land for themselves. To make matters worse, our last Mexican governor, Pio Pico, quietly issued fraudulent grants after the conquest, antedating them to make them look valid. The effect is to cloud every Mexican grant in the state.

"Now, the Treaty of Guadalupe Hidalgo provided that all Mexican private property would be absolutely respected, but that hasn't slowed down Gwin and his cohorts, who would like to make a killing. Gwin's bill proposes a land-grant commission that would adjudicate disputed Mexican claims—including land owned by everyone present. It's clothed with the rhetoric of fairness and does provide avenues of appeal to higher courts, but the burden of proof lies upon the landholder, not the government. We're guilty of squatting on public lands unless we can prove otherwise. Every Californio is squatting unless he can prove otherwise. Gwin's bill is certainly popular; it's overwhelmingly supported by the hordes of Americans who've arrived here."

"How much of California's held by grants?" Weber asked.

"It's hard to know. Somewhere between ten and fifteen percent. It's hard to know exactly until the state is surveyed."

"You mean eighty or ninety percent can be patented the usual way—by preemption—but Gwin's backers want the rest?"

"Exactly. Now, it's true that the Californios have the choicest land, along the rivers, the fertile bottoms."

Sutter sighed. "I've already lost land. And now they'll take the rest. Much of the gold in the northern districts was taken off my land. How will I get it back? Who guaranteed it? The government in Washington?"

"Several hundred millions of gold—no one can say how much for sure—has already been taken from public land, as well as private holdings. But Congress hasn't lifted a finger against it," Larkin said.

"What did Benton say?" Stevenson asked.

"Old Bullion says it's confiscation and he'll fight it. But he's antislavery and unpopular in Missouri, and now he's a pariah in his own pro-slavery party. Not much help there."

"Where's Frémont?"

"Beside his father-in-law. I made him a millionaire, you know, and he'll listen to me."

"You did?" asked Jarvis.

Larkin sighed. "In eighteen forty-seven Frémont gave me three thousand dollars to invest in a California estate. I bought the Mariposa grant for him. He didn't like it, complained that it was nothing but worthless mountains—until he discovered it was loaded with gold. Oh, how he changed his tune."

They laughed for the first time that day.

"We'll be destroyed unless we can stop this," Weber said.

"That's why I've gathered you together. Every one of us'll suffer." He paused, as if shaping the words he would use. "I've been a consul and trader in Monterey for years, and I've come to love our Mexican friends. They're a joyous race. Land and livestock are their wealth, but they lack cash, apart from a few *reales*. They had a barter economy. Defending themselves before this commission will grind them to dust."

He paused, reflectively. "Perhaps that's a difference between me and the Gwin faction. I care about these people, my friends and neighbors all of my years here. This is a cruel, dastardly business. It's my hope that those of us who came here ahead of the American conquest—even you, Captain Marble, and you, Colonel—would find the same sentiment in your bosoms."

"I do!" exclaimed Sutter.

Stephen Jarvis thought of the Estradas, the Chávezes, and all their relatives and the humble people who depended on them for a livelihood. They had rejected a Protestant cooper's apprentice as a mate for a daughter, but that didn't matter. He loved her still, and his soul yearned to protect them all against this land grab.

"You can count on me," he told Tom Larkin. "The Estradas may not want me for a son-in-law, but they can count on me, too."

"I'm glad of that, Stephen. I've meant to tell you that Rita Concepción Zamora is living in Monterey with her aunt and uncle. I learned of it only at Christmas."

Jarvis gripped the arms of his chair to hold himself steady.

CHAPTER 67

E very man present at that lunch knew that public sentiment opposed them. The newcomers itched to take land away from the Mexicans, and reminded themselves around their campfires that four years earlier these Californios had been the enemy. Senator Gwin's land-commission bill was enormously popular and was being trumpeted in the *Alta California* and the *Pacific News* as the embodiment of justice. Racial feeling had crept into it, too. California's new mining tax, which imposed low rates on natural-born Americans, and punitive rates on the foreign-born, was really directed at the Sonorans, Chileans, Chinese, and Sandwich Islanders who had flooded into the goldfields, and only incidentally the Australians and Frenchmen, Englishmen, and others of European ancestry. The law even imposed its ferocious tax on the Californios, the original settlers, who were not natural-born Americans. Already the new law was generating chaos and bloodshed in the goldfields, and things would get worse.

"Well, then," Thomas Larkin summed up, "we've agreed to this: we'll seek amendments in the Gwin bill that'll put the burden of proof on the government. We'll try to amend the bill to make the primary purpose of the commission the rectification of overlapping grants rather than challenging the legitimacy of the grants. We'll work with Senators Benton and Frémont to modify the bill. We'll defend not only our own properties, whose titles came down through the Mexican grants, but those of the Californios as a matter of conscience. And we'll keep in close touch. As for myself, I will open my purse as generously as possible in this cause."

That suited Stephen Jarvis perfectly. He owned large chunks of land, including a piece of Captain Weber's estate at Stockton and numerous city lots in Sacramento, which were based on Sutter's grant. The probable confiscation of Californio grants outraged him.

The meeting broke up mid-afternoon, in time for Larkin to catch a coaster back to Monterey, and others to catch steam packets up the rivers. Jarvis caught his old friend and mentor Larkin at the door.

"What do you know of Rita Concepción?" he asked.

"I haven't seen her. But José Jesús mentioned her when I stopped at his tobacco shop. I've no more particulars, Stephen." He grinned. "They marry for life, you know. And even if things go sour they stay married and live separately. But I'm sure this is just an extended visit. Rita always loved the Chávezes."

"I don't expect ever to see her again, Tom. She's lost to me. I just want to know how she is; what she looks like. . . . Whether she has children. I'm out of her life, but I'll always be thirsty for news."

"I understand. I'll let you know if I learn anything else. You'll find someone, someday, Stephen. There are lots of women flooding in now."

"I wish I could interest myself in one. This was a good meeting. Maybe we can deflect some of this greed with a few amendments."

The guests vanished, and Jarvis faced his partner across a littered dining table. The old salt, with the face that reminded him of sun-blistered white paint, grinned evilly. "You can't conquer sin," he said. "Greed'll roll across this state, and ere long the poor Californios'll know that their days are over and the new barons have arrived."

"You make it sound inevitable."

"Only thing I know is that when lust or greed or any other major vice takes hold of a whole people, there's no stopping it;

it runs its course like a disease, leaving the mark behind, like a face full of pox."

"The Yankee New Englander speaking."

"The Marbles weren't Puritans. We came later, out of Yorkshire, all of us Church of England, and raised hell. Some of us went into the rum and slave trade." He leered at Jarvis, as he often did. "Ye made a partner of a rough man."

A rough man, maybe, but not a healthy one. Now and then Marble stopped cold, as if paralyzed, and then began to speak again.

"I couldn't be more content with a partner," Jarvis said. "Between us—unless disaster strikes—we must have a million dollars in assets in the company, and that doesn't include what we've taken out."

"I don't care about that. It's the game that counts. I meet those incoming barks and steamers before anyone else—pay a signal man on Telegraph Hill to keep watch. The dunnage is usually sold to Jarvis and Marble before the ship drops anchor. I've chased off rivals by brandishing a big Colt dragoon." He laughed heartily. "Well, mate, have ye anything on the table?"

"Yes. I'm thinking we should buy up farming equipment and look to the day when the goldfields start fading out. There's a hundred fifty thousand newcomers, and more arriving with every ship. They'll be wanting to start up farms and businesses. A fellow asked me to help him start a farm the other day, and I did. The state needs vegetables.

"But I'm thinking we should expand in other directions— sawmills, hard-rock mining, and even look at railroads—right now they're impossible because we have to import every rail and every spike as well as the engines and rolling stock. I'd love to start a railroad."

"I catch your drift. Buy the equipment and sell it dear, and reap double. We can sell pumps and steam engines just as easily as anything else."

Jarvis grinned. Marble grasped ideas swiftly. "You want to plunge?" he asked.

"Aye, let's plunge."

They reviewed accounts and inventories, profits and the lickings they had taken, and called it quits late in the day.

"I'll walk ye to Portsmouth Square, Stephen."

"I'll be fine."

"Sure you'll be, except San Francisco isn't what it was. There's restless men afoot. A bunch of hooligans called the Hounds are running wild. They're old New York Volunteers, too. You probably know a few."

"We had some rough ones come out of the city."

"Well, they wouldn't stop at sticking a dirk in ye, even if you were with the outfit."

"Does Colonel Stevenson know of it?"

"He does, and he fumes at 'em, but there's not a lot he can do. They're mustered out. He has no command of 'em now. He's urging the alcalde to ship 'em back East."

They hiked along the waterfront in twilight, without being troubled. Something in the rolling swagger of the old ship's master, or the bulge under his pea jacket, may have deterred ruffians. When they reached Portsmouth Square Jarvis was amazed by the crowds, and by the light glowing from every window in a place that had become the heart of San Francisco.

"Ye never saw unbridled sin before, eh, Stephen?"

"It doesn't look very sinful."

"Well, ye can enter any club—like the Eldorado there, or Dennison's Exchange, or the Bella Union, and lose your stake in moments, or addle your brain with likker, or find yourself a doxy for hire."

"I don't want any of that," Jarvis said.

Something almost feverish radiated from the gambling emporiums. Jarvis peered through the open double doors into dazzling interiors, so lush he could barely believe his eyes. Curiously, he plunged into Dennison's Exchange, into a whirl of light from the chandeliers, and numerous green-clad tables. A fine mahogany bar and back bar lined one wall. Serving girls carried drinks to tables. Cigar smoke drifted past the lamps. Occasionally a black-clad tinhorn at a table rang a silver bell, summoning a serving girl to bring a round of drinks to his customers.

The nudes startled Jarvis. On every wall hung paintings of voluptuous nudes, lacking even diaphanous drapery, plainly erotic. But none of the women took notice, and few of the male customers.

"Well, Jarvis?" asked Marble.

"I can see how these places stay in business," Jarvis said. "And where all the gold goes."

He watched miners crowd around a faro layout run by a woman named the Yellow Rose, not young but beauteous in her own way, and daringly dressed in a decolleté white silk blouse, her flesh creamy. But if her dress, or undress, weren't enough, she was plainly enjoying her company, her liquid brown eyes warm upon each of her players. Jarvis detected a soft Southern accent, and thought that she might be from New Orleans.

A young bearded miner in a hickory shirt and slouch hat, probably heading for the States on the next Panama steamer, laid an entire poke on the seven, to win, and waited while she drew the turn from the faro box. He let it ride for three more turns, and then lost it when the seven lost. The poke moved to a pile before the Yellow Rose, and Jarvis noted three other pokes there, all fashioned of the same leather. The miner plucked another out of a purse strapped to his belt, and laid it on the queen.

Jarvis watched, horrified, as the queen lost, and another poke slid to the dealer's hoard. This man had done well in the mines, and had already lost several thousand dollars. He might not be heading for the States after all, if this kept up. The Yellow Rose rang her bell, summoning a serving girl, who swiftly plied the miner with another golden-colored drink. The dealer pretended to sip, and continued the play. She had reached the hock, and removed the deck from the box to shuffle it.

"I've had enough," Jarvis said to Marble. "I can't stand to see fools throw everything away."

They toured the Bella Union and the Eldorado, finding more of the same: gaudy gambling parlors with flocked wallpaper, gilded cornices, fluted and enameled wood, and everywhere, desperate or amused males throwing away months of hard labor at the turn of a card. At the Eldorado the women were more openly brazen, and once in a while a serving girl would simply vanish into the night with a customer.

Jarvis remembered when there were few such women in California. Even the legendary fandangos, which Jarvis had watched several times, had been conducted with dignity and propriety.

Marble paused at the open doors, peering into the darkness

of Portsmouth Square. "Always pays to keep an eye out for cut-purses," he said. "They're around. The gambling halls don't let 'em in—bad for business, but this time of night, the streets are crawling with 'em."

"I just have to cut across the square, Caleb. The Parker House's over there."

"Ah, well, then, Stephen. I'm glad we had a talk." He cocked an eyebrow. "You want to build a gambling den and get rich?"

Jarvis laughed. "Caleb, when I scrape my jaws each morning, I don't mind looking at myself in the glass, even if I have ears that'd shame an elephant."

"Aye, I catch your drift. Me, I don't scrape my face, but I've been in a few scrapes. . . . I'll be seeing ye, then."

"Caleb—"

"I'll be seeing ye, mate."

Jarvis watched Marble vanish into the darkness.

CHAPTER 68

n ancient nun Rita Concepción had never seen before silently escorted her through the rectory to the priest's study, and cleared her throat at the door.

Father Juan Montalvo looked up, surprised, and set down his quill.

"Señora Zamora!" he said. "*Bendito sea Dios.* A surprise. You are here to visit over the holidays."

The nun vanished in a rustle of black skirts, and Rita Concepción entered shyly. She had so much to say to her old spiritual counselor.

"And how is Salvador?" he asked, ushering her in and clamping his hands over hers a moment with a warmth that bespoke ancient loyalties and affection.

She managed a small smile. "He is well."

He stepped back and eyed her. "Señora, I know you, and I know every nuance of your voice. There is difficulty. If I may help you, or counsel you, or if we may pray together, call on me."

"Sí," she said softly.

This time he examined her closely. "You are not happy. I think maybe Señor Jarvis still lurks there, in your heart, like a ghost who won't go away and give you peace."

"Sí," she said, wearily.

"And now you grow unhappy with Salvador. But things are always better than they seem. Are you a mother yet?"

Desolation welled through her and tears brimmed in her eyes.

"Ah, ah, I will keep quiet and listen. If this is something for the confessional, I will get my stole—"

"No, no, I will just talk." She didn't believe it would help much. Nothing would. She had wasted a fortnight at the Chávez home, unable to face the world. Scarcely anyone in Monterey knew she had returned. Her aunt had tried to take her to Mass, but she had resisted. One thing about being a married woman, she discovered, was that she now had sovereign power. She could do and be what she chose while the maiden Rita Concepción could only comply with the bidding of her married elders. For days she had stayed in her little alcove, her heart adrift, not so much melancholic as helpless and uncertain. Life and joy had fled her. She could not respond to her bright-eyed cousins, or the affable talk of her uncle or the chatter of her aunt, who began prescribing teas and herbs she acquired from the *curandera*, and burning candles before her favorite saints, especially Saint Jude, patron of hopeless cases.

The padre slumped back in his chair, a gesture decidedly not Hispanic, and waited. But she hardly knew where to begin. She decided upon the worst.

"Salvador is seeking an annulment."

Father Montalvo absorbed that without saying a word.

Swiftly and brutally, she told him everything that had happened. "Now I wait," she concluded.

He blinked solemnly, his gaze off somewhere, his mind obviously weighing what he had heard. *"Gracias a Dios, señora,"* he said at last. "You have come to me and told me this for a reason?"

A chill passed through her. Something had changed. She didn't know what was different but she knew that this priest was not the priest who had been such a strong, kind presence when she was a maiden. She had become a woman and now he faced her as a judging man. Perhaps that was it: She was witnessing clerical judgment for the first time. She drew her thick rebozo tighter over her shoulders.

"I seek your counsel, Father. I am lifeless inside of me, and . . . empty."

The padre simply waited, his head back, the pulse in the vein at his temple like the ticking pendulum clock she had seen in Thomas Larkin's home.

"I feel sorry for Salvador," she continued. "It makes me sad. He is a good and kind man. He wanted a happy marriage and did not get it. He feels cheated. He came to the marriage full of dreams, and now he blames me."

"Is it pity you feel, or guilt?"

"Both. I pity Salvador, and I feel I am the cause of his unhappiness."

"Guilt is a sign of a violated conscience. Perhaps you need the sacrament. . . . If you wish, I will meet you in the nave."

"No!" she cried. "I tried to be a wife." She glared at him, shocked at her hostility. She didn't want all this poking of a dead marriage. Why couldn't the church leave it alone? "Don't tell me my suffering is God's will," she snapped.

He lifted a hand, as if to stop the flood of words.

"Do not tell me I wanted this. Do not tell me it is my fault. I did not want to marry him. It was all arranged by fathers. Do not tell me I am to blame. I do not want lectures."

All the while she spoke, Father Montalvo sat straighter and straighter in his chair, invoking his innate pastoral authority under siege.

"Do not tell me to go back. Do not tell me I should stay married. Do not tell me I should live in a casa where I am not wanted. Do not tell me I should be glad to be wed to a Mexican. I will not listen."

He gestured helplessly. "Señora, I can help in one small way. You are here. Father Narváez is no longer your parish priest. I am. I will arrange to have a fair copy of the decree brought here directly."

She nodded.

"When you are ready, come to confession. Say the beads."

"I am not ready," she said. "And do not tell me my soul is in danger. That is what you were about to say, is it not?"

He rose. "Señora Zamora, it was good to visit with you," he said, rounding the desk to escort her. "Sister Teresa will see you out."

She stalked into wan sunlight of the last day of the year. "Señora Zamora! Señora Zamora!" she said to the chill wind. "It is always the woman's fault. A woman's will counts for nothing. She is married off by men. A woman's desire counts for nothing. If she is married to a man she doesn't desire, it is her fault. *Virgen santísima!*"

When she pushed open the massive door of the Chávez casa she discovered her entire family within. She should have expected it. They often came to Monterey to welcome the new year. But her mind had been elsewhere. She spied Hector, leering at her, and Benito, and Santiago with his new wife, Trinidad, who looked pregnant. And her father, gazing at her contemplatively, along with Socorro.

They would attend Mass this evening and might even stay up to hear the gaiety of the church bells. Tomorrow the Chávez casa would be open to all guests, a groaning table in the grand *sala*, and all of Monterey would stop in. Tomorrow she would see old friends, like Teresita and Soledad and their husbands and *niños*, and others she knew, like Thomas Larkin and his wife, Rachel, and maybe a few more *americanos* who would be the targets of Hector's sarcasm.

Juan Carlos greeted her and she sensed that her news was well known among them. No doubt Salvador had written his aunt Socorro. Her stepmother simply gazed smugly, faint malice around her lips.

"Well, it's the little mother," Hector said. "I heard you were back. You have fled the casa Zamora."

So Hector was going to be nasty. She despised him. "Hector, you may address me as the señora Zamora," she said, using her newfound status ruthlessly.

"Salvador writes that he is seeking an annulment. Another bright honor for the Estradas."

"Hector—the matter does not concern you."

Surprisingly, her uncle rescued her, and salvaged the afternoon. "*Basta. Basta!* Let there be peace in the casa Chávez," he said simply. "We are all a family, and we are here in the presence of God, at this time when He closes one page of his Book of Life and begins another. Let Him not put another black mark upon the page of this year of Our Lord. *Cuidado!*"

That quieted them, but Rita Concepción could feel things seething and swirling, especially in Doña Socorro, who oozed malice, no doubt having absorbed Salvador's version of events. Salvador would not have written of an unconsummated marriage, but of his belief that Rita's vows were falsely given, a fraud before God Almighty. Rita smiled at her stepmother, dangerously, boldly, and enjoyed the faint surprise in the woman's face.

"You look very thin, Rita Concepción," Socorro said gently. "I see no signs of blessed motherhood. It is a pity. See how Trinidad glows with the life in her."

Socorro was probing, and Rita Concepción was tempted to say something that would hurt. "I would like a child," she said. "It is a pity."

"Ah, but perhaps you were not so eager to have one."

"Those things were up to Salvador, Mama."

"Yes, and now it is too late."

Rita Concepción peered about to see whether this grilling was being observed, but the rest were all talking among themselves. She turned away, feeling Socorro's malice on her back.

The afternoon played out that way. When at last the bells announced that it was time to walk to the *iglesia,* Rita declined. She needed to be alone.

They did not press her. Had she not been a señora, they would have insisted. But she had a headache and wanted to lie down. She was losing her family. Hector had been cruel all afternoon, exercising caution only when José Jesús was within earshot. Benito and Santiago tried awkward conversation and retreated. Even her father, who truly loved her, had turned solemn. So it was going to be like this the rest of her life, outcast and unforgiven, the only Estrada ever to cause a scandal, a woman in disgrace with the Holy Church and all of California.

She waited for them to leave and slid to her pallet. Later she heard them all return and begin the feast that would carry them into the new year. She did not know what 1851 would bring to her, but she wouldn't surrender hope. She felt anger, but she also felt something steely building within her. She would do what she must.

CHAPTER 69

C aleb Marble died the afternoon of January 20, 1851. The news reached Stephen Jarvis the next morning, moments after the *Senator* docked at Sacramento City, when Jared Broome, Caleb's general manager, brought it to him.

It desolated Jarvis, though the death came as no surprise. "Tell me about it," he said.

"Well, sir, we found him last evening when we were closing the warehouse. I always bring the day's accounts to him. And there he was, peaceful, in his bunk. He left instructions, sir. He saw it coming. A note on the table. And a letter to be given to you."

Broome handed Jarvis the wax-sealed letter.

"His note instructed me, sir. I called Quinton, the mortician, who's preparing him for burial at sea. He figured he wasn't in good grace with the Episcopal Church but asked for a memorial service anyway, and I made those arrangements promptly, just before catching the *Senator*."

The news seemed almost too much to absorb at once. "Please wait out there for me, Mr. Broome, while I read this."

The young man vanished, and Jarvis slowly broke the wax seal, pulled out the letter within, and read:

It was dated January 7, 1851.

"I see this coming. The seizures—I call them blanks because they blank me—are coming often and lasting longer. One of them will carry me off.

"This is being witnessed by Broome and will serve as a will, as well as an instruction. The proceeds from my quarter of the company go to my wife, Anna Gatewood Marble, East Point, Gloucester, Massachusetts. I've already written her of my imminent departure; that letter went out on the *Panama* January 4. Please follow with your own word to her.

"You will need to reorganize the company to deliver my portion to my widow, and you have my implicit trust that you will proceed with all deliberate speed. I request that my share be converted either to bullion at twenty an ounce, or dust, at fifteen an ounce, and shipped insured by Adams and Company. Sorry to put you to the trouble, Stephen, but you will emerge with a new company and a large fortune.

"I've left instructions with Broome. Bury me at sea. I want clean salt water, not mud and worms. I'm exiled from the Church of England, but talk them into a memorial service if you can. A mariner sees God on the water.

"Take from my cabin any small memento of me, and let it be my presence in your future life. You came to me in a moment of mutiny and ruin, and made these last months a pleasure. Sincerely, Caleb Daniel Marble."

He had a wife!

From the time in 1848 when they met, until now, he had never mentioned her and had given the impression he was alone in the world. But some lonely woman had been waiting on the Massachusetts shore all these years, a lamp in her window for the sailing master who never came home. Jarvis felt a wash of melancholia. What made men roam, and abandon their women, the true treasures of their lives? He would never understand.

He knew, intuitively, that this business could not be reorganized because he could not replace Marble, and that the Jarvis and Marble Company was doomed. The ship's master had been the perfect partner, a buyer with an uncanny sense of what would sell in the gold camps and a gift for getting it. When the news of a ship rounding Clark's Point flashed down from Telegraph Hill, he ran to his lighter and met the vessel, always with a bottle of good brandy and a pocketful of half eagles, and often the transaction was completed before the sails were reefed. It had been a perfect match: Jarvis with his distribution skills, Marble with his purchase and supply skills.

All that remained would be to find a buyer among his rivals, or dismantle the company in pieces. That, too, hit him hard.

A wife, Anna. What was she like? Had she given up on Caleb? Had he ever written to her? Would her letters be found in his quarters on the old ship? He doubted they would. Somehow, his life with Anna had ceased long before. Now a quarter of the company would be converted to gold and shipped to this woman Jarvis had never heard of.

How little he really knew about Caleb. They had always talked business, and only rarely had he talked of his sailing days. When he talked, it was always of foreign ports. Jarvis didn't know Marble's age, but it had to be in the sixties, old enough to be Jarvis's grandfather. He had never seemed like an elder, though. They had dealt with each other on equal terms, except once in a while when the imperious tone of a ship's master, the absolute lord upon the open sea, crept through the conversation, and at those moments Jarvis had listened carefully and usually retreated.

He didn't feel like doing anything except retreating to his room at Sacramento, but matters required attention. He found Broome waiting for him in the foyer.

"When does the *Senator* sail?" he asked.

"At four, sir."

"We'll be on it," Jarvis said. "I've a lot of questions. Inventory, orders, commitments. You can tell me on the way to San Francisco."

"Yes, sir. It's mostly in good order."

"Did he ever mention Mrs. Marble?"

"I didn't know he was married, sir."

"You witnessed his will and instructions?"

"Yes, sir. I didn't read them. But I watched him sign that letter with his steel-nib pen, and then I signed."

"All right. You're going to be in charge of everything in San Francisco for a while, Mr. Broome."

"For a while, sir?"

"The partnership is going to dissolve. I can't promise you a position for long. But I'll help you relocate. You've served loyally, and so have several others."

Jared Broome absorbed that quietly.

The next morning the *Senator* glided up to the new Long Wharf, and the two hurried to the old beached vessel, where they systematically crated everything in Marble's cabin. Jarvis found no letters from Mrs. Marble. For his memento he chose a fine brass-and-walnut barometer. The rest of the day he reviewed the books and received San Francisco's merchants and leading lights, who dropped by one by one with their condolences.

He was one of the members of the company who bore the heavy casket up the gangway from the Long Wharf to the deck of the southbound *Panama*. An Episcopal priest returning to the States read prayers and collects and would recite another when the ship had bucked the tidal currents, passed through the Golden Gate, and reached the open sea, Marble's ocean grave. Few attended; Marble hadn't met many San Franciscans, and prided himself in being vaguely disreputable. Jarvis listened, watched the fresh wind toy with the coats and hats of the mourners, and then left when the ship's whistle announced its departure.

From the wharf he watched Caleb Marble sail one last time to a foreign shore. He felt hollow. Then he hiked back to Caleb's cabin, and set to work, feeling odd psychic pain, not only for Caleb, whose strength and cheer he missed, but for the company, that complex, pulsing, galloping thing he and Marble had created and nurtured.

Early the next day he headed for a shabby wooden building that held the offices of Adams and Company. From his lair there, Daniel Hale Haskell ran the brilliantly devised express company that had blanketed the Sierra Nevada, and given miners inestimable service. The company not only delivered letters and valuables to miners in the camps, but also bought their gold if they wished to sell it, or shipped it if they wanted to send it to the States, charging ten percent for the shipment and insurance. Its word was inviolable and tens of thousands of argonauts entrusted it with everything they had prised out of the cold rivers. More than any other company, Adams had reached the camps. Haskell had been at it since November 8, 1849, and his company gathered strength each month.

Instantly, Jarvis was ushered into Haskell's grubby office.

"I've been expecting you, Stephen. My condolences. Marble was a confounded genius—a Yankee genius." His emphasis on the word *Yankee* left no doubt of his prejudices.

Jarvis listened to the familiar Haskell twang. The Adams company had done Jarvis and Marble's banking, among other things.

They talked in circles for a while and then Jarvis broached the subject on his mind: He offered the entire business to Adams and Company. Haskell listened impatiently, shaking his head.

"The fact is, I don't know your business, Jarvis. And it's all I can do to run this one. I'm an expressman. I've become a banker. I can't be a major wholesaler and merchandiser too. We've got to be specialists."

"You're my only hope to sell it whole. You're the only company in California with the means."

Haskell shook his balding head. "No, you'll have to dismantle it, I'm afraid. You'll have plenty of buyers for the pieces, and maybe it'll go for more that way. Now, I'd be interested in some of your stores in the diggings. A lot of those towns have an Adams Express Office sitting next to a Jarvis store. It's a waste of real estate."

"We can do some business, then, Daniel," Jarvis said. "But I'll spend another day or two sounding out some prospects here."

Through the next months Jarvis liquidated the business, a gloomy task that kept him irritable. His rivals and former clients circled around him like sharks, offering fifty cents on the dollar, but Jarvis coldly rejected every offer. He evolved a strategy to hold the buccaneers at bay. He held on to every store in the camps in spite of offers for them, and when he couldn't liquidate goods at a decent price, he shipped them to his functioning stores. To keep the stores well stocked he even bought merchandise from other suppliers.

That turned out to be the key. He swiftly emptied his San Francisco warehouse, sending everything inland on his sloop. The camps still demanded everything; he had only to get his inventory there. But once in a while he did manage a major sale. Collis Huntington, an aggressive Sacramento City hardware man, offered a fair price for every piece of hardware Jarvis possessed, as well as every farm implement and odd piece of machinery. Jarvis accepted the deal, and with the stroke of a pen he sold a third of his inventory without loss.

Each month he totted up his profit from the liquidation, put three-quarters of the gold in Haskell's safe, and shipped Anna Marble her quarter through Adams. He thought of nothing the whole while but liquidation and a fair distribution to the widow who had been an unknown ghost in the partnership from the beginning. One great day he auctioned the San Francisco warehouse and realized a tenfold profit from it. That same spring day he sold the old hulk of the *Gloucester* to the city of San Francisco for two thousand dollars. The city needed a jail, and the old hulk would do. But he hated the transaction, hated dealing with politicians and relied heavily on Colonel Stevenson to see it through.

One of his biggest headaches was the real estate. The company owned riverfront property in Stockton and Sacramento. It owned the land Jarvis had promised to that farmer, McQueen. Jarvis didn't know how to deal with that one, and finally deeded the section to McQueen for a hundred dollars, which McQueen eventually came up with. Given the appreciation of the riverfront acreage, the loss didn't matter.

But as the summer neared, Jarvis came to the end. He auctioned his Sacramento City waterfront warehouse for a handsome profit, sold his sloop at a loss, and finally sold the stores in the camps: some to Adams, some to the men who ran them.

One July day, the last shipment of gold went aboard a Pacific Mail Company steamer, along with a letter certifying that the liquidation was complete. The widow Marble would be almost two hundred fifty thousand dollars richer. Jarvis had over seven hundred thousand from the company plus various properties he had purchased from the partnership over the years, mostly city lots and buildings. He was virtually a millionaire.

Jarvis and Marble Company had vanished from the world.

He watched the steamer carrying that last payment to Anna Marble back into the bay and belch smoke, peered about himself as he stood on the Long Wharf, and died a little. Nothing held him in California.

He could go back to the States as so many other argonauts

had done. Most of the men who had come to this far shore to win their fortunes were returning to their homes in places like Connecticut and Ohio. It struck him that he had no more business in California. It had become a place of ghosts and memories. He had no future there. It would be best to have Adams ship his gold east and take passage on the next mail steamer. A young man with his assets could do well in the New York Stock Exchange. He stared at the alien city, so cold and heartless, so empty of anything he wanted. The next monthly steamer day would find him aboard.

PART VII

1851

U lysses McQueen rested on his hoe, watching the low clouds—outliers of another Pacific storm—scud east where they would collide with the Sierra. He didn't mind the storms. They brought him rain. They also brought cool weather, but so far, nothing that might freeze his crops.

He returned to his hoeing. His enemy was the demonic native grass that threatened to engulf all his crops unless he hoed ruthlessly every day. It simply refused to surrender to his plow when he had cut through the soft virgin sod last June.

Farming in the central valley turned out to be far more difficult and mysterious than he had imagined. First there was the weather: a fall and winter monsoon and blistering dry heat all summer. What should he plant, and when? Very early, he realized he didn't know and couldn't find out. He would have to proceed by trial and error.

That summer and fall he had broken the land in ten-acre plots and planted them with whatever seed he could find, mostly bought from Californios. Onions filled one plot, cabbage another, potatoes another, yams another. Various squash and melons and cucumbers occupied small plots, and he tried some tomatoes even though he was planting late in the season. He didn't know how they would come out. He had quit plowing and harrowing after preparing forty, which were all a single man could handle and then some. In time he would know what would prosper during the mild central-California winter, and what needed more sun and heat. And he kept a wary eye on the insects, wondering what plague would ruin what crop.

But his mind had soared with the prospects. If he could grow some grain, he might start some poultry, and if he could find the pasture, he might run some sheep or cattle. Nothing seemed impossible. California was truly a place of dreams. Something in the very air inspired flights of hope and optimism.

He had a square mile of flat land north of Stockton to work; land yet to be surveyed, and without certain boundaries, the description merely stating that its northern boundary was the Calaveras River, and its western one the wandering bank of the San Joaquin River. Since the riverbank was a morass of tules, and sloughs penetrated his land, he couldn't even be sure of his lines. So it had been an act of faith to set his moldboard into the coarse grasses and begin that first furrow through loose umber earth.

Near what he took to be the south line, a low swell of land provided the only relief from the ruthless flats. There he had built a rag house, sailcloth on a wooden frame, and had driven a well into the water table a few feet down. It wasn't a pretty place, but he fancied that some trees would help. This flatland lacked the scenic beauty of the bay area, or the Sierra, but it seemed rich with promise. From the summer day he arrived, he had labored even more than he had at the gold-bearing bars of the mountains, at first enjoying his solitude, then haunted by it.

After the first week, when he knew he could make something of the place, he had hiked to Stockton and written a letter to Susannah. He hated to write gloomy letters describing defeat, but this had been different. It was as if something that had choked him had suddenly given way, like a bursting dam. Awkwardly at first, then joyously—he penned his letter on the counter of the local market—he described his bad luck in the goldfields, and then his chance to raise vegetable crops in an area starved for produce, and his encounter with a powerful California entrepreneur, Jarvis by name, who had set him up as a truck farmer.

"Susannah, I need a little more time," he had concluded. "You are always in my thoughts. This is a golden land. I want you here. I want to meet my daughter. Soon, after some crops are sold, I can pay for your passage. I've learned some lessons and know what to do with myself and how much I treasure you. I can give you a good life here in this new land. Here I am, with 640 acres of land, give or take a few swamps, and I need only you and Margaret to be complete. Your loving husband, Ulysses."

He had never written a letter like that before. Every time he had tried to write her, the words had been stiff and he couldn't think of anything to say. But this was different. Maybe with the next letter he could send some money through Adams and Company. He sealed the letter, left it with the storekeeper, along with a dollar for the expressman to take it to San Francisco. They were saying the mail was faster now; this letter might reach her in two months.

Now, in the winter of 1851, he toiled between his rows of onions and potatoes. Here and there the fat bulbs of his onions poked from the cool earth. He would harvest them soon, and ship the entire lot to Jarvis, who would no doubt make a killing in the gold camps. The potatoes were almost ready to spade up, and soon Jarvis would make another killing, selling them for a dollar each to the argonauts. Ulysses hoped he might get two bits each for them, but maybe that was wishful thinking.

As he hoed, he thought of Susannah. He hadn't heard from her. He had left word of his address with a passing teamster, but he lived in terrible solitude, and he feared that no one in all California knew how to find him. He lived scores of miles from the nearest diggings, alone in a world of flat horizons, vast skies, and solitude.

How was she doing in Mount Pleasant? How was his dear girl, Margaret Temperance? She would be walking now, and talking too. He ached to meet her, lift her up, and feel her heaviness. It would be cold there now, not like this mild climate. He hoped his women were warm and comfortable, and that the McQueens had finally accepted Susannah and Margaret into the family. But the thought made him uneasy.

When the light faded, Ulysses wearily plucked up his hoe and headed for his tent-house. It would be chill tonight and he had no firewood for the sheet-metal stove. He would have to head for the riverbank and cut dead limbs from the thickets of live oak and alder and brush there. But first he would harness up and drive to Stockton. He was out of a lot of things, and would get them from Bart Goodfellow at the mercantile, and check his mail.

The February dusk was settling when Ulysses reached the waterfront district, but the lamplit stores remained open. At Goodfellow's he discovered he had mail, a fat envelope from Stephen Jarvis, and owed a dollar to the expressman who had left it. Within he discovered an executed deed, "to be reconciled with public surveys when those are done." The note from Jarvis said he was dissolving his company and liquidating holdings including the real estate; that when McQueen could pay a hundred dollars, that would be payment in full, but the deed would be unencumbered by a mortgage in any case.

So now he owned his section. And could sell his crops wherever he could, providing only that he pay Jarvis that modest sum. He ached to tell Susannah that he owned an entire square mile of California land.

"Is that all the expressman brought?"

"That's it, Ulysses. Nothing from your wife. Have you let her know? Have you put out word with all the expressmen? You might write Adams and Company."

"I'll do that," McQueen said. "I've been so busy getting the place going and putting a roof over me and pounding wells and all the rest, I didn't think of it."

"Well, an Adams man comes in here every couple of days, right off the steamers. You just write out the information—that you're here and that you used to be at Mok Hill, on Big Bar—and I'll give it to him. I guess there must be a heap of mail backed up somewhere for you."

McQueen penned the information and left it with the storekeeper. He wished he had done it earlier, but the expressmen had been so good at tracking down miners in every obscure canyon of the Sierra that he had assumed they would be just as efficient elsewhere.

He dug potatoes all the next day, amazed by their size and quantity. Forking them up was a delicate labor, and he cursed every time a prong cut into a one. But those wounded ones would keep him in potatoes for months if he could find time to dig a root cellar. And they would provide sets for the next crop. By late afternoon he had a wagonload, his first successful crop. It might yield several hundred dollars in Stockton. Wearily he drove his burdened wagon back to his canvas house, just in time to discover a trotter drawing a black buggy coming smartly over the plain.

He recognized Bart Goodfellow.

"Ulysses!" Goodfellow cried. "I talked to the Adams man. Do you know they've been looking for you for months? They thought you'd gone east. The reason is, your wife's waiting for you at Mok Hill."

"My *wife?*"

"Let's see," Goodfellow said, consulting a scrap of paper. "Yes, Susannah Strawbridge McQueen. That's who's looking for you. The Adams man said she's been there for months, putting word out from one end of the diggings to the other."

"Susannah? Here?" He couldn't believe it.

"I guess she is. I told the Adams man to get word up there. He'll detour to Mok Hill first and let her know. He sounded plumb excited, getting you two back together."

Ulysses wondered whether this Susannah was his, and thought it might be a mistake. But the expressman had gotten the Strawbridge name. She was only fifty miles away! "I've got to get there, Bart. I've got to catch the next stage. I've got to find her." He paused, realizing that this merchant had come four miles with the news. "I haven't thanked you," he said.

Goodfellow's eyebrows beetled up and his eyes focused on the wagon. "Well, as it happens, McQueen, I came at just the right moment. Now there's a way you can thank me, and that's to sell me those hallelujah-amen-Glory-to-God spuds. I've been paying forty a hundredweight when I could get them, which is almost never, and I'll do that and clean off your account, too. There's five hundred pounds in there, unless I miss my guess. You get a wife; I make a killing. I'll wagon these into the camps and watch them melt off the wagon bed."

Ulysses laughed. "Bart, when does the Mok Hill stage leave?"

"Not until eleven, after the steamer gets in."

"I'll be there. It's a deal. Take the wagon and leave the buggy. Buy me a coach ticket, and put my profit on your account."

Goodfellow chortled. "It sure is funny what a wife does to a man," he said. He left the buggy and trotter with McQueen, and took his wagonload of Glory-to-God spuds into the twilight.

McQueen brimmed with questions. Why had she come? How had she survived on Big Bar? How long had she been there? What would she think of this barren place? And what would her news be?

He entered his rag-house and realized it was a rotten hellhole. His own body was little better. His clothes were rags, his hair was unwashed, his face was unscraped. Wildly he set to work on his place, sweeping debris off the dirt floor, cleaning off the surface of his crude plank table, scrubbing encrusted pots and pans. But it didn't do any good. The rag-house looked no less grubby. And he had no clean clothes. But in the morning he could get some ready-mades from Goodfellow, and a shave and haircut on the same block.

All that evening he tidied up, split stovewood, limed his privy, and tried to think of something to say to her. In a quiet moment he knew this reunion wouldn't be easy. Maybe it would hurt. He hadn't written her for months at a time, and she was going to ask a lot of questions. He wished he had done better. He should have tried. It didn't take much to send a note now and then, and let Susannah know how much he loved her and longed for her. He regretted every opportunity he had let slide by. Too late now, he thought. He only hoped that things would smooth out, and that she still loved him. He hadn't been a good husband. He couldn't understand himself, and wished he had been a better man.

CHAPTER 71

 usannah McQueen sold the last of her huckleberry pies to Gil Waggoner who urged her to take a *big* pinch for it.

"Gil, if I coat my fingers with lard would it help?"

"You've got lady-fingers, Mrs. McQueen, and they don't really raise a dollar."

She laughed. Waggoner had gotten the last of this batch. The miners always appeared within minutes of the time she pulled them from her oven twice a day, some mysterious telegraph— the fragrances of cooling pies perhaps—summoning them from their long toms.

She had done just fine at Big Bar, though the future remained a puzzle and she worried more and more about Ulysses' disappearance. She had tried everything: notified Adams and Company that she was looking for him, advertised in the *Alta California*, sent word out with every miner who packed up for better diggin's somewhere else, and contacted the teamsters and packers who brought supplies to the camps. And she had written the postmasters in Sacramento City and San Francisco.

But Ulysses had vanished, and now she was facing decisions she didn't want to make. His disappearance over seven months ago had become an aching mystery. Was he dead? So many miners had vanished, some of them murdered, a few dead of an accident in some hidden gulch, some of them lost to the Miwaks or Yokats, who had grown increasingly angry at the invasion of their ancestral home. Most had died of the plagues that swept the camps, dysentery in particular. Many of the dead were unknown, and were buried in unmarked graves because no one could put a name to them.

Ulysses was either dead or had taken passage back to Mount Pleasant, expecting to find her there. Anticipating that possibility, she had written her mother asking that word be sent immediately if he turned up there. Mail was moving miraculously faster now. She had heard it took only thirty-four days for a letter mailed from New York to arrive in San Francisco via the Isthmus. Her mother had replied, but had no news.

Much to her surprise she was enjoying life at Big Bar. The miners had gathered around her as if she were the very essence of all their wives and sweethearts and daughters and mothers, protecting her, paying her generously for her cooking and sewing and caring for the various injured men— someone was always getting hurt—and settling disputes. In the fall, when the nights grew cold, she had attempted to move upslope to Mok Hill, where a solid, thriving, boisterous town had sprung up. But the miners of Big Bar had other notions. One November sabbath fifty or sixty of them built a proper cabin for her, with a plank floor, solid log walls, oiled canvas roof, and a window with real glass in it. They had even installed a cast-iron kitchen range. So she stayed on the bar. It never got very cold anyway, not like the winters in the northern diggings, and the winter never resembled the sort she was used to in Mount Pleasant. As the weeks passed, she even found herself accumulating cash. Those pinches of dust added up. She sold her dust to Adams and Company, which gave her negotiable receipts that were coin of the realm in California, and could be cashed anywhere in the country.

The miners called on her for all sorts of Christmas pastries, which she somehow provided. They were a delightful boyish lot. Most of them avoided words that offended her, and if they drank, they never showed it in her presence. If these men were wild, they had carefully hidden it from her. She knew there had been some melees between the Americans, French, and Chileans in their separate gulches, and some of the fights had been brutal.

Miners came and went at Big Bar, but there were still a handful of Stevenson men, veterans of the New York Volunteers who had founded Mok Hill. Most of the miners gathered into small groups and worked long toms now that the easy pickings were gone. Whenever a newcomer appeared, she sought him out and asked about Ulysses. But no one knew of him. As pleasant as life had become in a world in which she was the only female, she knew she had to bring this phase of it to an end. It had no future, and at bottom, her labors were drudgery. She loved the scent of pine and the rush of crystal water, but she wanted more civilization. That meant San Francisco.

In her darker moments she thought of getting a divorce on the ground of desertion, if that was valid in this new state. If Ulysses had simply abandoned his wife, as many men here did, she needed to free herself of him. She had discovered that some miners had little intention of ever returning to their families. At first it shocked her, but in time she ruefully conceded that these men were having a marvelous time. It was time to go to San Francisco, wait a few more months, and then consult a lawyer. The thought of divorce desolated her. She had always loved Ulysses, but she didn't intend to let her life slip away pining for him. She knew she could start over; she had learned on her trip over the Isthmus just how much courage she really had.

Then one day the Adams and Company expressman, Billy Case, burst into camp and beelined straight to her cabin.

"Mrs. McQueen, I've found him, that rascal. Yep, ma'am, I have done found your one and only, and he's barely fifty miles away."

"Billy!"

"Ulysses McQueen's plowing a parcel of land north of Stockton."

"Billy! How do you know?"

"Because Goodfellow, at the store there, told me."

"Oh, Billy, does he know I'm here?"

"Yep, he knows now. I reckon you'll see him soon. Maybe today or tomorrah. He'll come a-sailin' in, I expect. Maybe on the Stockton stage this afternoon. You oughter go meet it."

"Oh, Billy . . ." She reached for her poke. "You take a few pinches."

"Oh, no, Mrs. McQueen, I fetched my heavenly reward just by the look on your face. You lovebirds. What a reunion you'll have. I guess the camp'll give you a whoop. It'll be a honeymoon for the McQueens."

He was seeing what he wanted to see, she thought. "Thank you, Billy. I can't tell you how much this means to me."

That afternoon passed in a strange haze. Her feelings tumbled this way and that. A part of her feared the reunion, though she was desperate for it. The word flashed through camp, and miners slipped to her cabin to congratulate her. But they acted like strangers now, and she spotted an odd look—perhaps resentment—in the eyes of some. For once her pies weren't snapped up as fast as she pulled them out of the oven. The men she had bantered with all these months had gotten almighty polite.

Frantically she swept her cabin and scoured every surface. She had only a cracked hand-mirror, but what she saw in it dismayed her. Her youth and beauty had vanished there in Panama, and now she beheld a gaunt, knowing woman, with a firm set of the mouth, determination in her eyes, and disillusion written about her lips. Her matted hair needed washing, and her dresses were in rags. Swiftly she set water to heating, closed her door—a signal to the men in camp that she wanted privacy—and began to make herself presentable, all the while wondering why.

Oh, Ulysses! What if he wasn't on the stage? Should she go to him? *No.* Let him come to her. She was tired of chasing a man who was always a few steps ahead. *Let him prove that he cares by coming to me now.* And if he doesn't come today or tomorrow or the next day, then what? She had no answer to that, but the thought made her mood bleak as an overcast day.

That endless afternoon she washed her hair and sewed a hundred rents in her clothing and heated up an iron on her stove and pressed the gray woolen dress she intended to wear to a reunion that might feel more funereal than joyous. Still, currents of delight eddied through her. Ulysses! Oh, it would feel so good when he held her. She felt so confused, sometimes exultant, sometimes angry, sometimes wrapped in pain when she thought of her baby eaten by worms in her grave— the baby Ulysses had abandoned when he walked down the lane.

The stage was due in Mok Hill around the supper hour, but she had dressed in her best long before. Suddenly she couldn't stand Big Bar, so she walked up the hill an hour early, needing Mokelumne Hill and its urbane life. It had continued to bloom, with thousands of miners still pouring in from all over the world, changing almost daily from its founding in 1848 when some of the discharged soldiers dug gold from the nearby bars and gulches, and the regiment's colonel even made himself alcalde of the new village. She would be glad to escape it, though. It had turned wild.

As she walked the rutted streets, drawing more attention than she wanted from woman-hungry men, an idea formed in her mind: She would engage a room at the new Hotel de France on

Main Street. She couldn't bear the thought of three hundred miners at Big Bar observing her reunion with Ulysses. The gracious yellow hotel with its white enameled galleries would be the place to meet him, no matter what a room might cost. And a place for her to wait if the stage should be late. Hesitantly, because she had never engaged a hotel room before, she entered, and approached the clerk.

"I'd like a room for my husband and me tonight," she said, blushing.

"We're booked up solid, ma'am," he replied. "Always booked up weeks ahead."

"Oh, thank you . . ." She turned away.

"Well, of course, if you have the dust, we always keep the Mokelumne Suite available for special occasions. But it's eight dollars."

"Half an ounce? For one night?"

The clerk nodded.

Still, reunions didn't come often. Feeling almost giddy, she withdrew her poke and let the man measure a half ounce of dust on his fine brass gold-scale. Then she signed the register: Mr. and Mrs. Ulysses McQueen.

It turned out to be a haven, a second-story room with a view over the clapboard buildings along Main, and Center, and Church Streets, and the wooded valley of the river not far beyond. She felt better, closeted there. She hadn't really thought until now about how Mok Hill was changing, and what sort of male was roaming its alleys. But it was high time she did think of it.

She sat rigidly until five-thirty and then walked to the foot of Main Street where the Adams and Company express office stood. In the low winter light she waited, her pulse high, until five-forty, when the wine-colored Concord stagecoach drawn by six spirited mules rumbled in, and the Jehu tugged the lines. The coach settled on its thoroughbraces as if life were leaking out of it. The light door opened, and the first man out looked like Ulysses. Yes, it was Ulysses, but browner and leaner, and so changed she barely knew him.

"Ulysses!" she cried.

"Is that you, Susannah?" he asked.

They stood staring at each other, a wall of ice between them.

CHAPTER 72

lysses McQueen saw her there in the soft light, and barely knew her. Susannah had become an angular, unsmiling adult. And yet she was smiling. How could she be smiling and yet not smile?

"Susannah!" he cried, but as he stepped to earth, he stopped. Something as solid as a wall of glass stood between her and him. He stood, paralyzed. Around him, passengers stepped off the rocking coach and stood waiting for the Jehu to unload their luggage from the boot.

It was the oddest thing, seeing her smile and her delight, but knowing she wasn't smiling at all.

"Hello, Ulysses," she said softly, the words boring through all that glass. Then the barrier shattered, and he leapt to her and embraced her.

"Well, well," she said. She hugged him and then worked free of his arms.

"I never expected you," he said. "Let me look at you. Why, you've changed, Susannah."

"Yes."

"How was the trip? You must've come across the Isthmus."

"It was hard."

"Where's our baby girl?"

"She's dead."

"Dead? Dead?" His first child in her grave? He had never met his baby girl and never would.

"Cholera?" he asked softly.

"Chagres fever."

"She died in Panama?"

"Yes. I almost did, too. A very kind woman cared for me."

"Susannah, I'm so glad you made it. If I had known you were coming . . . I would have been mad with worry."

"Would you?"

Her question lanced him. Somehow, in his mind all these

months she had just been there, back in Mount Pleasant, cheerfully tending the farm and raising the baby and waiting for him to return.

"I was fixing to send for you," he said, desolately. "I wrote you a while ago, telling how things've gone. I guess you didn't get the letter." He sighed. "Tell me about her," he said. "Tell me everything. What she looked like, who she took after, all that."

"She was a beautiful child, Ulysses. She took a fever on the road from Chagres to Panama City, and died. She was buried in a common place outside of Panama City. When I was well enough, my friend took me there. It wasn't a pretty place."

He choked up. "You almost died, too? Coming after me?"

She nodded.

"Why did you come after me?"

She hesitated. "Because . . . to see whether . . ." She couldn't finish what she started to say, and he sensed she bit back rebuke. She hadn't said an unkind word, and yet he knew there were things on her tongue going unspoken.

"I've so much to talk about," he said. "Let's go to a café and talk, and then go down to Big Bar."

She shook her head. "I've engaged a room for tonight. We'll go there. I'm not hungry."

"A room?"

"At the Hotel de France. I didn't feel like returning to Big Bar tonight."

He followed her to the new place, carrying an old carpetbag that contained everything he had brought. She led him to a second-floor room and they entered. Within, he hugged her again. This time she hugged back, clinging to him with an ardor that wasn't apparent on Center Street. But he sensed a reserve in her. Still, she hugged him and her hands traced his shoulders and neck.

"You've changed, Ulysses," she said, drawing back and examining him. "Tell me everything. Tell me what you didn't—" Again she bit off her sentence. *Didn't write.* He knew the ending of that sentence, and knew also she was trying hard. This reunion wouldn't groan with recriminations.

She sat on the bed, and he on the sole chair. He hadn't seen a room like this one in the gold country. Its enameled plank floor gleamed. The woodwork had been painted white. Canary-colored paper lined the walls.

"Tell me everything that happened at Mount Pleasant, and your trip," he said. "Don't leave anything out."

"I will, but not all at once."

"I got some letters from you," he said.

She didn't reply, and he knew why. She had received so little from him. And for that reason she had come here, seeking a husband who had vanished. And for that reason they had lost a child. . . .

She began talking softly, and he heard gentleness in her tone. She wasn't condemning him. On the contrary, she was reaching out to him, seeking to renew an old love. She told him about the gradual alienation of the McQueens, the brothers' snide comments about Ulysses, and then the time when Stanford insisted on naming the baby. That was the last he had heard from her through the mails, and all the rest was new to him.

She told him about the pressures she had endured, and the harsh isolation after she had resisted, and Stanford McQueen's shocking decision to evict her and disown his son. She talked about her trip down the river, her passage to Panama sharing a tiny cabin with a New Orleans woman.

"But Belle turned out to be a lovely woman, with her own courage, and I don't think the way I used to about people like that, Ulysses. She saved my life, but that's not why. She had a beautiful spirit."

"I've learned a few things too," he said.

Then she came to the trip across the Isthmus, the swamps and forests and monkeys, and the fevers. She and the child had both taken sick at Gorgona, and by the time they had reached Panama City the baby was gone, and she was at the brink of collapse. Her cabinmate had seen to everything and nursed Susannah back to life.

He felt a sorrow so deep he couldn't speak. She had come because she had heard nothing from him for all those months. He had lost a baby girl because he hadn't picked up a pen to write her, and he had almost lost her, too. A few letters from him would have assured her. But he had always found excuses;

she would always be there, smiling and happy back in Mount Pleasant.

"Susannah, I let you down."

She peered at him, searching for something, her eyes warm. Then she continued. He learned that she had supported herself comfortably on Big Bar, well protected by his old friends as well as new men, and had even put some money aside.

So he had her story from the time he had walked down the lane in March of 1849 to now, two years later. She had come to him. She had not given up in spite of his neglect.

Then he told her of his hard trip west and his life in California, especially the disappointments. Of shoveling gravel in icy water from before dawn to after dark, of the sheer blind luck in finding gold in one spot and not in another, of shifting friends and shifting loyalties, terrible prices that ate into profits, winter cold, sand in food, blistering summer days, and a life without domestic comforts. He told her about falling into his tent at night too tired to cook a meal, too tired to wash his clothing, too tired to build a cabin.

He paused, summoning the courage to tell her of his last desperate attempt to get a few dollars ahead, when he left all the dust he had on Asa Wall's faro table. He stumbled through that, watching her closely. She squinted sharply at him at first, but then when he told her how that terrible episode had set him on the right track, about his appeal to the wealthy entrepreneur named Jarvis, and his farm, her face softened again, and he even saw tenderness in it. He was glad he had confessed his worst secret, a thing he would have hidden from her if he had won at Asa Wall's table.

"Now I know," she said softly.

They dined at a ramshackle wooden café, returned to the hotel, and slipped into their dark room, where Ulysses scratched a lucifer and lit the coal-oil lamp, turning the wick down to stop the smoking.

She vanished behind the dressing screen, and he saw her dress come over her head, and heard the rustle of things, while he slipped out of his clothing and into a nightshirt. She emerged in a plain white cotton nightgown.

She approached him, her face soft, her hair loose and free about her shoulders, her gown concealing her from the neck down. "I'll tell you about our baby," she said.

"I want to know everything about her—who she took after."

"She took after me," Susannah said. She climbed into the small bed, and he climbed in beside her. "She chased the tabby cats and hardly ever got cross. She learned a few words. I told her that someday her father would come home."

She smiled at him, not at all angry or hostile, and snuggled close to him, taking his hand and pulling it to her breast. She fell asleep that way, holding him, comfortable with him, and yet still distant. He listened to the stillness, the occasional creak of the wooden hotel, the soft sound of her breathing. She was here. He loved her.

He lay beside her, unable to sleep. Tomorrow they would head for Stockton, and out to his vegetables, and the rag-house he had built. The uncomfortable shack would dismay her. The flat fields would oppress her. But maybe the promise of it would awaken something in her, especially when she saw the rows and rows of greens he had planted and nurtured. Maybe she would be willing to begin over. He had spent his youth in the camps, and now he was building a different sort of life, and wealth, on the fertile ground of the Central Valley of California. A man's life this time; a life that offered something to a woman.

Could he win her back? He thought so, but it would take a while. She cared deeply. All this evening, she had avoided accusation, and had listened eagerly to the long story of his progress. When he told her of his farm, she had smiled at last. She loved him, even if she wasn't quite ready to say it. And he loved her. He would never again take her for granted, never ignore her, and never leave her.

CHAPTER 73

S usannah thought that Ulysses' farm was the bleakest place she had ever seen. She stood on the faintest of hills, six or eight feet above a relentless flat. Half a mile west the land vanished into marshes that bordered the San Joaquin. To the north and east she saw nothing but flats that marched toward a hazy union with the sky. South lay Stockton, raw and ugly. Her new home, such as it was, consisted of canvas on a framework, with an earthen floor and no furniture but a narrow bed, a homemade table and a single chair built of poles.

"Not much to look at," he said as she studied all this.

"It's not Mount Pleasant," she replied, her mind's eye seeing the Iowa country with its wood lots, gentle slopes, little creeks, and verdant pastures to delight the eye and lift the heart.

He led her out into his fields, and there she beheld rows of potatoes, onions, squash, melons, and cabbage, fighting to survive the relentless grass that wouldn't surrender its age-old dominion to Ulysses' moldboard. "It needs hoeing. I can never keep up," he said. "Virgin land's like that."

But she saw something else. The spiky onion stalks grew tall, and she could see enormous bulbs popping through the soft soil. She walked the rows of bright green potato plants and saw no blight. The melons were struggling in the winter sun and she thought it might be the wrong time to grow them, but the cabbage was doing fine. He had harvested one plot and another would be ready in a month or so. Their leaves were being gnawed by some bug, but she thought he would have his crop anyway.

"You've worked hard, Ulysses. Forty acres is a lot for one man."

"It's a lot for two men," he replied. "I started with grassland. No one's grown a crop here before. I'm trying a little of everything to see what grows. If I don't keep it hoed, it'll be grass-land again right quick."

"You've shown the world what can be done here. Do you have two hoes?"

He looked so delighted that she smiled with him. "I can get another in town," he said.

They strolled back to the canvas-walled house. "You know, Ulysses, nothing'll make this a pretty place. Not trees, not shrubs, not flowers. I'm hoping that we don't stay here long. There's such beautiful land in California. I'd like to see the Sierras from my window. The country we drove through this morning, so green and hilly, with those live oak groves . . . I'm hoping we can start there someday, and build a big white frame home with high ceilings to free the summer heat, and high win-dows to let the breezes through—a little more like Mount Pleasant but not a whole lot. This is different, and I love the new."

"Whatever you want, that's what I'll try to do," he said. "I can sell this for a good profit. I've proven it'll grow crops. It's close to the river and shipping'll be easy. It's just the place for some brothers, or a father with several sons. We can buy a place nearer the diggings, and I can wagon our produce to the camps."

She smiled at him in a way that sent a wordless message to him, and he caught her gaze and its meaning. "We can start over," she said softly.

"Yes, start over." She watched the emotions that crossed his face, and saw them all: joy, fear, remorse, hope, dreams. Ulysses had changed. She found herself examining a person she didn't know well. She liked what she saw. Ulysses seemed to draw his strength from a different place now.

"If you were to write me a letter now, what would you tell me, Ulysses?"

He looked stricken. The question had reached to the core of things, as she had intended. But he gathered his courage and finally ventured a reply taut with feeling. "Well, I could go on about the ways I failed you and how bad I feel, but that doesn't get us anywhere. I guess I'd just say I love you. I'd like to start over now. I've made my mistakes, and now I want to get on with living, and give you and our children the life we want."

"I would like that."

Golden light poured through the tent-cloth, turning the room into a magical shadowless place. The golden light burnished Ulysses, turning his deep tan into amber liquid. It caught his face, and she saw a man who had been transformed. As much gold emanated from him as from the filtered sun. The canvas shivered slightly in a zephyr. The warmth of the sun reached through the cloth and bathed her in beauty. She knew that as long as she lived, she would always wonder how the golden light had gathered there and caught them both in it.

She saw his arms open, his hands eager to hold her, and she stepped into them and drew him tight, even as his strong arms captured her. The time of reconciliation had come and gone, and now she felt only the yearning to begin.

PART VIII

1851

T ime dragged for Rita Concepción Zamora. Everything in her mind centered on the annulment. When she received it, she would be free. When it came, she would seek Stephen. When it came, she would stop being angry at the church. She would move, and not burden Tía Maria anymore. When she was given her annulment . . . maybe life would start again.

She lived for the day, scolded the slow priests who were handling her case at their leisure, if at all, and making her suffer through the weeks and months and seasons. *Sí*, it was Salvador's annulment, but she wanted it more than he did. He was suffering too. A few months ago, when her brother Santiago came to town, he stopped to see her. He had always been the most affectionate of them. And at that time, just before the feast of Navidad, he whispered something that didn't surprise her. Salvador had taken a woman Rita knew, the wild Paloma Ortega, and had gotten her pregnant, and in the spring there would be a bastard child. That amused Rita. She was happy, in a way, for Salvador, whose manhood was now beyond question. But she hoped the news hadn't leaked to clerical ears. It might affect the annulment.

She joined the altar society and embroidered vestments and washed the altar cloths as penance for her anger toward the church. She helped Tía Maria care for her brood, and that made it all right to be there. Her aunt was happy to be pampered; she always said she never had a moment to put her feet up and relieve her varicose veins.

But still the minutes and hours and days crawled by. Ever since the *yanquis* made San Jose the capital of California, Monterey had shrunk into a small, sleepy village, enlivened only by the occasional trading ship that called in the bay, most of them doing Thomas Larkin's business. Even the coastal packets stopped their daily shuttling to San Francisco, and now one came only on each *martes*. She no longer had the chance to improve her *inglés*, except on the occasions she ran into Señor Larkin himself, and made a valiant stab at it.

When that happened, she always made inquiry about Stephen Jarvis, not caring what he thought or whether she was still the señora Zamora.

"Yes, señora, I have news of him," he said one day near the presidio. "His partner, Marble, died, and he's dissolving his company. It's a loss for me. I did a lot of business with him."

"But what will happen?"

Larkin answered cheerfully. "Who knows? He has a fortune, and California begs for development."

"Has he . . . found a wife?"

"The last I heard, he was a resolute bachelor."

"Tell him I inquired about him, and that I wish him . . . I wish I could see him."

"I'll do that, señora."

She walked back to her home frightened. Things were changing. Maybe she should write him. But what would she say? "I, the señora Zamora, await an annulment and pine for you? I have worn nothing but mourning since the day of my wedding." No. She must outwait the maddening canon lawyers. She felt helpless. Why must she submit to all these authorities? Was it really for her own good, as they all said, or was it because they loved to dominate the lives of others?

One June afternoon Padre Tecolote summoned her. It was a day made in heaven, alive with summer light. Sea lions played in the bay, making white furrows. She hadn't seen much of the priest for months. Some tension had crept into their old, cheerful friendship, and she had avoided him. She loved him in a way, but he was the church, and the church was irritating her.

The annulment! She dressed carefully, brushed her hair, and sailed into the sunlight only to plunge into the gloom of the rectory minutes later.

"The news you have been seeking has come this hour," he said, waving at a document in church Latin on his table. "But it is well to consider the decisions of the church the work of God, and to be grateful always, no matter what the consequences.

For the church is the one true instrument of God, and illuminated by the Holy Spirit."

She waited patiently.

He peered at her owlishly. How often she had compared those big, wise eyes, and hooked beak, and his expression of patient waiting, to the night-bird.

"The church fathers have denied the annulment," he said.

She swam through darkness.

He pulled wire-rimmed spectacles over his nose, and read. "The señor and señora shall, with the grace of God, remain man and wife. They are validly married. No grounds exist to annul. Both parties agree that Señor Zamora is not impotent, and that removes one ground. The question is not whether the marriage has been consummated, but whether one or the other party is incapable of consummating it. If there is no impotence there can be no annulment. The other ground, whether the señora made her marriage commitment sincerely, is disputed. She swears she did; he says she didn't. The presiding fathers have chosen to believe that the señora, vowing eternal wedlock before God, did not defraud her husband, and the proof is that this proceeding was brought by the husband, not the wife. The marriage is valid. In the name of the Father, the Son, and the Holy Ghost, amen. Done this seventeenth day of April, Anno Domini eighteen fifty-one, the see of Durango."

She could barely breathe.

Padre Tecolote pulled his glasses off and smiled gently. "Now, Rita Concepción Zamora, it is time to make a good marriage. Your loving husband, your true husband in the church, awaits you in Sonoma. This is good and right, and pleasing to me."

"I don't want to be married to him," she said.

"Your reward will come to you as a faithful daughter of the church."

"What if I get a divorce? I have grounds."

"I have heard the gossip. Adultery is a serious sin, but it is not a ground for annulment."

"I am talking about a divorce in the civil courts."

"You will always be married to Salvador." He leaned forward. "Rita Concepción, do not defy God."

"I am not defying God! I am—"

"It is a grave matter to deny one's self the holy sacraments."

She stood suddenly, sick of this, sick of Monterey, sick of Father Juan Montalvo Pérez. He lifted a hand.

"My daughter in the faith, I have known you all your life. I have been your confessor. I know your soul. We are losing you. Do not lose us. I beg of you, not as your spiritual counselor, but as an old friend—"

But tears blurred his image and his words.

"Adiós, padre," she said.

"Adiós? I was afraid of that. Please do nothing rash. Please weigh this carefully, talk to your elders, surrender your pride."

But she had heard too much of this, and whirled away, her heart tumbling in her chest.

She fled from the shadows, into the plaza, hardly knowing why her feet carried her down a lane to the house of the former American consul and great trader Thomas Larkin. She found him there with a seaman, and backed away.

He stared. "Señora Zamora, something seems to be wrong."

"Oh, I'll come again."

"No, stay. Captain Ariel and I are about done. We've been checking his manifest. He's the master of that schooner out there, unloading some whale oil and china silks for me."

"Come in, madam. I'm just on my way out," the captain said.

She waited as the captain concluded his business, and then turned to Larkin. He bowed slightly.

"Where is Stephen Jarvis? I need to know. Please, if you know, Señor Larkin . . ."

"In San Francisco. He's sailing for New York in two or three days on the mail steamer."

"New York?"

"He's leaving California. Liquidated everything. His note says he'll become an investor."

"When? What ship?"

Larkin looked puzzled but he plucked a note from a stack of papers and studied it. "The *Oregon*, the Pacific Mail Company steamship, day after tomorrow."

"Why is he leaving? Do you know?"

Larkin remained silent a moment. "It's not for me to say,

señora. I cannot speak for him. But you might ask yourself some questions. Why did he liquidate his company? He could have reorganized it. And why does he feel he must depart this land he loves so much?"

The questions answered themselves. "Oh, *válgame Dios!* I must go. How can I get there? The packet no longer comes each day."

Larkin studied her, his gaze absorbing her anguish. "Am I to play Cupid again? Perhaps it is not my business."

"I must go to Stephen."

Larkin seemed hesitant. He stood there, weighing it, and shrugged. "It's not my business. You and Stephen are a mystery. But I can help, Señora Zamora."

"Por favor, por favor . . ." she whispered.

"The schooner will head up the coast in two or three hours. I can arrange it with Captain Ariel. With a fair wind, you'd be in San Francisco this time tomorrow."

"Oh, yes, yes."

"Shall I have him send some seamen to your house for luggage?"

"Oh, yes. How can I thank you?"

He smiled. "May I consider it a wedding present?"

She laughed because she was so nervous and couldn't think of anything else to do. "If it would please you," she said. "Where is he staying?" she asked.

He consulted the note, and shook his head. "I don't know."

"I will find him. Wherever he is, I will find him."

She clasped the trader's hands in her own, fought back tears, and fled into the bright day, weeping her way across the plaza, welling tears as she entered the Chávez home.

"Dios mío!" cried her aunt. "What did that priest do to you?"

"He freed me."

"Your marriage is annulled."

"No, they say I am married to Salvador forever, through all this life and all eternity."

"Ah, you will go to him now."

"No, I am going to Stephen Jarvis."

It shocked her. *"Toma!* You are married forever to Salvador and you are going to Jarvis." She stood squarely with hands on hips, blocking Rita's path.

"Help me get my trunk. The sailors are coming for it."

"The sailors? *Madre santíssima!*"

"I love you, Tía, and José Jesús. You have been so kind to me. Now I will cause another scandal. I will go to the man I love, if he will have me."

Her aunt clucked unhappily, while her eyes smiled at Rita Concepción, and the moment dissolved in comedy. "Ah, ay, now I will be roasted in hell for this. Now I will listen to Padre Tecolote's unhappiness. He will say I failed you, and endangered your soul, that is what he will say. And I will have to put up with my man for a month. Ah, ah, how will I ever explain it to your father, eh?"

But she was following Rita Concepción to her little alcove, where they heaped everything into the battered old trunk. Then they dragged it to the door, and Rita hugged her aunt and wept into her shoulder.

A while later two seamen arrived, took her trunk and her to a lighter, and rowed her to the schooner. The *capitán* escorted her to a tiny stateroom, and before she had settled in it she felt the schooner heel to the wind.

CHAPTER 75

Rita Concepción huddled all night in a café on the Embarcadero. She had only a few *reales*, not enough for a room. But a room didn't matter. She wouldn't have slept. So she sipped chocolate, dozed, and kept an eye on the comforting black bulk of the *Oregon*, faintly visible through the grimy glass window.

She had found no place to store her trunk, so it rested beside the steep iron side of the steamship, as if it belonged there. When she had arrived, she learned from the purser that passengers could board beginning at noon. She would have a long wait. She had wandered the wicked, hectic city, looking for hotels where Stephen might be, and had boldly inquired at several. Finally she fled the hotel area around Portsmouth Square.

She would wait at the gangway and not one mortal would board—not one—without her knowing it.

Before she had debarked from the schooner that afternoon, she ended her mourning. She slipped out of the black linen dress she wore, folded it and set it on the bunk. She removed the black underclothing also. Then she washed herself, brushed her hair until it glowed, and pulled over her white cotton dress, the one with lace. It had slumbered in her trunk for a long time, and she welcomed it as she would a beloved friend. Even in June, San Francisco would be too chill for such a gauzy dress, but she knew what it did for her, and she would wear it, along with the gray rebozo for a little warmth. She buttoned it tightly to her neck, and felt joy. Her body glowed in the ebullient, flounced white, and that was how she wanted to come to him. She performed one final, ritual act: she slid off the gold band on her left ring finger, and dropped it into her little *bolsa*.

Now, through the weary night, the rebozo was a comfort. She drew it tight, and threw the tasseled ends over her shoulders. When daylight finally returned, she ate a small meal, a pastry and some rich black coffee, and walked the Long Wharf, still comforted by the great iron ship that creaked and groaned in the ebb tide. She refused to think of what might happen if she missed him. But she wouldn't miss him. Even less would she think of other possibilities: Whether he might have a Yankee woman on his arm. Whether he would simply be embarrassed and eager to be rid of her. She knew him better than that.

Sometime around noon she would find him. She sat on her trunk and waited, ignoring the stares of seamen.

The morning dragged. Then, at eleven, a lacquered black carriage drawn by a smart trotter headed out the wharf, its iron wheels rumbling hollowly on the planks. Behind the driver sat Stephen Jarvis.

She leapt up, sudden panic boiling through her. The barouche wheeled around and stopped. He started to step down, saw her, and froze.

"Stephen!" she cried.

"Rita Concepción Zamora," he said softly. "You've come to say good-bye."

"Stephen, take me with you! I love you forever."

"But Rita—"

"See? No ring!" She thrust her left hand up to him.

"You're not married?"

"Oh, Stephen . . ." Dread pierced her. "Yes, according to the church. Forever, they say. But no, not in my soul. I want you, only you." She waited, terrified, while he registered that.

He looked bewildered. Feelings played across his face like sun and black-bottomed clouds, while her mind froze. "I can get a civil divorce," she ventured. "There wasn't time. Salvador, he— There are grounds in your American law. There was . . . Salvador wanted an annulment. We finally heard from the archbishop of Durango—that is where the court of canon law is. It took forever. Stephen, *Dios mío*, don't leave me now."

This time he smiled, warmth flooding his face, something tender and boyish rising in it. He looked so grand to her, so sweetly homely with those big ears and awkward gaze. He might be a *rico* but he didn't seem like one. He was just the same man she had met at the rancho Estrada.

"Sit here in the carriage with me," he said hoarsely. "Tell me everything. Do you know—can you imagine—how much I love you, and what it meant to lose you?"

She nodded and settled beside him, her hands clasping his, her tears flooding into her white cotton bodice, his hands gripping hers as she told about the arranged marriage to Salvador Zamora, and all that had happened.

He listened closely. *"Amor,"* he said. "Will you be happy defying the church? Will you regret it someday, and feel remorse? Will you look at me sadly that day?"

She nodded. "It is possible," she said. "But Stephen, I do not run from God—only from what my stepmother arranged. And if I offend God, maybe he forgives, *sí*?"

"You'll be denied the sacraments, I guess."

"Ah, Stephen, you are my sacrament on this earth. Maybe heaven smiles upon us. I want to think so." She stared into him, loving the gravity in his face. Her Stephen was a serious man, who saw beyond the moment. Then a gentleness suffused his face, and she saw humor in his eyes.

"Rita Concepción, I was going to New York, via Panama, but we don't have to. We could go somewhere else."

"It doesn't matter. Go where you will go, and let me come with you."

"*Let* you! Ah, God, how I've waited! We can be married somewhere after you get a divorce."

"I don't want to wait for a divorce. I don't care about that. All those laws and rules. If you will take me, I would like the ship's *capitán* to marry us. Tonight! At sea!"

"Now? At sea? While you're still married to Zamora?"

"*Sí!*"

He laughed, and she laughed. "That's the best proposal I've ever gotten. Do you care where we go?"

"Oh, no, Stephen. Go anywhere."

"We'll fly to the moon and build a cottage on it. Let me talk to the purser. He's getting ready to board people."

She watched as Stephen talked with the man in the piped blue uniform. Then she saw Stephen slip the man a double eagle, and the man vanished up the gangway.

"The *Oregon*'s bound for Panama City," Stephen said. "It connects there with the *Star of the Andes*, which goes on to Valparaiso, with a stop at Callao. I've asked him to book you and get us the best stateroom. He'll talk to the captain about marrying us. Well? How about Valparaiso?"

"Oh, Harvis, anywhere. Chile, Argentina, Peru, Tahiti. What does it matter?"

"Maybe we can find a rancho in Chile, and a fast new mare you can call Plata."

"Estéban . . ."

"Maybe our own *hacienda* on the Argentine pampas?"

"Oh, Estéban Harvis," she said, the tears welling out of her eyes again.

They waited impatiently until the purser trotted down the long gangway and came to them. "We've a suite for you. It took some doing. You're both booked to Panama City. You'll have no trouble getting a stateroom on the *Star of the Andes*."

He surveyed them cheerfully. "Captain Clement Jarkow will be honored to perform the ceremony at nine this evening, after dinner with you as his guests. Come this way, please, and I'll have your luggage brought directly. That's your trunk, ma'am?"

She nodded, speechless.

Stephen Jarvis lifted her in his arms and carried her up.

AUTHOR'S NOTE

The early California figures who appear in this story, particularly John Augustus Sutter (Johann Augustus Sutter), Thomas Marshall, John Bidwell, Thomas Oliver Larkin, and William Tecumseh Sherman, have all been depicted fictionally. I have attempted to capture their personalities, but the scenes in which they appear spring from my imagination. I have, however, stayed as close as possible to the actual events and conditions of the early gold rush.

Stephen Foster's great 1848 song, "Oh, Susanna," was not actually written about California or the gold rush, even though it was instantly adopted by the forty-niners. The original goes like this:

> *I came from Alabama with a banjo on my knee,*
> *I'm going to Lou'siana [sic], my true love for to see.*
> *It rained all night the day I left,*
> *The weather it was dry,*
> *The sun so hot I froze to death,*
> *Susanna don't you cry.*
> *Oh, Susanna, Oh, don't you cry for me.*
> *I come from Alabama with a banjo on my knee.*

The California-bound argonauts invented their own verses, some of which have been recorded in this novel.

The California gold rush is one of the best-documented events in American history. Several hundred diaries or sets of letters are extant, and these are still being published. The argonauts were remarkably well educated and left behind them some memorable literature.

Adams and Company, the express service that appears late in this novel, was a brilliantly operated company that provided important services to the miners throughout the gold-rush country. It safely transported California's gold to the Philadelphia mint, or delivered it in the East. It was soon superseded by an even better and magnificently conceived company, Wells Fargo.

Senator Gwin's California land commission was signed into federal law in March 1851, and from that moment the fate of the Californios was sealed. While the commission did ultimately confirm the validity of 604 Mexican land grants out of the 807 it examined, the costly litigation involved in defending their land, and the endless appeals, averaging seventeen years, broke the backs of the native Californians and destroyed their culture. One of the victims was John Sutter himself, who lost the land under his fort and died impoverished and bitter.

While the last Californio governor, Pio Pico, did not help matters by making fraudulent grants to Californios after the conquest, the federal commission's work, and the ulterior motives behind it, remain one of the darker chapters in American history.

I am indebted to that gifted novelist Jory Tecumseh Sherman for inserting the idiomatic Spanish into this story. I am indebted as well to the protean editor, historian and biographer Dale L. Walker, who supplied numerous valuable leads and ideas, as well as a copy of a newly published gold-rush diary that became a research bonanza for me, that of Dr. Israel Shipman Pelton Lord, a forty-niner who recorded details helpful to his contemporaries and to a future novelist.

—Richard S. Wheeler
September 1995

Historical fiction available from

THE SINGING SWORD • Jack Whyte
In Book Two of the Camulod Chronicles, Jack Whyte tells us what legends have
forgot: the history of blood and violence, passion and steel, out of which was forged
a great sword…and a great nation.

GOLDFIELD • Richard S. Wheeler
"Mixing history and melodrama with fast-paced storytelling and frontier detail,
Wheeler paints a vivid picture of life in a turn-of-the-century Nevada mining town
called Goldfield."—Publishers Weekly

STRONG AS DEATH • Sharan Newman
The fourth title in Sharan Newman's critically acclaimed Catherine LeVendeur
mystery series pits Catherine and her husband in a bizarre game of chance—which
may end in Catherine's death.

CHAPULTEPEC • Norman Zollinger
The Gone with the Wind of Mexico. This is a tremendous saga of love and war, and
the struggle for Mexican freedom.

JERUSALEM • Cecelia Holland
An epic of war and political intrigue, of passion and religious fervor, chronicling the
fall of Saladin's empire.

PEOPLE OF THE LIGHTNING • Kathleen O'Neal Gear and
W. Michael Gear
The next novel in the First North American series series by best-selling authors
Kathleen O'Neal Gear and W. Michael Gear.